Dar

I,
REMBRANDT

I,
REMBRANDT

A Novel
by
David Weiss

ST. MARTIN'S PRESS • NEW YORK

Library of Congress Cataloging in Publication Data

Weiss, David.
  I, Rembrandt.

  1. Rembrandt Harmenszoon van Rijn, 1606-1669—Fiction.
I. Title.
PZ4.W429Iad   [PS3573.E415]   813'.5'4   78-21352
ISBN 0-312-40261-9

TO
BETTY BUCHAN
and
HELENA O'NEILL
who must live in a world of books

My work is myself
Anyone who ignores that
Ignores me

GOD I WILL BELIEVE IN YOU TODAY

GOD I will believe in you today
since I must believe in something
and I do not believe
    in myself today

You will be my substitute
    for myself today

It is only on rare occasions
like this
    that I borrow you this way

Whenever you feel as I do
and you do not believe
in yourself that day
you may borrow me
    in the same way

None
not even God
should be without faith
    for a day

And in that way
we will be equal
to each other
and that is the best kind
    of faith

        —Stymean Karlen

I STOOD in my studio and sought to absorb myself in the two portraits I was painting, but I was distracted by my anger. I, painter and etcher of Amsterdam, who assumed that my work was all that I needed to sustain me, who took exceptional care only with my pen and brush, was so upset I could not focus on the pictures I was painting. While I was glad that I resided in a fine mansion on the Breestraat, a street with character, and full of potential models, these advantages did not lessen my anger.

I thought indignantly: The Reformed Church of Amsterdam is wrong. They had accused me and my housekeeper, Hendrickje Stoffels, of sin because we were living together without being married and they had ordered us to appear before their Council of Elders to stand trial.

And because she was pregnant they had also accused her of adultery.

This charge angered me most of all, and now I strode up and down my crowded studio to relieve my rage and to decide what to do.

I recalled how I had ignored their first summons—I had not believed that we were sinners, whatever the Church declared— but when we had not responded the Council had repeated their charges. However, the second time the elders had accused only Hendrickje. This summons had frightened her, and she had told me that she must obey the Council of Elders, but I had persuaded her to ignore them once more.

The third time she was accused she was terrified. These charges were conveyed in person by her minister, Pastor Hoag, to stress the gravity of her sins and to remind her that she was also guilty of adultery. He had added that if she failed to appear this time she would be denied Holy Communion and that any children born illegitimately would not be baptized.

These warnings shook her profoundly. She said to me, after the Pastor left, "Calvin preached that unbaptized children are infected with evil and become servants of the devil," and while I retorted, "That is false, as is his doctrine of original sin," it did not abate her fear or halt her need to appear before the Council of Elders.

Since she was pregnant, the Church's admonitions were threatening to her. And because the seed she bore was mine, I felt responsible for her, and so I could not stop her from appearing before the Council now.

Her submission troubled me. Did she think that I was evil, too? That, as the elders implied, I was not a good Christian? I would match my belief in Jesus against anyone. But how could I prove that to her?

Hendrickje was dressing in her most sober garb to impress the elders with her piety despite her condition, while I was waiting for Pastor Hoag, to arrive to take her to the hearing. He was escorting her in person to be certain that she answered the summons this time. I had agreed to this unwillingly, only to please her, for I detested this situation.

Yet I felt that I must observe her appearance before she left with the pastor. My eye would know if her garb was suitable. There was no one in the house to fetch her, and I cursed the circumstances that had forced me to send my one remaining apprentice, Daniel, and my thirteen-year-old son, Titus, in search of oils so that I could finish the two portraits I was painting. Infuriated and distracted by the Church elders, I had not noticed that my stock of oils was used up.

I gazed out a window at the Breestraat in the hope that the fog that hung over Amsterdam was lifting, but when I saw that the air was still moist, heavy, and gray, I repeated a favorite jingle to myself.

> "The great town of Amsterdam
>   Is built on piles, until
> The day the whole place tumbles down
>   Then who will pay the bills?"

This brought a smile to my face, the first relief I had felt this summer morning, but I still wished that the city was not so damp. The fog made my hands ache so much it was difficult to hold a brush.

Then I remembered that the natives were proud that they had been able to build the city on sodden land, although, wherever they dug, their efforts usually found water at a depth of just a few feet. And so while it was July, at the height of the summer, the day was still dank and there was no trace of the sun. This also annoyed me and yet, I told myself, I must make the best of the bad weather, Amsterdam was the center of the art world. Thanks to the city's success as a seaport and a trading center, more art could be seen and bought in its auction rooms than anywhere else in the world. I did not have to travel to Venice to see Titian; there was plenty of his work here. I could even purchase it, when I could afford it, and study it closely. I prized this blessing.

Looking for the pastor, I noticed there were many pedestrians on the Breestraat, several with paintable faces; a coach halted nearby, but I knew it could not be Hoag's, it was elegant, in the French style.

Hendrickje, entering the studio for my approval, interrupted my reverie. She wore a black outfit that hid her appealing soft skin, lovely complexion, round, pleasant features, and her plump, well-shaped, feminine figure. Her white cuffs and collar, although they were in the current mode, were too stiff and starched. Her thick, reddish-brown hair, which I loved to paint, was worn back on her head primly and tightly, denying the beauty that attracted me. She was of medium height and I observed that her clothes obscured the signs of her pregnancy—she was about six months with child—but I was not ashamed of this situation and I disliked that she seemed to be, hiding this fact every chance she got.

Her appearance offended me. I felt that it was not worthy of my taste that she should look so drab. She sensed my mood, for she said, "Master, I want to go in peace."

I muttered, "How can you when there is none in their hearts?"

"If I do not appear they will refuse to baptize our child."

"If we do not marry they will reject you, whatever you profess."

"Master, I understand your difficulties."

She blushed as she said that, but I felt that however earnestly she pretended to comprehend why I could not wed her, at least under my present circumstances, she did not agree with me. I said, "I still think that you should not respond to their summons," although I was shaken, too, by the Council's severity. "They will only make you feel worse."

"I must go. They will excommunicate us if I do not come this time."

"They cannot. I am not a member of the Reformed Church anymore."

"Hoag is my pastor. Do you want me to give up my faith, too?"

"Of course not. I believe in Jesus as much as they do. I have painted Him as much as any artist in the Netherlands. I am always searching in Him for an expression of my faith." And sometimes that was confusing.

She insisted, "Master, their disapproval will damage your reputation and cost you commissions. Most of the rich burghers belong to the Reformed Church. They are the most influential people in Amsterdam."

I did not reply. I was tired of this conversation.

There was a knock on the front door and Hendrickje hurried downstairs and soon after she returned with Pastor Hoag. I had not moved. I realized that it was not oils I needed but energy. Twenty years ago this would not have happened to me. Then commissions had come to me from the most profitable quarters; I had wed an heiress and had bought a grand house and stocked it with art treasures and many apprentices had sought my instruction. I had felt admired and exuberant. Painting and etching had been my excellence and I had overflowed with energy and I had thrived on expectation. There had been so many faces to paint: Saul and David, burghers and beggars, and the Bible and Amsterdam had supplied me with many subjects. I had regarded this as my inheritance and I had used it fully. But now, as I saw Hoag staring at me grimly, I was unable to focus on my work and this added to my resentment of him.

I sought to revive myself by regarding him as a painter. But he did not stimulate my eye or my hand. His face was fleshless and his pointed features too rigid, and he reminded me of a cackling black crow.

He began, "Heer van Rijn, I am glad to find that you have heeded us finally. This is a grave business. I would not have come otherwise."

His cold, inflexible eyes frowned and said authoritatively to me: You are infected with sin. You will be damned unless you deliver yourself into my hands. Repent. On your knees. Cringe.

He added, "Your neighbors have complained about your household."

"Do I make too much noise? Do I disturb them?"

"This is not a time for frivolity. You have put this peasant girl in a family way. This is our third summons."

Leave off, I wanted to cry, have mercy, you are only one voice and a slanderous one! But Hendrickje looked so frightened and tearful that I said instead, "We have been busy. And then my housekeeper has been ailing."

"We know that you are not always responsible. That you are . . ."

I interrupted him abruptly, "Pastor, I am acquainted with my reputation." I knew I was considered rude, impatient, not one to suffer fools, quick to rebel against authority and tradition, profligate with money, but I did not need his views for my accounting. "I may not go to church regularly but I have as much of Jesus in me as you do."

"We are not pleased that you prefer the Mennonites. They are a surly, unbending sect, a danger to the Commonwealth. They reject the taking of oaths, military service, the carrying of weapons. They never would have defeated the Catholic power of Spain and won our freedom."

I retorted, "You do not like them because they do not educate preachers, but use for this purpose their most honorable and just men."

"They preach according to their caprice. They are blasphemous."

"At any event," I said angrily, "Whether I am a Mennonite or not is no one's concern. I am as good a Christian as anybody."

"That remains to be seen. At the moment you are not behaving as one. Come, Hendrickje Stoffels, you have delayed long enough!"

But as she started to obey him, I motioned for her to stay. She wavered, seeking to preserve the balance between us, and Pastor Hoag, glaring savagely at me, brought forth an official paper and read:

On July 4, 1654, members of the Council of the Reformed Church of Amsterdam, gathered together in plenary session, have decided that since a certain Hendrickje Stoffels has been residing in concu-

(6)

binage with the painter called Rembrandt van Rijn in the latter's home on the Breestraat, she is to appear before the consistory of the Elders within a week to explain her scandalous conduct. If not, she will be excommunicated.

I felt that Hoag had added the last threat on his own, but it was enough to persuade Hendrickje. She evaded my plea to remain and followed him out the door. Then suddenly she reappeared and cried out, "Master, I left dinner for you in the kitchen should I be delayed. Your favorite pea and prune soup, and herring, cheese, and beer."

I was pleased, despite a feeling that I was being deserted, but I said, "You should invite Hoag. He always goes where his stomach takes him."

"You must not anger him." But when I looked as if she were rejecting me, she added hurriedly, "I will try not to deny you, whatever happens."

"I do not expect you to," I said curtly, although I was not as certain as I sounded. "Now leave me in peace. I have work to do."

Long after she was gone I remembered the stricken look in her eyes. I could not work, although I tried. I, who had been able to toil without rest and to repaint a picture a hundred times, who had labored under the most difficult conditions, could not touch the two studies I had been doing. My portrait of the patrician Jan Six was good as far as I had gone but I had not gone far enough. And my half-figure study of Aristotle observing the bust of Homer was wrong; it was not sufficient to give him compassion; he needed more. I told myself that the light was too dim, that the paint was smeared, that I required more yellow, but I knew it was more than any of these things. I felt tired, old. I had marked my forty-eighth birthday just a few days ago. I had worked in sunshine and darkness, shivered in the cold and damp, suffered sickness and death, I had been praised and scorned, I had been rich and now I was poor, but, somehow, I had been able to disregard all these things when I was nourished by the strength of my work. This afternoon, however, waiting for her return and the elders' verdict, I could think of nothing else.

(7)

But gradually, as I surveyed my collection, my spirits improved. I was stimulated by the portrait by Titian that I owned, the small head by Michelangelo, Giorgione's *The Samaritan Woman,* one of my favorites. I studied Palma Vecchio's *Rich Man,* such an undervalued artist, I thought, and I was gratified that I had displayed his work to advantage.

I could not give up these pleasures willingly but as twilight came and Hendrickje was still absent my anxiety about her increased.

Just before nightfall, while I was still in my studio and feeling the paint on the face of Aristotle with my fingers—which I usually trusted—the sun broke through the fog. As it shone on his features the light reminded me of a golden leaf I had found. That sight had given me much joy. This leaf had become my treasure until it had withered and even then I had been unable to rid myself of this crumpled fragment. And now I realized what dissatisfied me. The paint on Aristotle's face was too heavy, as thick as my finger. Yet the yellow was not strong enough, lacked passion, and had too much green and orange in it.

I told myself that I must go deeper into the yellow, be decisive. I was contemplating this when I heard footsteps on the stairs. It must be Hendrickje, I thought with relief, Maybe she had escaped with a reprimand.

I was disappointed when Daniel and Titus appeared, although I was glad they had returned finally, although much later than I expected them. I anticipated an apology for having kept me waiting so long.

Instead, Daniel, my twenty-two-year-old apprentice, flushed as he said, "Master, we had difficulty finding the oils you requested."

My son, whose delicacy worried me, added, "Papa, we walked over much of Amsterdam. It was tiring. Where is Hendrickje?"

"At the hearing. They keep her too long. As you kept me waiting."

"Have you eaten? She must have left you something."

"I am not hungry. Where are the oils?"

Daniel said slowly, "Sir, we could not find all the colors you wanted."

"Did you get yellow?"

"Master, you did not ask for yellow."

"I need it for brightness. You should know that."

"Not everyone has the yellows you prefer."

"That is no excuse. What is the true reason that you have failed me?"

"Papa, do not be unreasonable," Titus said. "We were able to obtain some of the oils you wanted."

"Neither of you are answering my question." They were so uneasy that I knew something was wrong. Daniel glanced at Aristotle, Titus at Homer; two foolish youths, I thought, trying to deceive me. "What is it now? They do not approve of my subjects? Or is it that my style offends them?"

"Master," Daniel said awkwardly, his discomfort growing, "the times are hard. The war with England has affected trade. Most of the money goes to digging ditches, fortifications, and ships of war."

"And I have many debts. Were you refused credit?"

Daniel did not answer, but Titus said, "Papa, we were able to borrow pigments from your old friend, Jan Lievens."

I said furiously, "We do not paint alike anymore! You should not have gone to him! He imitates Van Dyck now! Gloss is all that he knows. Since he returned from England his colors do not suit my palette."

Daniel remarked, "Master, the yellow is the same that you use."

"Is it of good substance?" I asked suspiciously.

"The best. Sir, Lievens' portraits are the fashion now."

But mine were not any longer, I thought angrily; the young were cruel, sometimes unwittingly, often stupidly. However, my apprentice looked so uncomfortable I did not chide him. I took the yellow from him and tested it with my thumb. It possessed a consistency I could endure, although it was not what I preferred. I applied a dab of it with my forefinger to Aristotle's face to illuminate it and while this did not satisfy me, at least, I thought, it was a step in the right direction. I asked, "How much did these oils cost?"

(9)

"Master, Lievens offered them as a gift. With his compliments."

I grumbled, "I do not want his charity."

Titus cried, "Papa, they were all that we could get! Do not ask for the impossible. He gave them as an expression of his friendship."

"Past friendship," I mumbled, but to myself. My son, who was still beardless, had endured so much in his brief thirteen years that I could not push him harder. Yet I had to know, however painful it was, another vital fact. "Daniel, is my credit gone?"

"It may not be that. The times are difficult."

"And I am considered even more difficult? Is that what they tell you?"

He did not reply, and now my brief burst of energy was gone. The sun faded and Daniel lit a brace of candles but I could not paint; their light was uncertain, false. My anxiety about Hendrickje grew. I wondered: Had the elders jailed her after all? Pastor Hoag had behaved like a warder and these keepers of the public morals were strict.

We were sitting in the kitchen trying to digest the prune and pea soup she had left when we heard the front door open. I sat tensely, not sure who it was. When I saw that it was Hendrickje I sighed with relief and I rose to welcome her, but she evaded my arms as if they were unclean and sobbing, she thrust a document into my hands. I read:

> Hendrickje Stoffels, having appeared before the sitting of the Church Council of Amsterdam, admits she has engaged in concubinage with the painter, Rembrandt van Rijn, and is therefore severely reprimanded, exhorted to penance, and is forbidden the sacraments of the Lord.

She was crying so sadly that Titus sought to comfort her by putting his hand on hers, but she thrust him away, too, shouting, "You must not!"

Daniel said, "Miss Hendrickje, it cannot be that terrible."

"It is worse," she sobbed. "I am not worthy. Forgive me, Master, the elders say that I am living *in Hoererif.* In whoredom."

No one spoke. I was stricken by her pain.

She wept, "I have sinned and my seed will be damned."

Daniel whispered, "They could not be so cruel."

She whimpered, "You would not know. You do not belong to our faith."

"That is not just!" Titus exclaimed. "Daniel feels like we do."

"What is just? Only Jesus is just and He has deserted me."

I affirmed, "He forgave Mary Magdalene and many others."

"And I am a poor peasant girl, who can barely read and write, and only because you have taught me. It is no wonder our first child died. This one will be punished, too, and suffer the same fate."

I was not certain that I believed this and I tried to change the subject. "Hendrickje, your soup was excellent."

"Yet you hardly touched it."

"I was thinking of a new subject. Daniel, set up a canvas, and Titus, you help him." I yearned to be alone with her and to console her, to say, I care. But even after I heard them moving about in the studio I could not utter these words. Instead, I said, "Tomorrow morning I will paint you as a character from the Old Testament."

"As the whore of Babylon?" she asked tearfully.

"As I feel you. And see you."

"With my bulging stomach. God will not forgive me."

"The curve is fitting and it will complete you as a woman."

Nonetheless, I doubted that this consoled her, for when we went to bed she moaned and she sounded in such torment I awoke her. I did this as gently as I could and when she felt my touch she kissed my hand in gratitude. But when I embraced her, excited by her warm, soft body, she recoiled and sobbed, "Not tonight. It would be unseemly."

I was angry at the elders for spoiling my pleasure and I clutched her amorously. I longed to deny their power over us.

She still did not respond as I desired and as she usually did, but continued to withdraw, asking tearfully, "Master, do you love me?"

I thought, What an expressive face!

She repeated, "Do you love me?"

I replied irritably, "That is not a thing to discuss." Yet I sensed that Hendrickje would only give herself when I said that and I could not. Not yet. Not ever, perhaps. I had given my heart to my wife, Saskia, and it had been shattered by her death. I was not sure that I could afford such a risk again. Yet I did not want anything to distract me from the view of Hendrickje that I desired to paint tomorrow morning.

I prayed that God would be merciful, despite the elders. I turned away from her, hoping she would find peace in sleep. But she got out of bed. Alarmed, I asked, "Where are you going?" Was she leaving me?

"I forgot to put the food away. I do not want it to spoil."

My anxiety, however, increased so much that when she returned I had to ask, "Hendrickje, are you going to leave me?"

She did not answer, sitting on the edge of the bed, pensive and melancholy, but in a posture I had to paint, her breasts as full as I had ever seen them. Then, as I started to ask again, she blurted out, "How can I leave you? I am bearing your child."

HE HAS A QUALITY

He has a quality
It is outside of anything he does
It persists stands up even outside him
But it is all around him
It never joins
It never separates
Yet it is always There

How can a quality have so much
Be so near
       And so far
And so sure
And so There and so There
And have a mind of its own
So all of its own So all of its own

              —Stymean Karlen

THE next morning I was still afraid that Hendrickje, despite her protestation of fidelity, would flee as soon as she realized more fully the severity of the elders' judgment. So the instant Daniel, Titus, and I had finished the breakfast that she had cooked and served, I ordered her to join me in the studio where they had prepared my materials for working. I thought: She is a natural housekeeper, she is most content when she is occupied with our household duties, and now she has come to regard modeling as one of them. I wanted her to be too involved to meditate on the consequences of her pregnancy and the threats of damnation.

She followed me upstairs reluctantly. But at least she obeyed me.

I was brusque, to hide my feelings. I knew I must hide my own doubts from her, or she would never have the will to defy the Church Council, as I intended, although I was not certain that I would be successful. I sent Daniel into his attic studio to instruct Titus in the use of chalk and crayon in the hope that this would spur my son's flagging interest in sketching, and so that they would be usefully employed and out of my way, giving me the privacy I treasured.

But while the mist had lifted and there was sun in the studio today, which I saw as a favorable omen, I could not find a subject she fitted.

She sat where I placed her, near the high window where the light fell on her face, but she was still all in black, covered from her wrists to her ankles by her garments, and the outline of her body disappeared under the weight of her clothing. She was modeling without individuality, hiding her personality from me, giving me nothing to feel. Annoyed, I detested poor models, I curtly changed her position.

"Please, try to be civil," she whispered mournfully.

"You are too grave," I replied sharply.

"I feel damned, Master."

"That is only in your own mind. Now be quiet so that I can decide how to pose you." I altered the elevation of her head, raising it so that I could see her features better. "That is an improvement," I told her, but I realized that she was still too stiff. There was no joy in her.

The past few weeks came back to me, reminding me that as her body had grown thicker the Portuguese Jewish ladies who were our neighbors had warned us to be careful; my Mennonite friends had prayed for a healthy delivery; and most of my Calvinist acquaintances had avoided us.

As I drew her I continued to feel that her inner truth was denied me. I thought of the many views of Jesus that I had depicted and I asked myself: Had I done them out of the needs of my spirit? Or for effect? I recalled what I had read of Him: "He was rejected and despised, a man thrown out, an outcast." Was I ever close to that view?

There was a cramp in my arm as I sketched her with pen and

ink. The last few years I had come to prefer that to chalk and crayon, it was more precise, but I was shaken by the pain that had spread to my fingers. I wondered if this was a visitation from God.

Hendrickje saw me rub my flesh and said, "It is a chill." Without asking my permission, she got out of her model's chair, prepared a hot application—she had equipped the studio for such a purpose—and as she spread it on my arm the pain vanished.

Suddenly I knew I was moving in the wrong direction with the Council. I was using Hendrickje poorly. I said, "I must find a reply before they crush our spirit. One worthy of Jesus."

"He forgave Mary Magdalene."

"That is not appropriate here."

"Then why did you ask me?"

"You could be more understanding."

At my rebuke she became so melancholy and pensive that it reminded me of how emotionally she had sat on her bed the night before, how her nature had taken on such a dramatic and human aspect that it had illuminated her face and her figure. I ordered her to move into our bedroom and to disrobe. Afraid that she would refuse, for she wavered, I picked up my sketch pad and led her to the part of the bed where the light was best. She went unwillingly, but I was grateful that she did not resist.

I behaved as if this was the most natural request in the world, and when she saw the heightened excitement with which I viewed her, she undressed, halting only when she came to her undergarments. But that was not enough for my needs. I said, "Your shift is wrong."

"Master, I thought you wanted me to model as if I were bathing."

"I have done that already. It was only a preliminary study."

It was evident that she did not agree with me, that behind her humble manner she was proud of this intimate oil sketch but I had no intention of portraying a burgher's wife whose chief concern was the coming and going of ships. Her present appearance was wrong. Although I had painted only one life-sized nude that pleased me, that was my need now.

(15)

"Hendrickje," I declared, "You must not be ashamed of your body."

"It has betrayed me."

"Then God betrayed you, for He created you."

Bewildered, she moaned, "You are blasphemous."

I was trying to prove I was not. But I was shaken and I halted.

"Master, why not paint yourself? That should please and distract you."

I reflected: I had made so many self-portraits I had lost count of them. I had done them to practice facial expressions and because I was my best model. I was available whenever and however I desired, and for other reasons I did not wish to dwell on. I knew that people thought my appearance plebian, the true son of a father who had been an ignorant miller. That I was considered ugly, ill-favored, with my thick lips, flat nose, broad forehead, heavy chin, wrinkled skin and gray fluffy hair that made me appear older than I was, as if I had been old always, even in youth, although then I had been often a gay, exuberant young man. These days everything seemed to add to the impression of age: my bulky shoulders, my squat shape, my wide, hairy hands and my blunt, solid fingers. Only my eyes, perhaps, I reflected, still suggested the vitality associated with youth; they were the most expressive part of me. Yet I usually preferred to paint old age; it often revealed the most about human nature. Today, however, I did not wish to convey myself. I wanted to give Hendrickje faith in herself, I must paint her as I felt her.

It was not my inclination to be polite and I said curtly, "This study is to be a nude. I do not want to hear any more objections."

She trembled at being naked, but once she was nude, I drew her, using my pen, making many preliminary sketches. She was about thirty—she was not sure when she had been born but she guessed it to be in 1625—and it was the age I needed. My many drawings became a record of what I was feeling, thinking, and seeing. Yet at the end of the day I still did not know what the subject of this work should be.

At the kitchen table I presided over dinner. I began it with a simple prayer and Daniel and Titus sat with me while Hendrickje waited on us. I asked her to join us but she said that she would eat afterward, that this food must be carefully prepared. I wondered why the meal required so much time and effort, since she had cooked the national dish of the Netherlands, *hutsepot,* a combination of chopped mutton, green vegetables, and prunes, sprinkled with orange juice and boiled with ginger.

Daniel ate heartily, but Titus picked at his food, which worried me. I was pleased that he had become a pretty lad with fine features and large, appealing eyes, but I was worried because he was thin and slight; I was afraid that he had inherited his mother's frailty. It was Daniel who was sturdy, with a tall, firm body and fair complexion.

My apprentice said that my son had shown some progress in drawing, but when I examined what Titus had done I was unhappy. It added to my doubts that either of them were sufficiently gifted, but I was glad that my son had a seat, a spoon, and a knife of his own. Most Dutch fathers insisted that their children sit separately or stand at the table and eat only with their fingers. I did not like Titus to do this; I did not think it was good for him, although occasionally I picked up my food with my fingers when I was occupied with my thoughts, as I did now.

My greasy hands smeared Titus' drawings and Daniel said, "Master, you have spoiled them. I worked hard to get Titus to do these sketches."

"Not hard enough," I growled. "You are trained to be useful. It is a condition of your apprenticeship that you keep me supplied with oils."

Daniel said, "Sir, I have done my best."

"It has not been good enough. I am starting a new life-size study and that requires a full palette. I expect you to supply what I need."

Daniel said, "I am not sure I can," but Titus said, "I will, Papa."

"How?"

Titus looked bewildered and this time it was Daniel who said, "We may find a way. Titus, we must not disturb your father any longer. Come to my room and I will read to you."

Titus replied irritably, "I am tired of the Bible. You never read me the interesting parts. Papa can draw a child pissing, or gamblers fighting over dice, or a courtesan awaiting a visitor, but I am not supposed to know about such things. No wonder I fall asleep over my sketch pad. He is as strict as the elders. And as unreasonable."

My first impulse was to punish him, but he had suggested a concept I had to pursue before I lost it. I said imperiously, "I will take care of your disobedience later, Titus. Now I have work to do."

As I read the Old Testament and the storehouse of stories that fascinated me, I recalled that Hoag had said, "You do not behave like a Christian," yet I believed in Jesus. I told myself that as a painter there could not be any light unless there was darkness, no darkness unless there was light. And so it was with human behavior.

When I found a subject that stimulated me and suggested a response to the elders I felt it was a miracle. For it was also a painting I had wanted to do for a long time. I read it aloud to see how it sounded.

> And it came to pass in evening tide, that David arose from off his bed, and walked upon the roof of the king's house, and from the roof he saw a woman washing herself and the woman was very beautiful to look at. And David sent and sought after the woman. And one said, "This is Bathsheba, daughter of Eliam, wife of Uriah the Hittite." And David sent messengers, and took her, and she came unto him, and he lay with her . . .

The next few weeks I was suspended in time. Nothing mattered to me but my life-size painting of Bathsheba. Hendrickje modeled for me, sitting on our bed as I remembered her, in sorrow and doubt, while I saw her as Bathsheba in the latter's own moment of conflict, when she had just finished a bath and had received the summons from King David. It was a crucial moment in Bathsheba's life. She was balancing her loyalty to her husband against her passion for the great king.

I drew many sketches while Hendrickje sat for me day after day, often shivering, often drooping with fatigue, her stomach slowly but clearly growing larger, yet my conception did not completely satisfy me. I labored feverishly so that I would finish before she became too swollen with child. I ate sparsely, usually late at night when I was too tired to work any longer, but only so I could have energy for the next day's painting. I knew that Daniel and Titus were in the house, for they supplied me with oils, but I did not ask them where they had obtained the pigments and they did not volunteer any information. If there were any visitors they kept them away from me. When I was in this kind of a mood I was not to be disturbed. It was Hendrickje who created problems.

Her uneasy attitude said that she doubted it was decent to be painted naked, that this would prove even more that she was a whore no matter how piously she prayed.

One dark afternoon the oil lamp went out and when I scolded her for allowing this to happen, she cried out, "I am a virtuous woman. I have not been touched by anyone else since I entered your household."

I was painting her heavy breasts faithfully and with feeling, they were a record of her life; when they sagged they spoke of having endured much. This life-size study must be more like her than she was herself. I said, between brush strokes, "You must not move. It hinders me."

"Then how can I fix the lamp?"

"You should have seen to that before we started."

"Master, I cannot do everything."

"Your mouth moved. It changed your expression. For the worse."

She sobbed, "I am being punished because I sinned."

Enraged, she was sitting clumsily, I shouted, "What kind of a God do you believe in if you think He can be so cruel?"

"Master, you expect too much from me."

"Put oil in the lamp. That will alter your posture and ease your body." And that would give my hands a rest.

She did as she was told, but as she returned to her modeling posture she declared, "You do not truly care what happens to me."

I thought bitterly, That was the difficulty, I cared too much. I loved my models when they satisfied my brush, if there was love in the world and sometimes I doubted that, yet I did love those that I painted, even though that love might die when I was finished painting, and frequently did.

"You like me best when I scrub the marble floors, polish the statues, lay out the linens to dry, clean the dishes, set the table, do . . ."

"Quiet!" I shouted. "I like you best when you sit still!"

She managed to remain motionless for a whole hour but that did not help my faltering brush. I wondered if my failure to find a conception that satisfied me was God's punishment after all. Suddenly I halted, telling her that we were finished for the day and she could dress and serve dinner. But I did not join Daniel and Titus at the table; I had to examine Bathsheba in privacy. I decided that her figure was not natural and that her expression was not memorable but commonplace.

I recalled the first time I had seen a Titian portrait, a drawing by Leonardo, Caravaggio's use of *chiaroscuro*. They had been revelations that had stimulated me. And I had assumed that she would consider it an honor to be painted as Bathsheba, not a crime. Hendrickje Stoffels, I mused, with her full, womanly figure, stronger than Saskia, but not even sure who her father was. No wonder she felt vulnerable.

Then I noticed black smoke with the disagreeable smell of peat pouring from the fireplace. When I heard a knock on the door I opened it unwillingly, annoyed that I was being disturbed.

Hendrickje stood there, saying, "I was afraid you might suffocate. We could smell the smoke below."

"It is the poor fuel. Why did you use peat?"

"We have no more beech logs."

"And cannot afford them anymore," I suggested irritably.

"Master, I brought you cheese, bread, beer, and a salad of radishes and cucumbers. You cannot go without food all day."

There was such concern on her face I was moved, and I said, "When I finish, I will take you for a carriage ride wherever you want to go."

"Take me to church. Please."

"I do not belong to the Reformed congregation anymore."

"You were married in it."

"That was Saskia's wish."

"But I am just a poor, humble serving girl while she was a rich heiress and an aristocrat."

She looked so forlorn that for a moment I wanted to laugh at her, and yet her feeling was genuine and that I could not ignore. And now I knew another of her grievances, if not all of them. I said, "I paint you as Bathsheba because of my regard for you."

"As you feel, not as I feel."

After she left, I pondered what she had said. I realized that she was more gentle and thoughtful than I had painted Bathsheba.

I returned to the picture as if we were starting again. I tried to treat her kindly, like a good Christian. I told her to model as she felt.

But when she was subservient, I said curtly, "Hold your head straight, do not slump, you are flattered by King David's attentions."

"I do not see how this answers the charges of the Church elders."

"You should consider it an honor to be painted this way. Nothing is more interesting than human beings. Your emotions are the essence."

She gazed at me with an expression of wistfulness, yearning, and doubt. I had never seen her look more appealing, I thought with joy, She held her head too high still, but that could be remedied. I asked her, quietly, to incline her head forward.

When she did, she possessed the natural fluidity I sought and expressed the emotions that she shared with Bathsheba. Now I painted swiftly. I had found a view I could trust. The inclination of her head downward, the lowering of her eyes gave her the melancholy, pensiveness, and modesty that were of supreme importance to me. It was inevitable that I added several details to complete the design. I liked particularly when I put in her hand the letter that had just arrived from King David and at her feet a servant to give her a sense of what she truly was.

The excitement of the work absorbed both of us now. This was not a classical nude I was painting, not a pagan goddess, voluptuous, but only ornamental; my Bathsheba was soft, warm, mortal flesh. And as Hendrickje sensed that I cared for her, that this was my way of showing it, whatever else I said or did, she was nourished. Her features, especially her eyes, were rich with feeling and reflection. Very few nudes were ever thoughtful, I told myself, most of them did not have an idea in their pretty heads, but my Bathsheba brooded intensely about her situation. The more I painted, the more I was convinced that this was the way Hendrickje felt. I was glad that I owned an abundance of yellow, thanks to Lievens' gift; with my new conception it became the most vital pigment in my palette.

When I finished this picture, I wrote on the back, "Overpainted," to indicate I had painted on top of my original conception. "That is," I said to myself, smiling for the first time in weeks, "anew."

Later, after I had rested from my exertions, I summoned Daniel and Titus to the stuio to view it. I told my apprentice, "Hang Bathsheba in the best light, so she can vouch for herself." Hendrickje did not join them, although she had been invited too, as if she were ashamed to be seen naked before anyone else, now that the excitement of modeling had ended. But I was curious about their opinion even as I pretended to be indifferent. I liked Daniel's taste and I longed for my son to understand what I was attempting.

There was an inquisitiveness in Titus' eyes, as if he had wondered what Hendrickje looked like naked, almost a kind of meanness, which I tried to ignore. Daniel was fascinated, as if a veil had been rent.

It was not my custom to ask an apprentice his opinion, even a perceptive one such as Daniel, but I had no one else. I asked, "Does it confuse you?" Suddenly he looked apprehensive.

He hesitated, then replied slowly, "No, Master."

"But something troubles you. What is it?"

"Sir, are you going to offer this picture for sale?"

"Why do you ask?"

"The nude is not in the fashion."

"The devil with the fashion. I painted it for myself."

"It is expressive, sir. But it is not for me to judge it."

"No," I stated emphatically, "Nor anyone else." There was nothing more for me to hear about Bathsheba, I decided, for in this work I had expressed myself. I had lived through an extremity of feeling, even of physical pain, but I had glimpsed desire and shame and, perhaps, truth.

Titus said, "Papa, you had callers while you painted this."

"From the clergy? That scarecrow, Pastor Hoag?"

"No. Others. Jan Six sent a messenger to ask when his portrait would be done and there was another inquiry from the Sicilian nobleman, Don Antonio Ruffo, about his *Aristotle*. They sounded impatient."

"They can wait."

Daniel said softly, "Master, their money is needed."

I said grimly, "I already owe Six a thousand guilders, so he will take his fee out of that loan, and only God knows when Ruffo will pay me."

Daniel murmured, "Probably when he receives his painting."

I sensed something else was wrong. "What is troubling you now?"

Daniel was silent, so Titus said, "Papa, your credit is not good."

"I know that. But I am not to be hurried."

"The oils you requested were very difficult to obtain."

"You got them. They were adequate."

"Only because Daniel gave his apprentice fee of a hundred guilders to you a year in advance. That was why we were able to buy them."

I did not know whether to feel outraged by his charity or to be grateful for his generosity, but I was stunned by my lack of funds. I knew that my affairs were in a confused state, but when I painted I felt as if I held the whole world in my hands. I grumbled, "Daniel, I do not approve of your gesture."

"Sir, it was the only way I could help you finish this painting."

"I doubt the painter's guild will approve of what you have done."

"Then we will not tell them, will we, Master?"

"I will make that decision, Daniel. I will return to *Aristotle* and you can notify Jan Six that he can come back for more sittings."

"Sir, I thought his modeling was done."

"His face needs retouching. I am not satisfied with it."

"When should I tell him to come?"

"At his pleasure!" I shouted. "That should satisfy him!" Then I was sorry that I had lost my temper, for Titus was on the verge of tears and Daniel was so upset that I was afraid he was going to leave me. I needed them, although I could not admit that fact; it would be too humiliating, and I already felt humiliated almost beyond enduring. I said, more gently this time, "Daniel, please put the studies by the window so that I can view them properly, tell Hendrickje to prepare some soup, bread, and cheese, and after I eat I will know better how long it will take me to finish these two commissions. And any others that might come my way."

Titus shifted uncomfortably and muttered, "Papa, she is not here."

Daniel hurried to add, "But she left dinner for you."

"Where did she go?" I asked apprehensively.

"She went to church, sir."

"Church?"

"Master, it is Sunday."

I had lost track of the time. I said, to hide my confusion, "She was forbidden to go by the elders."

"She thought that if she was penitent they would admit her."

"Fool! They will use her gesture as an excuse to humiliate her more." I started for the street instead of the kitchen, disgusted with her and possessed with an overwhelming desire to flee from my difficulties.

"Where are you going, Master?" Daniel asked anxiously.

"Where I can breathe." Where I could get away from my troubles, I cried within. I closed the front door behind me quickly and firmly before I could change my mind, and strode down the Breestraat to the center of the city, the Dam. People were everywhere, for it was a clear, sunny July afternoon, a rare day in Amsterdam, and they were taking advantage of the extraordinary weather. I did not halt until I reached the new town hall that was being finished in the Damplein. Then, as I stared at this grand edifice which was supposed to illustrate the supremacy of Amsterdam, I wondered if there would be any work in it for me. Once it was done, I was sure paintings would be commissioned for its galleries. One of those could restore me to favor. But I doubted I could wait. This vast rectangular structure with its bell turret and dome was still several years away from completion. And who would speak for me?

I lost interest in the town hall when I saw an aged man leaning against the walls of the Bourse, the trading center of the United Provinces. He was eating a dried herring with ferocity, as if it were the first thing he had eaten in days; he was so ravenous, so dramatic, I had to sketch him. I was grateful for my habit of always carrying a pad and pencil with me. I must capture this beggar's face. He leaned into the glow of the summer sun as if it were life itself. I sketched his wrinkled skin, seeking to capture the bite of his mouth, the dirty rags he wore and which served as his napkin, and the suffering in his features, so expressive of his poverty and old age.

When I finished this sketch I was in a better humor and I could return home. I had not wasted the day after all. I was hungry myself now and I wanted to share my dinner with Hendrickje, Titus, and Daniel.

They were at the kitchen table but no one was eating. Daniel and Titus were trying to console Hendrickje, who was in tears.

I asked, "What is wrong?" and she replied, as one bereaved, "They denied me the sacraments. They would not even allow me in the church."

She was so grief-stricken I was frightened for her. She went to church faithfully every Sunday and I seldom did and she was the one condemned. Much good her faith did her, I thought angrily. Then I shivered. Had something broken in her? What hope was there for us?

I took her gently by the hand but she pulled away from me, sobbing, "They meant what they said. My child will be damned."

Whatever doubts I had, I could not accept such a harsh view of Jesus. But how could I convince her? And myself?

Daniel said, "They shut the door in her face. They would not let her inside."

Titus said, "Papa, is that the Christian thing to do?"

"No," I replied sadly, "I do not believe that it is."

"I do," she whispered, "I will die as I have lived. In sin." She wept and hid her face in her hands as if the heavens would fall on her.

I pulled myself together and spoke slowly. "Hendrickje, we must find a church that will accept you. There must be one in Amsterdam."

"None," she moaned, "that are Christian."

Nobody moved for a time. Then I stood up and declared, "We have work to do. If the Calvinists do not baptize our child, someone else will." A painter bore two existences within him, I thought, the existence he desired and the existence that was, and often they did not meet. "I will speak to Jan Six. He is one of the most influential men in the United Provinces. I will finish his portrait quickly. That will please him. As will *Bathsheba.* He is a man of taste."

I could not tell whether I had brought Hendrickje out of her melancholy, but she raised her head from her hands, stopped weeping, and warmed some *hutespot* on the stove. The food was burnt, but I did not criticize her. I ate as eagerly as the beggar had, hoping that would show my regard for her, and approval, and I was pleased that Daniel and Titus joined me.

I MUST KNOW

I must know
what else you were
and who else you are

Dont you want to know
what else you were
and who else you are

No one is just what they were
and who they are
I must find out even if you dont

Or what you were
and who you are
will never know themselves

—Stymean Karlen

WHEN Jan Six arrived at my studio I was working on his portrait. It was a week after Daniel told him that I needed him for another sitting, and as I saw him I was even more certain this was essential. This was the first time we had met in a month and I observed that he had changed, in some ways his face had become a stranger's. Although this rich linen merchant was youthful, in his mid-thirties, his skin had become harder and heavier, his chestnut-brown hair longer and thicker. I thought wryly, This was an expression of his social position, it was the poor people and the peasants who wore their hair short in the Netherlands. And there was a reserve in him that I had not felt before. While we exchanged polite compliments, he waited stiffly for me to start.

I said, "It is good of you to come," and he replied, "I was

surprised. I thought my portrait was done."

I reflected, I must know what else you were and who else you are.

the poem preceding

He no longer suggested the patrician who had withdrawn from his family's prosperous business to devote himself to collecting etchings, paintings, books, to publishing his own verse tragedy, *The Medea*, whose title page I had illustrated as an act of friendship; his present manner was that of a burgher determined to excel in civic affairs. I desired to talk about light and shadow, motion and stillness, space and mass, and he discussed my delays.

"Rembrandt," he said suddenly, quite exasperated, "Are you deaf?"

"Why, my lord?"

"You are not listening!"

"My portrait of you is not finished. You have altered."

He regarded me as if I had reproached him, which in a way, I had.

I wondered, Do you want to know what else you were and who else you are? Blessed it is to be a painter and to have a painter's eye to see.

He declared, "What you have done is suitable."

"But not satisfactory, sir. I should have drawn you more."

"You drew me a hundred times. More than enough."

"I made some mistakes. It was wrong to paint you in an insufficient light. Work done in winter always requires an extra effort. Now that we have the long days of summer and a bright sun I see you better."

"My friend, I am satisfied."

"Be patient, sir. It will not take much longer. Now, if you will stand just as you are." The patrician had made a gesture to go and I liked the movement of his hands in the act of putting on his gloves. "Incline your head forward, please. It gives you a thoughtful look."

For a moment I thought he would refuse, then he assumed the posture I requested. I opened the windows so that the light would fall directly on his face and I heard the milkmen and the bakers starting their rounds.

They were dragging their handcarts noisily behind them,

shouting, "Beautiful milk! Warm milk! Sweet milk! Barley biscuits! All hot! Fresh bread rolls!" And the housewives were yelling back, "How much?" although they knew the price. I heard Hendrickje bargaining on our front stoop, and I closed the windows abruptly to shut out the commotion, although this lessened the light. I saw a mouse under my easel and a cloud of dust when I stirred but I knew what I wanted now. My eyes gave Jan Six existence, nothing else. I concentrated on his features. He was smiling reflectively, and my yellow softened his face and illuminated his skin and expression.

After he stood an hour, he demanded to know, "When will you be done?"

"Soon." Even more now, I must know who he was.

"My friend, I am very tired."

I was exhausted. I had put so much of myself into this day that my energy was gone. There were moments when I felt it was impossible to go on and yet I could not halt when I was this close to my intention. Then Six stirred restlessly and I was terrified that he would shatter his pose just as I reached my conception. I said consolingly, although I longed to chide him, "You should be tired. But you have modeled excellently."

"I had to. I cannot come for more sittings."

"Sir, you do not approve of this portrait?"

"I am busy with my civic duties. I cannot spare the time."

Six was always concerned with such affairs; there must be other reasons, I decided, why he could no longer model for me.

"Rembrandt, you must finish today."

"I will finish when it is right."

"Is it ever right for you?"

"Rarely. But it is possible that this portrait may be."

"You are too critical. Even of yourself. You will never finish."

He regarded me sadly, and it was precisely the expression I craved.

"Just a few more minutes, please. I will not be much longer, sir."

Excited, in a state of grace, I forgot my fatigue, everything but the vision before me. Now that I knew what I desired I worked with a freedom that stimulated me. My yellows caressed him as

I imagined. Nothing was lacking. I painted with single brush strokes, in the most economical way possible; I was putting his essence on the canvas and that was enough.

When I finished, I said, "This is the work of a friend, not a thing apart from ourselves."

I could not tell whether he was involved the way I was. This work was my life, what I loved the most, and he stared at the portrait blankly, as if he had decided not to commit himself. I could not ask him what he thought of my work, it was not worthy, but I had to talk to him about Hendrickje, I owed it to her, and he did call me a friend.

I said, "Sir, I have some difficulties with my family situation."

"That is common knowledge," he replied curtly.

"It is unfair. My housekeeper is accused of adultery when she is pious, kind. She desperately needs love, not condemnation."

"I am not her judge."

"The church elders are. My lord, tell them that she is virtuous."

"Good." For an instant I saw the old Jan, the friend who had invited me to dine at his country house, who had prized an album of my etchings, who had lent me a thousand guilders in an hour of need, who had recommended me to other patrons, whom I had depicted today. Then he shifted uneasily, declined the chair and the goblet of wine I offered him, although he drank copiously, and stated pontifically, "You should listen to the elders."

"I tried," I responded, "but they would not listen to me."

"Deliver yourself into their hands and you will be saved."

I regarded him incredulously.

"They are chosen people. They are our spiritual leaders."

"Not mine, sir. I do not belong to their church."

"You say your mistress does. Give her child your name. Marry her."

"I cannot!" It was out before I could contain myself.

"Why not?"

"My wife left half of her estate to my son, the other half to me, but with the proviso that if I marry again my half reverts to her sister."

He asked skeptically, "Is that the only reason?"

No, but I could not expose myself any further. If I wed again,

I would have to go before the courts and become enmeshed in numerous documents and oaths. And I could not turn over everything I owned from my wife's estate when there was hardly anything left of it. There never had been as much as others assumed, but I had to keep up appearances if I wanted to keep up my credit. I turned to the portrait in the hope that it would revive my flagging spirits, but the gray overcast that had spread across the sky darkened my colors, even my yellows, and I was disheartened and full of doubts.

He added, "And you must consider your son."

I said softly, "I do. I hope he will succeed as a painter."

"In a disorderly household? My friend, you put a heavy burden on him."

"They get along well. Hendrickje is considerate and affectionate."

"But do you know how he truly feels about her? Do you, Rembrandt?"

Whatever I professed, I was not sure. Daniel seemed to accept her, too, and yet here, also, I was uncertain suddenly.

"You should have thought of these things before you became involved."

Before I could reply, Titus ran into the studio, followed by Daniel. My son was upset while my apprentice was angry. Titus exclaimed, not seeing my visitor, "Papa, I tried to paint a still life like he ordered, but he does not care for my apple and orange."

"Master, the boy refuses to complete anything."

"There are too many leaves, Papa, and I do not like their color."

I asked, "What about the work itself?"

Daniel said, "Some of it is satisfactory."

Six, who was standing concealed in the shadows, stepped forward and declared, "It is obvious that the child needs a mother."

Daniel said, "Sir, Mistress Hendrickje treats him as her own."

The patrician turned to my son and asked, "Child, what do you think?"

"I do not like to paint in oils. It weighs my brush down."

"No! No! I mean about your housekeeper, Hendrickje Stoffels."

"She makes me wash too much but I like her plants."

I interrupted, "She has taught him how to cultivate them. I

(31)

wish he were as eager to learn about painting. She is very good in the garden."

"So that is all there is to it," Six said caustically. "Rembrandt, no wonder you have many difficulties. I am glad the portrait is done."

"I am, too, sir," I said. I was determined not to give him any more advantages. "Daniel, will you ask Hendrickje to prepare dinner. And Titus, I expect you to help her set the table."

My son frowned, but my tone was so authoritative he obeyed me.

After they went downstairs, I made one last plea. "My lord, for the sake of our friendship, unless I presume, tell the elders that Hendrickje is a good Christian and worthy of the sacraments."

"You do not presume. But I am powerless in this matter. For myself, I could accept your irregular arrangements, but public opinion is critical of you, there are many in Amsterdam who do not approve of your situation."

Stupid, misguided fools, I reflected, living like blind folk, gossiping—because they had nothing else to do—about a poor peasant girl from a small village. Five years ago she had come to Amsterdam to find work as a maid and a friend of mine had recommended her to me, chiefly because she was clean and her full, womanly figure pleased me as a model, and I was a widower who needed help. What had followed had been inevitable. And her tenderness with Titus had made him feel less like an orphan and had strengthened our bond. Now I felt that she was a fixture in my household.

Six said, "I would like the portrait delivered as soon as possible."

Since he had not mentioned the fee, I had to do so, although that made me uncomfortable. "Sir, I believe we agreed on five hundred guilders."

"I beg your pardon. My understanding was that the price was three hundred." Six stared at me with severity, then suddenly his tone grew conciliatory and he added, "However, I can make an adjustment."

"That is not necessary," I retorted proudly. I hated to bargain; it was humiliating. Moreover, I did not want to sound as if I were begging. "But, sir, I would appreciate if you would apply the fee to the debt I owe you."

He talked about the difficult business conditions in the United Seven Provinces. Because of the war with England and the failure of the tulip trade, there was very little good will in Amsterdam and no cash or good securities, and thus, it was sensible to use what one possessed.

I stopped him suddenly. "My lord, do you want all of the thousand guilders I borrowed now?"

"That is not the issue. These conditions forced me to transfer your debt to the iron dealer, Gerbrandt Ornia. Now you owe the money to him."

Because I had become too poor a risk for Jan Six, I thought angrily. No wonder his manner and appearance had altered, but I said, "And Ornia wants the thousand guilders immediately."

"I do not know. This is out of my hands. Rembrandt, nothing has changed between us. We are still friends. That was simply business."

"Where does this leave the art dealer, Lodewijck van Ludick, who was trusting enough to stand security for me? Is he still responsible?"

"I would think so. But, as I said, it is out of my hands. I am sorry, but circumstances forced me to do this. At least, you own this house."

Not actually, I thought, I had paid only half of the cost of thirteen thousand guilders when I had bought it fifteen years ago, and now, with the accumulated interest, I owed eight thousand guilders on it. Yet it was no use exchanging bitter words with Six, although I felt betrayed by him. Whatever I said, he would find an excuse. I lit a brace of candles and held them close to his portrait for a final examination.

He stated emphatically, "I am sending servants for it this evening. Before you change your mind and paint my face again."

I did not answer. Careworn, pensive, and breathing hard, I found comfort in what I had painted. Warmth glowed from the flesh tints of his face and hands and suggested a radiance that was life itself. More content, I reflected, *This was what you were, whatever you are now.*

"Remember, Rembrandt, no more scraping and polishing."

"Or . . . ?"

"Or I will not accept it."

I shrugged.

"Come, my friend, do not be a fool. Many people, important people, will see it in my house. It could lead to more commissions."

Ten years ago that situation would not have been of any consequence to me. But it mattered today, unfortunately, and I said, feeling that I was surrendering something precious, "The work is ready for delivery."

"Splendid. When the picture is hung and I am sure that I am satisfied, I will send you three hundred guilders."

"Sir, you have doubts about this portrait?" The more I surveyed it, even with half-closed eyes and in an insufficient light, the more I was certain it was one of the best things I had done. "Exhibit it in a strong light, so it may be seen from a distance. It will look better thus."

"As you say."

"My lord, you have not uttered one word about the work itself."

Jan Six smiled thinly, put on his gloves as I had painted them, for now he possessed an advantage over me, and announced, "You are my favorite Netherlandish painter. If only you were more practical. . . ."

An hour later my painting was gone. Once a painting was gone, like so much of my work, I felt it was gone forever, and I was afraid I would never see this one again. I wished I could afford a gallery of my own where all of my work was around me, but I knew that was an impossible dream. Good-bye, dear, kind, blessed friend, I whispered as Six's two liveried servants bore his portrait out of my house, You were fine company while I painted you, the best company, giving a meaning to my life.

When I did not come downstairs for dinner, Hendrickje found me sitting in the dark, mourning for my painting in a corner of my studio, and she put her arms around me and said softly, "You and I—you and I—that remains."

WHO AM I

Who am I
alone to explain
what the centuries say
through me

I am their silent messenger
who cannot hear the message
I carry for them

And yet
my instinct tells me
It is not futile

—Stymean Karlen

CANALS and bridges, markets and mills, inns and church spires, trees and windmills, I had to view all of them as I strode toward my picture dealer's rooms the next day. While I resolved not to allow anything to interfere with my visit to him, there was so much that was worth seeing in Amsterdam I was tempted to stop and to sketch. I carried my pen and pencil with me, as always, and when I came to a fish market I paused.

I was fascinated by its color and animation, by the intensity with which a fishmonger bargained with a fisherman, by the tilt of the sailors who had brought in the barrels of herring, eels, and lobsters, and the way they rolled when they walked, as if they were still at sea. I yearned to capture that angle of vision, obliquely. Then my attention was attracted by a young, womanly housewife carrying a basket of cod, whiting, and sole, who resembled Hendrickje. But it could not be her.

I had left her a few minutes ago, scrubbing the pavement in

front of our house with passion. I had warned her not to work hard because of her pregnancy and she had replied, "This is God's work," as if that assured her good health, and she had added proudly, "Our front stoop is spotless." Since she had seemed more content than she had been for some time, I had nodded and said, "I am going to raise money."

Recalling this decision, I tore myself away from the visual delights at the fish market and did not pause again until I reached the shop of my picture dealer. His district had been given the name of his trade, as was the custom in Amsterdam—Glassblowers' Canal, Wine Harbor, Spice Street were familiar and friendly places to me—and I was pleased that Art Dealers' Corner was regarded favorably by those who bought pictures.

His shop was new, of fashionable brick on a paved street, and the walk was lined with large elms and lindens, which indicated that his situation was prosperous and his merchandise marketable. Yet I was not sure how to approach him. In the hours that had passed since the departure of my beloved portrait of Jan Six, I had pondered this, but I was still assailed with doubts. I was not certain that he believed genuinely in my work.

Years ago, I recalled, I would not have faced this situation.

When I had come to the city in 1631 from my native Leyden, an ambitious twenty-five, I had not intended to stay, but my mind had been changed by Hendrick Uylenburgh, picture dealer, supervisor of an academy for young painters, and a retired painter himself. Twenty years older, this stocky, affable sponsor possessed connections with affluent burgomasters and aldermen, clergymen and councillors, doctors and merchants. He had persuaded me to settle in Amsterdam, saying that it had replaced Venice and Antwerp as the center of world trade. As a sign of his favor he had given me choice rooms in his own home on the corner of Zwanenburghwal and Breestraat, next door to where I lived now. I had been encouraged by the opportunities he had afforded me, especially when he called my work "excellent." I had also met my future wife, his first cousin, Saskia, in his house, and as long as my good friend had lived I had prospered.

But now? I sighed and shook my head wearily and looked around once again to collect my thoughts. There were times when

I still loved Amsterdam, and this was one of them. I could see the harbor in the distance, a forest of masts from all over the world. The warehouses were packed tightly along the canals and filled with grains and spices, timber and cloth. By their side were the gabled dwelling houses of the wealthy, often the owners of the warehouses.

Yet it was the haggard, strained face of the rat catcher across the street that I wanted to sketch. I shut my eyes to erase his features from my view. I knew I must not delay any longer or I would not have the will to confront my art dealer.

Cornelis Eysbert van Goor was not surprised to see me, as I had expected.

Youthful-looking, although he was in his thirties, he was dressed immaculately in the French fashion, with long breeches decorated with ribbons and knots. I observed that his clothes were costly and appropriate to most of the pictures that hung on his walls.

He said, "I am glad you came. I just received a letter from the Sicilian nobleman, Don Antonio Ruffo. He complains that you are taking longer to finish his *Aristotle* than you promised. I am concerned."

"Van Goor, he ordered it directly through me."

"You employed me as your agent in this matter."

"I needed someone to take care of the business details."

"Which I have done," the picture dealer stated triumphantly, "I have already written Ruffo, assuring him that his work is on its way."

"How could you take such a liberty? It is not finished!"

"Would you prefer to lose this commission? Ruffo is influential, rich, a devoted art collector . . . a valuable patron. It is unusual that he should prefer a Dutch artist to an Italian. You should feel honored."

I grunted. No one could tell me when I was done but myself. Van Goor's gray eyes were cold, his smooth features unwrinkled, his brown hair long and carefully combed. Not a feature here, I thought, worth painting. Or his opulent oak furniture, solid and ponderous, or his large French standing mirrors. I noted that most of the paintings on the wall were by Lievens, my former colleague, in the style of Van Dyck, and two pupils of mine, Ferdinand Bol, whose modish elegance I viewed with distaste, and Goveart Flinck, who sadly, was imitating Rubens.

"Knowing you are impractical, I wrote the following to Ruffo."

He handed me a copy of the letter and I read with amazement:

My lord, I have transmitted to the captain of the ship *Bartholomeus* a crate with your painting that you call, *Aristotle Contemplating the Bust of Homer*, which, as you shall see, God willing, is in the cargo.

Due, for the painting by Rembrandt, for the making: florins 500	
for the crate, and nailing it shut	" 5.12
for the transport, weight 20£	" 6.
for the loading and weighing fee	" 2.13
for the bill of lading N 120	" 1.64
for (loading) on board the ship in Trexel	" 1.68

I wanted to throw these details into his face but I desperately needed the money. Then he said, "I know that you are virtually finished. One good day's work would have this painting ready for shipping."

"Who told you that, Van Goor?"

"I have sources of information. I am looking out for your interests. I wrote Ruffo that the crate was consigned to him on June 13."

"And now it is the end of July?"

"Exactly. He will blame the delay on the shipment. According to Ruffo himself, he is paying you eight times what he pays Italian artists."

"The painting is worth more than five hundred guilders."

"Be satisfied. If he is pleased he will want more work."

I resented Van Goor's manner. I changed the subject. "Van Goor, I have several new paintings I want to sell."

"How can you expect me to do that when I cannot deliver a painting you have already contracted for?"

I wavered. I felt he was blackmailing me, but his auctions sold.

"If I am to be your agent, I must possess your confidence. Give me your word that his *Aristotle* will be crated this week and I will labor devoutly for your interests. The ship is to sail next week and if your painting is not on it, there is no other bottom for a month."

I hated to bargain, yet he had a point. I said, "I will do what I can if you place a nude I have just completed in your next auction."

"There is no market for nudes these days in the Netherlands."

"This one is worth exhibiting."

"Who does she represent?"

"Bathsheba."

"You will paint Jewish subjects. No good will come of that."

"But," I retorted angrily, "If I disguise the Jew as St. Paul, who was also a Jew, there may be a market."

"That depends. Biblical subjects are not in fashion either." But when he saw that I was not giving in unless he did, he added, "I will do what I can with your *Bathsheba* if the *Aristotle* is on its way to Sicily by next week. Don Antonio Ruffo is a great opportunity for you, Rembrandt."

"When will I receive the five hundred guilders?"

"After the work arrives at Ruffo's palace in Messina and he can decide whether it fits. You must not hurry him. It is not right. Tomorrow I will come to see your *Bathsheba* and to crate Ruffo's *Aristotle.*"

"No, no!" I cried, panic-stricken. "That is too soon."

"You promised . . ."

"I never promised. I said I would try." I estimated hurriedly, "Today is Monday. Come Friday, late. But while there is still sun in the sky, before twilight, so you can view it in the softest light."

"Remember, the ship sails next Monday."

The next few days I labored like Prometheus to finish *Aristotle* to my satisfaction. No other motive moved me. Ruffo had commissioned this portrait of "a philosopher" over two years ago and had left the choice of subject and treatment in my hands. Now, as I approached completion, I wondered if I had been too ambitious. I believed that the Sicilian nobleman would have been content with a single half-figure of Aristotle; instead I had included Homer. Yet, I assured myself, it was fitting for the philos-

(39)

opher to contemplate the bust of the poet in his pursuit of wisdom. And this was my way of expressing it.

When Van Goor arrived at my studio to collect the picture for delivery, I realized I would never be completely satisfied with this work. I was not certain I had achieved my intention, but I reasoned that the composition should suffice for its purpose. I had deeply involved my feelings, not my learning. I believed that Aristotle and Homer did possess an inner brightness, that they would be felt.

I sensed that the art dealer did not share my view, that he preferred richer, more beautiful colors, for he stared at the painting with perplexed eyes, as if, in his opinion, something was wanting, but he said, "It will do. It is satisfactory." I felt he said that because he was determined not to allow any excuse to delay further delivery of this work.

He added, "The subject is appealing. Ruffo should be pleased."

I was not interested in his opinion. His presence trespassed on my thoughts. He had become an intruder whose talk of art was an irritating presence; now I was certain that he could not see what I saw.

He grumbled, "You asked me to view your nude. Where is it?"

"In my salon." I led him into it without another word.

He was impressed with the splendor of the long oblong room with its oriental rugs, dark beamed ceiling, the three tall casement windows draped in damask, the highly polished wood of the wainscoting, and my collection of Seghers and Brouwers. Now that these painters, who had died in poverty, were dead, their work was valuable. He said, "If you need money, you should sell your Seghers and Brouwers."

"Who said that was necessary?" I asked angrily. The moment it was known that an artist was in need the value of his work depreciated.

"Rembrandt, you are unusually eager to sell your work."

"Here is the *Bathsheba.*" Daniel had hung it by the window as I had ordered, but I was still not sure that was right; the light fell unevenly.

The picture dealer regarded her without expression. Then he said, "There is no interest in the nude in Amsterdam. Unless it is by Titian."

"You do not want to exhibit this painting?"

"That is not what I said. The body is plastic and the shading in the background is good. You must simply realize it may not be saleable."

"Will you try?"

"What else do you have that can be exhibited?"

I took him into my storeroom. It was cluttered with paintings stacked against the walls, some finished, some unfinished, some to be reworked, some I no longer cared about, and a few that I liked to look at from time to time. There was dust on many of them, for no one was allowed in here except with my permission. Folios of drawings and etchings were on the carved table in the center of the storeroom, others were in boxes and racks with discarded palettes, brushes, paint rags. In a closet that was open so I would be reminded what was in it, I showed him some of my favorite ornaments. There were earrings, brooches, bracelets, strings of pearls—I loved the sparkle of jewelry—marine shells, medals, fans, bows, arrows. But when I saw his disgust with the disorder that prevailed, I stated, "I know where all my work is. I list my pictures as portraits, landscapes, religious studies, other subjects, and my drawings and etchings by genre. I keep them in separate albums under the headings: animals, figures, nude studies, landscapes, copies, and sketches of statues. And I possess a large quantity of unclassified work."

"Do you expect me to go through all this now? It would take forever."

"Van Goor, I have several biblical studies I have done recently."

"That has become a poor market since Calvin forbid the putting of pictures in our churches. And private persons, for the most part, have stopped buying them. If you have something decorative, medium-sized, and pleasant that would fit into a home I could show that."

"I have several portraits."

He did not seem interested but he asked, "Who are the subjects?"

"My son, a man in a golden helmet, my friend, Dr. Ephraim Bueno."

"The Portuguese Jewish physician?"

I nodded.

"You do not help yourself by painting Jews. That is not the proper task for a Christian painter. You favor Hebrews too much. Do you have any new works that deal with Christ?"

"Our Lord is the subject of several pictures I am working on now."

"Show them to me."

I found the two I liked best and put them on easels for his inspection.

He examined them quickly, then stated coldly, "I am disappointed. You do not display much wit. Jesus is too Jewish."

I replied strongly, "He is not Jewish enough. But I am working toward that end."

"Rembrandt, you injure yourself with your indifference to public taste."

"But Jesus was Jewish," I protested, "And spiritually, He was a rabbi."

"You are blasphemous. But you must have something I can sell. Ruffo is not a fool and neither is the Honorable Jan Six."

"I just delivered the burgher's portrait to him. Perhaps he will permit you to exhibit it. That might bring some orders."

Van Goor muttered skeptically, "That is not likely. The patrician likes to keep his art for himself. Do you have any landscapes?"

"A few." I showed him several, although they were no longer one of my favorite types of painting.

After he studied them and more of my pictures, he decided to exhibit two landscapes, a portrait of a boy that Titus had posed for and which he said had some charm, a young woman leaning on a door in the style of Titian, who, he felt, could be taken for a daughter of a burgher, and, as a concession, one of my favorite works, *Christ at Emmaus*.

Jesus came closest to my view of Him in this group painting, but I suspected that the picture dealer decided to show it to prove to me that my vision of Jesus was wrong, that it was too Jewish. At the last moment he also agreed to put my *Bathsheba* in his auction; again, I felt, to teach me a lesson. I concluded, while he arranged with Daniel for the delivery of *Aristotle,* that although he was critical of my choice of subjects and the way I painted them, he still thought there was money in my brush.

When Van Goor was gone, I mentioned this to Daniel, who had come into the storeroom to arrange for the shipment of the chosen works to the auction, and, to my surprise, he said, "The picture dealer is right."

"Why?" I wondered unhappily, Was even my apprentice betraying me?

"The market for Jewish subjects is poor."

"I did not expect you to say that."

"Because I am Jewish?" Daniel smiled sadly.

It was not a thing I ever brought up. I was interested in his gifts, scanty though they were, not his choice of pieties.

"Master, not all Dutchmen object to Jewish themes, but many do."

"Do you?"

"My view is of no account, sir."

"It is to me. Do you think that Jesus should be depicted as a Jew?"

"That is not an easy question to answer."

I disliked his evasiveness and I exclaimed, "You are a coward!"

He replied solemnly, his eyes averted from me, "It is true that the civic authorities have granted the Jewish community freedom of worship, but they have forbidden any criticism of the Christian religion."

"That is no reason for your family trying to be more Dutch than the Dutch themselves!" I exploded irately. "That is stupid!"

He said abruptly, "My father and I have never denied we are Jewish."

"Perhaps. But both of you behave like Dutchmen."

"Why not? We were born here."

(43)

"And so you avoid irritation more than exposure to your roots."

Daniel's discomfort grew and he changed the subject, saying, "I will never be able to send off *Aristotle* in time if you delay me."

"Blast *Aristotle!* Do you feel guilty, admitting you are a Jew?"

Startled by my loss of temper and shaken by my accusation, Daniel moved suddenly toward me, as if to deny that by striking me. Then, with an almost incredible effort of his will, for I sensed he was furious, he restrained himself and said softly, "That is none of your business."

"It is my business, since you assist me when I do subjects from the Old Testament. And my concern." But I stopped shouting, less angry now.

"Is that why you took me in as an apprentice?" he asked intently.

"Young man, you have not answered my question."

"Sir, do you want *Aristotle* crated now? The *Bartholomeus* sails on the tide Monday. The picture has to be loaded off the North Holland island of Trexel, since the ship is too big to sail through the Zuider Zee. I must deliver it immediately or it will miss the sailing."

His desire to change the subject was so strong I could not chide him any further, at least not now. I nodded, having regained some composure.

He added, "I will also prepare the works for the auction."

"Even though you think they will not be sold?" I asked mockingly.

"That is not what I said."

I still felt quarrelsome; I was on the verge of losing my temper again. It had been a trying day and I muttered darkly, "Everyone wants me to paint with caution. Yet when I try to borrow on my work, doors slam in my face."

Daniel said, consoling again, now that the attack on him had ended, "Master, you can borrow on your future. You will be a rich man then."

"Much good that will do me. I cannot borrow on the present."

Before he could reply, there was a violent commotion below. I heard a man's brutal voice raised against Hendrickje and her hysterical response. I ran downstairs, Daniel close behind me. Two men confronted her in the kitchen and I could tell by the severity of their black garb that they were the servants of the elders who were known as "The Brothers," paid spies and informers used to persecute anyone considered a heretic.

The leader, a middle-aged man of forty, sneered at the distraught Hendrickje, who was backed against the stove. "You are a creature of the devil. You will be eternally damned if you do not marry."

I shook my fist at them and rushed toward them. They backed away before I could hit them and I swore that they were the devils.

The second Brother snarled, "Van Rijn, you are profane."

I shouted, "You profane my house. Get out!"

They hesitated, but when Daniel, who was tall and muscular, joined me and I picked up a poker to emphasize my words, they retreated to the door. Then, just before they fled out the rear, the leader yelled, "We are taking your whore off the church register! She will languish in hell! She is committing a mortal sin! And you will end in the devil's arms, too!"

Stricken, Hendrickje threw a long brown cloak over her shoulders and started after the Brothers to beg for mercy, but I stopped her, saying, "You must ignore them. They are vultures."

She moaned, "Master, they speak for the elders."

But when I put my arm affectionately around her waist, although she had swollen so much it reached only halfway, she grew calmer. She sat down, while I asked, "I wonder who informed on us? The draper maker, the chimney sweep, the milkman, the grocer's delivery boy?"

"All the neighbors know," she mumbled.

"An apprentice Calvin, probably," said Daniel. "Where is Titus?"

She remembered suddenly. "He tumbled into the canal! I sent him to fetch some cod. Children were playing by the side of the water, he joined them, and one of them pushed him in."

"Deliberately?" I cried out, my temper flaring again.

"I do not think so. But I cannot be sure. We are not honored in this neighborhood." When she saw the anxiety on my face, she added hurriedly, "Titus is fine. I sent him upstairs to change his wet clothes. He is just scared. He cannot swim."

Neither could I, I thought, I had never had time to learn.

Daniel said, "I could teach him. I learned when I was in London."

"No!" I exclaimed. "He has more important things to learn. Hendrickje, did Titus say a neighbor's child pushed him into the canal?"

"He does not know who it was. It was from behind. But he said it might have been a prank, the children laughed so. A sailor fished him out."

"I will show them. I will take you, Titus, and Daniel to the auction. People will see that we are a family." I knew that she desired to be seen with me as a companion, that would give her the proper station in my household, and should suffice. I added, "I will take a day off from my work," feeling proud of my sacrifice. "And do not worry about being taken off the church register. I have been ready to give up that connection for years. They will not tell me how to live. They lack compassion. It was God who saved humanity by sacrificing his son Jesus Christ for our sakes. Our Lord loves us. I have shown that over and over in my work."

I stated that as emphatically as I could, but doubts remained. Titus joined us at the dinner table but he refused to talk about the near drowning. Daniel said that he was not hungry and he returned to *Aristotle* to finish the crating, while Hendrickje told me, "It is not fitting that I accompany you to the auction. I am not your wife."

Her vacillation was more than I could endure after the strains of the last few days and I sought escape in my work. Absorbed in my thoughts as I ate the cod Hendrickje had cooked, I decided that I could no longer paint Jesus as a Dutchman or an Italian or a Spaniard. I could hear Daniel hammering on the crate in the studio and I was glad I kept a large supply of nails in my house and that he was Jewish. He was in the true line of Our Lord, I reflected, however he wavered about that, and he might serve as a model, at least as a start, for a subject developing in my mind.

Then his hammering stopped, shaking me out of my reverie. Titus was drying the dishes Hendrickje cleaned, and I hastened upstairs to see if my painting was properly packed for shipment.

Daniel said, "It is done. *Homer* and *Aristotle* are on their way to Sicily."

I grumbled, "Hardly anyone will see this painting there."

"You may be wrong, Master," he replied, "Ruffo should be proud of it."

"Do you truly think so?"

"It is a magnificent work, with a sweep and authority that is grand."

"I hope you are right, but it is out of my hands now."

SOME DAYS I WEAR

Some days I wear
such piercing dagger colors
I blind the eyes of the sun
And the sun has to
protect its eyes

This instinct of mine
is just like the sun's
And neither of us will ever know
why
we need to be this way

The world would die
without the sun
Yet the sun
does not know this

The world would not die
if I did not shine
But I know this
And yet I have to shine
just like the sun

—Stymean Karlen

HENDRICKJE, if you do not go to the auction with me, I will not go!"

A week later I stated this with such vehemence that she gave in, for she knew that I would not be fit to live with if she disobeyed me.

"And do not wear black!" I shouted, "We are not in mourning!"

So she put on a pretty velvet bodice I had bought her because I liked its violet hue. The sleeves were blessed with vertical bands to lengthen the look of her body and to lessen the contours of her pregnancy. Her dress was a rich brown that I chose because it favored her complexion, and it was trimmed with yellow to brighten her hair and her eyes. When she was dressed I gave her a string of pearls to adorn her neck. I fancied the way they shone and wanted no one to assume that we were in need.

When she stood before me to find out if I approved, I nodded and said brusquely, to hide my pleasure lest she become vain, "I must paint you in this costume. It suits your person."

She smiled gratefully and whispered, "You are not ashamed of me?"

"That is a foolish thing to say. You are my companion."

"Will the world acknowledge that situation?" she asked anxiously.

"Those who are my friends will. The others are fools." Satisfied with my reply, I turned to see if my son and apprentice were suitably garbed.

Titus wore brown, too, as I had directed; it matched Hendrickje's clothes and fitted his fair, delicate coloring. Daniel was dashing in his red doublet and blue cloak, quite bravura for a resident of Amsterdam, and while his choice of colors heightened his good looks I was uneasy.

I was not certain that he was dressed sensibly. He wore too much red for me; I would have preferred more yellow or gold. But he was so gratified with his appearance that I did not criticize him. I gave him my approval and finished my toilet.

Determined to express the way I felt, I donned a flowing, sumptuous yellow cloak that glittered like the sun. Then, for contrast, I added a patch of white at my neck and a sash of orange around my ample waist. These colors were good to see—genuine work could be done with them and they gave me a feeling of well-being, a feeling I rarely had these days. Next, I, who was often shabby and careless in my dress, put the final touch to my wardrobe, a soft, large, round brimmed hat which I tilted over my right eyebrow to suggest an air of insouciance.

I loved hats. They were essential to me. They completed a person.

Now I was prepared, I thought resolutely, for almost anything.

It was a mild afternoon and we walked, for I wanted to observe my surroundings. I had a touch of regret, for it was a beautiful day for painting, bright and sunny, and perhaps I was wasting it, yet I yearned to see my work exhibited and the Italian masters that would be on view.

I placed Hendrickje close to me, with Titus next to her to express his affection, while I put Daniel on my other side. We passed people I knew and a few greeted me, but most of them gazed past us with a studied indifference. I ignored this stupidity, pretending that it was of no consequence, but still it angered me.

Hendrickje mumbled despondently, "I should not be with you," but I retorted, with a magnificent flourish, "You look lovely. These fools are not typical. It will be different at the auction."

Daniel agreed—I felt to lift her flagging spirits—while Titus wanted to skip over the cobblestones, impatient with my stately stride.

But when I started to chide him, Hendrickje halted me, saying, "It is natural that he should be full of animal spirits."

He blurted out, "Papa, will there be anything to eat at the auction?"

"Probably. Influential patrons will be in attendance."

"Is that why we ate so little at home? I am hungry."

Hendrickje said, "Titus, it is good manners to arrive hungry. Then we can partake of the food and drink as polite guests should."

That appeared to mollify Titus, while, when we approached the Art Dealers' Corner, I tried to make Hendrickje feel comfortable. I took her by the hand and escorted her inside with all the dignity I possessed. It seemed to soothe her agitation. But nobody noticed our entrance.

A circle of men stood around Van Goor—whatever women had come must be elsewhere, I reflected apprehensively—and the men were engaged in an animated conversation. No one was looking at any of the work on the walls. I was annoyed; this was sacrilegious, and Hendrickje whispered, "Master, be calm."

I hastened to assure her, "I am not in the least upset," although

I was, and I added, "Let us see what Van Goor has put on exhibition."

I avoided the chattering men as if they had the plague and surveyed the main auction room. The art dealer called his galleries after the style of the decoration and this one was known as The Adam and Eve Room. The ceiling was adorned with mythological paintings of the Creation and they were framed by finely carved stucco. The wood-beamed walls were whitewashed to flatter the work that was hung, and they were lighted by a large glass chandelier that was set in the center of the ceiling. I liked the floor best, a mixture of soft-hued tiles in blue, orange, green, brown, and yellow.

Suddenly nothing mattered but the Titian portrait in front of me and the sketch of the figure beside it. I was charmed by the curve of the arm on the parapet, the movement in the flowing sleeve, the richness of the blue in the fabric, the strength of the black cape that matched the subject's dark hair and beard, and the penetrating eyes that met mine. I could not afford this portrait, regretfully, but the sketch, since it was done by a Venetian instead of a Florentine, might be attainable. I could learn from this Titian drawing; the Venetian had performed stunningly.

Even so, perhaps because I was comparing myself to him, I heard Hendrickje ask Daniel, "Where is our master's work?" and his reply, "In the third gallery. This one is for the Italians: Titian, Raphael, and Caravaggio. The second is for Durer, Van Dyck, Lievens, Bol, and Flinck."

I snapped, "You must not interrupt me when I am viewing. I will lose my concentration. It is not fair to the work I am observing."

There was a sudden silence and I turned to a Caravaggio. Some of his figures were too contorted for my taste, but I preferred his painting to the Raphael that dominated The Adam and Eve Room. Many in Amsterdam said this son of Urbino was the best painter of all, but his palette was often too pretty for me, as was this *Madonna and Child.* Sometimes I liked his composition, but I did not care for his visual imagination.

Many paintings bored me but this Caravaggio illuminated the

darkness. I could do without Caravaggio's tricks, but his audacity and passion excited me. I was admiring his able use of *chiaroscuro* when I felt a tap on my shoulder. I pivoted angrily, but when I saw that it was Daniel I controlled my temper.

He said, "Your lady is uncomfortable. No one is talking to her."

"Where is Titus?"

"He has gone in search of food, to the reception room where the other ladies are. Hendrickje is afraid to go there alone."

She was standing next to the Caravaggio that attracted me, her eyes downcast. After I told Daniel to watch Titus, I hastened to assure her that we were welcome. To prove this, I took her by the hand and led her toward the group around Van Goor. As we approached them, I was shocked—they were all people I owed money to! I wondered, Was that the reason they were here? Had they come to see if I would sell any pictures?

They were all dressed alike. Even Van Goor had discarded his fashionable French garb in favor of sober colors and dark accessories, long breeches, knitted wool stockings, and the gray cape and violet doublet that served many purposes. For a moment I felt that we were peacocks next to their sedate attire, but then I was glad that I had taken care with Hendrickje's outfit, for I saw that several admired her dress, although they would never admit it. The men, who had been laughing heartily, became silent as soon as we reached them. I decided that they had been gossiping about my situation with her, and so, while she had met most of them before, I introduced her as "My lady."

Van Goor frowned, as if to say, Do you want to spoil my chances of selling your work? Six greeted her politely and the others were formal, but they did acknowledge her presence, which was what I desired.

Van Goor said, "We were discussing the illegitimate children of Prince Frederick Henry. Who do you think will paint them as a family group?"

Six asked, "Rembrandt, have you been approached?"

"No!" I replied angrily, feeling insulted, that somehow, this was aimed at my situation with Hendrickje, that they were mocking me.

"You should not be offended. The House of Orange is the most revered family in the United Seven Provinces. They are our heroes."

Not mine, I reflected, but perhaps these men were trying sincerely to find out if I had been approached by the influential House of Orange. I had painted important work for Prince Frederick Henry, even if it had been twenty years ago, and he had reacted favorably. I said curtly, "It is too late. His children are grown. And he is dead."

"It is never too late," said Van Goor. "Now that his children are legitimate, there is talk of a family group. A good painter could reconstruct this work from previous things that were done."

"I am not interested. It would be second-rate work."

While they argued whether this was true and Hendrickje stood silently, for this was not a subject considered appropriate for a female to discuss, their presence reminded me of the money I owed them. To my uneasy mind, which yearned to be free of these loans, Six still represented a thousand-guilder debt, although he had transferred this obligation to the iron dealer, Gerbrandt Ornia, who was at his side. Next to him was Christoffel Thyst, the heir of the man who had sold the grand house on the Breestraat to me; I guessed that the sum owed him came to eight thousand guilders, more or less, but probably more. I had borrowed from Six to pay the interest on this debt, only to have to use his money for other needs. Then I had borrowed four thousand guilders from Cornelius Witsen, the fat, short, pompous burgomaster of Amsterdam, with the intention of giving that to Thyst, but that, too, had been diverted to new bills.

I was amused that Witsen was by the side of the stiff, thin grain merchant, Isaac van Hertsbeeck. The four thousand guilders I had obtained from him had been for the burgomaster, but again, this loan had gone elsewhere.

For unpaid grocery bills, I reflected, and doctors' bills, bakers' bills, bills for clothes and costumes, bills to frame makers and dealers in pigments and palettes and brushes, and for copper plates and printer's ink and so many more bills that I had lost track of or had tried to forget.

No wonder they were assembled here. I decided that they were at this auction to judge whether they could retrieve any of their funds through the sale of my work, although it was unlikely that they would buy anything, and to judge my future prospects, if I had any. Then I was depressed. My affairs were so disorderly, so complicated, I was getting a headache from reviewing them. And their conversation did not lift my low spirits.

Six stated, "Gentlemen, I had to abandon my family business to remedy our civic affairs, they are so untidy. We never should have fought the English while they were astride our trade routes. It was stupid."

Van Hertsbeeck, whose thinness was accentuated by Witsen's fatness, added, "My corn trade lags, prices are rising, even herring is scarce."

Witsen said, "And some banks will fail. Conditions are hard. The English covet more of our trade. It is no time to invest in art."

"This condition will pass," Van Goor said hurriedly.

"The Italians will always be valuable," Six reminded his colleagues.

"Is that not so, Rembrandt?" Witsen asked me.

I shrugged as if I did not care, although I did. I was more concerned that no one was speaking to Hendrickje and I knew that she would not say anything unless she was addressed first. I thought grimly, I would be happier with my fellow craftsmen. I was turning to go when Daniel reappeared and said, "Master, may I show your lady the galleries?"

I answered, "If she will not mind."

Hendrickje said softly, "I will be honored."

Daniel bowed to her. Now I was grateful for his fine clothes and dashing colors, for he was the gallant as he responded, "I am the one who will be honored. Master, we will look at your pictures in The Damask Room."

But even after they were gone I was still uncomfortable. I felt that these men, even the contained Jan Six, wanted to shout at me, When will you pay, when? And that they were more worried about this than I was.

Witsen asked, "Rembrandt, why have you avoided Italy?"

"I have learned enough in the Netherlands."

"Your work would be worth more if you had studied there."

"I prefer Amsterdam. It sustains my brush."

"Our best artists have worked in Italy."

I thought impatiently, I have not only illustrated Holland, I have illuminated it, but I tried to be patient as I explained, "It does not matter where one studies but what one sees. It is easy to travel to Italy and to gaze on Florentine sunsets and Venetian canals and colors but that has nothing to do with what I am. Or what I become."

"Nonetheless, most of our Dutch masters have studied in Italy."

"Sir, I think it wise to find my subjects in my own region." Even though, much of the time, it was the country of my mind and imagination.

Van Hertsbeeck said, "I agree with my good friend, the burgomaster. For a Dutch artist to become a master he should work in Italy." When Jan Six expressed the same opinion, Ornia, who had been silent, did so also. Then Thyst and Van Goor made it unanimous, although I was not sure the picture dealer meant it, for he changed the subject.

He asked Jan Six if he could exhibit the portrait I had just done.

"No!" The patrician replied curtly. "My collection is private!"

And included some of the best things I had done but I did not press him either, although I felt that it would have been to my advantage if he had consented. It would have convinced some of these doubters that I was still capable of doing a fine portrait.

Six added, "Rembrandt should have other work that is worth viewing."

Van Goor declared, "Of course. And they are for sale."

I did not like the critical expression on the face of Witsen or Van Hertsbeeck's obvious agreement with him, and I was still provoked by their assertion that Italy was necessary for my brush, and so I exclaimed, "Painting does not depend on where you see your subject, but how you see it and convey it." Van Goor was desperately trying to halt me but I was not going to heed him; I was tired of being lectured and chastised for being independent. "I must get my stimulus from my own country. Furthermore, if the Italians care so much for their masters, why do they allow them to be sent abroad? The best work of Titian,

Giorgione, and Raphael is to be found in Amsterdam—except for the paintings done on the walls of churches—for here there is a market for them. Italian art needs us more than we need them."

I felt that I had given them clear and concise reasons for my views, but their response was a shocked silence.

Just as I was certain that no one would speak, as if I had maligned their most cherished prejudices, Jan Six said abruptly, "Let us judge for ourselves Rembrandt's argument." He motioned for all to follow him into the third gallery but I stayed behind. I was not inclined to hear their comments, especially when I owed them money.

I was in the second gallery, The Gilt-Leather Room, poised before an engraving by Durer—I did not care for the other work, even the two portraits by Van Dyck—but Durer was a man I could feast on, when Thyst appeared suddenly and whispered, "Rembrandt, my patience is not eternal. Do you have any commissions? You have not even paid the interest on your mortgage this past year. Soon it will be larger than the principal."

"Give me five or six months and I will pay it."

"You promised that last year. I have not seen a single stiver."

"Whatever I get from my *Bathsheba,* I assure you, will go to you."

"No one will want it. She is gross. Now if you painted like Titian . . .?"

"Did you look at her carefully?"

"Carefully enough! Fancy putting your mistress on public display! And I am not the only one who feels that way. Do not forget, if you do not reduce your obligation on my property soon, I will foreclose."

With that, Thyst strode away. I saw Ornia approaching and I sensed that he was going to ask for money, too, and so, to evade him, I hurried into the third gallery and tried to blend into the crowd. Although most of the viewers were in the first two rooms, there were about a dozen people gazing at my work, mostly strangers, the others had returned to the main gallery for the auction of the Italian masters. I was relieved that Ornia had not followed me, as if he desired a better opportunity to accost me, and I noted that most of the spectators were looking at my *Bath-*

sheba. More out of curiosity than genuine interest, I felt, but at least it had caught their attention.

Then, to my dismay, Pastor Hoag entered the gallery and went straight for me. I was stricken with forboding but I had to take the offensive. I said, "How dare you send your vultures into my house?"

He looked puzzled and he replied, "I do not know what you mean."

"Two of your Brothers threatened my lady with hell-fire and damnation."

"They were doing their duty," he retorted piously.

"I threw them out. And if they come again . . ."

I left it unfinished purposely so he would ask, "What will you do?"

"Hoag, I will not be responsible for the consequences."

While the pastor, shaken by my defiance, searched for an adequate response, I saw that Van Goor had used cheap candles to light my work instead of the expensive tallow candles in the other galleries, that it was badly hung, and the damask drapes shut out the sunlight. I missed the sun, it shone too little in Amsterdam as it was, and so when it did, as today, I yearned for its warm, piercing brightness.

Then Hendrickje, Daniel, and Titus came into the room with some friends and I was relieved that they were talking animatedly. Before I could join them, Hoag blocked my way, having recovered his equanimity, and he stated, "I have come to warn you that our patience is exhausted."

"So is mine."

"Do not joke, Van Rijn. We will expugn your mistress from the church register if you do not marry her and legitimatize her child."

"Someone will baptize the baby."

"I doubt it. We are Calvin's country and The Reformed Church is his instrument. We do not tolerate heresy."

This was a serious charge and I could not ignore it. I considered myself as good a Christian as anyone, and yet, I wondered, had I in some way deviated from the faith of Jesus?

"It is no accident that your religious pictures are not in demand."

I responded by pointing to my painting *Christ at Emmaus,* which hung near us.

He grumbled pedantically, "It is too passionate."

"But Jesus was passionate!" I exploded. "That was why He cared!"

"This is not for you to say. You take excessive liberties. Take your painting of Bathsheba. It is erotic, immoral."

I said, "Then so is the Bible."

"Do not distract me. It is no wonder that you and your woman are living in sin. You will both end in hell if you continue to paint this way. It is ungodly, heretical."

"Is that why you came to this auction?"

He said proudly, "I know a good picture when I see it. Even your friends, the Mennonites, would be ashamed of some of the subjects you paint. Dogs fornicating, defecating, peasants pissing, puking. If you do not mend your ways no one in my church will buy any of your work."

In some ways this was the most serious charge of all, I thought angrily, for most of my potential patrons belonged to his church.

"Consider carefully. Heresy is a crime against the state."

I fled from his presence before the doubts that he had aroused could overwhelm me. I was deeply conscious of the supremacy of God, the evil of sin, the majesty of Jesus, and that wickedness often prevailed, and I had tried to express that through the Bible, and my own insight, but had I failed? Had I been arrogant? Or heretical? He had rapped my knuckles harshly, yet was there something to what he had said?

I was grateful that for the moment, at least, I could escape from these thoughts as I joined the group around Hendrickje, Daniel, and Titus. She was smiling for the first time today. Ordinarily, I considered the men she was talking to my friends, but now I was suspicious of everyone.

Then, as was my habit, for faces fascinated me, I merely nodded a greeting so I could examine their countenances for signs of change.

I was pleased to see that Abraham Francen, the apothecary, was holding Titus by the hand affectionately as he joked with Hendrickje, and that his features were still soft and unlined and his long, brown hair as attractive as ever. I was also glad to see the lean and courtly Lodewijck van Ludick, a print seller who had stood surety for my loan from Jan Six. Although both of these men were of my generation, neither had aged prematurely as I had; fortunate men, I thought. Isaac Joost was another friend that I felt at home with, for his square, blunt face reminded me of my own, and although he was much younger, he was compassionate, and devoted to my brush.

Francen was saying, "Hendrickje, you must be feeding Titus cleverly. He has grown positively plump. I hardly recognize him."

"It is the Master's wish," she said, but she looked gratified.

"Here are the Dutch pictures that matter," Joost declared. "Not the elegant, high-finished paintings in the Art-Leather Room. Rembrandt, you have forgotten more than Lievens, Bol, or Flinck has ever known."

"I do not like comparisons," I said sharply.

"Everyone indulges in them."

"I am not everyone. But I appreciate your feeling, Joost."

Titus said suddenly, "Papa, the women in the reception room would not talk to me. What have I done wrong?"

"Nothing, son, nothing." I had had enough of this auction. "Let us go. I have seen what I came to see."

My son did not want to leave. He said, "I want to see if anybody will buy my picture."

"You will hear if anyone does." It was unnatural, I thought angrily, to accept being ignored in favor of inferior painters. I had suffered many humiliations but this was one that I was determined to avoid.

Francen said, "Titus, I have already asked for your portrait."

My son grinned and said, "What will you do with it?"

"I will hang it in my parlor where I will see it every day."

"Thank you. Papa, will you paint me again?"

"If it suits my brush." I observed that we were the only people viewing my work now and this upset me too, especially when I saw that the other two galleries were crowded. My friends accompanied us to the door, where Van Goor stopped us and asked us to remain.

Tempted in spite of my irritation, I paused, but Hendrickje exclaimed, "Master, I am tired, frightfully tired!"

I realized that she had no more strength to endure the scorn of most of the guests. That worried me, for Saskia had said the same thing just before she had fallen fatally ill. I tipped my hat to Van Goor to express nonchalance and said, "I am not needed here."

Ludick, who had been unusually quiet, said, "I will stay. If you do not mind, Rembrandt?"

"Why should I mind?" I retorted, but I was surprised.

"I want to see what is sold."

"You do not have to explain."

Van Goor drew me aside and whispered, "Do any of your friends want to purchase any of your pictures?"

"Francen, I think. Van Goor, how much is the Titian drawing?"

"You cannot afford it. You should pay your debts first."

"How much?" I repeated.

"I had intended to ask four hundred guilders, but for you, under the circumstances, since his drawings are not in the fashion, I might consider . . ."

I interrupted. "I will give you three hundred for it. No more."

"Everyone desires his nudes. I told you that *Bathsheba* would not sell."

"If Francen wants my portrait of Titus ask for three hundred guilders."

"You will owe me a commission. I will ask for five hundred."

"Bargain as you will, but I will dispose of it only if you sell me the drawing." Now, with the biggest flourish I could summon, I raised my hat to that agreement while he shrugged, as if he were not sure he could do this. "Have there been any inquiries about my other paintings?"

"Only about the landscapes. As I told you . . ."

I cut him short. "You have told me enough. Good day."

Van Goor withdrew to attend the patrons who were waiting for the auction to begin, and I started out. At the last moment Francen and Joost changed their minds and decided to stay. Francen said he wanted to be sure that no one else obtained the portrait of Titus, although I doubted that anyone else would want it, and Joost added that he thought I might prefer to be alone with my family and that he intended to bid for one of my landscapes, which would fit appropriately into his parlor.

Evidently that gave Daniel the courage to say, "Master, do you mind if I remain, too?"

I did, but I exclaimed, "Of course not!"

"My father is coming and I am eager to guide him. I may be able to persuade him to buy one of your paintings."

"That is not necessary. No one should have to be persuaded."

Daniel said apologetically, "He has to learn what is a good picture."

"Do not apologize. Never apologize."

Hendrickje and Titus followed me out of the auction; Titus, I sensed, unwillingly. I was so eager and impatient to be away from what had become adverse criticism of my work that I walked ahead of my family. I was very lonely. No one else was leaving the auction and I felt deserted.

AN EMPTY CANVAS IS

An empty canvas is
like a new day to fill

Is like a new world
to create in your own way

Is like a great unknown
to explore and discover

Is like a past civilization
to imagine and redefine

Is like so many things
but not like an empty canvas

An empty canvas is

—Stymean Karlen

THE auction was a success. Van Goor made sure that I knew this.

I was doing my preliminary drawings for a new portrait of Jesus —it was the only way that I could free myself of the disgust that I had felt after the auction, although I had not yet decided on a model—when the art dealer stopped in to tell me that the Italian masters had fetched the highest prices ever known in Holland, and perhaps the world.

He announced triumphantly, "Despite the poor business conditions, I obtained thousands of guilders for the Titian, Raphael, and Caravaggio."

I shrugged to indicate my indifference and went on working. He asked incredulously, "Rembrandt, you are not interested?"

"No."

My disgust was vanishing, for I was doing what I loved, and I had lost track of the days since the auction in my absorption with Jesus, which I preferred—I hated to be dependent on time, it was a kind of servitude—but it must have been several weeks later, for he added irritably, "I expected you to visit me and find out what happened. Finally, I got tired of waiting. My Dutch masters sold, too."

I did not respond.

"Van Dyck, Lievens, Durer, Bol, and . . ." He paused deliberately.

Lifting my eyes away from what had become the ruin of my drawing, his entry had fatally distracted me; I thought, He has another reason for being here; and I grumbled, determined not to give him the satisfaction of showing any interest in my own sales, that would make me subservient to him and the marketplace, "How can I work when you interrupt me?"

"You do not care what happened to your pictures?"

"Van Goor, you are pale, you should be in the sun more. It shines so seldom here that you should take advantage of this nice weather."

"What would you know about it, closeted in your studio like a hermit?"

"The sun is good for my work."

He said skeptically, "With all the darkness you use?"

I reminded him, "Out of darkness comes light, out of light comes—"

"I know," he interrupted quickly, "you have told me that many times. Do you want the Titian drawing you mentioned?"

This was a different matter. "Yes."

"You have not come for it."

"I gave you my word. Did Francen buy the portrait of Titus?"

"On the spot. I convinced him that it was worth five hundred guilders."

"You overcharged him. But he meant well."

"Rembrandt, you are not concerned with what you sold?"

"You will tell me." I would have liked to have used him as a model; he was animated when he was not pouting, but he lacked the spirit I needed for Jesus. As he stared at me, I realized I was incomprehensible to him, a mystery he could not fathom.

He complained, "You do not appreciate my efforts on your behalf."

"I do," I replied quietly, "when you employ them."

"I did at the auction," he stated proudly, "I also sold a landscape to Joost for two hundred guilders, *The Girl at the Window* to Ludick for another two hundred, and I even managed to dispose of your *Bathsheba.*"

Surprised, I cried out, "You said there was no interest in her!"

He grinned, pleased that he had obtained an advantage over me, and added, "William van Dorn purchased it."

"Daniel's father?" I had not expected this.

"He came with your friends, Rabbi Manasseh ben Israel, and Ephraim Bonus, the Portuguese Jewish doctor, and when your apprentice called their attention to *Bathsheba* and they approved, he bought it."

So that was why Daniel had remained, I decided, but why had he hidden this sale from me? "Did Van Dorn give any reason for buying it?"

"The Jew said that *Bathsheba* represented the glory of King David."

"Are you sure that Van Dorn genuinely desired this painting?"

"I do not ask my customers such stupid questions. He paid me promptly. Three hundred guilders. In cash."

"Now I can buy the Durer engraving, too," I said eagerly.

Van Goor sighed helplessly and said, "You are hopeless."

"It is one of the finest engravings I have ever seen."

"It is a thousand guilders. You must pay your debts first. You owe virtually everyone of consequence in Amsterdam."

"There is time for that."

"Not as much time as you think. Witsen, van Hertsbeeck, Thyst, and Ornia are men of business. They will not wait much longer. Particularly since two church elders asked me to withdraw your work from the auction because of your present household circumstances. If you do not mend your ways, no one will buy you except a Jew or a Roman Catholic like Ruffo."

Angrily, I stormed, "Are you referring to my lady?"

"Call her what you will," he answered cynically, "your way of life makes you a great risk. That I have been able to sell any of your pictures is an accomplishment. You are no longer the fashion."

"Despite our national reputation for tolerance?"

"Do not confuse the issue. We tolerate other faiths but we do not tolerate a lack of faith. That is heresy. However, in spite of your scandalous behavior," he concluded proudly, "I did sell you."

Van Goor was a good Dutchman, I thought wryly, He would not allow piety to interfere with profit, and I was still profitable, if only occasionally. I asked, "Will you deliver the Durer with the Titian?"

"No! Even with what you sold, you would still owe me hundreds of guilders for the Durer. I cannot take that risk. You borrow from van Hertsbeeck to pay Witsen and in the end you pay neither of them. At the auction your creditors considered attaching whatever money you received. It took much persuasion on my part to dissuade them from that step, to point out that if they cut off your earnings now you would not be able to work, and thus, they would lose most of what they had lent you."

I did not want to destroy what might be my last chance to sell. I said, "I appreciate your efforts. When will I get my fees?"

"I will apply two hundred guilders from Van Dorn to the Titian."

"You told me that he gave three hundred for *Bathsheba.*"

"One hundred is my commission. Francen, Van Ludick, and Joost said they will pay soon. Are you working on anything else that I can exhibit?"

"A portrait of Jesus."

"Such subjects are difficult to sell, often impossible."

"Did you have any inquiries for *Christ at Emmaus?*"

"My customers said it is too dark. One of the reasons you are no longer popular is that you have changed your style. Now the bright and elegant manner of Van Dyck is preferred. I could have sold anything of his I had. You demand too much from your viewers."

For once, I thought grimly, the picture dealer might be right. I went to the head of the stairs and called up to the attic for Daniel to usher him out. Then, as he arrived promptly because of the urgency in my voice, I said, "Van Goor, I will have Daniel pick up the Titian drawing."

"What about the work you were doing when I entered? May I look at it?"

"No."

"I could offer a suggestion or two. Make it more saleable."

"Good day. And Daniel, after you have taken care of our estimable picture dealer, will you attend me?"

I returned to my drawings, but my hand felt numb. I was accustomed to making many sketches, but van Goor's words worried me. No matter what I did, my debts multiplied and threatened to destroy my concentration on my work and added to my doubts. Once I doubted myself, I doubted my work. I pressed so hard upon my red chalk that it crumbled in my fingers.

Daniel returned and as he stood in the doorway his sensitive features appealed to me, yet to use him as a model for Jesus seemed wrong, he was too worldly, too concerned about the glory of being an artist. I asked him abruptly, "Did you persuade your father to buy *Bathsheba?*"

"I persuaded him to view it. The decision to buy it was his own."

"Why did he make this decision?"

"Master, the subject is Jewish."

"Was that the only reason?" I asked skeptically.

Daniel smiled slyly and said, "My father may have been influenced by the fact that Jan Six, whom he admires, has a collection of your work."

Daniel looked so satisfied I changed the subject. "Today I must put my affairs in order. Summon Hendrickje and tell her to bring me whatever bills she has."

To convince myself that I meant what I said, while he was gone I collected all of my bills. Years ago, I had started to put them into a long oaken box, but it had overflowed and since then I had stuck my bills into whatever was about me at the time. After I took the oblong box from the shelf, I found bills in my smocks, in my doublets, behind drawings I had discarded, attached to other papers, and folded into corners and crevices of the studio. Some of them were so dusty I could not decipher them, on others the writing had faded from age and neglect.

By the time Daniel came back with Hendrickje, I was sitting at my studio table behind a pile of papers that was my tower of Babel, which spoke to me in many tongues but none, I felt, that were my own.

Hendrickje carried a market basket full of other bills, chiefly for the day-to-day things like bread, milk, and herring, but there were some for pots of paint, canvases, palettes, prints, ink, and crayons. Suddenly I wanted to flee, I wanted to be anywhere but here. I sensed that I could not bring order out of this disorder; it would take the rest of my life and I did not have that much time to spare from my work.

Hendrickje opened the window to let air in, the studio had become hot and stifling, and a gust of wind blew many of my bills aimlessly about on the table. For an instant I considered ordering Daniel to start a fire to burn all this trash. Instead, containing this impulse with effort, I said to Hendrickje, "Splendid! Soon we will know how much we owe!"

She asked somberly, "What about the big debts? What you owe Thyst, Witsen. I cannot find them. Have you lost the accounting for the house?"

I turned to Daniel, but he shook his head to indicate that he did not know where they were and I had forgotten where I had put them.

She said, "A few days ago there was an emissary from Thyst asking for the interest on the mortgage. I put him off by telling him you would give him that when you were paid for your sales at the auction. I am not sure he believed me but he went away. But only for the time being."

I asked, "Has anybody else come for money?"

"Almost every day. We have fallen behind with the baker, milkman, grocer. We need money for food and necessities. Master, did Van Goor give you any guilders for the sales at the auction?"

"No."

Daniel said, "Begging your pardon, sir, but what about the money my father gave him? I know that he paid in cash."

Hendrickje's face lit up for an instant as if a ray of sunlight was on it, only to become grave when I said, "I used it. For a necessity."

I would not explain further, I could not explain how much that Titian drawing mattered to me. But she looked so miserable that I could not rid myself of the obsession that I was responsible for her unhappiness. I could not purge my poor, old, tired brain of a vision of the church council grinding her down into a devastated ruin. Then their dismissal of my Christianity hurt painfully. Without faith I doubted that I could go on. To divest myself of this terror, I walked over to an old globe of the world and spun it around. Unused for a long time, it creaked and fell off its axis.

I said slowly, "Hendrickje and Daniel, separate the bills the best way you can. So, at least, I will know where the most immediate demands are. I must go out. To clear my head."

She said woefully, "These debts are God's punishment for our sins."

Assuming the kind of faith I felt that we needed, I replied piously, "Hendrickje, if an infinitely good and wise God has chosen to visit us with afflictions we must not complain. If we allow them to produce melancholy, it will prove fatal to our health. Such things are not to be altered by sorrow or complaints. It is sensible to compose the disorder of our minds by applying our thoughts to things that are more agreeable."

I was not sure she understood what I was saying, but Daniel remarked, "Master, you must be careful. A long walk could exhaust you."

"Not as much as these bills!" I growled. With a rage that astonished even me, I tore up the drawings of Jesus with sudden savagery while Daniel and Hendrickje watched in horror. "I must find him elsewhere!"

She asked, "Will you be back for supper?"

"I will be back when I will be back." But when I saw the dismay on her face, I kissed her. Brusquely, it was true, but for the first time in the presence of someone else. Then I shouted, "Daniel, I expect you to make sense out of this nonsense," motioning at the pile of bills with a sweep of my hand. Before either of them could protest, I rushed out, but only after I had grabbed my sketch pad and pencil.

I wanted to avoid the city, which I felt had attacked me, and so I strode hurriedly until I reached the countryside. Only when I began to feel an affection for what I saw was I able to view clearly again. I halted for a minute to sketch a haystack that loomed like a mountain on the flat, even land. I was following a waterway which reminded me of the ever-present sea, and the soil which was below the level of the sea, and the dikes and the other efforts that had gone into the maintaining of these banks to protect the lowlands from being flooded. We, the Dutch, I told myself, treasured every inch of our earth, even when it was nothing but clay and turf, as now, and in many places not even that, but simply mud. I forgot my bills as I halted to draw a tree by a small bridge over a rural canal. I loved trees and their expressiveness, this oak had roots like legs, branches like arms. One enormous root in particular fascinated me, I saw it as a huge toe. Then my attention was caught by a clump of trees that were tinged with light and shadow. The wind rose, a storm appeared to be approaching, yet the sun continued to shine. These three trees were animated and alive as their leaves moved with the wind in a graceful dance. I felt that they possessed a charmed life as I sketched them passionately. Just as suddenly as the storm appeared it vanished over the horizon without harming a single twig. And when a leaf fell I picked it up and stuffed it into a pocket of my doublet.

By the time I came back to my house on the Breestraat I felt almost amiable. Dusk was falling but I had learned that I could still draw. I could imagine Daniel laughing at that idea and replying, Master, you are better known as an etcher than as a painter, you are the best there is, you cannot doubt this, but what he did not know, what I could not tell anyone, was that without faith I was nothing. Every line I drew was an act of faith. I still felt far away from the conception of Jesus I was seeking but at least, as I approached Hendrickje, who smiled when she saw me enter the kitchen, I knew I must paint Him as my gift to her. That was reason enough. Although I realized I had other motives, too.

Titus, who sat at the supper table, complained, "Papa, she would not feed me until you returned. And I am very hungry."

"Hendrickje is right. We must act as a family."

"But I never know when you are hungry."

"I am now. I had a splendid walk. I must take you next time."

"And make me draw? When I want to play?"

That was my play and had been even in childhood. Yet, eager to keep Hendrickje happy, I did not scold Titus. I asked, "Where is Daniel?"

Hendrickje said, "Upstairs. He has not come down since you left."

I shouted, "Daniel, I have something to show you!" He hurried in, looking tired, and he said that he wanted to discuss my debts, that he had put them into some order, but I cut him short, saying, "I have more vital matters to discuss. Look what I did today. Do you like them?"

This excited him, it was not in my nature to ask another's opinion of my work, least of all, an apprentice's. As I spread out my day's work on the kitchen table between the crockery and the pewter, Hendrickje and Titus crowded around us, curious to see how I had spent the rest of the day, while Daniel exclaimed, "Master, everything you draw is so alive!"

"See, Hendrickje," I added gently, "if God has given me such a gift, He must be wise and good."

Titus lost interest and repeated his demands that he be fed. In the commotion that followed, I could not tell if she agreed with me. Then Daniel reminded me, "Master, you must pay attention to your debts, or you will lose these drawings. When can we review your bills?"

"Later," I said curtly. I took out the leaf I had found and fondled it for a moment, enchanted with its blend of green and brown, and then I placed it by my side and thought, It has a language all of its own.

The next day, having reflected on my affairs while I had lain beside Hendrickje in the large four-poster bed that I had inherited from Saskia, I did not wait for Daniel to itemize my debts, that would have been too painful, I would never be able to work if I knew all the sorry details. Instead, before he could tell me how much I owed and to whom, I gave him orders with such authority that he could not disagree with me. Hendrickje had clutched my hand so intensely while we slept that I had to relieve her of some of her anxiety over the household bills.

Daniel listened carefully as I stated, "Francen, Ludick, and Joost's purchases should total nine hundred guilders. Do not allow Van Goor to take more than three hundred for his commission. Then, with the remaining six hundred, apply that as follows. One hundred to each of my chief creditors, Thyst, Witsen, Van Hertsbeeck, and Ornia, as—you must tell them—an expression of my good faith and my desire to pay them back. Give the art dealer another hundred to conclude the purchase of the Titian drawing, and the last hundred to Hendrickje for household expenses."

"In that order, Master?" Daniel questioned.

"In that order," I answered emphatically. "I want to ease Hendrickje's worries, but first, I must stop any threats of foreclosure."

"I doubt that any of these creditors will be satisfied."

"It should give me more time."

"What then, Master?"

"No one will let me work in peace," I grumbled, "Not one, not even . . ."

Daniel responded as I hoped: "Sir, I will do my best."

"Good."

"One other thing, Master. What about the money from Jan Six?"

"He may apply it to the loan. If not, I will find a use for it. Now fetch me the Titian drawing before Van Goor changes his mind." But Daniel did not move and I cried out, "What is wrong?" I was so eager to start a new painting of Jesus that I could hardly restrain myself.

"Will you look at my work? You have not seen it for a long time."

There was so much emotion in his voice I realized this was an urgent matter to Daniel. Yet I feared that my judgment would hurt him, he had not shown much talent and I doubted that he had improved. Hendrickje thought that I regarded him as a son, but that was not true. I liked his nature. He had come back from London in spite of an education that had created valuable connections for him and he had joined me when other apprentices were deserting me. But I hesitated. I felt uncomfortable.

"Sir, how can I help Titus if I cannot help myself?"

"Keep working and I will observe your efforts at the appropriate time."

"My father wants to see what I have done and to know your opinion of it. He prefers that I go into the family business, but I have dreamed of being an artist all my life. It is the only thing that excites me, that makes me happy. And if he comes here, he may buy more of your work."

According to our contract, I did not have to heed Daniel's request, he was supposed to serve me in return for my instruction, to do all sorts of menial tasks, to grind my paints, to mix my oils, and never to complain. But since I felt obligated to Daniel for his efforts on my behalf, I agreed to look at his work.

We climbed to the attic together. Many pupils had studied with me and in the past the spacious attic had been divided into cubicles, each one filled with an eager apprentice. Today the attic was filled with only dust and silence. And Daniel's quarters shocked me. They were a rubbish heap of costumes, hangings, and hats, as if it was from these things that he chose the background for his work. He apologized for the clutter, stuttering that he fancied the variety of fabrics and colors, but I sensed that he had collected what I had cast off in an effort to find self-expression by imitating me. I pretended that this did not matter and I asked to see the latest work he was doing.

His self-portrait was intelligent but without life. I saw that at a glance, but I examined it intently to indicate that I was interested.

He asked, his voice trembling, "Master, is it worthy of your studio?"

"Interesting," I murmured. I did not know what else to say.

"Should I show it to my father?"

William van Dorn might not know the difference, I reflected, and Daniel, like most apprentices, had painted himself flatteringly as if failure was impossible. I sneezed, my nose full of dust.

Daniel asked anxiously, "What is wrong, sir?"

"Some people are concerned every time I sneeze. Your quarters need a thorough cleaning. What else are you working on?"

"I am teaching Titus to draw animals. He likes them. What will you tell my father?"

"That you are industrious. And that you paint like most apprentices, in the style of their teacher. Be more individual. Where is Titus' work?"

Daniel showed me a dog that my son had painted. It was even worse than my apprentice's work, but I hid my disappointment, merely saying, "He should work harder. I fear that Titus is inclined to be lazy."

"Master, he is still a child. He is only thirteen."

"When I was his age, even while I was in Latin school in Leyden studying Ovid, Cicero, Virgil, Horace, and Caesar, I was using my free time to draw. I never had time for games. Drawing was my play."

"I was not aware that you knew Latin, sir."

"It enabled me to enter the university of Leyden, one of the best in Europe, but I left to pursue art. When I came to Amsterdam I used the Latin form of my name, Rembrandt Harmensis Leydensis. But for many who try to be artists, learning can be an affliction, can bind their hands."

"Master, is that one of my problems?"

"Sometimes. Forget your classical English education. Painters are not scholars. Be spontaneous, intuitive. Trust your feelings more."

"Will that help my craft, technique? What rules should I follow?"

"There are no rules. Just practice and hard work. And knowing how to see. When does your father want to look at your work?"

"When it is convenient for you, Master?"

"Try another subject first. Paint Titus and have him paint you." An idea was forming in my mind, but it was still too nebulous for me to be certain that it had value. "Now fetch me the Titian drawing."

By the time he returned with this coveted work I had set up an empty canvas in my studio that I was eager to fill. He informed me that Ludick, Joost, and Francen had paid for their pictures, but I was more concerned with the view of Jesus I had to find. I said curtly, "You know what to do with their money. Now do not allow anything to disturb me."

I did not hear him leave, the Titian drawing absorbed me, it was the quintessence of seeing. I laid out my crayons, red and black chalk, and pens to decide what instruments to use. But first I must know how I was going to see Jesus. I told myself that Our Lord must be tender—I needed His compassion—but He must also be human.

However, although I made many drawings of Jesus that day, the canvas remained empty. It was easy to express His outward actions, but it was difficult when I came to the search for His inner feelings. I wanted the viewer to be absorbed in the meaning of Jesus, not in His manner.

My sandglass ran down, marking the twelve hours I had worked on this subject, and I had to light an oil lamp to see at all. Exhausted, I halted, for my hands felt numb. I closed my eyes, which burned from fatigue, and tried to shut out my mistakes. Whatever I had found, I had not found His spirit. I sighed and draped the empty canvas so that it would not remind me of my failure. I put away my drawings so that they would not compel me to continue.

Hendrickje called me for supper and I shouted back, "I will be down!"

I left my studio without a look back. Otherwise, I felt, I would never be able to stop. Yet, as I sat down at the kitchen table with my family, Titus, Daniel, and Hendrickje, I kept thinking of the empty canvas and that I must fill it.

THE POOR CIRCLE

The poor circle
It can go only inside itself
Never away

The poor line
It can go only away from itself
Never inside

—Stymean Karlen

FROM then on I labored daily and incessantly on my new portrait of Jesus. Once again my time was measured only by what I accomplished. The Titian drawing continued to stimulate my hand and I filled a folio with sketches, but the canvas remained empty. None of the faces that I conceived satisfied me. I used crayon, then chalk, and finally, my favorite pen and ink; I tried a variety of expressions, but the problem was, I did not trust what I was doing. My results did not move me. With all of my concern for my subject, I was not expressing my faith in Him.

I was in the middle of another conception—I had lost count of how many drawings I had attempted—when Daniel asked to speak to me. It was a gray, overcast afternoon, with sharp gusts of rain pelting against my windows, and the light was poor, not fit for a Jesus that I wanted to burn with a bright flame, but Daniel was bursting with news. So I motioned for him to enter the studio, although I covered what I was doing. "What is it?" I meant to be friendly but I sounded curt.

"The money due on the sales of your work in the auction has been paid."

"Is that all?" In my view this did not justify his interruption and my frown indicated my irritation.

"No, Master. But I was able to do what you ordered."

"Are Hendrickje and her household needs taken care of?"

"Yes. And the others, too. Do you want to know how they behaved?"

Not actually, I thought, but I realized that I had to show some interest or he would discard the burden I had placed on his shoulders. I asked, as he desired, "So my creditors accepted the hundred guilders?"

"Indeed, although Thyst said it did not even reduce the interest on the mortgage, Witsen grumbled that it was just a drop in the bucket, Van Hertsbeeck said he could not wait much longer and Ornia was dissatisfied."

"Creditors are never satisfied. But they will wait now," I added, with an assurance I did not feel. "You look as if you have more news."

"How can you tell, Master?"

"You are eager to speak. What is it, boy?"

"Jan Six has paid for his portrait. Three hundred guilders. To you. He could have given it to Ornia to apply against that loan."

This was a pleasant surprise. Perhaps this indicated, I reflected, that he still had friendly feelings toward me.

"Sir, you need painting supplies and this money takes care of that."

"It is not necessary." I took the guilders and peremptorily dismissed him before he could argue. I hid the money, deciding to save it for an emergency, possibly for my Jesus, a comforting conclusion.

Meanwhile, Hendrickje grew large with child but since there were no new threats from her church elders she seemed content to concentrate on having a healthy birth. Titus was curious whether it would be a boy or a girl, and I sensed that secretly he preferred a girl, which would give him superiority in the household, although he insisted that it did not matter. Occasionally I instructed him and Daniel in drawing while they worked on their portraits of each other, but I did not ask to see these paintings, afraid they would upset and distract me. Most of the time I left them to their own devices. I saw only a slight improvement in their work but I tried not to be concerned. I prayed to Jesus to forgive my preoccupation with Him, and sought to make this work worthy of my faith, but I did not make any genuine progress on His portrait.

As summer blended into autumn and my lady's time approached, I paused in my labors to refresh my tired brain, thinking that perhaps I should put aside the subject of Jesus for the moment, and Daniel asked me if I could spare an hour for his father. I had forgotten about this proposed visit, two months had passed since we had discussed it. My impulse was to say no, that such a visit would not serve any useful purpose, but he looked so imploring I wavered. And when he added that his father wished to discuss a possible commission I consented.

The appointment was arranged for a Sunday afternoon, which was a day of rest in Amsterdam, even for its Jewish inhabitants, and I agreed to be the host to William van Dorn, who was being accompanied by two of the prominent men I knew in the Jewish community, Rabbi Manasseh ben Israel and Doctor Ephraim Bonus. I had painted portraits of both of these men and Daniel said that they would help make his father feel comfortable and influence him in my direction. I liked the rabbi and the doctor and they should make me feel more at ease also, and so I accepted this situation willingly.

Hendrickje cleaned my reception room until it was spotless, although she moved with difficulty; she was nearing her ninth month of pregnancy. After she finished I placed my recent paintings where they could be seen to advantage and hoped that my visitors would like them.

On a cloudy, chilly Sunday afternoon, with everyone in my household wearing their most sober clothes—only I put a dash of color around my waist and at my throat, I could not resist the lure of yellow and orange—I met my visitors with as much attention as I could muster. Part of my mind was still on my empty canvas upstairs, but I wanted to observe them carefully and I greeted them cordially. I was hopeful that possibly I might find a model for Jesus among them.

(77)

Rabbi Manasseh ben Israel led the others in, as befitted his position in the Sephardic Jewish community, but I was more interested in William van Dorn's appearance, for he might desire a portrait. Daniel's father had altered since he had brought his son to study with me two years ago. Now he seemed as much a Dutchman as any I knew. The rabbi moved with gravity, with unction, while the doctor focused at once on my work with pleasure, but William—who Daniel had told me had been named after the heroic Prince of Orange—entered with an impatience that verged on rudeness. His blue eyes, yellow hair, and fair complexion heightened his fleshy, red-faced features even more than I remembered. I wondered where he had inherited his appearance; I felt that a Northern intruder must have infiltrated into his family; most of the Jews I knew were dark.

I expressed my pleasure at his visit, and he retorted briskly, "I am equally honored, Heer van Rijn," but he did not sit as I suggested.

He strode around my reception room as if he were taking an inventory of my situation, while the others acknowledged my greeting politely and sat down, although Bonus continued to stare intently at my work.

Facial contours fascinated me and I noted that Bonus' features were round, the rabbi's square, and Van Dorn's regular. But I realized that their differences were more profound than these variations of line.

Van Dorn's features were energetic; I saw this in the firmness with which he gripped his cane. And where the others wore simple, plain black-and-white clothes, he was dressed elegantly. His fur cap, his blue doublet, his lustrous silk cloak were all of the most costly quality.

I thought regretfully, There is nothing of Jesus in him.

I turned my attention to the rabbi, who had folded his hands in a gesture of silent prayer, recalling that Jesus had been a rabbi, at least in spirit, but I saw nothing of Him in Manasseh ben Israel either. He was of medium height, inclined to be stout, and with his long gray hair looked too old for my purpose. And I did not care for his venerable deportment or his air of certitude, although he could be eloquent.

Bonus came closest to my vision with his animated eyes and his compassionate manner. But that was not enough, I knew, for he was also too old, too settled for my view. He was the smallest of the three men, and thus, he wore high-heeled shoes to compensate for his shortness, and his brown hair, which should have been gray, was so brown, thick, and wavy, I was sure it was a wig and I did not like to paint wigs.

Van Dorn was restless and he said suddenly, "Van Rijn, my son will not show me anything he has done. Does he waste his time?"

"I doubt it. You must not hurry him. He needs time."

I did not feel that I had convinced him and I was grateful that we were interrupted by Hendrickje serving my guests tea and cake, for I did not want to pursue this subject. Yet I did not like the intent way the doctor observed her swollen figure; I felt that he was critical.

Van Dorn sampled the tea and said with satisfaction, "It is good. It must come from the East Indies."

Daniel said, "On one of your ships, Father, no doubt."

"Probably," he said proudly. "They carry many cargoes. Van Rijn, do you think that my son is wise to abandon my thriving business?"

"That is not for me to judge."

"He is my only child. My other boy died in childbirth with his mother. I never expected Daniel to want to be an artist. All my family have been merchants. Oh, I am sure it is a worthy occupation, but . . ." His voice broke for an instant with surprising emotion and then he caught hold of himself. "Does he have any gift for art?"

"I said it is too early to tell."

"He has studied with you for two years. That should be enough."

Daniel cut in, "Please, father, you came to discuss other subjects."

Van Dorn asked Manasseh ben Israel, "Rabbi, what do you think?"

"My good friend Rembrandt is a splendid teacher. Your son is lucky to study with him. But I am disappointed that your son has stopped coming to my classes at the synagogue. He was one of my best students."

"Father, I know the basic questions."

"No one knows all of them. You must attend our rabbi."

Daniel was uncomfortable, as if he did not agree, and I wondered if he had any faith. A lack of religious faith was considered the worst sin of all in Amsterdam, worse even than being a Jew or a Catholic.

Bonus spoke suddenly, "William, we did come here for other reasons. And do not reproach me or disapprove. I delivered Daniel. In some ways I know him longer and better than you do. Ever since I can remember he has wanted to draw and paint. He should have his chance."

"I have given it to him. I sent him to the best school in England so that he could have the education of a gentleman, where he was regarded as a Dutchman instead of a Jew, which afforded him considerable advantages, even though our esteemed rabbi frowned on that. To compensate, when he returned I had him enter our synagogue school, but now he never goes."

Daniel lit the logs in my fireplace to evade answering and I was glad he had the foresight to obtain logs instead of the foul-smelling smoky peat—it showed that I could still have luxuries —and I realized that I could not afford to lose him, whatever his limitations as an artist.

I stated forcibly, "Heer van Dorn, you must give him more time."

"What has he done lately?"

"I will show you." I took him to a corner of the reception room where I had hung Daniel's self-portrait and his view of Titus, although he had said that they were not good enough to hang with my pictures. Sadly, he was right, these portraits were no better than his previous work, but his father might not know, merchants rarely did.

Van Dorn peered at the two pictures, then said, "It is so dark here."

Purposely, so that they could not be examined too closely, but I replied, "You can see the features. They are clear, accurate."

"Yes, they bear a likeness to our sons. But who would want to buy them?"

I shrugged.

"Unless you put your name on them. He is part of your workshop."

"Heer van Dorn, I pointed out that he must not be hurried."

Bonus said quickly, to change the subject, "William, you did come here to consider a painting from the hand of the master himself."

I asked, "Are you interested in another *Bathsheba*?"

"Oh, no!" He flushed, embarrassed for what he had blurted out, and added, "I am happy to have that work, since it is a tribute to the taste of King David, but now I would like to have work that would rival that owned by the Honorable Jan Six."

Daniel said, "Father, the Master just finished a portrait of him."

"Something like that would interest me."

I said, "The sitting will take time. Can you spare it?"

"Could you do it from a sketch? I am very busy these days."

"No," I said bluntly. I had thought we were going to discuss serious things, not bargain over time. I must control my own work, if nothing else. Suddenly I no longer wanted to show him the work I had hung in the reception room. "I must get to my new canvas. Will you excuse me?"

"May we see it?"

I hesitated, not sure how to respond.

"Heer van Rijn, we would be honored."

But what were his private feelings? I almost trusted Bonus' interest and the rabbi was curious, but would this shipping merchant understand? Then I was seized with a wild idea. Ignoring the work I had placed so carefully for their attention, I took them upstairs to my studio.

I kept the empty canvas covered whenever I was not there and they waited so intently the slightest sound could be heard. Then, with an abrupt gesture, I pulled off the drape. The sheer unexpectedness of the empty canvas put them momentarily in a state of trance.

Even Daniel was puzzled, then Bonus chuckled, the rabbi looked offended, and Van Dorn, feeling that he had to say something, murmured, "Is this what you would use for my portrait? Would it be as large as Six's?"

"This canvas is intended for a portrait of Jesus Christ."

They were all open mouthed now.

"Do you have any suggestions?"

But they had become self-conscious, Daniel, too, and I realized that this could be a touchy subject, especially with Jews.

Yet something compelled me to continue. "I want my portrait of Jesus to be accurate, to show Him as He was, Jewish and a rabbi."

Bonus exclaimed, "Extraordinary! You want to give Jesus a Jewish face!"

"As was His nature. Rabbi, what do you think of such a conception?"

"No one will approve. And certainly not your Christian friends."

"What is your opinion?"

"I do not mix in the affairs of our neighbors. Rembrandt, I cannot afford to offend the burghers who have allowed us to live here peacefully."

Van Dorn said sharply, "Our rabbi is right. Such a conception, fostered by our community, could cause a scandal and damage us."

I asked Daniel, "Do you agree with your worthy compatriots?"

"Master, you do not need my argument. At the right moment your canvas will speak for itself. Whatever subject you choose."

I could have embraced him for that; instead, embarrassed by the emotion I felt, I growled, "I hope so. Gentlemen, thank you for your time and attention. Now I must return to my new canvas. Will you excuse me."

The rabbi and Van Dorn, pained by my rudeness and my outrageous conception, exchanged shocked glances that indicated they thought I was mad. And so they could depart with a feeling of righteous indignation. They did not pause at my reception room to look at my pictures. However, at the door Van Dorn turned to his son who was escorting him and declared, "I will pay for your instructions here only on the condition that you attend synagogue regularly and study with our rabbi."

"Father, I need all my time to practice drawing and painting."

"If you are not in the rabbi's class next week I will withdraw my aid. You do not seem to have progressed much and my Dutch friends do not respect a Jew who does not follow his faith."

Daniel glanced at me for help, but I could not defend him in this matter.

Bonus suggested, "Heed your father. He is all you have."

"And ten merchant ships," I heard Daniel mutter under his breath but he nodded and managed to say, "I will try, Father."

"You have one more year to become an artist. Then the money stops."

"What about the commission you wanted to discuss with the Master?"

"I will consider it. But if he insists on depicting Jesus the way he has mentioned, I cannot in good conscience support him."

I started to disagree with him and the rabbi halted me, explaining piously, "My good man, as you know I have valued your work. I have used your etchings for my writings and your portrait of me hangs in my house. But my people are here only on sufferance. As it is, we do not have the privileges of citizens, although Holland is the only country in Europe where we are not persecuted. We cannot risk that, even if you can. We must be discreet." Then he left with Van Dorn.

Bonus did not want to discuss their views, except to say that while they were popular they did not necessarily prevail. He asked for permission to look at the pictures I had hung in the reception room.

I gave it, still stunned by their opposition, and wondered if I should put aside my conception of Jesus, perhaps forever.

After he had examined each picture intently and thoughtfully, Bonus said, "Rembrandt, you are painting even more beautifully and expressively than before. I wish I could afford your work."

I did not respond to his hint. I was in no mood to bargain.

"One thing more," he said, "Your lady looks due. I would feel privileged to attend her and to guide a child of yours into the world."

I knew that he meant well but I was still upset over what had just happened and I said curtly, "Doctor, there is no rush."

"She lost her first child. You must not take any risks now."

"It was not my fault. The midwife was careless and inefficient."

"All the more reason that you should have a physician this time."

"I will make that decision when it is necessary. Good day, sir."

Bonus sighed regretfully and said, "May God help you."

I could not turn back to my empty canvas when Hendrickje's birth pangs began and she had to take to her bed. It was a few days after Bonus' warning, and when she could not serve me I knew that her time had come.

She writhed and moaned, her face contorted with pain, and I frantically ordered Daniel to fetch Tulp, one of the most eminent doctors in the land and a notable patron of mine in the past. An hour later Daniel told me the elderly Tulp had said that he could not attend Hendrickje, that he no longer visited patients. In my anxiety, for she was worse, I sent Daniel to Arnold Tholnix, whom I had portrayed in a painting and an etching. He was the Inspector of the Medical College of Amsterdam and he should know what to do. Daniel returned with the unhappy tidings that Tholnix did not deliver babies, that it was unseemly.

"Why?" I was distraught and close to despair. Hendrickje appeared on the verge of collapse; I had never seen her look so dreadful, so pale, so short of breath and energy. I was terrified. "Does he consider her unworthy of his attention? Because of our situation? Is that it?"

"He said to use a midwife, that childbirth is their work, that it is immoral for a man to view a woman's body, to see her private parts."

"I do not trust them. Hendrickje lost our first child with one."

"Master, why not try Bonus? He lives just down the street, near St. Anthoniesmarkt. I can fetch him quickly."

"Do you think he is dependable?"

"He delivered me. Remember?"

I had forgotten. I exclaimed, "Summon him. If he will come."

Daniel assured me that Bonus would but as I waited by the side of a suffering, convulsed Hendrickje, I did not share his optimism. I could think of many reasons why he would not attend her, while she sobbed, "I am being punished for my sins. The Brothers were right."

"You must not believe them!" I shouted. "Jesus is merciful!" Yet at this moment I wondered if she could survive and whether He truly was. I held her hand to give her strength and hope while I wished I had some to sustain me. How long we waited I could not tell, but when Daniel appeared with Bonus it seemed as if an eternity had passed, although the doctor was out of breath from hurrying. He was only half-dressed, without his wig; his doublet was unbuttoned, and he wore slippers instead of high-heeled shoes.

He was a little man, but I was grateful for his presence. Hendrickje's misery was frightening.

I asked with many misgivings, "Doctor, is there any hope?"

"We will know better after I examine her."

He did this with a gentleness of touch that could have held a paintbrush and then he sent Daniel for a midwife who lived next door to him. I began to protest and he halted me. "We will need her after the infant arrives."

"Poor Hendrickje," I murmured.

She recoiled at the unexpected sight of Bonus leaning over her to wipe the sweat from her eyes and mumbled, "He is not of our faith," but I assured her that would not make any difference, "After all, Our Lord was Jewish, too." Puzzled, distracted, she forgot her misery for a moment while Bonus sought to soothe her so that her spasmodic convulsions would become more regular.

The midwife came quickly, as if used to such emergencies. She was a heavy, round-faced middle-aged woman; Jewish possibly, I thought, from her swarthy skin, but she knew what to do.

Bonus ordered everyone out of the bedroom but the midwife. As I waited apprehensively in the hall, I heard him say encouragingly, "Easy now, my lady, easy." Her screams started again, but soon I was surprised by a sudden stillness. Then I heard another cry, shrill and loud.

A minute later the midwife opened the bedroom door and announced, "Heer van Rijn, you have a girl."

I prayed, dear God, let this one live! I remembered the three children that Saskia had lost and Hendrickje's fear and I asked, "How is she?"

"The infant looks healthy."

"No, I mean my lady."

"As well as can be expected. You called the doctor just in time."

Daniel went downstairs to feed Titus and to tell him that he had a sister, which seemed to please him, while I waited to see Hendrickje and my daughter. When Bonus let me in the midwife was cuddling my daughter, who was quiet now, and Hendrickje had fallen asleep. I was glad to see that my daughter looked sound and the doctor assured me that both mother and child were doing fine, but that the midwife should remain with them until my lady could get out of bed. I agreed—I was so grateful I would have done almost anything he suggested—and I gave the matronly woman five guilders, although Bonus said that two were the custom. When I offered him a handful of coins out of my scanty store, he did not speak for a moment but stared at me in silence. Finally, when I tried to put all the coins into his hand, he declined them, murmuring, "This has been my pleasure, Master. It is an honor and privilege to deliver a child of Rembrandt's. I will return tonight to see how they are doing."

When Hendrickje was able to talk coherently several days later, her first words were, "Master, we must baptize our daughter at once."

"As soon as you are able to accompany us."

"Speak to Pastor Hoag. Perhaps he will relent now that it is a fact."

"I doubt it." But when she grew breathless and faint, I added hurriedly, "I will if it is possible. Now you must rest."

She lay back for a moment, then suddenly she exclaimed, "Do you want this child?"

"Very much."

"Even though she is a girl?"

"I have a son and a girl will be a welcome change and resemble you."

"What will you name her?"

"Cornelia."

"After your mother?" she asked in amazement.

"Yes." The devil himself could not change that. And to prove to her that I meant what I said, I handed her a simple gold ring. As she examined the band with wonder, I told her, "Hendrickje, it was my mother's. Wear it with my blessing and hers."

I put it on her finger and she smiled so sweetly and embraced me so passionately that I felt at this moment we could withstand almost anything. The ring fit and shone a bright yellow in the morning sun.

WHY SHOULD I KNOW ANOTHER'S JUDGMENT

Why should I know another's judgment
of you

What do I know of those judging you
It would be meaningless to me

If a wise judge judged you
And I would deem him to be wise

If his depth was an exact depth
to mine
well . . .

But even then
what would another's judgment of you
add to you

And give me something
Or give you

except a boundary
around you
holding you in

—Stymean Karlen

To make sure that the community knew that we had a
child and that I cherished her and her mother, I indulged in one
of the most ancient customs of my homeland. The day after
Cornelia's birth I hung on the front door of my house a wood
placard covered with red silk, and trimmed with lace, to an-
nounce the birth of our child. I added a square of white paper in
the corner to indicate that our infant was a girl.

A week later I gave a reception to celebrate the birth and I
invited friends to pay their respects to the mother and the child.

This was also a custom in Holland and again I followed the traditional rituals. I put on a feathered hat of quilted satin, which signified that I regarded myself as the spouse of the woman who had given birth to my child, and I dressed our daughter in a ceremonial flowered dark-green costume.

Hendrickje was out of bed now, but Cornelia was in the care of the midwife, Wilhelmina Baask, which was also a tradition. Yet it was my lady, garbed in the finest, most beautiful gown that she owned, in colors I had chosen, sky-blue and garnet-red, who presented the child.

I was determined to establish the strength of our situation. No one was going to make me feel guilty or ashamed if I could help it.

Titus and I stood by her side while Daniel ushered in the guests.

I was grateful to those who came, and I observed them carefully. The first to appear were Van Ludick, Joost, and Francen, who entered so close in time to each other, it were as if they had agreed to come together. Soon after Rabbi Manasseh ben Israel and Doctor Bonus arrived. Then they were joined by the print dealer, Clement de Jonge, whose cheerful, square face was dear to me, and a fine goldsmith, the gray-haired, bearded Jan Lutma, who was known as the Elder, since he was seventy.

I was not surprised that Pastor Hoag, whom I had invited, had not appeared, but I was disappointed that Jan Six and his father-in-law to be, Doctor Tulp, who had been my good friends, failed to come. Van Goor dropped in briefly. I felt that he wanted to see if there were any prospective buyers for my work in attendance. It was encouraging to know that he believed it could still be sold, and I was pleased that he was cordial to Hendrickje. Near the end of the day two of my creditors arrived, the iron dealer, Ornia, and my landlord, Thyst. They were more curious than congratulatory and I thought that they had come chiefly to judge my circumstances, but they had the grace not to mention the money I owed them.

I offered toasts to the good health of Hendrickje and our daughter and most of the guests joined me. Many of them spoke to her and I tried not to be annoyed at the few who avoided her.

I saw some raised eyebrows because of the presence of my Jewish friends at what was considered a Christian ceremony, but if there was any criticism of my family situation I did not hear it.

Thus, I assumed this reception would comfort Hendrickje, and I was dismayed when she did not recover fully from the strain of childbirth as I expected.

Afterwards, despite the devotion I had given her, she complained that she was depressed, that no matter what my friends said or pretended, the church wanted baptism to be done quickly after birth or the devil would seize our daughter's soul. I thought this was an evil, cruel, immoral view but I could not lessen her apprehension. To have Cornelia christened as soon as possible became her overwhelming desire, and so, while I changed the subject, afraid that she would worry herself into an early grave, and I still did not agree with her, I came to the conclusion that I must satisfy this need in her or I would never restore her to good health.

So, without telling Hendrickje, I decided to try to persuade Pastor Hoag to perform the baptism in return for a proper show of reverence and contrition on my part. It was an unpleasant task but I saw no other way to live with her and I did not want to lose her.

I carefully chose the time to approach him, a Saturday when he should be home preparing his sermon for the Sabbath. I dressed with the utmost sobriety to avoid offending him, avoiding all traces of the colors I treasured. My heart was heavy, for Hendrickje had taken to bed as soon as she had fed me, and while she insisted that she was only tired and simply needed rest, I did not like the lethargy with which she had served me. I covered her with the warmest blankets we possessed, for winter approached and it was a cold, gray day, and the logs in the fireplace were not sufficient to heat the entire bedroom.

I told her, "I am going to do some sketches in the countryside."

She nodded, but I could not tell if that mattered to her. Then she muttered, "Only baptism will wash away our daughter's sins."

I was horrified by this concept and I replied strongly, "That is not so."

"It is always so. All of us are born with original sin."

"I do not believe that. Jesus is compassionate, not cruel."

"We are all sinners. We must all be cleansed. Baptized."

"Hendrickje, you must not feel like a sinner. I do not feel like one."

She was not listening to me, mumbling agitatedly, "Without baptism our daughter will not be a Christian. She will be eternally damned."

For an instant I thought of telling her about my mission, then I decided not to, afraid that I would fail and that the disappointment would be too much for her and confirm her guilty feelings. I said in my most conciliatory manner, "I will find a way to satisfy Our Lord."

"With your work? It is not sufficient. It is not enough."

It was difficult for me not to be annoyed, but I managed to say, more gently than I felt, "Rest, Hendrickje, that is the best medicine."

Our midwife had become Cornelia's nurse because of Hendrickje's poor health, and she was with the baby now, who had fallen asleep in her arms while Wilhelmina sat in a meditative attitude. I told her to do whatever her mistress requested, and she accepted the assignment cheerfully.

Reassured a little, I told Daniel to take care of Titus and for both of them to draw figures from the Old Testament. I was interested in which subjects they would select. I said I would be back later in the day and I left without another word.

Pastor Hoag's house was a fifteen-minute walk, near the Blauwbrug, a bridge over the Amstel at the edge of the city. I knew this neighborhood intimately. I had sketched the bridge, the fishing harbor, the boats, and the countryside a number of times; they were favorite views of mine.

Today, however, I paused at a nearby inn to reinforce myself. I doubted that Hoag would receive me cordially, although repentance on my part might help. Several drinking bouts were developing under the broad wooden beams, although it was still morning, but I avoided the gin that they were gulping down. I kept away from the middle-aged fishermen, who were angry at their lot—a new war with England threatened their livelihood—and were shouting toasts to anyone who was against the war, spilling their drinks as they smashed their glasses in their rage, their faces purple, their bellies inflated.

There was nothing here that I wanted to paint, but by my second beer I felt better.

I thought that maybe Bonus was right—he had examined Hendrickje regularly and he had said that she would recover in time—and on my third beer I was tired of drinking alone. I had not touched the empty canvas since the birth of Cornelia, disturbed by her mother's condition, but had done chores, rearranging my studio, studying half-finished works, yet since I was not at peace, I had been unable to settle on any subject to do. This was unusual; I was alone too much, I decided. Then music started from sawing violins and screeching voices and a robust young woman grabbed my wrist, inviting me to dance with her, shoving me into the crowd in the middle of the tavern.

She whispered in a hoarse, guttural tone, "Just a guilder, sir, I will do whatever you wish, my lodgings are nearby," and I pulled free from her embrace and fled. She glared after me as if I were crazy and she screamed, "Cheap bastard!" But I was sober again and revolted by her excess of flesh; her breasts were so big they had almost knocked me down.

By the time I reached Pastor Hoag's residence the chilly air and wind had cleared my foggy senses. I arranged my clothes so I would look neat, a rare situation for me, and I wiped off the remnants of the beer from my mouth and approached his front door.

I was startled by the smallness of his house. Although this was one of the most prosperous neighborhoods in Amsterdam, where many of the rich lived in four-and-five-story mansions, his dwelling had just two stories and the second had only a single casement window. Then the building was more wood than brick and needed painting badly. A dull brown varnish covered all the wooden parts to give them a shine and to protect the surface against the constant damp air, but only added to the houses's ugliness.

Nonetheless, in spite of my growing apprehension, I had come too far to turn back and I knocked. When there was no response, I banged on the door loudly, over and over, as if to express my urgent need, and so I could not change my mind, and suddenly it opened.

Pastor Hoag glared at me agitatedly, evidently he had slept late. He was in his nightcap and slippers and muffled up in a dressing gown, and his face was even more bony and yellow than before. He looked worried, and I observed that his head was bald and that he smelled of brandy. For once he was not cold or inflexible, and yet he moved to dismiss me, obviously not wishing to talk to me in his present condition.

I put my booted foot in his door before he could close it and said urgently, "I must see you now. It is important."

"I am very busy. I am working on tomorrow's sermon."

"But you just woke up."

"I labored so late last night preparing it, I overslept. The woman who attends my four children—I am a widower—is little better than a slut, but I cannot afford better. I do not have a grand house like you do."

Somehow, I had assumed that Hoag was a virgin. To find him a widower with four children was as astonishing as my presence here.

"What do you want, Van Rijn? I only have a minute to spare."

"I want to review my family situation with you."

"And to repent?" Suddenly he was animated and his eyes became intense.

"If certain things could be agreed on."

"I do not bargain. The Lord's sacraments are not for sale."

"If you baptized our daughter it would mean much to me."

"How much?"

"Sir, you just said that it is not a matter of money."

"Van Rijn, you are such a sinner."

"Perhaps, but I am also a Christian."

He hesitated, as if he did not agree with me, but suddenly a gust of wind threatened to disrobe him. I could see his long, scrawny, bare legs, and he began to shiver and abruptly he motioned for me to come inside. The floorboards creaked under our footsteps and it was very dark in his parlor. He threw open his shutters but dust was everywhere and it was still so dark he had to light an old oil lamp, and it confirmed that he was poor, only the poor used these contrivances.

I asked, "Pastor, where are your children?"

"My housekeeper, the slut, took them to my sister's this morning so that I could get some sleep. I am exhausted from their clamor."

"Could your sister take care of them?"

"She has two of her own. And her husband is at sea. I have no time to waste. I assume you came to make your mistress into an honest woman."

I pretended that I did not understand what he meant and he shouted, "That you intend to marry her!"

I answered softly, "I told you, Reverend, that I cannot."

"So why are you here? There is no other solution."

"I thought that if I admitted that my circumstances are unfortunate, that I am willing to apologize if I have offended the church elders . . ."

"And then we would baptize your child?"

"Yes, Pastor."

My submission must have restored his arrogance, for his manner became severe and he stated critically, "You are insane. You violate the sacred tenets of our church, yet you assume you can be forgiven whenever you choose."

"Jesus forgave. The heart of Our Lord is His mercy."

"Do not instruct me. Women were not created for the pleasure of sinful flesh, but to protect the sanctity of the family, in our case, the Dutch family. If you want your child baptized by us, you must marry."

"But if, as I said, I cannot?" I trembled as I asked, but I tried to sound firm. Hoag was so censorious it was terrifying.

"You will suffer the consequences of your immorality."

He had not asked me to sit and I doubted that I could, the two austere chairs in his parlor looked so uncomfortable. Unable to humble myself any further, I turned to go. However, he stopped me and started to preach, and I thought, I must be his sermon for tomorrow, Master Painter Rembrandt van Rijn's sins trumpeted on high from his pulpit, whatever the disguise he used. But I listened to him.

"You give a reception to celebrate the birth of your illegitimate daughter when it is supposed to be given only for legitimate children. Yet you proclaim that on your front door. You defy the church. You are not content to hide your situation, as you should —you flaunt it."

"How did you find out?"

"Our eyes and ears are everywhere."

"Spies, you mean."

"Respected citizens, some of the most respected in the community." I wondered who had told him and I asked, "Was it Ornia, or Thyst, or—"

He cut me short, "I cannot tell you. They asked to remain unknown. But your impiety does not surprise me. It is in your lack of reverence for our Savior."

"That is not so!" I denied hotly.

"When you consider depicting Him as a Jew!" Hoag said scornfully.

"He was."

"Nonsense. Our Lord was born immaculately. He was God's son, not a Jew's. You even work on Sundays. I have seen you sketching by the bridge. Why do you have to paint Christ differently than anybody else?"

"Nobody knows what He truly looked like but I can imagine it." My imagination was potent and he could not take that away from me.

"You should have a right knowledge of Him, but you are a freethinker."

"I am a Christian," I repeated, and I could imagine His compassion and love.

"I doubt that. The way you paint Him, the way you think. . . ."

He was growing tedious and I stopped listening. I started for the door, thinking that we had nothing in common, even if we were Dutchmen and worshipped Jesus, when the pastor halted me once more.

This time, however, instead of chastizing me, as he had been doing, he confided in me, as if he had to unburden himself to someone, even if it was a sinner like me. He was saying, "At least you acknowledged my authority by coming to me."

I replied, "You are my lady's pastor. She looks up to you."

"She should," he cried out with a burst of emotion. "I have to open and close the doors of my church, ring the bells, keep the clock wound, the church clean, chase out the children and dogs who misbehave and preach the sermons. And for what? I live in poverty. In the country, at least, I would be paid in rye, milk, and cheese, enough to feed my family, but here, with the cost of everything rising, a hundred guilders a year is not enough to live on. You get more than that for a picture."

"Sometimes. When I am paid."

"I can hardly feed my birds. Come!" He led me to a little garden behind his small house and showed me two coops filled with pigeons.

I admired the independence and spirit of a gray one taking a promenade along the fence across the bridge, but he regarded that bird with contempt.

"You think it would appreciate that I fed it, but no, the moment it got loose it left me. What do you think of my black ones? They are unusual."

He pointed to the smaller of the cages, for that was what they were, I thought, whatever he called them, and I noted that his favorite dark birds were attractive, but not truly black, I saw white when they spread their wings, and I had no desire to paint them. "Pastor, you are fond of them?"

"I love them. I am a connoisseur of pigeons. At one time I also fed the sea gulls but they are greedy. They came to me only when I offered them food, otherwise, they had no faith, they were undependable."

"But your pigeons give you great pleasure?"

"Indeed. Not like humans. I have an exceptional way with pigeons. They trust me, except that scoundrel on the fence."

"You must have spent much time encouraging their faith and devotion."

"As much as was necessary. Do you like pigeons?"

"I have painted several. Of course your children share your taste."

"No! My oldest, who is ten, wants to eat them."

"And your youngest?"

"She is only three. She cries most of the time. Sometimes I think Our Lord is punishing me for not being able to rid our country of sinners."

He gazed at his flock with such intentness and love that I was silent, trying to decide what to do next when he spoke suddenly.

"Rembrandt, what do you want to name your child?"

He almost sounded friendly and I said quickly, "Cornelia, after my beloved mother." And to show, I thought grimly, that this union was permanent, with or without the church's sanction.

"That is a worthy sentiment. And you have shown some humility."

"Then you will baptize my daughter?" I asked eagerly.

"No! That has been settled!" But when he saw my disconsolate expression, he added, "However, a man who paints pigeons is not to be completely despised or damned. I know a pastor who might baptize your daughter in spite of the sinful state in which you are living."

"Is he qualified?"

Hoag sighed and looked sad and said regretfully, "Robert Ruismeer is not a member of the Reformed Church and I do not approve of much of his theology, he is inclined to be a Mennonite, if not in fact, in spirit, but he is a clergyman and a Protestant."

"I want Cornelia baptized in the Reformed Church, to please my lady."

"Impossible! I have no more time to waste on an unrepentant sinner. Do you want Pastor Ruismeer's address before I change my mind?"

Left with such a choice, I nodded yes. I was still skeptical about Hoag's help but he did give me Ruismeer's address on a slip of paper. It was within walking distance and I decided to visit him at once, while I had some energy left. I started to thank Hoag and he cut me off and ushered me out. Then he hurried back into his ramshackle dwelling before he could change his mind and take back the address.

I walked so fast I was out of breath when I arrived at Ruismeer's residence. It was a red brick house with wooden shutters and stepped gables on a gray, winding street paved with cobbles and shaded by linden trees, and although the neighborhood was part of Amsterdam it had the quiet and solitude of a small Dutch village.

The pastor answered my knock. He was in simple clerical clothes and when I explained who I was, he said, "I know. You are the Master Painter, Rembrandt van Rijn. I have seen you at auctions. Come in, please."

I was glad that he was my own age, vigorous, with a ruddy face, wide features, light-brown hair, a pleasant mouth and an open manner.

He led me into a spacious, well-lit reception room which was dominated by the paintings on the wall. He said apologetically, "There are none of your quality, Master, but they are excellent in their own way."

I had too much on my mind to examine them. I blurted out, "Pastor, can you baptize my daughter?"

"That depends."

"I am not married."

"I am aware of your situation. You are not an obscure artist."

"Does my family relationship offend you?"

"I would prefer to marry you first and to baptize later."

"That is impossible. I cannot marry because of my circumstances."

He looked distressed and said, "Too bad. That is unfortunate."

Feeling rejected, I asked, "Then why did Hoag send me to you?"

"He knows that I paint and that I am fond of painters. He does not approve of a pastor painting, he thinks it is contrary to the doctrines of Calvin, but he tolerates it in me because when we were students at the theological seminary at Leyden, I helped him with money and his studies. He was very poor and not good with his books." When Ruismeer saw the look of alarm on my face, he added quickly, "Oh, my work is not of much account, I would not think of showing it to you, but I have admired your art for a long time. Ever since the picture dealer, Van Uylenburgh, introduced me to it many years ago."

I felt a little better. This painter, teacher, and art dealer had been a dear friend and a strong supporter. And close to the Mennonites, I remembered. I asked, somewhat hesitantly, "Pastor, are you a Mennonite?"

"The name of our sect does not matter. It is what we believe that does. Our God is capable of pity, mercy, love, He is not the implacable, unforgiving God of Calvin. We have softened his harsh doctrines."

"How do you exist?"

"We are independent of the Reformed Church, we have rejected their dogma and authority. My income is helped by my wife, who is a public scribe, she writes a clear hand and is much in demand, which gives me time to preach, visit the sick, and comfort the needy and sore at heart. Our church is excluded from the government but we enjoy religious freedom as long as we worship God and Jesus Christ and pay our taxes."

"I worship Jesus, too, and yet you condemn my situation."

"I do not approve of it, but I do not condemn it. It is not for me to judge you, or to heed those who do. My duty is to perform His sacraments for those who honestly embrace His faith and mercy."

"Pastor, I believe in Him fervently. Will you baptize our daughter?"

"I am sure that you do. But there are conditions."

My heart sank and I cried out, "What are they?"

"The presence of the father is indispensable."

"Of course. I will be there."

"If there are any brothers or sisters, they must attend, also."

"My son will be by my side. He is proud of his baby sister."

"Finally, two sponsors are required. That is obligatory."

"I will do my best to obtain them."

"If you do, I will baptize your daughter a week from Sunday."

Since there was so much urgency in Hendrickje and myself, I did not go home but visited the man I considered as good a friend as I had, Lodewijck van Ludick, who had stood surety for my loan to Jan Six. He was in his print shop, as I had hoped, but when

I mentioned my mission he replied that he could not support a sect different from his own, it could ruin his business. Besides, he added, Ornia had been to see him recently to demand payment of the loan from him if I did not satisfy the iron dealer soon and he could not stand surety for me again. I was distressed but I was in too much of a hurry to argue. I rushed over to Francen's nearby apothecary shop, only to be informed that he was in Antwerp and nobody knew when he would be back. And Joost could not see me. He was in bed with a serious contagion and was not allowed any visitors.

Finally, at the end of one of the longest, most tiring days of my life, Clement de Jonge and Jan Lutma agreed to sponsor my daughter's baptism. Both men were astonished at my relief. They said that if they had not been available, I would have found other friends who would have been, but I did not share their certainty.

Night had fallen by the time I was able to tell Hendrickje my good news, but she did not get out of bed or show any signs of joy as I had expected. She said, "Cornelia must be baptized in a Reformed Church."

I replied, "Hoag stated that was impossible. So I have already accepted Ruismeer's services. I have made all the arrangements."

She burst into tears and for a moment I felt helpless.

Then I could no longer endure her excessive self-pity and I declared, "There is no time to argue. Pastor Ruismeer has agreed to perform the baptism a week from Sunday. My daughter will be there, whether you are or not." I strode away without another word.

Titus wanted my opinion of what he had drawn, but I did not like his sketch of Jonathan, this biblical figure was too Dutch. I found Daniel's head of David too noble, too refined for my taste, but both of them had worked hard. So, while my mind was elsewhere, I told them that they had spent their time sensibly; I hoped that I had, too.

On the appointed day for the baptism I dressed for it appropriately, as if this occasion were an accepted fact, and this persuaded Hendrickje to follow my example. She prepared Cornelia and

Titus for the ceremony and dressed herself with great care. She said she felt fine, although she was much thinner than she had been. Daniel asked to be excused, saying that his presence would be wrong. He looked so uncomfortable as he said this that I accepted his absence, although with regret.

Ruismeer's church was a simple gray stone edifice with two Gothic towers and a plain nave and altar and he baptized our daughter as if it were the most natural thing in the world. This eased Hendrickje's anxiety and she was aided by the way de Jonge and Lutma admired the pastor's grace.

At the last moment, Francen and Joost arrived. Joost was still pale and drawn from his illness but he said that he would not have missed this baptism for anything, while Francen told Hendrickje that she was blessed to have such a healthy child.

She was able to smile now, whatever her secret self felt. I thought with relief that nothing should stand between us now. When I took her by the arm to lead her out of the church, while she held our daughter with her other arm, I believed that we had proven that we were a family. Pastor Ruismeer was ringing his church bell himself to celebrate the baptism and I thought about the last thing we had discussed.

I had asked him, "Reverend, what do I owe you?" I felt that I owed him much.

"Master Painter, whatever you consider suitable."

I had nodded. I must give him a painting, I decided, when I could afford it. And now I could go back to myself and to my search for the truth.

THE COURAGE IT TAKES

The courage it takes to face
the emptiness

The cowardice one must have
to run from it

—Stymean Karlen

I decided to concentrate on reducing my debts. I put aside the Jesus I had intended to paint for Hendrickje, for her health had been restored by the baptism of Cornelia, and there was no longer any need to sustain her faith. Yet I was still discontented with myself; I felt that until I painted a conception of Jesus that satisfied me, there would be a void in my life. Then I disliked painting solely for the sake of money.

Nonetheless, I told Daniel to total my bills so that I would know how much work to do. I also gave him a day off each week to attend the rabbi's classes at the nearby synagogue. His father did not return; I felt that William van Dorn had decided not to have me paint him, which did not trouble me, since I did not find him a stimulating subject. I still intended to present Pastor Ruismeer with a work of mine in return for his services, but I put that off to pay accounts that were more immediate.

Soon after I assigned Daniel to his new task he approached me with his conclusions. I was heartened by the receipt of the fee for *Aristotle* and the news that the wealthy Don Ruffo wanted more work from my brush. I was trying to decide what subject to suggest to him, when Daniel stood opposite me in my studio and spoke before I could stop him.

"Master, I cannot wait any longer. I must talk to you."

"Not bad news, I hope," I said, even as I sensed that there was.

For an instant he was very still, as if he were holding his breath, and then he replied in an embarrassed tone, "Some of it is unpleasant. You owe money to more people than I thought. Even so, I have tried to put your affairs in order as you requested, but I cannot proceed until I know exactly what you owe."

"Exactly?" I laughed derisively. "No one knows precisely what I owe!"

"Possibly, but I have listed the most pressing accounts."

I would have infinitely preferred to pursue my work. It was sunny, which was rare for late autumn, and at the best business details bored me and at the worst were difficult and confusing. Must cater again. Must be their slave. Today, and the day after, and every day thereafter. But I knew that I had no choice. And he was so earnest I could not mock his efforts any longer. I put aside my plans for Don Ruffo and asked him more quietly, "What is most pressing?"

"Christoffel Thyst, for the balance due him on your house."

"He is always impatient." I dismissed him with a wave of my hand.

"Master, you must take him seriously. He was here the other day and he said that he cannot wait much longer. I think he means it."

"What does his bill total now?" I asked with resignation.

"He claims that with interest it comes to almost eighty-five hundred guilders. But what seems to worry him the most is that fourteen years after you bought the house, he says that you have not paid even half of what you owe him."

"I tried. I borrowed four thousand guilders from Witsen for that purpose. It was not my fault I had to use the money elsewhere."

"Witsen's loan, with accumulated interest, now totals, four thousand two hundred eighty guilders."

Shaken, I steadied myself with one hand on the studio wall and said, "I planned to pay him with the four thousand I borrowed from Van Hertsbeeck."

"And now, that merchant's debt, with interest, is also four thousand two hundred eighty guilders. Both men say that you agreed to pay them back within a year, that several years have passed, that you pledged your work as security. Is that true?"

There was reproach and shock in Daniel's voice, as if I had pledged away my life, and perhaps I had, I thought, and I nodded regretfully.

"Then the Jan Six loan, which Ornia holds today, has risen, with interest, to one thousand two hundred twenty guilders. And it, like the others, is overdue."

"Is that all?" I had to sound casual, although I was afraid that I was in a hopeless bog that would only get worse.

"It is not all. Here is a bill for nine hundred guilders, but I cannot make out the signature. Do you know to whom it belongs?"

I examined the writing but I did not recognize it. I stated, "Whoever it is, they will make their claim. Creditors always do."

"I have found other obligations for eight hundred forty-eight guilders, sixteen hundred and five guilders, and I fear that there are other debts. Then there is the money owed grocers, bakers, butchers, paint dealers, and—"

"Enough, Daniel! I believe you. What does it total?"

"What I can count comes to over twenty-one thousand guilders. Master, why not apply to these debts what you inherited from your wife, Saskia?"

Daniel looked so sympathetic I explained, "My share of it came to only twenty thousand guilders and most of it is gone. Saskia left the other half to Titus, adding that I should get the interest from it until he came of age or married. But she added a clause in her will—I have never known why, unless she assumed I could always provide for Titus—that has created a grave problem for me. *If I remarried, my half of the estate would not go to Titus, but to her sister, and with it, the interest on that half.* And there is hardly anything left of my portion or what was inherited by my son. The inheritance was never paid in full, the interest on Titus' share went to pay Saskia's heavy medical expenses, and then I had to support my brother and sister in Leyden to keep them out of the poorhouse."

"Does Hendrickje know the circumstances, the terms of the will?"

"Yes. If I wed her it would ruin me completely. It is impossible to raise the money that was left to Titus and the interest from his share."

"Maybe if you explain that to the authorities they will be merciful."

"That would only make matters worse. To account for where the money went, I would suffer constant litigation, swear many oaths, fill out countless papers, and not have a moment to do a stroke of work. What credit I have left would vanish. As long as people think there is money still coming to me, as long as I can keep up appearances, I can still borrow, I can still use my work as collateral. But the instant my credit is gone I will be thrown out of this house, all I own will be seized and sold, I will not even have collateral, and my creditors will fall on me like a pack of jackals. It will be the end of my work."

"Sir, that would be too dreadful to contemplate."

There were tears in Daniel's eyes and I was stirred by his response. Yet, I knew, some day I would have to tell him that his gifts were small, that he would never be more than mediocre. I rarely speculated about my own ability—that was for lesser artists—I had no doubts when I was properly aroused, but Daniel's passion for glory, characteristic of the young men I met, would leave him grievously disappointed if I judged his work unfavorably. So, once again, I put off the inevitable telling.

"Master, you must avoid bankruptcy at all costs."

"I am doing my best."

"What about the five hundred guilders you received from Don Ruffo?"

"Van Goor took a hundred for his fee and fifty for shipping expenses."

"They did not come to that much!" Daniel declared indignantly.

"I am in no position to argue with him," I replied wearily. "I am supposed to consider myself fortunate to have received what I did. Ruffo, who is very rich, says he paid me eight times more than he pays Italian artists. Are our household expenses in reasonable order? I would like to spare Hendrickje aggravation as much as possible."

Daniel itemized, "You owe for rice, cheese, butter, bread, beer, flour, dried peas, spices, salt, oil, meat, fish, eggs, fruit, vegetables, wood, linen, paper. Who do I pay first?"

"Give Thyst two hundred. That should quiet him by showing that I considered him first. And use the rest for the household."

"What should I tell the other creditors?"

"I will give them my work in return for their debts, and when I have it, cash. They must allow me more time. It is to their interest to do so."

"You could sell some of your art collection to pay your debts."

"Daniel, you sound like the devil himself!" I was horrified, then indignant at what he was proposing. "I would go bankrupt first!"

"Sir, you may if you are not careful."

"I will salvage my situation with my work." By now I knew what I had to do and I was determined to succeed in my new-found resolution.

From then on, most of my energy was put into work that I thought I could sell. I consulted Van Ludick and De Jonge, who had sold many of my prints, and they told me that there was a better market for my etchings than for my paintings. So I did some on Biblical themes, and landscapes and trees, and for my own gratification, another rat killer, a pancake woman, several beggars. The last group did not sell, they were regarded as inappropriate; potential buyers saw these subjects as an unpleasant commentary on the seamy side of Dutch life. But the others fetched a good price and I pocketed hundreds of guilders with a sense of relief.

I told Van Goor that I would paint whatever he thought I could sell. He said that it was about time that I came to my senses. He suggested that I use the myths of antiquity as Rubens did, but while I respected much of his work, I could not imitate anybody else. The picture dealer also said that I should paint histories and landscapes, but I was happier depicting my own family. I did a simple self-portrait to show that I was still in command of my faculties, and above any disasters. I saw Titus sitting at his desk in such an appealing manner I had to paint him, too, and since Hendrickje had blossomed with the baptism of our daughter, I posed her as Flora in one of my most cheerful pictures. Jesus, too, remained in my mind, and to express Him I did a painting of *St. John the Baptist*. Small, mostly in gray, I lavished my love of Jesus on it. I did other biblical subjects but Van Goor was unable to sell this work.

He obtained a few portrait commissions. Two of them were of my friends, De Jonge and Lutma; I could not charge them much, they had been kind to me.

The third was a merchant, Hans Ottman, who wanted me to paint his sixteen-year-old daughter. He paid me half the fee of two hundred guilders in advance, but when I finished the portrait he refused to give me the balance, saying it did not resemble her. Grimly, I replied that she liked to grin like a cat but that I had painted her inner feelings. The merchant retorted that if I failed to heed his wishes he would sue me to get his advance back. Van Goor advised me to give in, but I could not; I was unable to falsify my brush, whatever the consequences.

My behavior displeased the picture dealer. He said, "Your obstinacy will discourage possible patrons. Ottman knows many burghers."

There were no more requests for portraits from my hand. And during the time I labored feverishly to pay my debts none of my creditors agreed to take any of my work in return for what I owed them. All of them, without exception, wanted to be paid in cash, and I had very little.

I did not discuss this with Van Goor; I felt that would merely invite further criticism from him. Besides, now I had better news to tell him.

Many months after I had written to Don Ruffo, suggesting that a half-figure of Homer or Alexander the Great would be a notable companion for his *Aristotle*, I received an answer from him that excited me. I was meeting Van Goor in his gallery where my newest paintings hung in his back room, unwanted, but I could endure that better today.

"Listen," I said, "to what the nobleman has written me."

I read: "Master Painter, Signor Rembrandt, since I find *Aristotle Contemplating the Bust of Homer* beautiful in execution and done with taste and perfection, I would like another half-figure from your hand to go with that fine piece, possibly, as you suggested, Homer or Alexander."

"That will not sell your work here," Van Goor muttered, "although it is encouraging in Italy. Have you sent him any preliminary sketches?"

"Without being paid? No."

"It is a risk you have to take. You are in no position to bargain."

"Is that why he wants more work from my brush?" I asked defiantly.

"He is only one patron, although influential. It is difficult to sell your work in Holland. No one has made an offer for what I have hung. You lead a disorderly life and your work is out of fashion these days."

"Because I paint them as they are and not as they believe they are."

"I have tried to warn you to mend your ways, but I am beginning to think that it is futile, that you will never change."

I said curtly, "I have worked harder these past months than ever."

"With your irregular household, your impiety, your thick paints?"

"Paint is paint. How I use it is my business."

"Your method is not the fashion. Your colors are too thick."

"They are what my subjects are."

Van Goor sighed. "I tell you this for your own good. If you would listen to me just once you might still retrieve your fortunes before it is too late. But you must go your own way, heedless of anything else."

I thought, I am not irresponsible as he suggests. And I did not want to destroy one of the few places I might still sell my pictures. I asked, "What course of action do you recommend for me?"

"Van Rijn, I tell you this out of the goodness of my heart. There is much criticism of the way you live. You act as if you can do whatever you please, according to your own rules, but your fellow citizens are displeased with your behavior. Your impiety and immorality has offended the entire community. They mean to punish your brazen indifference to the rules of our society, your arrogant independence, the stubbornness with which you gratify your own taste rather than the public's. Even Jan Six, once one of your best patrons, no longer has any use for your brush."

That choked off my incipient answer. I reflected sadly that this was true. Jan Six had just wed the daughter of my old friend and patron, Doctor Nicholas Tulp, and I realized that I had fallen from favor when I had not been asked to paint the wedding portrait. Instead it had been given to my ex-pupil, the more fashionable Ferdinand Bol. I know that this was a slap in my face whatever I pretended.

"If you do not change soon it will be too late."

To say I would try would have appeased him, but it would have been a lie. But I did manage to remind him, "What about the work I have done this past year? I did follow your advice."

"When you paint works for which there is no demand: yourself, your son, your mistress? You are only deceiving yourself, no one else."

"I will send Don Ruffo sketches for a Homer and an Alexander."

"You had better do it soon. Did you know that some of your creditors wanted to attach whatever works of yours that I sold?"

For a moment I could not breathe, as if a hangman's noose was around my throat. Shocked, I asked desperately, "Who were they?"

"I cannot tell you. They came to me in confidence. I put them off, temporarily, on the promise that I would persuade you to mend your ways."

"How much time do you think I have?"

"Not much. If you do not satisfy your creditors soon, they will seize everything you own. I tell you this for your own good."

"Thank you. I will attend to them at once." I strode off, feeling like a shaggy and unkempt bear who was about to be chained and possibly, skinned.

And so, a year after I had started the struggle to save my house and my possessions, I sat down with Daniel again to review my circumstances. This time we met in my salon where I had hung many of my own pictures that I could not sell or had refused to sell. There were also works by my teacher, Lastman, who had guided me, and my recent predecessors, Brouwer and Seghers, whose work I respected, *An Image of the Virgin* by Raphael of Urbino, two drawings by Titian, *Two Little Dogs Done From Life* by my son, the only work of his that showed ability, and a good Caravaggio. There were also many busts, mostly of Roman emperors, but also of Socrates, Aristotle, Homer, and Alexander, and the best furniture I owned, a large oak table, seven Spanish chairs with green velvet seats, a marble wine cooler, and cardboard shades to give a diffused light to the chamber so that everything could be viewed properly.

Thanks to Hendrickje everything was in order. But I did not include her in this discussion—I did not want to worry her, and she seemed content as long as I managed to give her enough money to pay for our day-by-day expenses.

Daniel's summation was another shock. Despite the disappointments, I had earned over two thousand guilders, which would have been a fortune when I came to Amsterdam, although there had been years when I had earned much more, and still he told me that I was even deeper in debt.

"How could that be?" I asked. "I have tried to spend wisely."

"Even so, Master, you are spending more than you have received."

"I have stopped buying other work. I have concentrated on my debts."

"Interest eats up what you pay. In borrowing from one person to pay another, each time at an accumulating rate of interest, in the end you owe more than you paid back. The interest is growing faster than you can take care of it. The debts I estimated last year to be about twenty-one thousand guilders have risen to about twenty-five thousand. Thus, you have been unable to pay back any of the principal, and your main creditors, Thyst, Van Hertsbeeck, and Witsen have joined together and have informed me that if you cannot begin to pay back on the principal they will sue you. They could take all that you own, not only your house but your possessions and pictures, too."

"Is there any remedy?" How I wished I could labor with a free mind again. But Daniel was too serious to be ignored or put off this time.

"I suggest that you meet with your chief creditors."

"When I cannot pay them? That seems a futile gesture."

"It would show your wish to do so, your good faith." When I did not halt him, he added, "And I would offer them something tangible as security. Your personal possessions such as these in the salon."

His suggestion revolted me. They were my other self, my impulses, my fidelity to passing emotions, my approach to the truth of my existence, my ever becoming. Without them, little of myself would remain.

"Or they will seize them eventually anyhow. This way, you may be able to save them. You have no other choice."

I realized that he was right and I replied, "Arrange a meeting here with my main creditors: Thyst, Witsen, and Van Hertsbeeck."

Daniel did so, and a few days later I met Thyst in my salon. He had been chosen as the spokesman for the three chief creditors, since I owed him the most money and for the longest time. He did not take the chair I offered him, and before I could explain my position to him or offer him refreshments, he silenced me.

"Van Rijn, the time has come for your debts to be cleared up. Not only have you not paid any interest on the outstanding amount for the past four years, you have forced me to pay the taxes on this house, too, for the last two years. This is intolerable. I do not own the house, yet I am being put in the position of being responsible for it."

"What do you propose?" I asked hastily, a dull anger stirring in me.

"Sell your possessions to pay us. Many of them are valuable."

Although it was midday and I had opened the shades to light the salon, I felt that I was in the deepest darkness. He was surveying the contents of this elegant chamber even as he spoke, as greedily as a starving man contemplating food, yet he was wealthy, as were the other creditors. And these details infuriated me; if they occupied me much longer they would destroy whatever desire I had to work. But I mumbled, "I could try."

"Do more than try. Raise the money or we will go to court and seize everything you possess and you will be left with nothing."

"I understand," I said, with despair in my heart, but bowing my head before the force in him. "I will do what you ask."

Thyst relaxed a little then, as if he had not expected me to give in, at least so quickly, and he said, "You have a fine collection. You should be proud of it. You could make it into a splendid museum."

"I would prefer that for my own work."

Thyst regarded me as if I were mad. His expression said: A museum for one artist, one who could not even pay what he owed —how absurd! But he remarked, "We must stick to business. I have arranged with a notary to draw up a new agreement wherein you promise to pledge your personal possessions, such as these in the salon, as security for our loans."

I assented, although still unwillingly, feeling that I was being compelled by circumstances beyond my control.

But at least, I consoled myself, as I signed the necessary papers the next day, I had extricated myself from the immediate danger. I had no intention of selling any of my personal possessions. I decided that something else must save me.

Thyst was very pleased with himself and after we finished with the notary, he invited me to join him in a tavern for some drinks.

I accepted. I thought, Why not? I was thirsty and the beer was good.

I was disappointed when he ordered wine in a pewter jug to indicate that he was above using cheap spirits; I did not care for his taste. He had taken me to an establishment so respectable and dignified I felt uncomfortable. We sat in a large marble-flagged hall with ornate stained-glass windows, a tavern for prosperous gourmets, magistrates, and guild masters, although he did not suggest that we order any salmon, the specialty of the house. It was, I felt, too expensive to waste on me. And Thyst, whose face flushed quickly, was very careful with his change, saying, "You cannot trust the employees. They are always looking to cheat one. Were you serious about wanting your work in a museum?"

"It is the best way to view my work."

"No one will support you. Although," he added, putting a hand on my shoulder to show that he was a good fellow, "you could sell more if you only heeded popular taste. You are not a bad painter. If I were you, I would sell the Titians first. They should command a large price."

"I will consider it," I replied.

"Good," he replied. "I knew that you would listen to reason."

The wine he had ordered was too sweet for my taste but I sipped it, for he was trying to be a host. Then he chattered about the recent sea war with England and how it had hurt business and I stopped listening. I thanked him for his hospitality, put my copy of our agreement in my pocket, and I went home to start painting for myself again.

EVEN THOUGH I AM ONLY A STONE

Even though I am only a stone I know
Last night the moon shone yellow
At dawn the sun rose red
through the resting trees
And the leaves whispered in a cream tone

At dusk a bird flew down into the brown
Then a blade of grass grew a tall green
I heard a bee sigh purple wide
I saw the mountain blink one of its eyes

Among all these manifestations only I
I alone am stiller than death stiller
Yet my manifestation is as great as theirs
I have the sense of wonder to ask

WHY AM I SO WHY WHY WHY WHY WHY
AND WHAT WAS I MEANT TO DO
TO DO TO DO TO DO TO DO

Even though only I I alone
am stiller than I don't know what

—Stymean Karlen

I WAS writing Don Ruffo the next day to ask him if he desired any preliminary sketches of a half-length figure of Alexander and Homer that I proposed to paint for him, when Hendrickje announced a visitor that surprised me. It was the day that Daniel attended classes at the nearby synagogue and so she answered the door and admitted Frans Hals.

I was delighted to see my old friend and I put aside what I was doing, for he was one of those rare people worth being interrupted by. I asked Hendrickje to join us, but she said that she would only be in the way, that we must have much to talk about, we had not seen each other for a long time. I did not argue with her as she withdrew from the studio, but tried to make my fellow painter feel at home.

We embraced warmly and I gave him my chair, which no one else ever sat in. I observed that he had aged since I had last seen him and used a cane now. Yet, although he was in his seventies and his stocky figure had become plump and his thick hair white, his blue eyes were still clear, his round cheeks rosy, and his smile engaging. And there was the expression that I liked, animated and interested.

"It is good to see you, Hals!" I exclaimed. "What brings you to Amsterdam? I thought that you never left Haarlem these days."

He grinned and replied, "Curiosity, my friend, and business."

"Are you here to see about your work?"

"It is my first visit in years, but I could not come to Amsterdam without viewing what you are doing. You have put on some weight, I see, you still have some vanity about your clothes despite the paint smears on your smock, but your eyes are still good, I can tell by your work."

He was one of the few whose opinion mattered to me, and I said apologetically, which was unusual for me, "These works are unfinished." There were four pictures on my easels but none that satisfied me. "My completed work is downstairs. Would you care to see the latest ones?"

"I would be honored."

As I escorted him down my wide wooden staircase I saw the scratch I had made years ago on the top step with my heel. Saskia had died a few days before and in my despair I had kicked the stairs for not returning her to me. Now, Hals, who I had given up as lost, was by my side, walking more slowly than he used to, but walking just the same, and I was pleased by his presence and that he held my arm for balance.

Then, as he paused in the doorway of my salon to regain his breath, framed by the sunlight, I was apprehensive suddenly. I wondered: Had he come to borrow money? His breeches were baggy, the two pairs of stockings he wore to keep out the cold were shabby, and he had on a large floppy hat that was out of fashion and obviously borrowed. This reminded me that I had heard that he had gone bankrupt recently and had been forced to reside in the Haarlem almshouse. And while he looked eager, he was anxious, too. I waited for him to speak.

I felt that he was critical of the luxury of my large salon. Never mind the contents, I thought, you must think I am still prosperous, only a prosperous painter could afford such a lavish chamber.

Hals said abruptly, "This reminds me of two memories of you."

"What are they?"

"Once, as a young man, when I suggested that you study with me."

"I could not join you in Haarlem. I had to remain in Amsterdam."

"You made the right decision. You were too strong-minded to follow anyone else's style. It was selfish of me to want to influence you."

"You have. I have studied your work carefully. But I had met Saskia and I did not want to leave the city."

"Rembrandt, you should not have. You were the rage. Everyone desired your work. You were the most successful artist in Amsterdam. You had conquered. By the time you were thirty you could afford this salon."

"What is the other memory that remains?"

"The last time I saw you. Your wife was dead, you were no longer first in popularity, and you were painting better than ever. Yet you have kept all these elaborate and costly furnishings."

My tone grew curt. "Hals, they gratify me."

"But do you need such a great house? It must be a terrible drain."

"I bought it because it has excellent light. Other considerations were minor. Although I have enjoyed using this chamber as a museum."

He said, "That is a worthy purpose."

Yet he stood apart from me, subdued and silent. I did not move either and I was surprised and disappointed when he did not focus on my pictures but fastened his gaze on the Brouwers and Seghers that I owned.

He declared abruptly, "I am glad that you respect Brouwer's work."

"Very much. I have six of his paintings."

"Adriaen Brouwer studied with me but he painted in the style of Brughel. He loved the color of peasant life, the drinking bouts, the card players, and he raised his scenes out of the sordid with the beauty of his brush. But it is no wonder that he died prematurely at thirty-three. He could only get small sums for his paintings, he drank even more than me, he was rarely sober. He spent whatever he earned on drink and tobacco."

"His work has unusual power. I am privileged to own some of it."

"Rubens owned some of his pictures, too. Sometimes I think it is only the painter who appreciates a painter. I see that you also possess eight paintings by Hercules Seghers. You must like his brush, too."

"He was an etcher of genius and his passionate and melancholy landscapes are of importance to me. He was an original artist."

"I knew him, too. He worked in Haarlem for a time. But he was an eccentric, he kept aloof, he rarely saw anyone else, even fellow painters, as if he were living in a world of his own. He died in poverty, too, as have all the artists I have known except Rubens and Van Dyck."

"How old was Seghers when he died?"

"Forty-eight. Much too young."

"I am just past forty-eight. Often I feel far older."

Hals moved quickly, as if he did not want to be reminded of his age, and as he hobbled in front of my newest pictures his eyes were as animated and expressive as ever, although his face had aged.

I said, "I should paint you." I loved to paint old age.

"It would not work. I no longer have the patience to sit. I ache when I am motionless more than a few minutes, and I could not support myself in the days it would take."

"You could stay here. There would be enough to eat and drink."

"I doubt that I could stay sober. You know my reputation. I would have to drink to free myself of the tedium of sitting. I would treasure a portrait of me from your hand but it is too late. Now I must view what you have done. Undisturbed." He held up his hand for quiet.

I was silent while he examined my work and my mind returned to Saskia, who had liked Hals, she had said that he was a merry person. She adored merriment, it was her nature and her joy. Saskia had died in 1642, and yet I remembered her vividly. I could still draw her chubby, cheerful, fair likeness precisely. I loved Hendrickje, too, I reflected, but differently. Saskia was my romance, Hendrickje my necessity. But now Hals was speaking.

"Your portraits of your son and your mistress are moving but it is the self-portrait that I feel the most. But why do you depict yourself so harshly?"

"Truthfully, Hals, truthfully, the best way I can."

"It is a remarkable portrait, emotional and evocative, but your nose is bulbous, your cheeks are fat, your forehead is lined, your eyes are clear but weary, your skin is worn, aged. If not for the expression . . ."

I interrupted, "That is essential."

"It suggests so much."

"What about yourself? Have you done anything lately that you like?" I recalled fondly his portraits that I had discovered as a young man. They were among the best I had seen, indifferent to the ideal of classical beauty, free, vivid, genuine, mature, concentrating on essences, faces, hands, expressions, with powerful, sweeping brush strokes.

He seemed to have other things on his mind today and I had to repeat the question before he answered. But then he spoke with passion. "No, they have not buried me, although they have tried. I am painting again, after not having done a stroke of work for years. When I was declared a bankrupt and put into the almshouse, I had no desire to paint. I said to myself that I could not sell anything, so what was the use. Then I made a marvelous discovery. Being poor was the best thing that could have happened to me. Now I could not afford to buy all the expensive colors I had used when I was younger and prosperous, when there

(118)

was a papa or a patron to pay my bills. At seventy-five I realized that it was not my strength that had been wanting, but my imagination. Now I have to achieve results from only one or two pots of paint and I have learned—as your brush shows, my friend —to suggest tints rather than to state them in a multitude of colors. They say that my hand has become heavier and my colors darker, but the truth is, my palette has become simpler. Today I suggest rather than state. If you can do that honestly and humanely, as I see you have done, a few tints will suffice and your viewers will feel your brush even more movingly than before."

I nodded with an enthusiasm that I had not felt for some time.

He said with a sudden change of mood, "But I have talked too much about myself. My throat is parched and weary. Let us partake. There is a favorite tavern of mine, The Black Boar, between St. Anthony's Gate and the Jewish quarter, which serves a wide variety of refreshments."

I hesitated; I knew he was a heavy drinker, some said, a drunk. But that was also gossiped about me, although I considered my taste for beer no more indulgent than most of my Dutch friends, and so I agreed. After a word to Hendrickje to tell her where we were going, we took each other by the arm and descended into the street.

With the many layers of clothing that we wore to keep out the usual chill and damp, I felt as if we were two barrels waddling down the Breestraat, but gradually, as the sun warmed my back, my spirits improved. The weather was mild for late autumn and the neighborhood was warm and friendly. Hals eyed the canal, the high bridge, the lofty houses with fondness, but I was more interested in the itinerant vendors and the salt fish, sweets, and fruit they were selling, their faces were expressive with excitement.

Hals said, again with the abruptness that was characteristic of him, "Your piece of *St. John the Baptist* is admirable for your depiction of the listening faces. Most painters would have concentrated on John and slighted the others. But you did not."

"Thank you."

"Do not thank me. Thank yourself. You are still admired by many of our younger painters."

Hals was walking faster than I had expected in spite of his need to use a cane, as if he were hurrying to keep an appointment, but when we reached The Black Boar he paused at the entrance and announced, "I have asked three young artists from Haarlem to join us here. They have been eager to meet you ever since they learned that I knew you."

"Should I know their work?"

"They are much younger, in their late twenties, Jacob van Ruisdael, Jan Steen, and Pieter de Hoogh. Each gifted in his own way."

"I have seen some of Steen and Ruisdael's work. I liked it."

"Good. My young friend, De Hoogh, is equally gifted. But to support himself, this painter, he is about twenty-five, has had to become a footman in the service of a rich adventurer, Justus La Grange, and he is unhappy. Would you have a place for him? He is, as I said, gifted."

I could not dispense with Daniel, I thought.

"He would be willing to serve you as an assistant."

"I have an assistant who suits me."

"Ever since De Hoogh saw your golden light he has used it."

"Hals, I am not interested in disciples. Each one must paint his own way."

"Nonetheless, do not make up your mind until you view his work. He has brought paintings with him to show you. Will you look at them?"

I was tempted to refuse him. But I respected his taste, as I did his brush, and he had gone to much effort for this friend of his, and so, I agreed to view De Hoogh's work, although still reluctantly.

The Black Boar was very different from the establishment that Thyst had taken me to. It was a spacious cellar with simple furnishings, lit by candles that flickered and frequently went out, and as we stood on the thick stone steps inside the heavy oak door, Hals waved to three young men waiting anxiously at a large round table. I had been here before, this tavern was a favorite meeting place for the St. Luke Guild of Painters, but not recently. I recognized the pot-bellied stove in the center of the room, with the spout that was cut through the ceiling, the birdcage hanging near a window, the pictures of the House of Orange on the walls, the barrels of beer and the wine in leather bottles by the counter, and the plain dress of the customers. They were a mixture of working men and middle-class burghers, with a sprinkling of women and children and dogs, and I observed that almost no one was drinking alone.

As Hals escorted me to the table by the largest window in the tavern, where the light was best, the three young men who were sitting there rose as one to acknowledge my presence. Although I maintained that worldly honors were unimportant, I was moved by this gesture of respect.

My friend motioned for me to take the most comfortable chair, which was high-backed, with a velvet seat, unusual for this kind of a tavern, and when the others insisted, I did. I braced myself against the high back, uneasy about what was to follow—I did not see how I could help them when I was having such difficulty helping myself—but I could not leave now. It would be rude to Hals and I was curious about their work.

Hals sat in the other high-backed chair and the young artists arranged themselves on stools about us while he introduced them.

Pieter de Hoogh looked older than twenty-five to me, of moderate size, with dark, deep-set eyes, a serious way of speaking, wearing the modest garb of a servant and was engrossed in the pipe he was smoking.

Jan Steen was robust, ruddy faced, with square features, the most mature in appearance of the three painters, and was bearded and red-haired.

In some ways it was Jacob van Ruisdael's expression that invited my interest the most. He was brown-eyed and brown-haired, frail, and his voice was soft, but there was an intentness in him that pleased me.

Hals ordered Holland gin, grape brandy, and Dutch beer, while I wondered who was going to pay, these drinks were costly. When they were put in front of us with glasses and jugs, he stated eloquently, "I have been preparing for this occasion for a long time." He scattered a cascade of coins on the table for the waiter and cried out, "Drink! You, too, Rembrandt, it will not harm your brush!"

Everyone waited for me to begin, and so I did, with beer, which I preferred, and as the round was repeated, I gradually felt more at ease.

Suddenly De Hoogh said, "Master, I believe that you are a greater painter than Raphael or Titian, although they say that is blasphemy. You see with a dark lantern the world of our emotion and of our soul."

"Young man, you must not exaggerate."

"I do not exaggerate. You are first among us. Correct, friends?"

The others nodded, even Hals.

"If you would view my work I would be honored."

He was so earnest I could not refuse him, although I was uncomfortable again, afraid that I would dislike his brush, and so, have to hurt him.

His work was imaginative, I realized, Hals was right, De Hoogh was gifted. Not only was his craftsmanship excellent, he had an independent viewpoint and style. I took his two paintings over to the window where I could see them better but my opinion did not alter. He was attracted by light as I was—although these days I was considered a dark painter—and while his depiction of Dutch interiors was a little too meticulous for my taste, it was effective. He was clearly more gifted than Daniel.

He was fearful of asking my opinion and so Hals said brusquely, "Rembrandt, I am right? Agreed?"

Everyone was motionless, even Steen and Ruisdael, as if, should I utter a negative comment, it would be a sentence of death.

I chose my words carefully. "De Hoogh, it is unfortunate that you should labor as a footman. You should labor only as a painter."

He replied passionately, "Master, that is why I want to serve you!"

"Your brush is sufficiently mature to stand on its own."

"But I cannot support myself with it. If I could only assist you."

"No!" I said curtly. "That is impossible!"

"I am not gifted enough?" he asked tragically.

"That is not the issue. I have an assistant." I thought wryly, I have just promoted Daniel although he does not know it.

"I could be your second assistant," De Hoogh implored.

I could not afford that, but I could not admit it. I said, "I do not need any more assistants at the moment. I am sorry . . ."

De Hoogh looked devastated and whispered, "I am sorry, too, that I wasted your time."

"You did not waste my time," I said sharply. "Your work is fine."

"But in Haarlem and Delft, where my cloth merchant lives, there is no market for my work. He pays me very little, just room and board, and keeps my work for himself. In Amsterdam there would be more opportunity."

"Not as much as you think."

Steen spoke up. "Master, Ruisdael and I want to move here, too."

"Amsterdam's importance as a center of art is exaggerated."

"Yet you live here."

"I have become accustomed to the city. My roots are in it."

"You never paint the city. You go beyond that. In Delft and Haarlem, where I live, I have great difficulty selling my pictures. Most of them are unsold. I cannot even pay my baker with what they earn. The only way I can support myself is to follow my father's footsteps, work in his brewery and run a tavern to put food on my table. Amsterdam, with its trade, has become one of the great and rich cities of the world. There must be much money here."

"And poverty," I added. "In Amsterdam wealth marches hand in hand with poverty. For every rich merchant who builds himself a five-story mansion to display his affluence, a dozen country folk flock to the city in search of jobs they do not find. Employment is seasonal and most of them end up, if they work, digging ditches or fortifications."

Ruisdael said softly, "Yet it is the goal of most Dutch artists. Even of myself, and my brush is devoted to landscapes."

I replied, "Our esteemed colleague, who has brought us together, whose work honors us, has remained in Haarlem all of his life."

Hals said, "I am not sure I should have. I only remained because I had many children to raise, two wives to support, and I thought that when I became the favorite painter of the Haarlem burghers it was sensible to stay there. I even turned down Van Dyck when he suggested that I join him in England. But the last few years, since they have ignored my work, I have wondered whether I should have stayed in Haarlem."

I said, "The same thing could have happened to you in Amsterdam."

"It is because his brush has become dark," said De Hoogh. "The burghers are stupid and do not realize that it makes his work even more powerful."

"Stupidity is a dreadful thing," said Steen.

"And exists everywhere," I added. "As much in Amsterdam as in Haarlem."

They sat still, contemplating what I had said with intense feeling. Steen shivered, De Hoogh was mournful, Ruisdael looked grave and grim.

This was too much for Hals' ebullient disposition and he ordered another round of drinks, then a fourth, and now the conversation flowed as freely as the liquor. At first we talked shop, of the different methods of grinding paint, of new combinations of acids with which to treat our copper plates, then Hals took the floor with an abrupt tirade.

"People see the painter sitting at his easel between a pile of dirty dishes and soiled linen and they say, poor fellow, poor fool, while his wife cooks a thick bean soup to keep him warm. To them, he is a slovenly idiot, not willing to do an honest day's work, deserving his poverty and neglect. But his work saves him, since nothing else will."

I said suddenly, on my fifth beer, "I could paper my house with my unpaid bills. Should I be proud I am a Dutchman living in Amsterdam?"

"You should be proud you are Rembrandt van Rijn. It is a noble name."

"And has been in our family for only one generation. My father took the name Van Rijn after the river Rhine, to give himself an identity, and I have kept it since it suits my tongue." I paused, for Ruisdael had ordered oysters to keep him sober and as he squeezed a lemon on them its yellow color attracted me.

Hals continued, "The last ten years I have had few commissions. Two years ago, when I went bankrupt, they put me in the almshouse."

I asked, "How is it there?" I was thinking of myself.

"It could be better. It could be worse. Rubens and I were fellow students in Antwerp. He died a very rich man."

"But he is dead and you are alive!"

"Indeed! We must not think about money. Friends, this is a party." He stood up and in spite of his swollen ankles and his permanent limp he began to dance and he cried out, "No one will shoot me for my sobriety!"

He grabbed me and whirled me around and Steen joined us, then Ruisdael and De Hoogh. I felt like a drunken swashbuckler and I loved it.

When we finished I declared, "When I started I tried to paint like the old masters but they were too old for me. They say I have a reputation for avarice, but I only bargain when I do not want to sell. When it comes to keeping my pictures I am as avaricious as the worst miser."

"So am I," said Hals.

De Hoogh said, "I wish I could be."

"Now," Hals cut in, "no whining, no complaining."

Once again he proceeded to set the example, drinking, laughing, dancing, and I followed him, relieved to escape the pain of thinking about money.

By the time we left the tavern we were all drunk, even the serious Ruisdael and the gloomy De Hoogh. We held each other by the arm for good fellowship and to support ourselves, and as we emerged from The Black Boar into the sunlight and the crowded street we shouted and sang, we skipped and danced. Steen wanted to jump over the beer barrel announcing the contents of the tavern, De Hoogh wanted to roll it, Hals said that we should open it and drink from it. So we did, without asking anybody's permission, and after we sampled it there were more toasts, casual and comradely. Then the others insisted on escorting me home. Not to come in, they said as one, it was too late, but they declared that they were my civic guard proudly restoring me to my place of importance in Amsterdam. Each step we took seemed vital as we linked arms and staggered along the cobble-stones of the wide, neighborly street.

Passing the synagogue that was halfway between the tavern and my home on the Breestraat, I became sober suddenly. Daniel had just come out of it with three friends and one of their faces fascinated me.

There was my Jesus, I thought excitedly, he was holding a book and arguing with Daniel. He was dark in the bright sunlight, his olive skin a vivid contrast to his black hair that fell in a carefully combed curl to his shoulders, as if it were the one feature of which he was vain. I was also absorbed by his deep brown eyes, as lustrous as any I had seen, his long aquiline nose and chin, his high forehead and cheekbones, his wide, full red lips, his large, spacious head. He was slight, not tall, yet he carried himself erectly and he wore the fashion of the day, a black robe with a white collar. But it was his expression that enchanted me. He must be a rabbi, I thought, or studying to be one.

I clutched Hals' hand and halted him as I exclaimed, "Look!"

Hals and the others paused and followed my gaze, sobered for the moment by my passion, but none of them reacted the way I did. They were puzzled.

I said, "This youth has the face of Jesus Christ!"

Steen asked, "That young Jew?" He obviously did not agree with me.

"Yes!" But before I could stop Daniel and his friends they vanished around the corner. I felt empty, although my vision remained.

Hals ignored my excitement. He moved on to the steps of the synagogue where he could command the largest audience and he orated drunkenly, "Drinking is our blessing, our solace and our refuge. We drink to drive away care and to keep warm in our wet, cold climate. To escape from homes where women never wash themselves but clean our homes until they are spotless and unin-habitable. To avoid rheumatism, to acquire energy, to have pleas-ure, to forget, to forget . . . What was I saying, friends?"

De Hoogh said, "I would be glad to model for your Christ."

His face had enough suffering but not enough compassion. "No," I said, "Your expression is not what I want."

Steen volunteered but he was wrong, too, as I told him, while Ruisdael could hardly stand, he was so tipsy and without the endurance I needed.

Hals asked gruffly, sobered by my intensity, "Rembrandt, must you paint another Jesus Christ now?"

"Yes." I was positive once more.

"But you have devoted a large body of work to Him. Some of your views of Jesus are exceptional."

Thinking of the tenderness I had seen on the face of Daniel's friend, I replied, "But not what I want. I still have not captured the best expression."

Hals muttered, "The expression, always the expression."

"It is more important than the face or the features."

Everyone was quiet as if I had uttered a revelation. We walked silently and almost soberly to my home. I invited them in, but when Hals declined, the others did also, although, I felt, reluctantly.

I did not insist, preoccupied with what I had just seen.

Then De Hoogh made a final frantic effort to join me. He offered me half of what he earned on any picture that he sold while in my employ.

There was money in his work, I believed, properly displayed, but I refused. I added, "What time I have left, I must devote to myself."

This spurred Hals into stating, "They must not count the old man out."

At first I thought that he was talking about me, and then I realized that he was speaking about himself.

He added, "I can still paint when I can see. My hand does not tremble when I hold a brush. I do not need a cane to feel. Painting is breathing."

"Yes," I remarked reflectively, "yet once in a while I wish that I could start now with what I have learned, with an old head in a young body."

"Why?" asked Ruisdael. "You paint so movingly now."

"Much pain and difficulty and anxiety could have been avoided."

"I have those hardships already," De Hoogh said somberly.

Steen observed with a sigh, "We all have. But, Master, it has been a great honor to have met you. Your work is unforgettable. I will treasure this day as long as I live."

De Hoogh agreed with a sudden, unexpected smile that was like a ray of sunlight bursting out from behind a dark cloud, while Ruisdael said with surprising vigor, "Jan Steen is right. Your work is a shrine to worship."

Embarrassed by their praise and emotion, I coughed to clear my throat and to gain time to think how to respond. The three young artists stood like statues while Hals reached into his pocket and found a dirty piece of paper and a stump of a pencil and began to draw me.

Hals was as compelled as I was, I thought, and I smiled.

He whispered drunkenly, "The sun is strong here. I can see you now."

"I can, too," I said. "Thanks, friends, for the party and your company. All of you have stimulated me." Then, since everybody, even Hals, looked as serious as if we had just attended a funeral instead of a celebration, I could not bear to end such a nourishing occasion on a somber note. I contemplated them a moment with complete concentration and intense eyes, and then reminded them, with the widest smile I could summon, "Remember, we must always bark, bark, bark. As we did today."

"Yes," said Hals, grinning again, "We may be dogs but we must remain free."

We shook hands on that and went our separate ways.

SINCE WE LIVE

Since we live
in the heart
of God
Let us live
gently there
Not to wound
the body of God
Not to empty it
of God's blood
Which of us want
the death of God
on their
conscience

—Stymean Karlen

AFTER I sent my offer to Don Ruffo to sketch the heads of Alexander and Homer for his approval, I resumed work on my portraits of Jesus with fresh energy. It was the day after Hals' party and the expression that I had seen on the face of Daniel's friend continued to haunt me. The passage of time only added to my conviction that I must paint it. I told Daniel that I had seen him coming out of the synagogue with a friend who suited my brush and I ordered him to fetch this person to me.

When he recovered from his surprise, he pointed out, "Master, I was with three friends. I do not know which one you mean."

"The dark one," I said emphatically.

"They were all dark," he reminded me.

"This one had an unusual expression. The others were commonplace." I added impatiently, "You should know who I mean."

"What do you want him for?"

"To sit for the Jesus I have been struggling with this past year."

Daniel protested, "I doubt this is a good idea. My friends would be uncomfortable sitting for such a subject, it is likely that the rabbis and the members of the congregation will object and—" I cut him short.

"The subject does not concern them and I will pay him to sit for me. Do as I say and you will no longer be my apprentice but my assistant." That should spur him, I thought, that was a position he coveted.

"Because of my work, Master?"

"Because of many things," I said hastily. "You know that the situation between master and pupil is fixed according to the rules of the Guild of St. Luke. Your apprenticeship has lasted the necessary two years, now is the time for you to progress. But you are still required to do whatever I order. Fetch me the dark young man with the pointed face and the expressive features and you will be promoted."

"You must mean Joseph Lopez. He is studying to be a rabbi."

It was my turn to be critical. "What makes you so certain?"

"He fits the description you gave me."

"I did not describe him. It is his feeling that matters."

"He has that, too. He is devout and learned."

"Then he should be willing to sit for me. Tell him that I am a friend of Manasseh ben Israel, that I have done his portrait. Since Lopez studies with this estimable rabbi, he should want to please him." I was not sure I was being logical, but I persuaded Daniel.

Hendrickje cleaned the house so that it was spotless and so that Lopez would not be discouraged by dirt or evidence of poverty. When he came on the appointed afternoon, she thought that he was handsome and attractive, which, she said, was not always the same thing. She prayed that he would satisfy me and after she led him into my presence she retired into the kitchen while Daniel tried to make his friend feel at home.

I was upset. This was not the young man whose tenderness had caught my attention. Yet his appearance fitted the impression that I had given Daniel. Lopez was dark, with a slender, pointed face and long black hair that fell to his shoulders. The more I examined the rabbinical student's features the more paintable they became. But I was not sure that he fitted my conception. He was very righteous, too much, perhaps.

I asked, "Young man, did Daniel tell you what I desired?"

"Sir, he suggested that you wanted a model for a biblical subject."

"Does that please you?"

"I am proud to study with your friend, Rabbi Manasseh ben Israel."

"He was a splendid model. I enjoyed painting him."

"Where would you like me to sit, sir?"

"In the chair by the easel." Once he was there, I studied him intently. His face might do after all, but I was still not sure about his expression. I blurted out, "Did Daniel tell you that you would model for Jesus?"

"No! I am not certain that I can remain. Many will be offended."

"Jews or Christians, young man?"

"Both, sir. This is a sensitive subject."

"I do not intend to offend. I am simply interested in the truth."

"Sir, will the rabbi approve?"

"I think so." But suddenly it did not matter. Lopez was wrong; he was ill-at-ease, too righteous. My sitter must possess a profound tenderness, and I sensed this was beyond Lopez.

"If my rabbi approves, I will be glad to pose for you."

"Thank you." My voice grew hoarse as I added, "I appreciate your difficulties. Now you must excuse me. I have other work to do."

"When shall I return?"

"It is not necessary."

"You do not want me, sir, after I agreed to model for you?" Lopez was insulted, and Daniel was very uncomfortable.

"You do not fit my conception." I did not bother to say that I was sorry, I was not sorry but annoyed that I had wasted time, energy, and emotion. It was enough that this young man was wrong. "Good day."

The abrupt dismissal worried Daniel. After he saw his friend to the door, he exclaimed, "Lopez will never forgive me! Master, you were rude to him."

"I was brief. It is not the same thing. You fetched the wrong one."

"He fitted your description."

"It must have been one of your other two companions."

He muttered, "I will not ask them. I cannot risk offending them or I will not have any friends left. Besides, Elias is too busy with his studies and Baruch will not come no matter what you offer."

I had to persist while I possessed the energy. I knew that Daniel was not the sitter I preferred for my view of Jesus, he was too fair, too Dutch, but at this instant he was the only model I had. He stood with his chin in his hand, in an attitude of meditation, and there was compassion in him. I told him to hold this posture.

Astonished, he did, and I drew him quickly. I told myself that he must suffice, but this inadequate prospect caused me to pause. Not only was his complexion wrong, his features were too broad, too Dutch. No wonder I waver, I thought, he does not fit my view despite his sensitivity.

He said, "Master, if you want me to model for this subject, I will."

I sighed. It was no use. I put down my sketch pad and pencil.

"I am Jewish."

"You do not look it."

"There is no such thing!" Daniel cried out angrily. "Since the dispersion we look many different ways! I am as Jewish as Lopez!"

"Not in appearance. It is a pity."

Daniel was even more offended and he retorted heatedly, "It is not my fault that I inherited my father's complexion and features."

"That is not the issue. I do not want Jesus to look Italian as Raphael painted Him, or German as Durer expressed Him, or English as the English depict Him, or Dutch, as is the custom to picture Him in the United Seven Provinces. But only a fool explains."

I dismissed him so that I could decide what to do next.

The day Daniel went to study with the rabbi, I stationed myself outside of the synagogue, which was a short walk from my house. It was a Saturday when devout Jews attended services. This was the center of Jewish life in Amsterdam, and I stood in the shadows of a nearby warehouse where no one could detect my presence. I was familiar with this Portuguese synagogue; I had visited it as a guest of the rabbi; I had found subjects within it and I had even used the building as a model; but I did not want to enter it alone, that would make me feel self-conscious.

When the services ended and the congregation came out my excitement waned as no one emerged whose appearance attracted me. I thought sadly, These Jews are too Portuguese, too old for my purpose. I wondered if any young men attended these services, the congregation was so elderly. To lessen my impatience I drew two old bearded Jews who resembled figures in the Old Testament, but I felt no pleasure from this sketch. Weary from waiting, my body aching, especially my precious eyes, I decided to depart.

Suddenly I caught my breath. Daniel was leaving the synagogue with the three young men that I had seen last week, but today they were arguing and while the one I wanted as a model sounded reasonable, Lopez was speaking with bitterness. Yet when I saw again the tenderness that had moved me deeply, I realized that my emotion had not betrayed my taste or my reason and I could not retreat. I stepped forward as if I were meeting them accidentally. When we came face to face I was as surprised as Daniel, while Lopez recoiled from me as if I had the plague.

I said hurriedly, "Daniel, I was strolling along, looking for a subject to draw, this is a picturesque neighborhood, and . . ." I paused, waiting for him to introduce me to his other friends.

Instead, he replied, "Master, did you find any subjects?"

"None that pleased me." I focused on the expression that had attracted me and added, "What are your friends' names?"

"You know Lopez, of course."

Lopez grumbled, "He is mad," but I said quietly, "Of course." When Daniel paused and did not introduce me to the others, I stated, sharply this time, "Are you ashamed of your other friends?"

"No," said Daniel. "It is just that neither of them will sit for you."

"Perhaps they do not know me and fear to trust themselves to my brush."

"I am acquainted with your person," said the one I desired. "I have seen you with Rabbi ben Israel and Doctor Bonus. You are the painter, Rembrandt van Rijn. They speak favorably of your work. They say you are the best painter in Amsterdam, perhaps in all of the Netherlands."

"Then why is Daniel hesitant to introduce you?"

"Perhaps it is because I am having some difficulties with the rabbis and he is afraid that I will say something that will embarrass him."

"That is not so!" declared Daniel. "But, Master, when I asked Baruch to sit for you, I thought he might be the person you meant after all when you stressed his expression, he said he could not come."

"Why not?" I asked impatiently.

Baruch said, "I do not want to sit. I have better work to do."

"Are you a rabbi?"

"No. I am too young."

"A rabbinical student?"

"Not any more."

"Never any more!" Lopez burst out caustically. "Baruch means blessed in Hebrew, but he is anything but that. Daniel, as I told you and Elias, we must not associate with him any more. He attacks our faith, and indirectly, our Christian neighbors. He is a grave danger to us."

I found that difficult to believe. Baruch was even slighter than he had appeared at a distance, his manner was gentle and suggested a youth of sensibility, reason, and modesty. The closer I came to him, the more I felt that he fitted my view, that the spirit within him was precious.

Lopez said, "I invite all of you, even you, mad Dutch painter, to avoid him. That will teach him not to question the existence of God."

Baruch replied softly, "I do not question His existence. But I do wonder whether God is in one being or in everything. And I find it hard to believe in angels, or in some of the things in the Bible."

Lopez shouted, "That is heresy!"

I was not interested in theological differences. Baruch was the most appropriate model I had seen so far, everything else was irrelevant. I said, "Daniel, arrange with your friend to sit for me."

"Why should I sit for you? I have no desire to be painted."

"Daniel, bring him to my studio tomorrow."

Baruch said, "I have other things to do then."

I persisted, "The next day."

Baruch asked Daniel, "Is your Master always so insistent?"

"Only when he wants to paint someone."

To make sure that he did not take that amiss, I stated, "It is unlikely that you will do, but it is barely possible. Daniel, one of your tasks as my assistant is to find me the best models. I cannot continue you in this position if you fail me in this mission."

Daniel said, "Baruch, if you do not visit my master, he will never forgive me."

After a long, regretful sigh, Baruch responded, as if he were doing a favor for Daniel against his reason. "I will come to his studio. Tomorrow afternoon. But only once."

"Do not be late," I stated, "Winter is approaching and the light does not last long these short days. We must work when the light is good."

Lopez said scornfully, "Now I know that this painter is mad. Spinoza, do you have any idea what this lunatic wants to paint you as?"

Spinoza shrugged, "Why should that matter? He will interpret me as he pleases. It is evident he is a man with a strong purpose. He will, no doubt, tire of me as soon as he realizes that I do not want to sit for him and that I am a poor subject. I am doing this for Daniel's sake."

"Did Daniel tell you that he wants a Jew to model for Jesus Christ?"

"Why not?" Spinoza said simply. "He was."

"But you say that you do not believe in the divinity of Jesus. Or, for that matter, in anybody else's."

"What I believe does not concern the painter. It only concerns myself. That is what I have been trying to tell the rabbis."

Yet, I observed, although Lopez was struggling to provoke him, he remained gentle, almost tender, as if he did not hold the other's scorn against him. It was a mood I needed for my portrait. Their theological discussion bored me, I only half-listened, for it had nothing to do with how I painted. And when I saw that Spinoza regarded Daniel fondly, I asked him, "Have you known my assistant long?"

"All our lives. Our parents were old friends, we learned the alphabet together, and Doctor Bonus delivered both of us. We are the same age."

From the smile he gave Daniel, I realized that he might distrust me, but he did not distrust his friend. I said, "Then I can depend on you to appear tomorrow afternoon?"

"I gave you my word." It was the first sign of pride he had shown.

"Not everyone keeps it."

"I will. Daniel has defended me when no one else has, but I do not expect to satisfy you as a sitter. And surely you do not desire an unwilling subject."

Not a stupid remark, I thought, even for one who acts as if he does not care for painting. Such perceptiveness might prove useful. But I said, "Spinoza, I will decide whether you are suitable or not."

Then, as I was about to depart, Lopez turned to the third friend of Daniel's, who had said nothing so far, and stated ominously, "Elias Delgado, you are studying to be a rabbi, as I am. If Spinoza and Van Dorn will not listen to reason, at least you should. If his heresies reach our Christian neighbors, our situation here will become precarious."

Delgado's stolid face and irresolute mein took on an air of anxiety and he grumbled, "Spinoza, until now I have not mentioned your blasphemy to anybody else, but there is truth to what Lopez says."

"Because I doubt some of the things that I have been taught?"

"At least, if you kept your doubts to yourself it would not be so difficult. But when you tell them to us, which you should not have done, we are infected with your false doctrines and could be corrupted."

Lopez regarded Spinoza even more suspiciously. Spinoza looked dismayed but he replied softly, "My friend, I attack no one. If the questions I raise, as a fellow student, trouble you, I shall keep them to myself hereafter. But you cannot stop me from thinking, nor can anyone else. The mind goes its own way. And just as our ancestors fought for the right to believe, I have the right to disbelieve."

Lopez regarded him contemptuously and declared, "Spinoza, I hope, for your sake, you change your attitude. Otherwise, you will suffer. Either you will halt your heresies or others will." He glared balefully at Spinoza and then pulled an unhappy Delgado back into the synagogue.

"To report me, I suspect, to the authorities," Spinoza murmured. He did not seem disturbed, only resigned.

"Perhaps not," Daniel said consolingly, "Lopez talks a lot but he does not always mean what he says. I do not think he will betray a friend."

Spinoza replied, "He will not consider that a betrayal. He is too righteous for that. He will regard such an act as his holy duty."

For an instant an oppressive quiet pervaded the street in front of the synagogue, then it was too much for me. I said, "Young man, I will expect you at my studio tomorrow afternoon. Daniel will show you the way." He was so silent and withdrawn now that I wondered if he felt as solitary as I did sometimes or did he ever lose himself in the intensity of a vivid and burning desire? I hurried off with my short, quick, choppy stride before even the devil could change his mind.

I WILL PAINT
SOMETHING VIVID THAT I SEE

I will paint something vivid that I see
I will paint the two lemons glowing so
I will paint my gratefulness into them
for the scene they create for me

I will paint pathos into them
because they cannot see me
I will paint beauty into them
for their yellow forms

I will paint pain into their beauty
for the stabbing mankind will give them
I will paint meditation into them
because they cannot move away from harm

I will paint longing into them
for the safety of their mother tree
I will paint love into them that I feel
I will paint a soul into them that I paint
into everything that grows

I will paint a halo around them
for the crucifixion destined for them
I will call the painting Little Christs

—Stymean Karlen

WHEN Spinoza did not appear at my studio by the afternoon of the next day as he had promised, I decided he was not coming. I was disheartened, unable to start any other work, yet unable to give up my vision of him. The more I thought about his sensitive face, the more it attracted me. There was a vividness of expression about it that composed. If I could not paint that, I told myself, there was no sense to seeing. My feeling of impotence increased as the light of the short winter day ebbed and I realized that soon there would not be any sun to pose him in, that I would have to settle for less than I wanted, an intolerable situation.

Disgusted, I summoned Daniel to explain his absence, but he insisted, "If Baruch said he will be here, he will be. He is a man of his word."

I did not say that I had not expected him to keep his appointment with me, but grumbled, "He agreed to see me only to appease you."

"He does not appease anyone, even himself."

The severity of his tone silenced me for a moment.

"But it is possible that Baruch had to meet with the rabbis today. If that happened, they could have delayed him."

I asked, aggrieved, "Why did he not warn me of this possibility?"

"He does not want to discuss his difficulties with anyone."

"What are they?" That perhaps, might help me to paint him better.

"It is not for me to say. Baruch would not like that."

"I should start a new self-portrait," I growled. "There, at least, is a model I can depend on and I have only to satisfy myself."

"Whatever you do, Master, you satisfy only yourself."

I did not pursue this idea further but strode about my studio restlessly, while Daniel put my easel close to the dwindling light and acted as if his friend's arrival was inevitable. Nonetheless, when the door bell rang a few minutes later, he was as relieved as I was and he hurried to answer it. The sun was setting, the daylight was almost gone, and by the time Daniel ushered a breathless Spinoza into my studio I had to stare at him intently to view him accurately. I saw a look on his face that suggested, How the devil did I allow myself to be persuaded to come here? Yet I was glad to see him, for his dark, soft features still possessed the sensibility—human, tender, and subtle, and I hoped, unquenchable—that attracted me and transformed him into an unique being and subject.

I thought, Daniel must have been praising my work, for as Spinoza entered he tried to observe everything in the studio and he was obviously disappointed when he saw that my easel held only an empty canvas.

"Did you have far to come?" I asked. I noted that part of his breathlessness was caused by agitation.

"Not under normal circumstances. I live a short walk from here. I was delayed by affairs at the synagogue."

"What were they, young man?"

"They are of no consequence," he said, but there was such emotion in his tone I felt they were of great consequence to him. "My father died recently and I was arranging for a time to make a prayer for him."

Daniel's face brightened and he exclaimed, "Then you are not going to leave the congregation after all!"

"Not if I can help it, friend. Sir, I am sorry I have kept you waiting. I do not like being late."

"Neither do I," I snapped. "It is an inconvenience."

"Am I too late?" he asked, as if he wished he were.

"Not completely. Daniel, light the oil lamps. That will enable me, at least, to sketch your features. To see how they compose."

By now it was dark outside and I seated him in a chair next to the brightest oil lamp. But it flickered from the wind that sifted through the window and I was chary of it. Not satisfied, I moved him around until the yellow glow shone directly on his face. He obeyed me dutifully, but after he was settled he was still uncomfortable and awkward.

I thought anxiously, An unwilling sitter could be even worse than an unwitting one. Usually, I did not explain to my models how to pose; I preferred to capture them in a natural movement and position; often I felt it was better if the sitter did not know why they sat, that could make them self-conscious, stilted, obvious. But I sensed that Spinoza was different, that he had to comprehend what he was doing before he could do it. Trying to make him feel at home, I declared, "Your face is not as important as your expression. Think of what you were reading." I had observed that the pockets of his cloak were stuffed with books.

He nodded and he sat back reflectively, breathing without strain now, his agitation gone, while Daniel mixed my paints until I stopped him. Lately, I had dispensed more and more with preliminary drawings; these days I frequently painted directly on to the canvas; but now, I felt, sketches were essential. I motioned for Daniel to make himself inconspicuous, which he did, standing in the back of the studio where I could not see him and be distracted, yet where I could use him if it were necessary. I was prepared to draw vigorously; I was in my working dress, a smock that reached to my ankles, much like a monk's robe, with a belt around my middle that gradually fell to my hips as I worked, slippers on my feet for comfort, and a hat that gave me a sense of order and fitness and that protected my precious eyes from any strong glare.

I did not move much as I drew. I was wary of such movements. Only my eyes were as active as my hand, roaming over Spinoza's features. I sought to capture him in a variety of expressions, using my pad as a storehouse of my visual ideas. I drew rapidly, driven by the pent-up emotion that was being released in me, and I ran out of paper quickly. Without stopping, unable to stop, I picked up a funeral announcement and used the blank side, I drew on bills, a loan agreement, and gradually found a few things that I could use. His manner was without vanity, which I liked, inclined toward self-effacement, which could be overdone, I thought, and essentially tender. Yet even as I found an expression that approached what I was searching for, I sensed there was a core in him that was adamant, that would not give in, a hard center that was his truth.

Just as I was prepared to do serious work, he stood up and announced, "I cannot stay any longer."

"My God!" I exclaimed, "I have just begun!"

"I have other things I must do today."

"Daniel should have warned you that I would need you longer." When he did not sit as I ordered, I added in a conciliatory tone, "You must be cold and hungry. I will fetch some tea to warm you."

"I do not need tea. There is something else I must do tonight."

"You cannot desert me now! I went to such trouble to find you!"

"Why not use Daniel? We are the same age. We are much alike."

"Not enough." When he disagreed, I added, "You are like two lemons, the same in age and shape, but different in personality and expression. Daniel, show your friend some of my work while I obtain two lemons to illustrate my point." I wanted to choose them myself and Daniel should have time to persuade him to remain. "And I will get some tea and cake."

I hurried out before Spinoza could stop me; I felt he was too polite to leave without informing me. Hendrickje was in the kitchen, as usual, and I told her to give me two lemons, but she was not sure that she had any, which upset me. My mind was fixed on lemons for my illustration and nothing else would do. After we ransacked the kitchen, Titus, who was drinking tea to stay warm, recalled where he had gotten the lemon he was using, and found two in a cupboard behind some oranges he had painted.

Delighted with his powers of observation, I hugged him, which was rare. I told Hendrickje to make tea for my sitter, that should soothe him, and to bring it to the studio with whatever cake we had in the house.

I climbed the stairs slowly. I was tired and short of breath from my frantic exertions and I was composing what to say. Spinoza and Daniel, absorbed in discussing me, did not hear me returning. Under most circumstances I would not have thought of eavesdropping, but I feared that my sitter had had enough of my hand and he was telling Daniel why. If I knew his reasons perhaps I could rebut him and convince him to stay. I halted outside my studio door and listened intently.

Spinoza said, "He looks so old. I doubt that he will have the energy to finish this work. He must be sixty, at the least, if not more."

Daniel replied, "He has aged prematurely. He is going on fifty."

"And he is ungainly, squat in size, round in shape, almost gross."

"He is not feeble. His arms are strong from lifting many pictures."

"But he does not even look like a painter."

Daniel said passionately, "He is the best there is."

Spinoza answered skeptically, "Perhaps. But you would never

think so from his appearance. He looks more like a barman or a seaman with his bulbous nose, his double chin, his unkempt hair, his stubby, soiled fingers, his thick, hairy hands, and his untidy, sloppy clothes."

"You do not approve?"

"It is not for me to approve or disapprove." Spinoza's voice grew softer and I had to lean against my studio door to hear what he was saying. "Even if I sit for him only this one time, I want to understand a man who wants to paint me. This seems like such a strange house. His wife, who answered the door with you, looks so much younger than him."

"Hendrickje is not his wife."

I noticed that Spinoza did not say anything.

"Baruch, are you surprised that she is his mistress? Do you mind?"

"Does Rembrandt's son?"

"I am not quite sure. Most of the time Titus seems to accept her as a foster mother but once in a while, when the boy is peevish, I wonder. However, I think that he is devoted to his father."

Now I was listening with every fiber of my being.

Spinoza said, "His son is fortunate. I miss my father. Ever since he died last year I realize what a loss I sustained. I have no family left."

"What about your half-sister, Rebekah?"

"She is not family. She and her husband are suing me for my share of our inheritance. Her husband, De Casseres, is studying to be a rabbi. He says that my religious lapses and delinquencies, they are his very words, disqualify me from inheriting my portion of my father's property."

"I am shocked."

"I was, too, at first. But now I am fighting them. I do not want the inheritance but they are wrong. And they are telling everyone of what they call 'my heresies,' as if that will win their suit for them."

"Baruch, you should be more careful of what you say. Many people could betray you. Lopez, for instance, is not to be trusted."

"Should I lie? Bear false witness?"

"That is not what I said. But sometimes silence is a virtue."

I was impatient with this conversation. I had enough of religious quarrels and I was about to interrupt them when I heard my name mentioned again. I paused, for Spinoza's tone had become more favorable.

"However, there is one thing about Rembrandt that fascinates me."

"What is that, Baruch?"

"His eyes. They gaze at me so relentlessly, as if they are penetrating to the essence of my being. It is the one thing about him that is not old. They are so vivid it is remarkable."

While he halted to search for the precise phrase, I reflected sadly, My eyes were not as strong as he assumed; these days I suffered often from nearsightedness and drawing by candlelight gave me a dull ache in my forehead, which, I felt, came from exhausted eyes. I was worried more about going blind than anything else. It was one of the reasons I painted my own eyes vividly. The possibility of such a calamity filled me with terror. But I returned to Spinoza, for he was speaking again.

"When Rembrandt is observing me for his work his eyes take on a wonder and excitement that is almost childlike, as if he is seeing me for the first time and discovering many things about me for himself."

"Then you will sit for him?"

I could have embraced Daniel for that, but his friend said, "I cannot. I have to prepare my defense should the congregation attack me, and I think they will, and I do not share the painter's view of Jesus of Nazareth."

"That is not necessary. Allow him to make that decision."

"No, I cannot wait any longer. I have much to do. I must leave."

When I heard him start toward the door, I rushed in, smiling cheerfully, although I felt depressed. "Here are the lemons I mentioned."

He said, "I do not have time to look at them."

I disregarded that and I placed them on the table before him, saying, "See, one is wrinkled, one is not. One is ripe, one is not."

"Is that all?" he asked skeptically.

But he had halted, and I declared, "I will paint one with a

dazzling splash of yellow that will rival the sun."

"What about the other one?"

"I will paint into it the love I feel for it."

"Can you?"

"I can paint whatever I want into it. I can do that with any object that I feel." I sensed this was no time for understatement but for a manifestation of what I was, whether it was grand or incomprehensible. I felt possessed and now all the words I knew were not enough to express the life within me. I needed to illuminate what I saw. I sketched the two lemons until their outlines became personal, while they watched intently, as if they were being initiated into a mystery and we were fellow conspirators in this creation. Then I turned to my brush and to my beloved yellow. The lemons became as alive as anything I had ever done, compelling their attention like the moon and the sun. Then I said abruptly, "See how different they are. Just as every sitter is."

Spinoza murmured in amazement, "You have even painted a soul into them."

Daniel said, "Whatever is possible. Baruch, stay a little longer."

Baruch was still hesitating when Hendrickje and Titus entered with tea and cake. He was about to decline the refreshments until he saw the eager expression on her face. Then he accepted, saying, "Thank you, lady."

She said, "It is the best tea, sir, from the East Indies. And I brewed it myself and baked the cake. From a recipe my mother gave me."

"My mother was a good cook," he said proudly. He added sadly, "So I was told. She died when I was six."

Hendrickje's eyes filled with tears as she moved toward the door as was the custom, Titus behind her, when Spinoza's voice halted her.

He said, "Would you join us? The boy, too? It is so nice to be with a family. I have none since my father died last year. All my close relatives are gone except a half-sister and she has her own life."

I motioned for Hendrickje to sit down and for Titus to fetch more tea and cake and as they followed my instructions, we formed a group around the massive oak table in the center of the studio. Daniel cleared it of work materials so that there was space for all of us to sit and sip and nibble. Spinoza asked Hendrickje for the brand of tea, he said he liked it so much that he wanted to have some for himself, too.

She had difficulty writing it out for him—when she had come to me she could not read or write and I had taught her, but she still had difficulty with spelling—and yet he was patient with her slowness.

He said suddenly, "I do not like anyone to wait on me. I prefer to take care of myself. I make my own bed and I have learned to cook but I cannot bake, although I have tried. Madam, I do not have your talent for it."

She said impulsively, "Next time you come I will bake a cake for you."

"Thank you. It would be a good reason to return. It is delicious."

I had seldom seen Hendrickje so pleased, while Titus said, "She is a fine cook, the best we have ever had. Even her *hutespot* is tasty. Did your sister cry all the time when she was a baby, Heer Spinoza?"

"She was older than I was. To her, I was the baby. You must not mind your sister's crying. It is natural."

"I hope so," my son said, trying to sound grown-up. "She is starting to get hair and it is red, like Papa's used to be. Do you like sitting?"

Spinoza wavered, then said quietly, "I have never done it before."

Titus confided, "It is not hard when you get used to it. Papa uses me a lot, even more than Hendrickje. I am a good model."

"Very good," I said, "and so is my lady, when she has the time."

Hendrickje said apologetically, "You see, Heer Spinoza, this is such a big house that it takes much time and effort to keep it in order. Not that I am complaining," she said hurriedly, afraid that I would be displeased, although I was in a good mood, gratified with the way matters were going. "The Master likes to know where all his work things are."

I said, "I do know where they are thanks to you and Daniel."

"And me, too, Papa," Titus declared.

"You, too, son. You help me with many things."

"Heer Spinoza, if you want to learn how to sit I could show you."

"I would be honored, Titus, but I have so little time these days that I cannot come here anymore."

"Oh!" It came from both my son and Hendrickje and they looked so disappointed that Spinoza felt a need to explain.

"I have enjoyed your company but now it is time for me to leave."

As he stood up I did, also, and I said abruptly, "A first sitting is like a first night of love. It can be exhilarating and it can be tedious. Young man, you must understand this. I know that my nature is inclined to be curt, even rude, but I do not like waste. Not to use you would be a waste. Your expression orders me to paint you." That concept seemed to capture his imagination and he paused to reflect about it. And when I saw his profound thought and feeling I realized that I was right. His face was one of those that revealed the history of a race. But that was not enough. I also had to make him feel comfortable, to sit correctly. A reluctant or poor sitter could be worse than no sitter.

Hendrickje said, "Heer Spinoza, if the smell of paint bothers you, do not worry. You will get used to it in time, as I did. And I will have a fire going whenever you sit. And tea and cake."

"You are very kind."

Titus volunteered, "And I will be glad to show you how to sit."

Spinoza smiled broadly for the first time since I had met him and he said, "Master Rembrandt, you are fortunate in your family. Now I know why Daniel is here all the time and admires you."

I was pleased but I frowned. Compliments made me uneasy; I did not trust them. So I assumed my sternest demeanor and said with a pugnacity I did not feel, "You are certainly not the best model I have had."

He laughed. "I know that. I told you that from the beginning."

"But you might represent Jesus, if your spirit is right."

"Despite my different view of Him?"

"I am not concerned with a mere representation of Him, I am

(147)

concerned with His inward vision, the human yet spiritual substance of the man."

"Of the man?" he reflected intently.

Spinoza's face became spiritual; his cheekbones rose until they were as high as I visualized; his forehead widened like a temple of God.

He said, "You know I do not believe in Jesus of Nazareth's divinity."

"I will decide that. We must work on a better day, when the light is good. Daniel, when does the sun reach the studio these winter days?"

"Between ten and eleven in the morning, Master."

"Spinoza, I will expect you at ten so we have time to prepare." I said that with all the certainty I could command to hide my fear that he would not heed me, while Hendrickje, Daniel, and Titus regarded him imploringly.

He deliberated while my stomach trembled and I felt sick inside at the possibility that I would not have the opportunity I craved, and then he said slowly, "My presence here as a model could harm you."

I thought, What more could happen to me than has happened already, and I said, "If I do not worry about that, you should not."

Daniel said, "As the Master stated, you are right for what he sees."

Hendrickje said, "And if Rembrandt says so, it is true."

Titus added, "Then, as I told you, I will show you how to sit."

"That is for me to decide," I said. "I will expect you a week from now."

We shook hands on that and Hendrickje and Titus escorted Spinoza to the door, chatting like old friends.

DOES THE FISH

Does the fish
Living always
In the water
Know
When it is
Drowning

      —Stymean Karlen

MY good friend, Van Ludick, interrupted my plans for Spinoza's second sitting. The print dealer ignored Daniel's warning that I was busy and pushed his way into my studio, with which, he said, he had "great familiarity." I was reviewing the sketches of my subject that I had retained and I motioned for him to sit down. I assumed he would disregard the crumpled drawings on the floor that I had discarded, the paint rags, the stench of oil, the unfinished pictures that leaned against the walls, and the usual clutter.

Despite his urgency, I said, "Wait a minute until I finish this mouth and then I will be able to give you some attention."

Van Ludick squirmed and looked away, as if in this instant he could not bear the sight of my work, which surprised me, since he was an admirer.

I thought, A day without work was a day wasted.

He was visibly distressed and suddenly, although I was not finished, he blurted out, "Ornia is pressing me for the money you borrowed from Jan Six. Since I stood surety for this debt, the iron monger is holding me responsible for it. As the guarantor of the loan."

I was annoyed, for the print dealer sounded as if he could no longer rely on me, but I said, "Thyst and I signed an agreement, giving me more time to pay my creditors from the proceeds of my work."

He retorted, "Thyst represents only Witsen, Van Hertsbeeck, and himself. Your debt to Ornia is separate. Could you relieve me of this obligation as soon as possible? Otherwise the stigma will ruin me."

Exasperated by what I felt was both his self-pity and his exaggeration, I put down the sketches of Spinoza that I had decided to use and asked sharply, "Does Ornia seriously want you to pay him what I owe?"

"If you do not. Since I signed the note, he can force me to do so."

Van Ludick was nervous, which was not like him. I said, more softly, "Ornia knows that I am making an earnest effort to pay him and all the others. I gave him a hundred guilders toward my obligation to him."

"He tells me that was months ago, that the interest has accumulated so much since that you owe him even more than you did at that time."

"He will not have to wait much longer," I muttered. "After I sell a few more pictures, my position will be stronger."

"Ornia does not believe this. The iron monger claims that you are as unreliable with promises as you are with dates and money."

"Do you agree with him?"

"Certainly not. But you must admit that you deliver your work slowly. You finish reluctantly and often only when you need the money."

"I am reluctant to bow to the wishes of Philistines."

"Yet even your patrons sometimes have to beg for their work. Your creditors will not wait much longer. That is why Ornia threatens me."

Van Ludick was so stern that I asked, "How much time do you think I have?"

"Ornia talks of sixty to ninety days, but if you make a decent gesture in his direction you might exact six months from him. But no more," Ludick said solemnly, "You have put off your creditors for the last time. Soon it will be winter and tempers will be edgy because of the chill and the damp that never seems to end, the short days, the lack of sunlight, and the economic uncertainty because the tulip boom has broken. All these things cause people to worry about their money."

I added sarcastically, "And about an irresponsible old reprobate who refuses to do conjuring tricks for rich merchants, who has lost his virtue because he has not wed the woman he lives with, who might even fart when he paints, who never washes his smocks or his face . . ."

"Rembrandt," Van Ludick cut in fervently, "I am a lover of art and an admirer of your work but Ornia's note should be paid. I do not want to go bankrupt, too. It is too much to ask of a friend."

He had grown so pale I asked carefully, "What do you want me to do?"

"Put up your possessions to guarantee his money."

"I have done that already for Thyst, Witsen, and Van Hertsbeeck."

He looked at me in astonishment and exclaimed, "All of your things?"

"I think so. I am not sure of the exact wording of the agreement but Thyst seemed pleased with it."

"Why did you not tell me about this arrangement?"

"I did when I said I would make whatever prints you could sell."

"You did not tell me the reason. You simply said that you needed money but then you have needed money for a long time."

He shook his head with such doubt and despair that I cried out, "I cannot think of everything! As it is, it is difficult enough to work!"

"Your work is the remedy. Guarantee Ornia the money from what you sell until his obligation is paid. If you put that in writing, and give him something as an expression of good faith, he may wait a little longer."

I agreed to this proposal and later in the day, after I had washed my face and hands and put on my most respectable garb, I visited Ornia's office with Van Ludick. The print dealer was not sur-

(151)

prised to see us, which led me to believe that they had planned this meeting in advance.

His rooms were nondescript, without any character or distinction, as was his person and his clothes. He gave me the feeling that he had taken on my debt to Jan Six to do this rich burgher a favor, and to impress him and to obtain him as a customer. Appropriately enough, I thought, I saw a Lievens on the wall behind his spotless desk but nothing of mine.

Small, wizened, with a raspy voice, Ornia informed me, with Van Ludick standing at his elbow, "I must have my money. That is why I instituted a claim against the print dealer. It is simple justice. There is no other standard with which to judge you. No one can depend on you to pay back what you owe, and thus, I had to act in this manner. If you do not pay me something on account immediately, I will sue Van Ludick."

"I will do what I can."

"Your interest on the loan has risen to three hundred guilders."

While I felt that it was less than what Ornia stated, Van Ludick was so worried that I accepted the iron monger's figures. I agreed to pay the principal with four paintings to be valued at two hundred and fifty guilders each. I said that my pictures were worth more, but Ornia replied that Jan Six, who was a connoisseur, had paid only three hundred for his portrait and since then my work had depreciated in value. Once again Van Ludick's anxiety stifled my protest and when I assented to this condition, he was relieved and Ornia was pleased, as if he had outdone Jan Six in his ability to bargain. But he insisted also that I give him the three hundred guilders in cash now to express my honorable intentions. Otherwise, he added, he could not accept the proposal.

I handed him this money with reluctance. I had saved it for an emergency, but I could not resist Ludick's appeal that I acquiesce.

When we went to the notary to draw up the agreement, Ornia stated that the pictures must be delivered within six months, or he would not sign; he might not be a connoisseur, but he knew how long it took to paint a picture. Any decent worker could do four paintings within this time, he said, it was not healthy for an artist to procrastinate.

This was the most difficult condition of all for me to accept but by now I felt I had no choice. I doubted that I could live up to this stipulation, for everything in me rebelled against it, but when Ornia waved the thousand-guilder promissory note in my face it was like a sword at my throat and I signed.

Ornia took his copy of the agreement with smug satisfaction and said, as he examined my signature to be sure it was correct, "Rembrandt van Rijn, you are a risky investment but I am a good businessman and I will be able to sell your work at a profit to Jan Six even if no one else wants it. He still admires your work."

"Is that why I never see him now?" I blurted out. I had pretended that this did not matter, but it did, and sometimes it hurt me.

"Candidly . . ." Ornia paused for emphasis.

I wondered if everything else he had said was untrue.

". . . Six cannot afford to become involved with you anymore. He hopes to be burgomaster some day and association with you could ruin that prospect. He is embarrassed by your increasing financial and family difficulties. That is why he relinquished his loan to me."

Several days later, when I recovered from my shock at his statement, I turned to Abraham Francen and his brother, Daniel, for help. They lived in the Angelierstraat, which was close to the River Y, and I felt that they valued friendship more than money. I visited them at dinner time when they were likely to be at home. It was dark when I knocked but I was relieved to find them in and they seemed glad to see me.

Abraham Francen, who was the older by several years, appeared more careworn than I had ever seen him, his smooth skin had become lined, but he was still his thoughtful, urbane self, while Daniel, plump, energetic, with a strong will and a resolute voice, was in an excellent humor.

I felt at home here. I knew that Abraham was a devoted supporter of my work and that Daniel, while less passionate about it than his brother, approved of it, too. In return I had painted figures upon the cast-iron sign on the front of their house that showed that the owner, in his wisdom, was an apothecary. This was the custom and I had designed a blue mortar and a yellow pestle to signify Abraham's profession. It was one of my simplest compositions but the sight of it pleased me. Tonight I noticed that it had been washed recently, as if they were proud of it.

They were in the kitchen of their modest two-story brick house, finishing a dinner of red herring, which was considered a delicacy, and having cheese tarts for dessert, and Abraham asked me to join them.

"Thank you very much," I replied, "but I have eaten already," although I had not. I was eager to get to the matter that was troubling me and I did not want anything else to interfere with or delay it.

Daniel grumbled, "Rembrandt, I admire your work as much as any man, but my brother is insane in his devotion to it. He has such a passion for your etchings that he is willing to starve himself so that he can afford to own them. Even now, he has eaten very little, he is so engrossed in the etching you gave him of the three trees."

Abraham said, "What else are eyes for! Your work is my pleasure!"

This gave me the courage to tell them about the agreement I had signed with Ornia and that this worried me.

Instead of criticizing me, as I expected, Abraham replied, "I am glad that you came to us. My brother has just received a fine profit on an investment in the East India trade. How much do you need?"

The truth was, I thought, I needed at least ten thousand guilders to avert disaster, but that was such a huge sum to borrow I did not have the nerve to ask for that amount. I mumbled, "I believe a few thousand guilders would help me over the next few months."

"A few means three," Daniel said quickly, with a warning glance to Abraham that he must not offer more. "That is all I can spare."

"You are very kind," I said humbly, even as I was angry at myself for such deference, but talking about money made me uncomfortable.

"I trust that you will not mind signing a note for this loan and putting up your work as collateral." When Abraham regarded him reproachfully, he added, "It is the custom and simple common sense."

"You are right," I said. "All the others have done it."

Abraham interrupted, "I would prefer if they were etchings."

Daniel said, "We will insert that provision into the agreement."

Abraham said, "But we will lend this money without interest."

Daniel was unhappy at this prospect but his brother was so stern that he agreed, but he added, as if he still had to prove that he was a good businessman, "To include the etchings is sensible. There continues to be a market for them; it is the painting situation that is unreliable."

Abraham consoled me, "Rembrandt, one day your work will make you rich."

I was more occupied in saving my own life, and his optimism did not console me. After Daniel wrote out the agreement on the terms that we had discussed, to be sure that there would be no misunderstanding, although Abraham felt this was unnecessary, that I was a man of my word and could be trusted, I examined the etchings that Abraham had been viewing and suddenly I was upset. It was maddening, I thought, no matter how carefully I worked I seldom achieved my intention. These etchings were competent but they could be better. Abruptly, I asked to buy them back. Abraham was horrified, he said that they were his most precious possessions, that he could not satisfy my request.

I was tempted to yank them out of his hand, then I realized that he might never forgive such an act, and I valued his friendship. He also looked unhappy, which was unusual, and I added hurriedly, for now I saw what I had to do, "Abraham, I will etch you against the back window."

"How much will that cost?" Daniel asked suspiciously.

"Nothing. It is my thanks for not charging me interest."

Abraham said, severely for him, "Rembrandt, that is not necessary."

"But it is. Your most effective expression is on your face when you are examining my etchings. I must do you in the sunlight so that I can show you for the art connoisseur that you are. It will work fine."

"A good idea," said Daniel, while Abraham looked embarrassed and yet pleased by my enthusiasm. "You speculate with your work as much as I speculate in the overseas trade. Both of us are taking a risk."

I felt this was the first time the younger, more ambitious and purposeful brother respected me, and I replied, "Whenever I start a new work, it is a risk, a risk that I will not satisfy myself. But once in a while I am gratified. As you must have been with your investment."

"Yes. But not everyone is so skillful. Wilhem Beghen, the merchant I invested with, told me that not all shipowners can be trusted. That some pocket the money themselves or report losses at sea that may not have happened. You have to be shrewd and select a reliable merchant."

"I hear that some ships do not come home."

"Some. But ours did. I doubled my original investment in one voyage."

Abraham cut in, "Rembrandt, we will give you the money tomorrow."

"At our notary's office," Daniel said. "That should take care of your obligations to Ornia and carry you over your present difficulties."

"I think so." I accepted their invitation for tea. Yet even as I sat there, I felt in two places at once. I wanted to invest with Wilhem Beghen, feeling that only a large sum could solve my difficulties, and yet I craved to sketch Abraham, there was such animation in his eyes.

After I received the three thousand guilders in cash the next day I did not go to Ornia and erase this debt as I had intended. By now I had reasoned that since I owed over twenty thousand guilders, perhaps as much as thirty, and that the interest alone came to thousands of guilders, I needed more money to ease my situation. This could be the turning point of my life, I thought, with three thousand guilders I might make as much as six, then with six double that. The prospects could be infinite, if Daniel Francen had done so, I could, too. Money could have an active power, properly used, I told myself. What finally decided me was the realization that three thousand guilders was only a drop in the bucket and would only alleviate my financial distress but not cure it.

So I cleaned my boots until they were spotless and put on a clean cloak that was without paint stains and went to call on Wilhem Beghen. His was a familiar name. I had heard from Jan Six and Cornelius Witsen that he had handled their overseas investments and they were rich men.

I saw a gilded carriage standing outside of his office. It had his family name on it and a coat of arms and a liveried driver, which, I knew, only the very rich could afford. He was located in a new brick building, near the Bourse, the most prosperous part of Amsterdam.

As I paused to collect my thoughts, I also observed many reasons why many felt that Amsterdam was the wealthiest city in Europe. The harbor was filled with sailing ships from all over the world and there was feverish activity as the cargoes were unloaded by the port's lighters.

"Water has made us great," I remembered Jan Six saying, "it is the source of our power and our wealth. We have conquered the seven seas and now we dominate its trade. We possess the best ships and the best sailors. Our *fluits* are the finest merchants ships afloat, as are our herring-busses. There are profits ready to be made everywhere."

Buoyed by these reflections, I put aside the pessimism that had developed because of the collapse of the tulip boom and the recent war with England, and strode briskly into Wilhem Beghen's office where I was admitted into his presence after only a brief wait.

He was a slight, red-cheeked man of forty, with white hair and a cherubic smile. He sat behind a large, splendid desk and everything about him suggested affluence: the black-and-white marble tiles on the floor, the leather cushions on his sumptuous chairs, the thick, gold-trimmed Bible in front of him, the plastered ceiling with a mythological painting in the style of Rubens, and an opulent Venetian glass chandelier.

(157)

He recognized me even before I could introduce myself but as he welcomed me warmly, I had a feeling that he was thinking, Caught you at last.

When I told him the purpose of my visit, he said, "Master, you have come just in time. Two of my ships are leaving this week for the East Indies, *The Amsterdam* and *The Utrecht.* There is only one share left for each cargo. How much do you want to invest?"

I hesitated. Perhaps three thousand was too much. Suddenly I was nervous and apprehensive and I said, "I am not sure."

His hand had reached out to take my money and I noted that it was a bony claw, but he sounded like a truly beneficent and generous man as he said, "You will be investing in two of the finest bottoms in the world. Our profits have aroused the envy of all of our neighbors. Your friend, Jan Six, invests with me, and our estimable burgomaster, Cornelius Witsen."

"I know, but—"

He stopped me smoothly, "I understand. You want your investment to be a private matter. I will be the active partner, you will be the sleeping partner, and no one else will know of your involvement. Now how much should I put you down for? Ten thousand? Twenty thousand?"

"Two," I whispered, feeling ashamed before his supreme self-confidence to be offering so little, but I had decided to save one for an emergency.

"Two?" His scorn showed that he did not value that sum highly.

I was turning away when I felt his hand on my arm.

"Come, Rembrandt, you must not be touchy. I will double your investment in six months, and if you are patient, triple it."

The six months enticed me; I thought that was just long enough.

"You should be proud that you are investing in our national honor and prosperity. And grateful that I am offering you such a marvelous opportunity. I will put your money into the trade that yields the highest rate of return. In spices such as cloves, black pepper, and cinnamon. Because they are so scarce they have doubled in price in five years."

"What about the risk?" I ventured to ask. I was even more

excited by his enthusiasm but I was still afraid of losing the money.

"Risk!" He regarded me as if I had uttered a blasphemy. "Master, does my office look as if it has been losing money?"

I had to admit that it did not.

"Rembrandt, do you have the cash with you?"

"Yes."

"Good." When I handed him the two thousand guilders he added, "There is also a fee for my services."

"How much, Heer Beghen?"

"A hundred guilders per thousand."

I gave him that in cash out of the remaining thousand that I had left, signed the necessary documents to verify my investment, and left his office with his hearty congratulations on my wisdom ringing in my ears. Now that I had committed myself I was plagued with doubts. I was not sure that I was as astute as Wilhem Beghen said I was.

I AM ONLY A FLOWER

I am only a flower
but I have speech

And I say hello to you
my neighbor

And soon I will say
Happy Birthday
Your flower

      —Stymean Karlen

W HEN I reached my home I told no one of what I had done and I hid what I had left from the loan in the back of the canvas that I was using for my portrait of Jesus. I reasoned that it would be easy to reach if any more emergencies occurred, and safe, nobody should find it there, and I prayed that the investment I had just made would free me from the terrible debts and distractions that threatened to overwhelm me. I resumed my plans for Spinoza's sitting and it was a relief to return to work.

He appeared the next morning promptly at ten. Daniel ushered him in with an air of triumph, as if his judgment had been vindicated.

I could not scold my assistant. He had kept my best brushes soft and clean, and, since last year, supplied me with enough oils. I had not asked him how he had accomplished this; I was satisfied that he did.

I was prepared to start immediately, but Spinoza held a bouquet of flowers that did not fit my subject. Before I could question him, he explained, "They are for your lady. To express my appreciation for her hospitality. May I present them to her in person?"

I ordered Daniel to summon her, grumbling that we must not delay.

Hendrickje came quickly, as if she was hoping to be called, and when he gave her the tulips she flushed pink and thanked him warmly.

I growled, "You did not have to bring tulips, they are costly. Sweet peas or delphiniums would have been sufficient."

She marveled, "Where did you get such beauties this time of the year?"

"From the finest florist's shop in Amsterdam, madam."

"I have a passion for flowers. How did you know, Heer Spinoza?"

"Daniel told me."

I interrupted, "Now we must get on with the sitting."

Hendrickje said, "First, I must give him my recipe for the cake." Disregarding my impatience, which was rare for her, she handed it to him. "I had Daniel write it out, to make sure that it is clear. My mother told me that it has been in our family for generations."

Spinoza took it tenderly and said, "I will follow it faithfully."

"And when you finish I will have tea and cake for you. One can get very cold sitting, even catch a chill. Especially these winter days."

I felt that in some ways she understood him better than I did. They were closer in age, she was only a few years older. Or was it, I speculated, the maternal need in her that regarded him affectionately? I was a little jealous of that. So I declared gruffly, to hide my feelings, and I did want to do his face, the emotion on it was so real I could touch it, "We have delayed enough. We are actually simple Amsterdammer's and Hendrickje has many things to do today, herring to chop, beer to cool in a bucket of water, bread to buy from the baker, a fire to start in the hearth." I was chilled standing motionless and I drew my old blue velvet cloak around me for warmth.

Daniel said that he would start the fire, and Hendrickje took my hint and said, "The Master is right. The sitting is important."

But even after she withdrew Spinoza was reluctant to sit, reminding me that my son had promised to show him how this should be done. So, while I did not like giving in on this, I called Titus, who went directly to the chair that Daniel had put by the window and sat in it as if he belonged there, quite self-possessed. Yet his face was dirty and I told him to wash it.

He replied, "Papa, you have not washed yours."

"That is different."

"Why?"

"You must look clean today, like our young friend. Not because of what others think, but you must think more of yourself."

"Papa, you say that you like to paint persons as they are."

I was surprised that Titus remembered that, he was beardless, only fourteen. As I stared at him, trying to decide what to say next to him, I thought that he did resemble his mother with his fair skin, delicate features, and appealing eyes. He was fine to paint, as pretty as a flower. What bothered me was that there was an excitement in him that I had not seen before, as if this was one of his most substantial moments. I felt it was because of his desire to please Spinoza. Annoyed that he favored him, I declared, "Do not be impudent because you think you are needed. I can do without you. Now wash your face or I will wash it for you."

Spinoza said gently, "Titus, I washed my face before I came here."

I wondered why children often obeyed a stranger instead of a parent, for my son retired to his room and his wash basin, although unwillingly, and returned quickly, as if he had an urgency to participate in this grown-up matter. I observed that his ears were still dirty and his hands wet, and I pointed that out, so that he would not think he was deceiving me, but I was so eager to start I allowed him to sit this time.

He did so in a relaxed manner that pleased me while he confided to Spinoza, who watched him intently, "Do not mind when Papa growls at you. He does not mean it as long as you look the way he wants. As I do."

I was searching for a meaning to interpet and I ignored his words.

He continued however, to the audience he had, "I can sit where my sister cannot. She wets herself when Hendrickje holds her as a model."

"Titus, that is enough," I said abruptly. His words were distracting me and I needed my own vision. I must be in control of my work or it would come to nothing. He grumbled that he had just begun to sit but I cut him short. The sun fell on Spinoza's face with a golden light and I could not afford to lose this moment. I motioned to Daniel, who led Titus, still complaining, out of my studio.

Spinoza was embarrassed by my curtness to Titus, but I felt no concern for anybody else, there was too much to do. I was beginning to find a way to express the way I felt, and I had to explore these possibilities, whatever the risk. I seated Spinoza in the sunlight and told him to look up, as if he were gazing toward heaven. I was not sure that he agreed with what I was doing but he obeyed me. He was clumsy and I realized that I could only tell him what to do physically, I could not tell him what to feel. Yet I tried to make him comfortable.

Seconds lengthened into minutes, then into hours. Nobody disturbed us. I had drawings now that I could use, but Spinoza started to fidget, a dangerous sign.

Suddenly I shouted, "Be still!"

"My back aches and my leg is numb. I think it is asleep."

"Hold your tongue! When you speak your expression changes."

"You expect too much."

"I expect what I see!"

"No!" Spinoza said sharply. "We do not have enough in common."

"You are right." He was puzzled, not expecting this answer, and I added grimly, "Only when you get angry do you have a good expression."

"You are trying to provoke me."

"I am trying to draw you. When you are older and more experienced, you will understand better what I am doing."

He looked offended but he was also more animated as I desired.

"You must remember," I reminded him, "we have started from nothing."

"But you stare at me so intensely it makes me uncomfortable. I do not want such intimacy. You are looking into every pore of my body."

I decided that I would have to find in him what I wanted in myself. I must sit inside of him. I must live within the framework of his body. It must be what I felt about Jesus, not what Spinoza felt. With this awareness, I drew my final sketch for the day. Then suddenly I was congratulating him on a successful sitting and he was regarding me incredulously and rubbing his legs to restore life into them.

I said, as I called the others to join us for tea and cake, "It would be foolish to say that you are my best model but you are improving."

He replied, "I thought I was bad, awkward, graceless, unbelievable."

"It is a beginning. Beginnings are often difficult."

"May I see what you have done?"

"Not now. It is not finished and it would only discourage you. Today I put down only my ideas. I will show you the work when it is ready."

"How long will that take? I cannot come much more."

"I was teaching you how to sit. Next time we will work in earnest."

That upset him, but fortunately Hendrickje and Titus arrived with the refreshments, which soothed him, as did their presence. Then Daniel exclaimed, "Baruch, you have great patience to sit so long. Few of the Master's models can hold his attention for such a length of time."

Spinoza was pleased and I was glad that he had some vanity in spite of his natural modesty. This could be used to my advantage. And it was evident that he still enjoyed the company of Hendrickje and Titus.

Thus, I was surprised and disappointed when he said, "I cannot come next week." He added quickly, anticipating my question, "I am offering prayers for the dead, for my father, at the synagogue."

Daniel said, "Good. This means that you are still regarded as a member of the congregation and that a compromise is still possible."

"It is possible but not likely. Rabbi ben Israel is inclined to listen to me, but Rabbi Morteira is more severe. Master, do you know him?"

I said, "I have painted him."

"But do you know him?"

"Young man, I told you, I painted him."

"Then you are aware that he is not inclined to compromise."

"I know that he can be stubborn. But I could speak to him."

"No," Spinoza said decisively, "The less anyone interferes the better. You, too, Daniel. This is between me and the rabbis."

"At any event," I concluded, "I will see you in two weeks."

"How many more sittings will this portrait take?"

"That depends. I will pay you well for your effort."

Spinoza was angrier than I had ever seen him. He snapped, "I am not sitting for money. Or as a favor either," hushing Daniel. "I never thought I would find myself in the position I am in now but since I gave you my word that I would sit for you I will do my best to keep it."

Afterward, while I lay in bed next to Hendrickje, eager to caress her amorously—she had been helpful with Spinoza—she whispered, "You must try to understand him better. He is such a nice young man."

"That is why I am painting him."

"Did you see the gentleness with which he regards our children?"

"I see many things," I retorted impatiently. At this moment I did not want to discuss my sitter or anything else. I could not be celibate, it was against my nature, and it was a week since we had made love, I had been so distracted by other matters. I was grateful that her body was not flabby, that she did not have to keep her flesh in place with stays, that her belly was round and her breasts full. She started to speak again and I quieted her with a kiss of appreciation for the way she had treated my sitter. Then I caressed her thighs until they opened wide and now she was mine, completely mine.

When we finished and I handed her a heavy robe, for the bedroom had become cold, she asked, "May I wear your mother's band as a wedding ring when the young man comes? I do not want him to be uncomfortable."

I had noticed that she had developed the habit of fondling the ring I had given her but I did not reply, desiring to make love again.

"I know that we are not married, but in God's eyes we are, for we do not love anyone else and we have been faithful to each other."

"Daniel tells me that Spinoza does not believe in God."

"Daniel must be wrong. Do you mind about the ring?"

"No. Wear it if you want to. You were very good with my sitter."

This time she rewarded me with an expression of love that was the most passionate I could remember. And just before we fell asleep, she said, "We have not been to church together since Cornelia was baptized."

"I know." I was drunk from the sensations that flowed from the touch of her amorous body and I said, "We will attend Ruismeer's church."

"Will we be welcome?" she asked anxiously.

"I think so. It will be my birthday present for you. As were Spinoza's flowers."

"But I do not know when I was born. My mother said there were no records in our community."

"Then we will celebrate it now."

I was as good as my word. The following Sunday we dressed in our best clothes, and leaving Titus and Cornelia in the care of Daniel, we joined the small but intent congregation listening to Ruismeer's sermon. No one seemed to mind our attendance, as she had feared. It was as if anyone, whatever their background, who wanted to worship Jesus was welcome.

In doing this I felt that I was giving up whatever connection I had with the State church to which I had belonged, but I liked the simplicity of Ruismeer's words, his lack of dogma, his humility, and that he used the Bible in his own unique and individual way, as I tried to do. I was moved when he spoke of the humanity of Jesus, which reminded me of my Mennonite friends. He also stressed that Our Lord was a healer, not the avenging sword of Calvin. Yet he was not a Mennonite. He had theological training, and he wore the black, baggy breeches and long trousers typical of the Anabaptists, one of a number of dissident sects in Holland.

Ruismeer concluded his sermon with a quotation from a Dutch theologian that shook me. I repeated it to myself to remember it.

It was not the Jews, Lord Jesus, who crucified you. It is I, O Lord, it is I who have done that to you.

With each word I saw His face illuminated by the light of His love and mercy, and this was what I needed in my portrait of Him. Nothing else or less would do. Nothing, nothing, I assured myself.

I was so absorbed in this view that I did not hear the pastor address me until Hendrickje poked me with her elbow. Then I looked up from the pew into the smiling countenance of Ruismeer, who said, "Master, we are delighted to have you attend our services."

"I am honored, pastor," I replied, not to be outdone in civility.

"You must come more often," he said. "We need your support."

I probably needed his even more, I thought, but I said, "I am sorry I have been unable to give you the picture I promised."

"That is not necessary. How is your daughter?"

"Fine. We left her with my assistant and my son. We were afraid her crying would disturb the congregation."

"Bring her next time. Madam, you are looking fine, too."

I saw a glint of light on the wedding ring—as she considered it now—for she held it up to acknowledge the pastor and to display it so that he could see it. She bowed and said, "Thank you, Reverend, our daughter is fortunate to have been blessed by you."

"By Our Lord, my lady. I am only His humble instrument. Master, may I view your work some time? It would give me great pleasure."

"Whenever you want."

"I would not like to interrupt you. Or distract you."

"Come some evening. Although the light will not be good."

"Besides," said Hendrickje, "the Master never knows when he will finish. Rembrandt, could you spare a morning for the pastor?"

He had been so gracious that I tried to be, too. "As I said, whenever you can, pastor. Tomorrow morning if you like."

"That will be fine," he responded.

So it was decided. To my surprise Ruismeer was as impulsive as I was and while I did not like being interrupted, I was gratified by his interest in my work. And perhaps his view of Jesus would be useful.

I did not tell him that I was using Spinoza as a model for Our Lord, but as soon as Ruismeer arrived I showed him all my drawings of my new sitter except the last. I held that out as a final test of his judgment; moreover, it was personal and I was not sure that I wanted to show it to anyone else.

He said that their simplicity was splendid but that he desired to see my paintings, too. So I displayed what else I was doing in the studio and took him through my salon where most of my finished work hung.

He stated, "Master, it is a beautiful collection. All your work should be seen together. Like a family."

"I would prefer that they be preserved in such a way but when I say that to picture dealers they ridicule me and tell me that it is insane."

"They are insane. How many oils of your own do you still possess?"

"Finished?"

"That does not matter. Even your unfinished pictures should be seen together."

"I have not counted them. But I miss them when they are gone."

"You should. It is too bad that you have to sell them."

Although Ruismeer had grown grave, I observed that he still smiled frequently, unlike the other ministers I knew. For an instant I thought of him as my model for Jesus, his spirit pleased me, then I realized that he was wrong for this subject; he was too fair and too old, my age. Even so, I respected his feelings and for this reason I led him back to the final drawing I had made of Spinoza, the one that almost satisfied me, and asked him, "Do you think this is an appropriate view of Our Lord?"

He held this drawing up to the light and said, "The face is dark."

"Do you think that is wrong?"

"That is not for me to say."

I realized that it was not his criticism I desired but his approval. And that my depiction of Jesus had nothing to do with theology. I wanted to snatch the drawing away from him, but I was afraid I might damage it. In the light I saw the mistakes I had made. The mouth was much too tight. Too anatomical. Too clever. It was a man's mouth but not that of Jesus.

He said, "You must do Him as you see Him. Whoever your model is."

"Thank you." I tried not to be curt but I was. No one could help me, I decided, but myself; in the end, I knew, it always came down to that.

He gave back the drawing without having to be told, which was a relief. I offered him wine and cake, but he declined. He said that he had parishioners to visit who were ill and needed comforting.

"Will you supply that?" I asked, sarcastically, I feared, but I was irritated, it was impossible for me to be otherwise in this situation.

"I cannot be certain," he replied, quieter than I deserved. "But I listen to them and that seems to help. At least it eases them. Master, I hope I will see you and your family at our church again."

"I do not feel that I should have any religious affiliation now." I did not add that I feared it could stifle my intuition and emotion.

"You do not have to be a member of the congregation to be welcome. Come when you feel like it."

"What about the painting I promised you?"

"You promised me nothing. What was done for you would

have been done for anyone. My regard for your work is a separate matter."

After I escorted Ruismeer to the door I went to my dressing room and combed my hair differently, curling it so that it fell behind my ears instead of below them. Then I searched through my storeroom until I found the costume that pleased my eye and imagination. It was a heavy yellow cloak, Oriental in its splendor, a sumptuous fabric whose sparkle delighted my sense of touch and color. I also took a cane from my store of paraphernalia which was just the accessory I wanted. When I began to paint myself with all these ornaments it did wonders for my morale.

By evening I was engrossed in this new self-portrait. I painted directly on to the canvas, having withdrawn from the canvas of Jesus, which I had put into a closet to await Spinoza's return in two weeks. I was determined, with this picture, to assert my belief in myself.

I had applied a considerable amount of red to the face, but I had not completed the painting of the flesh, for this result, especially the cheeks, resembled an alcoholic burgher. There was too much ruddiness, I decided, too much stress on vigor. So I made the background darker.

"The yellow is beautiful," a voice said. "But the face is too old."

Disturbed by this unexpected interruption, I pinched my hand against the canvas and the little finger on my right hand began to bleed. Angry, I did not mind the pain but I could not hold the brush firmly, I turned on the intruder and saw Hendrickje standing in the doorway.

"When you paint yourself, you make yourself look worse than you are."

"I am painting what I am, what I feel, not just what I look like."

"Even so, you make yourself older than you are."

"I paint myself as old as I feel." I paused to shift the brush to my left hand, glad that I was skillful with both hands, for the blood had not ceased flowing and I feared that it would stain the picture. "Hendrickje, how can you be sure that I have not aged?"

She blushed as she murmured, "You have been loving lately."

"No more than you have been," I retorted, but I was pleased. She was changing, I thought, asserting herself in ways she had not dared before. Yet while I liked this spark in her, I did not desire criticism. I wiped the blood off my finger with a dirty paint rag and returned to my self-portrait without another word to indicate that I craved privacy.

When she saw the blood she was alarmed. She washed it off with water, although I said it was a trifle, but she replied that it could poison me, bathing it tenderly with a clean cloth until the bleeding stopped.

The red was appropriate to the sash I was painting, as it was to my flesh, and I wanted to resume, to use that part of my palette, but she said, "I came upstairs to tell you there is a message from Thyst."

My concentration was gone and I halted disgustedly and asked irritably, "What does our landlord want now?"

"His servant did not say. Do you think that we are being evicted?"

"I doubt that. He may have decided to accept a picture for my debt."

"I do not think so. The messenger said that it is imperative that you meet with Thyst as soon as possible. At his home tomorrow morning."

I put away my work with regret. From the tone and urgency of the summons, I had the feeling that this encounter with Christoffel Thyst could be more than just another distraction.

THE BLIND WALL LOOKED AT ME

The blind wall looked at me
but I knew the wall well
it saw through me
as I saw through it

I understood and walked away
knowing
it misunderstood me
as blind walls do

In a world whole
with blind walls

—Stymean Karlen

THYST resided in a mansion that he deemed worthy of his position. I saw that in the ostentatious manner with which his butler admitted me, and by the height of his huge home. In Amsterdam the wealth of the occupant was judged by the number of stories his house possessed and his had five, far more than the usual number. To reinforce this impression and as another indication of his wealth, he also had his family name and his coat of arms engraved on a pediment above his thick oak front door.

I was led into his salon, where he sat in splendor surrounded by lavish furnishings. It was my first visit here. Eager to know why he had summoned me insistently—it was obvious that I was expected, that he had assumed that I would come when he had ordered—I observed everything carefully. I noted that all of his household effects were luxurious: the oriental rugs, the leather-backed chairs, the tapestries, the porcelain from China on the mantelpiece, the silver-edged Bible by his side.

Although he wore a dressing gown to protect himself from the cold—the salon was chilly despite the logs blazing in the fireplace —he was garbed expensively. His sleeves were lined with fur and ornamented with gold lace. To show me, I felt, that he did not need my money, that he wanted my debt paid because of honor. I saw, too, that while he shivered from the draft my entrance caused, he had on just one pair of silk stockings, another sign of wealth, although they were without warmth. I wore two pairs of woolen ones to keep my legs from freezing.

This middle-sized, middle-aged burgher, who was younger than I was, although he looked older this morning, was so pompous, stern, and rigid that he did not ask me to sit down but left me standing, as if he were a judge and I was a culprit. He came to the point directly, very businesslike, stating, "I heard you got another loan. Why have you not paid me?"

Surprised, I stammered, "What loan?" I pretended ignorance to collect my senses. "How could you think that?"

He said knowingly, "I have sources of information. Reliable ones."

I looked into his eyes, hoping for mercy and understanding, but they were like ice. I equivocated. "I have several loans I made recently."

"Van Rijn, I know that you have just borrowed money. Five, six thousand guilders at the least, I have been told."

"It is exaggerated," I replied uncomfortably. Who could have informed on me, I wondered. Thyst was positive, arrogant, demanding.

"Yet you have not made any effort to reduce your obligation to me."

I retorted strongly, "I have done my best."

"It is not good enough. You are like a child in such matters."

"I put up my possessions as security."

"You make no effort to sell them. You are more interested in adding to your collection than reducing it. Despite what you owe. Your situation is becoming intolerable. It cannot be permitted to last much longer."

"How much longer?"

"Not much more. You are leaving me and my colleagues with

no alternative but to sell you out of your house and possessions."

"I am trying to meet my obligations."

"You are not trying hard enough. And now you borrow another six or eight thousand guilders and make no effort to pay us, your creditors."

"My situation is nothing like that."

"How much did you borrow now? Ten thousand guilders? Twenty?"

"Three," I mumbled, disturbed by this gross exaggeration.

"I knew it!" he exclaimed triumphantly. "You cannot fool me."

"You claimed that it was far more."

"What does that matter? I was right." He stroked his Bible fondly. "God will support the righteous. Your behavior is a scandal."

Thyst's features were slightly pointed, but otherwise nondescript, but in this moment he looked like a pig to me, with a nose like a snout, narrow green eyes, and a greedy mouth. Now I realized why I was sick of him. He was more sausage than man. And I did not care for his taste. I saw a full-length portrait on the wall behind his desk, only the rich could afford such large pictures, and it was by Lievens; I recognized his style, flattering, glossy, and dull.

Annoyed that I had not apologized, he continued, "Nearly seventeen years ago, I have the records in front of me, on January 3, 1639, you bought the large house on the Breestraat. Then you made money, and yet what you owed kept accumulating. You have become hopeless."

"I could lessen this with a painting or an etching. My etchings are still valuable." I found myself pleading, and now I hated him for forcing me into this humiliating situation.

"Van Rijn, I cannot realize what you owe on your work. I want cash. Your interest continues to accumulate, to say nothing of taxes."

It was a litany I had heard before and I stopped listening, but he brought me out of my reverie with the statement, "If you do not pay me, Witsen, and Van Hertsbeeck a substantial sum within sixty days we will seize your house and all of your possessions."

"Sixty days? That is not enough time."

"You have had almost seventeen years to pay for the house."

"Ornia has given me six months to take care of his loan."

"He is a fool. Unless you gave him the money you just borrowed."

"No. He has accepted my paintings as collateral."

"He is an even bigger fool than I thought. Where did your loan go?"

I was silent, oppressed by his unyielding, critical manner.

Offended by my refusal to tell him, he sneered, "You must have invested it in the East India trade. Everyone thinks they will get rich in it. But many ships do not return, much money is lost in it. It is very risky."

I longed to ask him why but I was afraid that he would take advantage of that, too. I said instead, "If we could compromise, I could have some money for you soon. Say, in about ninety days."

"Ninety days," he replied quickly.

Angry at myself, I realized that I could have gotten six months if I had persisted, but I never could bargain, I thought, that took more patience and greed than I possessed. I said, "Agreed. Ninety days."

I turned to go, weary from his questions, but now he was in a more expansive mood. He said, "Why not sell your house?"

I did not want to, I was attached to it, I felt toward it like it was a good and dear friend, but I replied, "It has excellent light."

"Is that all?" He regarded me with contempt.

"I could do pictures for my debts. My work is still respected."

"Borrow money on paintings not yet painted, or that will never be finished, or on those already promised to another party. No, I am not an idiot to invest in your work or your promises." He stared outside and growled, "It is raining again. It is always raining in this damned country. At the rate you are going you will only be able to eat eggs."

"A fried egg is the consolation of the poor man."

"Ninety days. No more. Remember. This time I mean what I say."

And in six months I would be fifty. But I must not complain.

I must start new pictures. Hendrickje had put Spinoza's tulips in the sun, when it shone, and watered them, and they had flowered under her loving care. As some of my work might. Despite the anxious moments.

Evidently my silence bothered Thyst, for he said suddenly, "I have been shopping for a gift for my wife. I considered a portrait of her by you but I decided on Lievens. Your brush is too dark, undependable. You will not paint her as we want. No wonder you do not sell."

I had taken so many sneers from Thyst, I could not endure any more. I said angrily, "I would not paint your wife if you asked me."

"Why not?" He was startled by my response.

"She is a poor subject, as you are. Without animation or spirit."

He glared and said savagely, "Do not approach Van Hertsbeeck or Witsen to pay me. They will not lend you any more money and it will only provoke them into quicker action against you and put you into bankruptcy. As you deserve. Borrowing three thousand guilders to spend on yourself when you owe everyone of consequence in Amsterdam money. You are irresponsible."

I was not sure what I deserved but as I left I was glad that it had stopped raining. I wanted to talk to the Francens about their loan.

Daniel Francen was away on business but Abraham had no idea who could have told Thyst about their loan, he assured me that he had not said a word to anyone about it. He wanted to talk about the etchings of himself that I had promised him; he was willing to sit for me whenever I desired.

As the day had turned dry it had become bitterly cold and I had shrouded myself in the hood of my cloak and put on mittens to protect my precious hands. Abraham, who was pleased to see me, insisted that I warm myself with hot tea. He also asked me to share some raw herring fillets which were a delicacy, but I declined. I was not hungry, just chilled and depressed by Thyst. Although I did not tell Abraham why, he sensed my despondency and he tried to lift my low spirits by stating how much he prized my work, especially my etchings. I knew he was repeating himself but I listened as if it were a first time, and I believed him, for they were hung in the place of honor in his parlor and I needed encouragement.

Gradually his cheerfulness and enthusiasm persuaded me to remain, although I had planned to continue on to visit Beghen, and so for the next hour we sat, drank tea, and talked animatedly.

I confided in him. "Abraham, I work chiefly to please myself but your devotion to my work helps me. Thank you very much."

"Master, I should thank you. Your etchings have sustained me through many dark hours. I doubt that I could live without them."

"Neither could I," I replied wryly. "I have carefully preserved the best of them in ledgers just for my own use. They are the result of many years of work. They are my ideas, my private record of my observations and feelings. I will give you some of them as a gift."

Abraham retorted with a rare flash of anger, "You must never give away any of your work. It is one of the reasons you are in such difficulties."

I sighed and said, "The reasons are more complex than that."

"Whatever the reasons, you must never stop working."

"I try not to stop. But to keep going is not always easy."

"I am certain that you will not allow anything to halt you."

I was not as convinced as he was. I needed time to restore my energy and my faith. Then I recalled my promise to him. As I prepared to leave, I assured Abraham, "When the light improves and we can depend on the sun, I will draw you as I suggested, examining etchings like the connoisseur that you are. That is when your expression is most effective."

It was too late to make my next call. Night had fallen and I doubted that Beghen would be in his office. But the following day I visited him to find out if he had told Thyst about the three thousand guilders.

The weather had changed abruptly and drastically, as it did often in winter, and it was filthy, snowing heavily and freezing quickly. To reach his office, although it was in the center of town, I had to make my way on streets that had become narrow icy ruts between heaps of snow and this added to my gloom. Then Beghen was disconcertingly brief.

He said curtly, "I have only a minute to spare. No, I did not tell anyone of your transaction. But it cannot be altered now. The money is already invested." How did he know I was having doubts about what I had done and that I wanted it back? "In the best ships in the world." That did not reassure me. "In a few months you will be rich." But I did not want to be rich, I just wanted to be free of the debts that hindered my hand. "However," he concluded, as he had his servant show me out, "others may have learned about your investment by seeing you coming from my office. You would not have visited me if you were empty-handed."

By this time I had committed myself too far to turn back. The snow was falling even more thickly when I reached the street, blotting out the sky and the landscape, but I turned toward the gallery of Van Goor, for it was nearby. I felt that only the picture dealer offered a possible solution to my dilemma. If he would meet me halfway, I told myself, I would be willing to compromise. He should be alone, so that we could talk as long as necessary—no sane person was likely to be out in such foul weather. And as I expected, there was no one with Van Goor.

He was in The Adam and Eve Room, admiring the mythological paintings on the ceiling, and I realized that in this, at least, he was sincere. His gray eyes, usually expressionless, glowed with animation. Despite the storm, he was, as usual, dressed immaculately, in keeping with his smooth, youthful skin and carefully combed brown hair. I, in my heavy, rough clothes, felt like a workman beside him.

I had not seen him in some time and he was surprised by my visit. He said cynically, "You must be in dire need of money to come here in such dirty weather. The devil himself would not be about today."

"I want your advice. To talk to you when no one else is around."

"Have you decided to heed me, finally?"

"I will try."

Since I was approaching him on such a miserable day I knew that he thought I was prepared to listen to him. And I did, until he suggested that I paint mythologies in the style of Titian.

Much as I admired the Venetian, that was impossible, and I said so.

"Then why did you come to see me?" His tone grew caustic.

"Van Goor, I said that I would listen to you."

"And the first proposal I make, a commonsense one, you reject."

I restrained my temper and said softly, "There are alternatives."

"You do need money. I was right after all."

I mumbled, "In a way."

"In a serious way. There are rumors throughout Amsterdam that your situation is desperate, that you are on the verge of bankruptcy."

That alarmed me more than I could admit; moreover, such an admission would put me at a grave disadvantage in bargaining with him. I said, "Another portrait of my son could sell. He is a pretty lad."

"I will consider that. What else are you willing to do?"

"More portraits."

"I am afraid to get any more commissions for you. Since you refused to do Ottoman's daughter as he requested, your already shaky reputation is worse. You have a reputation for doing what you please, for taking forever to finish, and sometimes you do not even accomplish that."

"My work remains so long under my hands because I seek the greatest amount of natural movement with the greatest degree of inward emotion."

"That does not interest my customers. They want to be flattered."

"What about my portrait of Six? He regarded it favorably."

"Has he asked for another work since?"

I admitted grudgingly, "No. But there were other reasons."

"That is another thing."

"I know. It is the way I live. You have told me several times."

He stated sternly, "But you make no effort to rectify your

(179)

personal situation, your fondness for Jews, your preference for the lower orders."

"My father was a miller. But he was also honest and decent."

"You misunderstand. It is true that the demand for art in Holland is large but the supply is even larger. The market is flooded, and so, it is also depressed. And you are flamboyant, unwilling to please." I sought to interrupt him, but he was in full flow, like the snow outside, and there was no halting him. As if, I thought, he had desired to say these things for a long time, and finally, I had given him the chance. "Do you think that you are more clever than the rich merchants who do not buy a picture until they are sure the price will be higher the next year? That you can ignore popular taste, refuse to do mythologies, genre pictures, histories, and survive? I have told you often customers prefer to spend money on things they can recognize and use. They are practical."

He had to pause for breath and I said, "Some have taste. Francen, Van Ludick, even Six and Tulp when they are not distracted by other matters."

"They are a minority. And you make your situation worse with your friendship for Jews. When I opened my gallery you were the favorite artist in Amsterdam, I sold everything you did, often for five hundred guilders a work, prices only Rubens fetched. You had income from your pupils, both in apprentice fees and in the right to sell their work. They came from good families, which also helped you. Now your only apprentice is a Jew. No wonder patrons keep away from you."

"Are you referring to Daniel van Dorn?" I asked indignantly.

"You know that Dutch law forbids Jews in our important occupations. They are tolerated here only because they understand Spanish ways, having lived in Spain, and they know how to outwit our ancient enemies. The painter's guild, St. Luke's, will never admit your apprentice."

"Who I employ in my studio is my own business."

"You do not listen to anyone, even when they give you good advice."

But I had come to earn money and I asked, "What could you sell of mine?"

"I could dispose of the Titian drawing you bought from me at twice the price you paid. You could realize a fine profit."

"It is not for sale."

"What about your Brouwers and Seghers? They are not worth as much, but now that they are dead you could realize something on their work."

"No."

He shook his head disgustedly. "Then why do you own them?"

"To look at and to love. They understood light and dark."

"You had better sell them before it is too late."

His tone had grown so ominous I asked, "What are you implying?"

"You have signed your collection over to your major creditors. If matters do not improve for you soon, they will seize it. As I told you, everyone is aware that your situation is desperate. But I could arrange to sell what you own of Titian, Raphael, and Michelangelo in Italy, Spain, and Germany so that just you and I would know. Both of us would realize a large profit and no one else would be the wiser. Then you could continue to paint the way you want to."

His voice had become very soft and I had to strain to hear him. His offer was tempting but I could not relinquish what I treasured. I said, as politely as I could, "Thanks for your efforts on my behalf but what you suggest is impossible." Before he could castigate me, I added, hurriedly, "But I have another matter I would like to discuss with you."

"I have no money to lend you. None to squander. Good day."

"Just a moment." I halted him as he moved toward his office. "Van Goor, have you ever considered an exhibition of my total work?"

He exclaimed, astonished, "Where I would show only yours?"

"Exactly. Everything hung in your gallery to be by my hand."

"You are saying . . . ?" He paused, still incredulous.

"That for one month you have a show of one man. Myself."

"What arrogance," he muttered.

"Then do it on a trial basis," I pleaded. "For a week."

He regarded me for a moment as if I were mad and when he recovered his composure, he shouted in his indignation, "Rembrandt van Rijn, even Bol, Lievens, and Flinck, who sell often, cannot dispose of everything they do, and would never suggest such an outrageous arrangement."

Disheartened, I was at his front door when he halted me.

He said, "However, I might still be able to sell an occasional work of yours if you listen to me. Don Ruffo continues to want your brush and I will be glad to take a first look at anything new that you do."

I was too tired to argue. I nodded and walked back into one of the worst storms I had ever known. As soon as I opened the front door of his gallery the wind caught me and dragged me outside. I was engaged with the elements and ahead of me was a great darkness, as if night had come in the middle of the day. There was no life on the streets, but I had no choice but to move on; I put my head down and plodded on. The storm was attacking with a senseless, destructive, continuous fury and I felt very vulnerable. Yet I dared not stop, to stop was to lose whatever ability I still had to keep going. I was encircled by walls that blinded me, but I pushed through them, wiping the endless snow from my inflamed, weary eyes, and moving when I could.

By the time I reached my house I had no idea of the hour, for day had merged into night. I was soaked, my hands were numb, which terrified me. Was God punishing me after all? I wondered dejectedly, to lose the use of my hands was the worst calamity of all.

Hendrickje, Daniel, and Titus were waiting for me anxiously and they welcomed me with obvious relief, my assistant saying, "Hendrickje was worried, but I told her that nothing would defeat you."

I did not share Daniel's optimism. I had held on, I thought grimly, because of my parents. As I had trudged through the blinding snow, I had remembered how my father, despite many severe blows, had worked to the end of his life, how my mother, too, had refused to give up, even when she had been driven to prayer when all else had failed. Staggering through the snow, other memories had kept me going: of the first time they had seen a drawing of mine and had not known what to do about it. Finally, they had decided that I must have the education that no one else in their families had ever had, and they had sent me to the University of Leyden. They had been dismayed when I had left it after a short stay to study art in the studio of a local painter, Jacob van Swanenburgh. Although they had been bewildered by my choice of a trade, they had paid for my lessons, they had even accepted my move to Amsterdam some years later, although it had not been their wish. I wondered how they would have felt about Hendrickje, Titus, and Cornelia, if they had lived. They had brought me up firmly but fairly. I remembered that fondly.

Hendrickje said, "You could have caught your death of cold."

As my mother had said when I had insisted on going out on a stormy day when I had been a child. "But I have not," I said, to reassure her.

In the heat of the kitchen my hands were no longer numb and I could believe again that God was good after all.

I AM ONLY A YELLOW LEAF

I am only
a yellow leaf
But I know
you love yellow
so you will
love me
will you

My sister is only
pink
and only a flower
But she came
with me
Will you love her
too

No one cut us
We just fell off
for you
Rembrandt
our genius
because you love
our colors

—Stymean Karlen

WHAT a relief it was to return to my painting.
The next few days, with Amsterdam snowbound, I was glad
that traveling was too difficult for anyone to interrupt me. As I
resumed work on my self-portrait, I accepted the cold, the damp-
ness, and with the end of the storm, the deep, sloppy slush and
the ever-present mud. I could do this as long as I was occupied;
it was the only way that I could escape from my debts. I was very

conscious of the fact that I was approaching fifty and the feeling that I was nearing the end of my life, and yet I resolved to paint this picture as if I were doing myself for the first time, although I had done so many self-portraits, sixty or seventy, at the least, that I had lost count of the exact number.

This must be the best that I had done, nothing classical, nothing elegant, but what I felt about myself. I discarded my romantic yellow robe and the red sash that I had used earlier and put on a plain brown cloak and a simple dark beret, but I could not look at myself with innocent eyes. I must paint from within my skin, nothing, no matter how ugly and unpleasant, must be hidden; I must be as truthful as I could, whatever I revealed about my inner self, I must paint myself as I am.

Ruthlessly, I fashioned my image as a bloated figure, although part of my unflattering size was because of the four waistcoats and trousers I wore to protect myself from the chill. Ruthlessly, too, I painted haggard eyes, a ruined skin, a ravaged face. I rubbed the red off my cheeks. I told myself that it shone and was untrue. I saw my person pitilessly, nakedly. I did not believe I had a need to paint a mask.

When Hendrickje entered with tea and cake to warm me she was shocked by my new self-portrait. Daniel joined us to supply me with sufficient oils for my palette and he was startled, too. It was evident they both disapproved of what I was painting. It was not my habit to allow anyone to alter my intention, but since I was doing this for my family I was concerned. If this did not represent me as they saw me, I had failed in my purpose. I asked Hendrickje, "What is wrong?"

"Since you ask me, Master," she said tentatively, then she paused.

"Say it. What troubles you?"

"Before you made yourself too old. Now, since you have dispensed with your costume, you depict yourself too harshly. You must not punish yourself."

Daniel volunteered, "You are too conscious of suffering. Your eyes are full of pain. It is not the way you look when you paint."

"How do you know the way I feel when I am working?"

"Master, it is in your self-portraits. In every move you make."

"Besides, Papa," said Titus, who had followed Daniel into the studio like a pet puppy dog, "you are different from anybody else."

"I know that."

"Yet you paint me attractively. You make me prettier than I am."

"Titus, I love you."

"And not yourself, Papa?"

Shaken by his candor, I paused. Yet he was regarding me affectionately, and so I did not chide him, but said quietly, "I paint you as I see you."

"Then why not paint yourself as we see you."

I smiled. My son, even at fourteen, was starting to sound like a man. He must want to feel grown-up. I said, "Titus, it is just your view."

"As is your view, Papa. Mine is just as truthful."

Titus sounded more mature than I had ever heard him. We had stood here many times together but never like this. Suddenly I said, "Son, paint me. Go ahead, as you think it should be done."

Hendrickje smiled encouragingly but Daniel was uneasy, while Titus took the brush from my hand and moved toward my self-portrait. But he did not apply it, as I expected, for he was well trained, dropping it at my feet, crying out, "I am sorry! I will only spoil it!"

I could not allow this situation to deteriorate. His interest had lifted my spirits, and I persisted. "Son, how do you see me? How would you paint me?"

Titus, now that he had recovered from his panic, replied quickly, "Papa, are you painting yourself at work in your studio?"

"Yes."

"Then you must paint yourself as emperor of all that you survey."

Daniel said emphatically, "He is right. That is the way you work."

Hendrickje chorused, "Sometimes, when you paint, you do look as if you could conquer the world. As if nothing then could injure you."

It was often the way I felt when my work was going as I wished. But that was not always. Yet they stood as a family now, sharing their view of me, and I decided to try to please them and myself.

"Papa, you are a king when you paint."

Thus, I thought, this portrait should be my defiance of the world. Creditors might deprive me of all my possessions but as long as I could work I was still Rembrandt van Rijn, Master Painter of Amsterdam. I was no more the actor practicing my facial expressions before the mirror, but a seeker after my self. I examined the portrait again and I realized that they were right and I was wrong. This work was not defiant, but vulnerable, melancholy, and now I knew what had to be accomplished. I thanked my son for his advice and dismissed them with a flourish of my brush and returned eagerly to this canvas.

After an hour of work I was dissatisfied. My concept was clear to me now, I must assert myself with authority and dignity, but other things were lacking. I did not miss my sumptuous costume, but I did miss the colors. I did not want to linger on the clothes, the expression was infinitely more vital and I yearned to stress that, and yet I found myself using yellow even for the skin, to reflect the sunlight on it, although there was none today and had not been for a week. And as I added a touch of red to the lips to give them life, I knew that I must assert myself for what I was: a painter who was seeking to express God.

While I rested from this labor and waited for Spinoza to return, I wondered about what I should paint for my creditors. This defiant self-portrait was too personal to please a patron and van Goor had advised me to do mythologies, landscapes, and histories. The difficulty was, every time I thought of something historical to do it was from the Bible, and that was out of fashion. No Reformed Church in any of the United Seven Provinces permitted religious art within its walls and so most of their parishioners felt the same way about their homes. And when I had done a mythology such as *The Abduction of Ganymede,* instead of making the child cherubic, as had been the classic ideal, I had shown the boy urinating, as I had believed he would, for he had been in a state of terror. Then I had been accused of being shocking and vulgar. The landscapes I had painted had been criticized, too. I had been told that they were too fanciful, gloomy, the fantasies of a feverish and disordered mind.

I did not know which way to turn. I assured myself that I sincerely wanted to sell my work but I could not do what I did not believe in.

When 1656 dawned a week later I was determined that it must be a better year than the past few. I was pleased that everyone in my family was in good health and by the way my new self-portrait was progressing. I had grown a mustache and a wisp of a beard to soften my features and I felt that I was doing a work that I could respect.

Seventeen years ago, on January 3, I had bought this house that I treasured, and I decided to celebrate that with a feast for my family. I took fifty guilders from the canvas where I had hidden the eight hundred remaining from the Francens' loan and handed it to Hendrickje. I ordered her to buy something special for dinner, "like *oliporigo.*"

"That is costly," she replied. "We should spend the money carefully."

"No, I do not want *hutespot,* anybody can eat that. I have been saving this money for a special occasion. You must spend every stiver." This was another kind of defiance and I felt better for doing it.

She could tell by my tone that I was not going to change my mind.

"People are starting to move about Amsterdam again. Take Daniel with you to carry the food, he is to be included in the festivities."

That made her feel better. She liked the idea of trying her hand at *oliporigo;* this was a stylish recipe, one that she had never cooked for me, and she was eager to prove that she was capable of doing so.

"Remember, all the meat must be fresh, whatever it costs."

She followed my instructions faithfully and returned with the best beef, capon, lamb, sausage, veal, pig's head, artichokes, and spices. Then, with considerable ceremony, she beat five egg yolks into this delicacy, and added sour wine and melted butter. She was as excited as I was when I painted a picture I liked and she stood contentedly over the stove as she boiled the *oliporigo* for many hours, while Titus set the table, not in the kitchen where we usually ate, but in the dining room. I had Daniel bring out my best table linen and silver, which I had not used for a long time. This was a wedding present that I had received from my mother, which reminded me that she had died on July 14, 1640, one day before my birthday and after fifty-one years of marriage.

It was one of the best meals that Hendrickje had ever cooked and I told her so while she served us. Cornelia lay in her crib, although she was starting to walk, while we sat on strong chairs, not the usual stools, and we used napkins, which was rare, too.

I was positive I had made the right decision, for everyone seemed happy. When Hendrickje wanted to return half of the money I had given her, I told her to keep it, to spend it on herself for a new bodice or anything else she desired. This gesture alarmed Daniel, but I hushed him, saying, "No talk of debts tonight. This is a festive occasion."

Hendrickje agreed, and when all the food was eaten, she took Cornelia out of her crib and showed me how she was teaching our fifteen-month-old daughter to walk. She explained, "My mother did it with me." Hendrickje held a rope above Cornelia while the baby toddled across the dining room hanging on to the rope to keep erect. Soon, I reflected, I will paint her when she can learn to be still. After several failures Cornelia was able to walk a few feet and I embraced her as a reward. Titus sniffed that he had learned to walk when he was even younger, that I had told him so. I did not recall having done this, but I did not correct him, he was in such fine spirits. Daniel had eaten with a relish I had seldom seen, generally he was a small eater, as if he worried that he would consume too much of my capital, but tonight he had indulged himself without hesitation. I felt that he and Titus were striving to outdo each other and show Hendrickje how much they appreciated her cooking. I had gorged myself, too, and I grew drowsy, for I had worked all day.

Hendrickje was washing the pots and pans, Titus had done the cups and earthenware plates, while Daniel had taken care of the silver, when I heard the warning bell sound on the street.

"Ten o'clock," I announced, as the guard's drum accompanied the curfew. "Time for bed, Hendrickje. You can finish tomorrow."

For once, she did not protest that she could not leave dirty things.

I blessed everyone, kissed Titus and Cornelia good night, patted Daniel affectionately on the arm, and after he climbed up to his quarters in the attic and my son went to his room, I took Hendrickje by the hand and led her up into our bedroom. When we had started to live together, she had not wanted to sleep in this bed, for Saskia had died in it, and she had said that it was bad luck, and she had been reluctant to make love in it. I had replied that it was common sense to use such a comfortable bed —I was attached to it, for some of my happiest moments had been spent in it—and tonight, I saw with satisfaction, there was no resistance in her. After she put Cornelia to sleep in a nearby cradle and drew the curtains around her, she came to me with all the passion I desired.

Spinoza arrived as he had promised, two weeks after the previous sitting. This time he did not bring any presents or ask for Titus' help. He was preoccupied, as if something was troubling him. Daniel greeted him anxiously, eager to talk to him, but he was silent, almost somber, as brief with his friend as he was with me.

I was relieved that when I placed him in the chair by the window, although his posture was still awkward, he remembered what he had learned and he sat more naturally. The sky seemed to be clearing, there was the possibility of sun for the first time in over a week and I was hopeful of accomplishing something of worth today. When I saw his face in the light I was convinced more than ever of the wisdom of painting him. If anything, the struggle he was having within himself heightened the expression I craved. I told Daniel to stop hovering about us as if he expected Spinoza to confide in him, and to prepare my palette with my usual colors.

"Master, you are painting directly now?" Daniel asked with surprise.

"Yes." I was curt. I could not explain that if I put off the actual painting any longer I might never have the courage to venture into this dangerous territory.

Daniel gave me a quizzical glance as if he disagreed with my decision, but he obeyed me, while Spinoza continued to sit, motionless and silent.

Now that the moment that meant so much to me had arrived I paused to reassemble my ideas and decide how to begin. I wondered if anyone else realized what an ill-matched pair we were. We were about the same height but I felt that this was the only way we resembled each other. I was heavy while he was slight. My thick, rough working clothes made me appear even bulkier, while his simple, neat black cloak gave his slender body an even slimmer look. Anybody in Amsterdam, I reflected, could tell that I was a malt miller's son while he was a philosopher. There were paint stains all over my smock but his garb was immaculate. I felt that my face was broad, plebian, gross, especially by comparison with his sensitive features. Only our eyes had something in common, for while his were darker and deeper than mine, we both possessed a penetrating gaze, although at the moment his seemed very far away as he stared out the window and into the distance.

I saw that his costume was wrong for my picture, that it did not convey the view I wanted to represent, but I decided to take care of that later and focus on his face. I was glad that he was clean shaven, I preferred that for this portrait, I wanted my Jesus to be youthful, as I felt Him.

No one said a word as I stacked my last drawing where I could refer to it. Sweat poured down my back despite the uncertain heat from the fireplace as I paced up and down to capture my sitter from the best angle. As I strode closer to him to observe him better, he became self-conscious and I muttered, "Do not pay any attention to me."

"What should I think of?" he asked, as if now he wanted to be helpful.

"Just meditate on your own ideas."

"But I do not believe that Jesus of Nazareth was divine."

"That does not matter. This picture is not a theological argument."

"Or that He was the son of God, except that we all are."

Was he trying to warn me not to paint him? I growled angrily, "Will you keep still!" I must select his most tender yet dramatic moment for the expression I needed, and so far, that had not occurred.

He asked, "Are your paintings true?"

"They are about truth."

He muttered, "That is what I am trying to find. It is not easy."

Perhaps I should allow him to speak. It seemed to make him feel better and to put him more at ease. I nodded and began to do his face as I had drawn it, but more tentatively than I usually painted.

He asked, "Do you think this picture will be good?"

"Young man, I thought that you did not care."

"I do not. But it is natural to be curious."

"No one can tell how it will turn out."

"Master, what does that depend on?"

"Myself, my subject, my sitter."

"You could find a better one than me."

"As I told you," I said impatiently, "I will decide that."

"What are you using as a source for your subject?"

"The scriptures."

"I do not believe in them. You should not have chosen me."

His words were starting to distract me. The sun had broken through the clouds and as it shone around Spinoza it formed a natural halo around his head. But when I painted that I smiled at my naiveté. This was the obvious way to portray Jesus, painters had done Him this way for centuries.

He said, "I wish I could believe that the wisdom of the ages lay between the covers of a single book, written thousands of years ago by a tribe of wandering shepherds, whose ignorance was only surpassed by their love for bloodthirsty tales and the conviction that they and they alone held the key to salvation. But I do not agree with this dogma. It is not reasonable."

"Will you please be quiet!" I shouted. "You move too much!"

"You are not listening to me!" He was upset, offended.

"I am not painting your ideas, I am doing your person."

"When will you be done?" he asked suddenly.

"When you allow me to work without interruption! Now be still! You gave me your word that you would do your best to model properly."

He sighed, as if he regretted that, and said, "That is right."

"Then keep your word."

He nodded, as if that, at least, was precious to him, and now he sat with some composure and resembled the young man who had attracted me.

It reminded me of how excited I had been the first time I had seen him. I moved him so that his entire body was bathed by the sunlight and I told him to be reflective, thinking of how that had succeeded with my portraits of Jan Six and Bathsheba, and he tried. Although this still did not produce the precise effect I preferred, it was an improvement.

I lost track of the time as the painting involved me. This work was making me acutely aware of myself: this subject must not preach and yet must be a rabbi with the vision of Jesus. By some miracle this subject was also myself. Loving Jesus, I squandered paint on His face, His presence possessed me. I forgot that my shirt was soaking wet with sweat, that the fire was going out, that my sitter must be growing weary and chilled. As the light ended and the sun vanished I cursed the short winter days, and then my sitter, for he stood up abruptly.

Before I could chide him, he declared, "I cannot sit any longer."

"What about your promise?"

"I am frozen, numb. May I see what you have done?"

"I am not finished." Now that it was dark, although I lit my candles, I was not satisfied with what I had done. It was just a start.

He stared at the canvas and looked surprised.

I asked, "Young man, you do not like the way I paint you?"

"I am not sure I understand it. Do you like what you are doing?"

"It is too early to tell." I called Daniel to arrange for the next sitting, and asked Hendrickje to bring tea and cake for our guest.

(193)

He declined the refreshments, saying that he was late for his evening appointment, dinner at a friend's house, and that he doubted that he could come again in spite of his promise.

Disgusted with his vacillations, I started to scold him and Daniel interrupted me. "Baruch does not want to tell you, Master, but he is afraid that his presence here could harm you." Spinoza tried to stop Daniel but he continued, although his friend was ill at ease now, "Baruch has been ordered to appear before the rabbis of the congregation because he has dared to question their teachings."

"Not publicly," he said. "Only in the privacy of my mind."

Daniel said, "Somebody informed on him. Lopez probably."

Spinoza said softly, "That does not matter."

In this moment he had the compassion that had been missing, but it was too late to resume and I knew he would not sit now whatever I said.

He added, "I understand the concern of the rabbis. They are worried about the effects of my doubts on their Christian neighbors. I had no intention of making my ideas public but once they confronted me with them I could not lie."

I said, trying to console him, "I went through much the same thing with the Reformed Church when I differed with them on some matters."

"But my situation is different. You believe in a personal God. I do not. I am considered a heretic."

This was more than I had bargained for and I was silent. I knew that in Holland one was permitted to be of a different religion than the established sect, which in itself was unusual, but not to believe in any faith was a serious offense, often a hanging matter. Atheism was the worst sin of all in Amsterdam, even worse than being a Catholic or a Jew.

Spinoza said, "So you see, for me to sit for you could have grave consequences. Especially when it is learned that you are using me as a model for Jesus Christ. You will be damned."

Daniel said, "I thought you did not believe in damnation."

"Not in the religious sense. But that does not stop man from trying to do it to us. It is not reasonable to pursue this sitting any further."

I growled, "You could be the right model if you wanted to."
Spinoza was silent.

"The light has been difficult, often wrong for my purposes, but you have not made my task any easier with your skepticism."

"Would you prefer that I believe in Jesus of Nazareth when I do not?"

"I am not talking about your view of Him. I mean your doubts about my ability to paint you as I conceive."

"I never said that!" he exclaimed.

"It is in your manner," I grumbled, "your lack of faith in my brush."

"You are challenging me. You are trying to provoke me into returning."

"You challenge yourself. Either you sit properly or you do not."

"Master Rembrandt, how simple you make things sound."

He would never sit for me, I thought wryly, if he knew how confused I often was, how many questions I had about my work, about myself, but one thing I believed, He was the best model for the rabbi that Jesus had been. Disagreeing with me, he was once again the animated figure that had fascinated me. This was crucial, the rest . . . I shrugged, thinking, Amsterdam was always being shaken by theological quarrels, it was the nature of the community, but not to paint him would be a sin.

Daniel asked, "Baruch, did any of the rabbis seem sympathetic?"

"Manasseh ben Israel was conciliatory, but he is going to England soon."

I said, struck suddenly with an idea, "I could talk to him. He respects my brush. I have painted him several times."

"No." Spinoza was adamant. "It will do no good."

"How can you be sure?"

"I do not want anybody to plead for me."

Daniel asked critically, "You want to be a martyr? A Jesus yourself?"

This brought a smile to his friend's lips and he said, "Of course not. That would not be rational. But I am able to take care of myself."

"Is that why you are in such trouble?" I asked.

"Master Rembrandt, you do not understand my situation."

"You do not understand my work. So we are even." He liked that, for he laughed, and I added, for I was starting to realize where I had erred with his portrait, "Will you continue to sit for me?"

"Despite the difficult situation I am in?"

"You said that I did not understand it. So if I am attacked for painting you, either as yourself or as Jesus, I will plead ignorance."

I was not sure I had convinced him but he said, "How long will it take?"

"When it is done."

"When will that be?"

"When I am satisfied."

"My situation could become impossible here. I may have to leave Amsterdam. What will you do then?"

"I will do you from memory if I have to. Now stop asking foolish questions. I will expect you at the same time next week."

"Then all I told you was for nothing," he said sadly.

"Not necessarily. It may fit the painting." I added brusquely, to hide my relief that he had agreed to return, "It is too bad that we have to work now. July is the best month for painting, the daylight is long and one does not get numb from the cold. That would be the suitable time to polish this work. Daniel, after you show our friend the door, I would like to speak to you."

When he did not return quickly I decided that he and Spinoza had engaged in a long conversation that I was not supposed to hear. I was annoyed; I felt their attachment to each other excluded me. Yet I saw that while they were the same age, Spinoza acted older, more maturely than my assistant, that he was closer to me in nature and in need. Then I assured myself that my envy of their friendship was unimportant as long as it did not damage the portrait. Nonetheless, I was relieved when Daniel finally came back and told me what I wanted to hear, that his friend would keep his word and continue to sit for me, if possible.

"What are you saying, if possible? We have decided that."

"You have decided, Master. Baruch has gone to live with van

den Ende. This skeptic is already considered a creature of the devil because of his criticism of Calvin and his reputation as a freethinker. I tried to dissuade Baruch from residing there, but he did not listen to me. He can be stubborn when something he believes in is attacked."

"Then you must continue to convince him to come here. As my assistant, it is your duty to do so." After that ultimatum, I dismissed Daniel.

Yet, I resolved, I must speak to the rabbis myself. I was of their generation, they should listen to me and realize that Spinoza meant no harm, it was his youth, his impulsiveness. I should be able to convince them of his decency despite his wrong-headedness and his need to shake his fist at heaven. Even as I planned this visit, I returned to my self-portrait. I was always available as a model, and now I could paint impulsively, whenever the need was in me. But after a few minutes I had to turn back to my portrait of Spinoza. With reflection, I saw even more clearly what was wrong. The tenderness and compassion that had attracted me was missing.

But I could not surrender my concept. There was not an hour that I did not think of it. Not the devil himself could stop me from thinking about it. I put both canvases away before I exhausted myself with pondering, and resolved to start a new work.

First, however, I knew that I must speak to the rabbis.

I went to water the flowers that Spinoza had brought two weeks ago but it was too late, they were dead and had been for some time. Yet I could not throw them out. They had withered and turned a dark brown but it was a color I could paint.

WHEN I ENTERED HEAVEN

When I entered heaven
I did not bring with me
the name of one wine
> Or of one fine soup
> Or of one flower
> Or of one city
> Or of one country
> Or of one hemisphere
> Or of one liar
> Or of one truth sayer

My blind instinct told me
that names
were not known in heaven

And then I learned
that heaven
did not have a name either

— Stymean Karlen

M Y meeting with the two chief rabbis of the synagogue to which Spinoza belonged occurred in the reception room of Manasseh ben Israel. It had been two years since I had been here and I was glad that it was still the province of the scholar, that books dominated what was the largest room in the modest, two-story house. As my host invited me to sit in his Dutch chair with its high back and low leather seat, on which he had put a thick cushion for comfort, I recalled his pride in his scholarship and his skill as a linguist. The books that lined his walls were in Latin, Hebrew, Spanish, Portuguese, English, and Dutch. I noted that while some of them were by his own hand and were works of erudition, there were also volumes on mysticism and messianic subjects. Since I had illustrated one of the books that he had written and had portrayed both men I was not surprised by their cordial greeting, as if they assumed I had requested this meeting for the same purpose. I had arranged it without consulting any-one else, wanting my mission to be a private one, and that was easy to do, for Manasseh ben Israel lived just a few doors away, and Rabbi Saul Levi Morteira resided close by, also.

After we sipped wine, Manasseh said, "Master Rembrandt, I still treasure your portrayal of me. As you can see, I have kept it in the place of honor." He indicated where it hung over his bookcase and I smiled to acknowledge my appreciation. "Your former pupil, Flinck, also depicted me . . ." I wondered if he was saying to me that I was not the only artist who wanted to paint him, or to show that he was influential. ". . . but although Flinck has become important and many official commissions come his way now, I prefer your work. You do a better likeness."

"Thank you, Rabbi." I was resolved to be calm and composed.

"I wish you could paint me again but I am leaving for England."

I had not offered to do him, I thought irritably, but wishing this meeting to go smoothly, I surveyed his appearance and Morteira's as if that were a consideration of mine. Manasseh's face had become stouter with age but he still possessed the grave yet amiable countenance that he cultivated for his many Christian acquaintances. He was reputed to have more dealings with the Christian world than anybody else in the Jewish community, and so I expected him to regard me benevolently.

But Morteira was grim. Dark-skinned, Venetian by birth, but of Portuguese extraction, as were Manasseh and Spinoza, he was shorter, thinner, and sharper-featured than his colleague. His spindly legs, fat belly, and cynical expression on his tight mouth reminded me of Pastor Hoag. His eyes were black, intense, and he watched me intently. Nothing else in him stirred. He appeared unwilling to move, as if he was distrustful of expressing any attitude in advance.

I was not sure how to begin. Then I decided to approach them as I approached the Bible, directly and straightforwardly. I said, "I have been using one of your students in my studio and . . ."

I paused. Morteira glanced knowingly at Manasseh as if to say, I told you so.

Manasseh asked, "Are you referring to Daniel van Dorn?"

I said slowly, "I am speaking about another pupil, Baruch Spinoza."

Morteira asked belligerently, "Did he ask you to speak for him?"

"No!" I said hurriedly. "He told me to keep out of this matter."

Morteira said severely, "Yet since you are speaking on his behalf, he must have informed you that he questions our authority."

"Only when I forced it out of him. And then just to explain why he was late for his sitting. He did not discuss his difficulties with me."

"See!" Morteira turned triumphantly to Manasseh, who was squirming uncomfortably. "I warned you that we must be stern with your protégé. We cannot afford to let him off with simply a warning."

Manasseh said apologetically, "Baruch is the best student I have ever had. He has an enormous desire for knowledge and at his age it is not unusual for a student to question a little."

"He does not question a little, he questions our faith."

"Baruch could change."

"He has already. For the worse. His views approach heresy."

"Morteira, we must be patient. He has the intelligence and the ability to become one of our most learned rabbis."

I interrupted, "That is one of the reasons I am using him as a model."

"For Jesus?" Morteira said critically, and even Manasseh looked skeptical.

I said determinedly, "Jesus was a rabbi, at least in spirit."

"We will discuss that later," Morteira said decisively, "Manasseh, you have taught Spinoza the Bible, the Commentaries, the Talmud, the Kabala, even led him into Maimonides, but instead of this guiding him deeper into our faith, your teachings seem to have moved him further away from our ritual."

"That is just your opinion, Morteira."

"Most of the congregation agree with me."

"Because you have labored to convince them."

Morteira said piously, "I have just put the facts before them."

"Whatever your excuse, we must not drive him out of the synagogue and we will if we are too rigid. Recently he made an offering for his father and he did read from the Holy Scroll. There is still hope for him."

"Is that why he has gone to live with a Gentile, Van den Ende? And worse, a freethinker? How can he pray in such a house?"

I sensed that Spinoza had become part of a struggle for power between these rabbis as much as a quarrel over theology. Morteira's expression had grown as unbending as Hoag's when he had condemned my situation with Hendrickje and this was too much for me. I said abruptly, "Rabbi Morteira, perhaps he went to live with this Latin teacher to study and to support himself as an instructor in this school."

"That is no excuse. Such behavior is disgraceful."

"Wrong, no doubt, but hardly scandalous," said Manasseh. "Van den Ende is a man of considerable learning."

"As if that justifies anything," Morteira sneered.

"It explains Baruch's attachment to him. He reveres learning."

"That does not excuse his views. Not only does he question our faith, he questions Christianity. What will our Dutch neighbors think? Enough crimes have been unfairly blamed on us already. We cannot afford to be accused of producing freethinkers."

Manasseh frowned, as if this was the argument that troubled him the most and he said, "Master Rembrandt, that is our main difficulty. We are in an awkward position in dealing with heresies that attack the fundamentals of the Christian faith in addition to the Jewish faith. We enjoy a religious toleration here that is denied us elsewhere in Christendom. This will be withdrawn if we allow ideas that might unsettle the religious and moral views of the established order. Morteira, could you try to persuade Baruch to moderate his opinions while we reason with him?"

"There is no reasoning with him," Morteira said somberly.

"We must try. Promise that you will while I am in England."

Morteira was reluctant to agree to that, but when Manasseh regarded him imploringly he nodded slowly and grumbled, "I will consider it."

"Good!" I exclaimed. "I will speak to him, too."

"What can you say? You have been accused of blasphemy, too."

"In what way?" I would match my reverence for God against anyone.

"You insist on depicting Jesus of Nazareth as a Jew."

"It is the correct view."

"I doubt that our Christian neighbors will agree with you. It will be one more thing they hold against us. Why do you paint us so much?"

I longed to slam the door in his face; it was none of his business, but as I stood up suddenly, Manasseh said quietly, "I do not share my colleague's opinion. I have been honored by your hand."

He, at least, deserved an answer. I answered, just as quietly, "Rabbi, I grew up with the Old Testament. My parents taught me to read every word of it until the scriptures became a reflection of our own fears and hopes, our sufferings and our triumphs. And the Jewish faces I see about me on the streets and in the synagogue are in the Bible. They resemble the figures from which they are descended far more than the idealized folk that other artists have painted. Moreover, much of the time they are the most interesting and picturesque faces in Amsterdam."

"You flatter us."

"That is not my intention. But it would be stupid for me to search for models elsewhere when they are all about me for the seeing."

"Is that why you asked Baruch to model for Jesus Christ?"

"It is one of my reasons." I could not reveal that I also felt a spiritual connection with this young man, that was a private matter and could embarrass me. "However, who I use is my own business."

"Yet you plead for him," Morteira said sarcastically, "even though you claim to believe in God and he says that he does not."

I shook my head sadly. Morteira could not trust his imagination but I had to. I said, "Everyone must believe in God as they see fit."

"No wonder you are in trouble with your own church, too.

Only in Amsterdam would you be allowed to live with such impious views."

I turned to Manasseh and asked pointedly, "Rabbi, you will be merciful with this young man? Please?"

"As you see, I am trying to be compassionate. But I am leaving for England soon and I do not know when I will be back. Ultimately, this affair will be in the hands of my colleague, Rabbi Morteira."

He declared, "I will give him one more chance to return to the faith of his fathers. At the proper time we will examine him again and judge his piety. If it still exists, I will find it."

I was not certain that I had accomplished anything, for Morteira still regarded me critically, but Manasseh escorted me to the door and said, "I have great plans in England. Cromwell, the Lord Protector, is favorably inclined toward my people. I hope to persuade him to admit us legally to his country. We have been banned from England since 1290. It is the most vital mission of my life. Do not worry about Baruch, I will persuade him to return to God. He has always heeded me."

Morteira remained unsympathetic. Although he joined us at the door, to be sure that his colleague did not obtain any advantage, he stated argumentatively, "Van Rijn, you should not have interfered."

I asked, "Rabbi, you were born in Venice, were you not?"

"What has that to do with this situation?" He was puzzled, annoyed.

"Did you become acquainted with the works of Titian?"

"I am not interested in painting. Calvin was right to forbid it from his churches. It seduces the faithful from the pursuit of piety."

"Then why did you want me to portray you?"

"Manasseh recommended you. I think he felt that it would create a bridge with the Christian community. I was not that much interested."

The other rabbi said, "Nonetheless, you have kept your portrait."

"It may be worth something one day. As his work was once.

Spinoza must preserve appearances or our situation here will become impossible."

As I left, Manasseh said, "God be with you."

I replied, "God is always with me." I doubted he understood what I meant but he smiled benevolently, while Morteira turned his back on me.

When Spinoza did not appear as he had promised, I was upset. I wondered if he had heard of my appeal to the rabbis and if that had kept him away. I asked Daniel, "Have you any idea why your friend has not come?" and he replied, "I have not seen him since the previous sitting. It is likely that he left Amsterdam. To compose himself and to prepare his reply for the rabbis in peace and quiet. As he prefers."

I did not believe this excuse but I did not say this to Daniel, who was having problems of his own. I felt an irresolution in him, as if he faced a crucial decision over his friend and he did not know how to resolve it. When I asked him if the Jewish community was hostile to Spinoza, he said, "It is worried about the persecution of Jews elsewhere. The Inquisition grows worse daily. This tends to make my people more determined to retain their faith and situation here. What work are you going to prepare for your creditors? They must be satisfied soon."

"Whatever is necessary. Do you think that Spinoza has deserted me?"

"I do not know. When he left last week he was troubled. No matter what decision he comes to about the synagogue, it will hurt him deeply. I hope he survives it without damage to himself."

The next day I resolved to dismiss Spinoza from my thoughts as my model for Jesus and to do other work to help me forget him. I put aside the partially finished canvas of him that I had been painting and my self-portrait and searched for new subjects. Annoyed by Spinoza's unreliability, I felt it was foolish to depend on models, that I must trust my own imagination which was dependable. Some of my favorite subjects were in the life about me. I saw a Jewish family standing outside of the synagogue, and the father regarded his sons with such affection, the scene reminded me of one of my favorite tales in the Old Testament, *Jacob Blessing the Sons of Joseph,* and I sketched them as the start of a study on this subject.

Later my imagination was fascinated by the sight of a slaughtered ox that hung from a wooden rack. It was suspended in the air and I was excited by the drama and color of the bloody carcass. I came upon Titus reading and the devotion on his face and in his hands that held the book developed into a painting virtually of its own accord. A simple portrait of Hendrickje followed to express my respect for her, and I liked the colors she wore and the pensive quality of her features.

While I was rummaging in my storehouse for accessories I was charmed by the glint of armor. I decided to use it in a painting. I was not sure whether the subject should be Mars or Pallas Athene or an Alexander the Great for Don Ruffo; I was determined to represent the brilliant light of shining objects; I was more concerned with this than making the flesh visible; I had done that many times before.

I could almost endure Spinoza's absence now. I loved starting new paintings, the first strokes of the brush when the paint was still alive and the problems had not begun. It was a happy moment when I was transforming a canvas into life, when I was using my imagination.

This delight lasted only a brief time. Once I became dissatisfied, which was usually when I realized how much further I had to go before I pleased myself, the struggles began. The more I learned, the more I had to learn. One moment I felt master of my material, the next the slave. Sometimes the paint was like clods of mud on the canvas, then inexplicably it caught fire and was like sparks in the sky. At times like these I did not know whether to laugh or cry, to hug myself with joy or thank God for the miracle I saw before me. Many of the strokes I made had no meaning, but occasionally a few suited me and spoke as I wished them to do.

The days became too short as I planned my work so that it would be sufficiently finished to show to my creditors. Surely some of the subjects I was painting should satisfy Ornia, as they had satisfied Jan Six, whom he looked up to. I was even hopeful that my brush would alter Thyst's indifference and lessen my obligation to him, also.

My mood improved also, for there were moments when I smelled the seaborne wind, when the sun shone despite the rigors of winter. I was grateful that when I needed sustenance Hendrickje had beer, a hard-boiled egg, and a strip of herring with buttered bread for me. Then I was able to resume my work with renewed energy. I also appreciated that she scrubbed the marble floor in my reception room for the creditors who would come eventually, that she bathed our daughter every day, while Titus and Daniel hovered near me unobtrusively, prepared to serve me when summoned; otherwise they kept a proper distance and silence.

Thus, when a visitor was admitted to my presence several weeks after my meeting with the rabbis, I realized that my family considered him important. I was in my paint-smeared smock, for I was in the middle of my work on *Jacob Blessing the Sons of Joseph,* but Dr. Johan Deyman did not appear to mind. This slender, brown-haired, middle-aged physician, who had succeeded my old friend and sponsor, Dr. Nicholas Tulp, as professor of anatomy for the Amsterdam Surgeons' Guild, did not gaze at my work in the salon, where I met him, as most of my visitors did. His mind was settled; it was evident from the directness with which he addressed me.

"Master Rembrandt," he announced, "our Guild will be honored if you paint our next public anatomy."

I was pleased, although I tried not to show it, afraid it would lower the price I would be offered. This was one of the most prized commissions in Amsterdam. I said cautiously, "Dr. Deyman, I appreciate your interest, but I am very busy now. I have many works in hand."

"Put them aside," he said brusquely. "We cannot wait. The subject of our anatomy is to be hung this week, and as you know, I must perform the anatomy immediately, in the next few days, before the corpse becomes impossible to use. But this should not be difficult for you. *The Anatomy of Dr. Tulp* that you painted over twenty years ago taught you whatever you need to know and we desire a work of the same quality."

"How much will I receive?"

"As much as Dr. Tulp paid you."

"Prices have gone up. Everything costs more. Oils, brushes, food . . ."

"We will decide that later. Will you do it for us? You will have a fine, healthy corpse to paint and this is a distinguished occasion. Many people of the highest importance in Amsterdam will be present to watch my dissection and it will remind them of the power of your brush."

I knew it was foolish but I had to ask, "Why have you chosen me?"

"Tulp recommended you. And anyone who saw the work you did for him knows you are the man for this. Master Rembrandt, I am not blind."

And I could learn more about the body and that was tempting.

"We are staging this anatomy with care. The subject is to be hung on the twenty-seventh of this month in a public ceremony, as is the custom. Then, on the following day his corpse will be put at my disposal, and we will sell tickets for ten stivers to anyone who wants to attend, while guild members and physicians over fifty years of age will be admitted free and have the choice seats."

"What part of the body do you intend to dissect?"

"That depends on its condition. But certainly the cerebrum, which, I believe, has never been done before in an anatomy painting. Are you acquainted with the work of Vesalius?"

"Yes. Although Calcar is reputed to have been the artist, some of his drawings of the anatomies are so skillful I believe that Titian did them."

"Good. We will expect you to include all the figures about the corpse."

"But the composition must be what I choose to do."

I felt he was going to refuse me, and I asked myself, what am I doing, with a feeling of panic in my heart, turning down the best commission I have had in years. He said quietly, "As a pupil of Tulp's, I have examined the anatomy you did for him many times. It is the best and most intimate view of the human body

I have seen. You will be allowed to paint the anatomy as you see it, as long as it pictures my dissection correctly."

I thought, with a sigh of relief, 1656 could mark a basic improvement in my life after all. I asked, "Who is the subject?"

"A young man, Joris Fonteyn, alias Black Jan. But you must not become involved in his person, it could cramp your hand and give you an unnecessary compassion. He is a hardened criminal, a beggar and a robber. We want a very large picture, at least eighty inches by one hundred ten inches, for it is to be hung in the operating theater of the Surgeons' Guild."

"I will put everything else aside."

"You must. We can only keep the corpse from decomposing a few days."

Later that afternoon I was arranging with Daniel to supply me with the materials I needed for the anatomy picture when Spinoza appeared.

Three weeks had passed since I had seen him; by now I assumed I would not see him again; I was surprised, then angry. This was the worst possible time to be distracted. Did he think that I desired him so desperately that he could come and go as he pleased?

His clothes were wet, for it had begun to snow, and while everyone in my family sought to make him feel at home, Titus hung his soaked cloak by the fire in the kitchen to dry, Hendrickje served him hot tea to warm him, and Daniel looked relieved, as if he, too, had not been sure that he would see Spinoza again, I waited impatiently for his explanation. It was too late in the day to use him and I was not certain that I wanted to. I was tired of catering to him, of having to coax an unwilling sitter to model for me; it was a practice I hated. I wondered, Why had he come back? I did not believe that it was because of the painting or because he had any feeling for me. Until I understood this, I doubted that I could paint him successfully. Or that I should.

He looked haggard, as if he had been suffering, and he mumbled, "I wanted to speak to Daniel. I knew I would find him here."

"Is that all?" I turned away from him with apparent indifference, and picked up a slice of herring to nibble on, although I was furious with him. I would show him that I did not have to depend on him. And this should tell me whether he truly wanted to sit for me.

"My sister has brought suit officially for my share of our inheritance and I need a lawyer. No Jew is allowed to practice law, but I thought, Daniel, because of your associations you might know one."

Daniel said, "Master, what about Louis Crayer? He represents you."

I grumbled, "I doubt that he will be interested in such a situation. Young man, where have you been? You did not keep your promise to sit."

"I am sorry but I was too distracted to model properly. I had to go away to think out many things. I could not do that in Amsterdam. I hope that I did not hinder your work."

"No one hinders my work," I said defiantly. Except, I thought, myself.

"Good. Perhaps I should not have come but you have been friendly."

"What about Van den Ende?" I asked with a touch of jealousy. "Why did you not go to that freethinker for assistance?"

"He is regarded with disapproval in Amsterdam."

And I am not? I reflected ruefully. But when I saw that Hendrickje, Titus, and Daniel were imploring me to be helpful, I said grudgingly, "I will send you to Louis Crayer. He is a good lawyer and an honest man."

"If it is too difficult I would not want to impose on you."

"Then why did you come here?"

"I remembered your hospitality and how you shared it with me."

"And you say one must always be rational."

"I try. But it is not always possible."

Now he looked very young and I realized that he was not yet twenty-four, without a father, family, or many friends or supporters, and I added, "Yet, as you said, nothing is too difficult unless we make it so."

"I hope that is true."

Daniel asked, "Baruch, have you been to the synagogue?"

"No, I went to Ouwerkerk, but I heard that Manasseh has gone to England and Morteira is in charge. It will be hard to approach him."

"Try," I suggested. "He might listen to you if your tone is right."

"Did you approach him?" he asked suspiciously. "I asked you not to."

"Is that why you are here? To question me? Like a Morteira?"

That brought a smile to his anxious countenance while Daniel said, "You cannot procrastinate any more. The longer you put off speaking to Morteira, the harsher and more unforgiving he will be."

"You are right." He added apologetically, "Master Rembrandt, I am sorry to burden you with my difficulties, but you seem interested."

"I am not a stranger to difficulties. Even over matters of faith. Daniel, give your young friend Crayer's address and add that I am sending him. That may help. The lawyer is devoted to my work."

"You are very kind," Spinoza said emotionally, for once not aloof from passion. "When would you like me to sit for you again?"

"I do not need to be thanked."

"I plan to remain in Amsterdam for the time being."

He was thinner, as if a part of him had been consumed by his difficulties. I was not positive now that he fitted my view of Jesus. Moreover, I could no longer be subservient to him. He must come of his own accord, or not at all. I said, "Settle your situation with the rabbis first."

"And if they condemn me. . . ."

I left his question unanswered. I had no answer, glib or otherwise.

Spinoza put on his cloak, although it was still wet, declined a second cup of tea, and said, curtly for one who was usually soft-spoken, "If my employment of your lawyer troubles you, sir, I will seek one elsewhere. I did not intend to interrupt your work."

"Young man," I said sternly, much as a father might speak to

(210)

a son, "If I gave you Crayer's address, I meant that you use it. Now stop wasting my time. I have an important commission to start tomorrow."

Hendrickje said proudly, "The Master is painting the public anatomy."

He said sadly, "I do not approve of hangings. They prove nothing."

Daniel said, "It will prove that Rembrandt is the best painter in Amsterdam."

"But if he is, why does he have to prove it?"

"Baruch, it is not that simple. Are you going to attend the hanging? Much of Amsterdam will be there. It will be quite a ceremony."

"No. Such affairs sicken me. If it were possible, I would prefer to bring the victim back to life."

All this talk was destroying my mood. I wondered whether I should witness the execution. Remembering the living man with the noose around his neck, it could distract me when it came time to paint the dissection. I said, taking Spinoza to the door myself to indicate that he was always welcome as a guest, "Whether or not we continue our sittings, young man, I want to know how your meeting with Louis Crayer turns out."

He did not answer that but asked, "Are you attending the hanging?"

I shrugged. It was not his affair if I did or not. As I shut the door behind him, I went to the window and watched him trudge down the Breestraat, and as he put up his collar to shut off the swirling snow that blew in from the sea, biting and icy, I wondered if I would ever see him again. What could he tell me that I did not know already? Yet, as I continued to observe him and meditate, I saw the brim of his black hat vivid against the bright whiteness of the snow. Was he going to take his punishment, I asked myself, or move toward being a different man, searching for another destiny? I knew that no one would ask for mercy for the hanged man. Only when Spinoza vanished from my sight in the storm did I return to my preparations for the anatomy.

DO NOT JUDGE ME

Do not judge me
by my coverings
The clothes I wear

I condescend to all that
To the most mortal of all
The fashions

Do not judge me
by my nudity
It is not an alternative
to clothes

It is only another
covering
But for my soul

I will not judge you
by your coverings
Only by your soul

—Stymean Karlen

I DID not attend the public execution but many in Amsterdam did.

When I arrived the day after the hanging at the *Theatra Anatomica* in the tower of the Weighting House of St. Anthony's Water Gate, where the anatomy was to occur, to arrange the composition of the painting, Dr. Deyman greeted me enthusiastically and informed me, "The execution was a grand and solemn occasion. A huge success. Everyone of importance in Amsterdam attended the hanging, the Lord Sheriff, the burgomaster, aldermen, many respected clergymen, doctors, burghers and merchants."

It were as if he itemized the nature of this audience to impress me and I said obligingly, since I did not want to lose this commission, although I was not truly interested, "Then the affair satisfied you?"

"Rembrandt van Rijn, you were not there!" He was shocked.

"It was not essential," I said hurriedly, as I sensed his disapproval. I wondered if my absence would have pleased Spinoza, then I decided he was in my mind too much, I must stop thinking about him and focus on the work ahead of me. But I was curious about whether he had seen my lawyer.

"Master, it was too bad you did not attend. It was a notable event. Once again we have shown that we have the will to punish evildoers."

I nodded, not wishing to discuss this any more, but to start my work. I walked toward the corpse, which was sprawled awkwardly on a rotating table in the center of the amphitheater. It was covered with a white linen sheet and draped with a black cloth. I hesitated to move these coverings, for Dr. Deyman was still involved in impressing me.

"This is the most vital anatomy to happen here since you painted Dr. Tulp's. Everybody who matters will attend tonight. You must remember what an occasion Tulp's was. I attended it as a young medical student and I swore at that time I would succeed him some day."

I remembered my painting *The Anatomy of Dr. Tulp* very well, although it had happened twenty-four years ago. Then it had been considered one of my best pictures. I wished Dr. Deyman would stop so I could start my work, but he seemed determined to inflict all of his knowledge on me.

"My anatomy marks the height of the winter season. It must be done when the weather is very cold, lest the cadavers putrefy too soon."

"What is the condition of this one?"

"The corpse is in splendid shape. I am performing my anatomy after sunset when everyone who wants to can attend. For reasons caused by the perishable substance I am laboring with, the anatomy cannot take more than five days. So I advise you to do your portrait of the cadaver between six and thirty-six hours after the execution, before the body decomposes and loses its resemblance to itself."

"Doctor, may I view it now?"

"Of course." He led me to the table and threw back the coverings. "I chose a criminal who has been strangled by hanging so that the body would not be defaced, and one who is neither fat nor lean, but properly constructed, with a good frame, so that his limbs and organs are of a generous size and distinctly visible to the spectators."

From the bulges under the coverings I had feared that the body would be too insignificant for a strong painting, bottle-shaped and bandy-legged. But this corpse was a fine figure of a man, with powerful shoulders, muscular arms, a massive head and thick red hair, as mine had been when I had been his age, and heavy, broad features. I had also expected to be repelled by the sight of a shattered corpse but, instead of a broken body, I saw that even in death there was a defiance and a passion in him that I wanted to paint. But the figure was placed wrong. Dr. Deyman had arranged the corpse sideways, as Dr. Tulp had done, but this was a different subject and I needed a better composition.

Dr. Deyman said, "I am dissecting the cerebrum, something never attempted before in an anatomy-lesson painting."

I replied, firmly now, "Then the painting must focus on the head." And the face, I decided, and so it would be a picture created in a totally new way from my previous anatomy painting.

Dr. Deyman was puzzled and he said, "I do not comprehend."

"Everything in the work will lead to your hands dissecting the brain."

"And to my face. My face is important, too."

I said impatiently, "Naturally it will be seen." I proceeded to turn the body around on the rotating table until it faced me, with the feet foremost, next I placed the doctor behind the head.

"Will everybody see me?" he asked anxiously.

"Everybody. Even better than Dr. Tulp, who was alongside of his anatomy instead of behind it. All eyes will focus on you."

"The patient should be located at the center of the theater on a high bench and in the best lighted portion so that the dissection is visible to the most spectators under the most favorable circumstances."

"It will be. It could make a splendid picture." But I was still not satisfied with the way the corpse lay. This did not fit its character. I shifted the body until it suggested the emotions that had been in the man, meanwhile, keeping Dr. Deyman at the head of the composition.

Then, while he said, "We will be seating the spectators according to their rank," I examined the chamber where I was to work, for its appearance would influence the tone and mood of the picture.

It was so haunted with aspects of death my hair stood up under my hat. Six human skeletons were planted around the eight concentric galleries like a forest of withered trees. They were chained together by copper wire and in their hands were fixed banners with Latin inscriptions that spoke mournfully of the dissolution of the human body. There were also pieces of human skin attached to the walls and other examples of morality. I glanced away quickly from these grisly reminders and observed that the rings rose obliquely and steeply with seats only on the first three rows. But all this focused on the oval space at the bottom of the anatomy theater, which was twenty-by-twenty-four feet in size, with the table for the corpse, and room for the anatomist and those who would be chosen to stand close to him in the position of honor and prestige.

"Of course," Dr. Deyman's voice brought me back to the dissection, "Everyone whose face is in the painting will pay you, as is the custom. You will realize hundreds of guilders if you portray them properly."

I knew that very well. I recalled the stir caused in Amsterdam by a previous painting of mine when I had done an unheard-of thing and I had not put in all the faces as they had been commissioned. And so, *The Company of Captain Frans Banning Cocq and Lieutenant Willem Ruytenburch,* which I had come to think of as *The Night Watch,* had been criticized.

I was commissioned by Captain Banning Cocq and the other seventeen members of his civic guard to portray them in all their martial glory, with their faces prominent and recognizable, but the subject of the painting overrode their wishes. Instead of giving each man the heroic proportions in the posed convention of the day, as they desired, I grew so involved with the brilliant contrasts of light and dark that their faces became secondary to the sweep and the illumination of my brush. The animation and drama of their situation stimulated me far more than their features. So I worked without restraint and when it was finished, it was one of the largest works ever seen in Amsterdam, thirteen-by-sixteen feet in size. It held not only the eighteen men of the civic guard, but many other figures who had entered into my imagination and my need to express the energy, color, and rush of a tumultuous event. Some of those who did not belong to the civic guard were more visible and vividly pictured than the men who had commissioned this painting, some of the civic guard could hardly be seen, and several had been omitted completely. But I had no regrets. *The Night Watch* was a work that gratified me.

While it was hung in the Kloveniersdoelen, the meeting place of the civic guard, and I received a hundred guilders apiece from the sixteen members who were in the painting for a total of sixteen hundred guilders, two did not pay me because they said that their features could not be seen. That was so, I thought, but when they asked me to paint them in, I refused, I found that offensive. I continued to receive excellent commissions, earning twenty-four hundred guilders for two smaller works for the Prince of Orange some years later, but my work began to be questioned. I was informed that the coarseness of my colors offended public morality, that I had cheated the civic guard by not presenting them more conspicuously. I did not care. I had more important things to think about. A few days after I completed *The Night Watch* to my own satisfaction I suffered the worst blow of my life. My wife Saskia died.

Dr. Deyman brought me back to the present. "I hope the faces of my associates will be clearer than they were in your depiction of the civic guard. A repetition of that will cost you whatever commissions the anatomy painting might obtain for you."

"I will do my best to please. This subject is different."

"As I said, you will be paid by the recognizable faces in the anatomy."

I remembered that Hendrickje said I was a poor bargainer—and perhaps I was, I hated bargaining, it was a terrible distraction and waste of time—that I was too soft, too eager for an exciting commission and too indifferent with a dull one, and so I said, "How much for each face?"

"The same as before. A hundred per person."

"There were seven observers in *The Anatomy of Dr. Tulp.*"

"There will be about that many in mine."

"Dr. Deyman, how much for the painting itself?"

He stammered, "The custom is . . ."

I cut him short, unable to give in any more, "Sir, I cannot count on individual taste. I must have five hundred guilders in advance, and five hundred more if the work is satisfactory and hung."

To my surprise, he assented, so quickly that I was annoyed that I had not asked for more. I sensed that I had undervalued myself once again. I did wonder since I had been approached so suddenly and on such short notice about the scheduled anatomy whether Deyman had asked others first, possibly Lievens, Bol, or Flinck. I decided, that for one reason or another, they had been unable to do this painting. Then, as the doctor stood behind the corpse as I had suggested, with an instrument in his hand, the drama of the scene absorbed me. I exclaimed, "Doctor, that is a good start, your hands are expressive."

"I have been told that they are adroit and learned."

"Fine." I must put the strength of the corpse into my sketch book. I made many drawings and only halted as the doctor grew tired. But when he wanted to see what I had done, I did not show my sketches to him. I said, "They are just a start. Notes. I will know better tonight when you start your anatomy whether they are suitable for further development."

There was a large crowd outside of St. Anthony's Gate that evening. The sale of anatomical tickets, even at the high price of ten stivers, was brisk, and by the time I arrived at the door many were being turned away. The collection pecuniary was being administered by two stewards, who did not recognize me, and I was refused admission until Dr. Deyman was summoned. He apologized and led me to the first row where I sat and faced the corpse as I had arranged earlier in the day.

I noticed that his pubic parts were covered with a white sheet, although no women were present; they were not allowed at public anatomies, it was not considered fitting. I wondered about this modesty. I thought, If God had intended the penis to be hidden he would have made it less conspicuous. I recalled that the cadaver in *The Anatomy of Dr. Tulp* had been draped the same way, and so I resigned myself to this prudery, although not willingly. I glanced around to absorb the atmosphere and saw Abraham Francen, who, as an accredited apothecary, sat in the first row, as did Thyst, Van Hertsbeeck, and Jan Six, as influential burghers, while Cornelius Witsen, the burgomaster, was placed directly behind Dr. Deyman, in a seat of honor, and Ornia stood in the rear.

I was pleased that my chief creditors were present. I hoped that this would convince them that my work was still in demand, that I could still earn enough to pay them back, given time.

Just before the ceremony was to begin I saw Bonus in the last row, but there was no one else from the Jewish community; apparently, as a doctor, he had received special permission to attend. Suddenly, to my dismay, Hoag entered with Ruismeer and they sat in the second row with the other clergymen. I did not like this; I feared that Hoag would persuade his friend to regard me as a creature of the devil.

Dr. Deyman commenced. Standing by the side of the corpse, he read an official announcement:

Right honorable Lord Sheriff, burgomaster, aldermen, distinguished doctors and councilors, worshipful clergymen, and learned burghers and merchants, on January 27, 1656, there was punished with the rope, Joris Fontejn, of Diest, who by the worshipful Lords of the Lawcourt, was granted us as an anatomical object.

He was applauded and he motioned for eight men to join him. I noted that not one of them held a medical degree. They were the administrators and officers of the Surgeons' Guild, and while their faces did not stir me, I was glad they were prosperous enough to pay me for their inclusion in my work. I reflected, If I were to make this painting memorable, it would have to be the corpse that provided the stimulation.

Dr. Deyman asked for a simple prayer, which he led, giving thanks to God for having preserved them from evil by the punishment of this criminal. I thought of St. Paul's terrifying admonition, "Death is the wages of sin," to remind everyone of the moral lessons of death, that life was transitory and that death had come into the world through man's fall, but I did not recall that Jesus had taught this.

Once everyone's piety was expressed Dr. Deyman began the anatomy. He stood under the chandelier, which had twelve *blaeckers* that shed an uneven light on the corpse, and first dissected the internal organs. This was the usual procedure, for they decayed rapidly. Everybody watched him intently, including the eight men from the Surgeons' Guild, although several of them shifted their position so I could portray them in a flattering manner. But I was more interested in the cadaver, which lay with its head on its chest. This suggested a mood of contemplation to me.

Soon there was a great cavity where his stomach had been and as the heart, kidney, and liver were passed around the audience for examination, Dr. Deyman stated, "Anyone caught helping himself to the organs will be fined six guilders and ejected," while I continued to sketch the body, seeking to illuminate both the terror and the majesty of death. I put the corpse's face into shadow, and its clenched hands and the broad soles of its feet became the strongest manifestation of its identity. I decided not to use the anatomist's knife at this juncture, it was too much like a butcher's, even though my own hand felt rough as I drew.

Dr. Deyman paused to refresh himself with wine from the silver gilt goblet that my old friend, Jan Lutma, had presented to the Surgeons' Guild to honor their services to medicine, there was more applause from the audience and my mind turned backward into my past.

It was 1631 and I stood in the parlor of my parents' simple brick house on a small street known as the Weddesteeg—Watering Trough Alley—in the north end of Leyden. I was waiting for my mother to appear so I could tell her that I had decided to settle permanently in Amsterdam.

Since my father had died the previous year, she had become the head of the household. To reassure myself that my departure would not be too much of a shock to her, I recalled that she had had nine children, two of whom had died in infancy, and that I was next to the youngest, and so, of no special importance. But I knew that was not true. I was the only one in my family who had been given an education; at the age of seven I had been put in Latin school while my three brothers had gone into the trades as a shoemaker, baker, and miller. And when I was fourteen I had enrolled at Leyden University, the first in my family to do so. I could still remember my parents' dismay when I had left after a few months to become an apprentice to the Leyden painter Van Swanenburg. And yet, when I had asked to study a few years later in Amsterdam with a better painter, Pieter Lastman, an artist with a national reputation, my father had taken me to him and paid my fee, although he could just afford to do so.

But to leave my home for good, especially now that my father was dead, was a more difficult matter. I wished he could be standing here; even if he disapproved, it would make the situation easier for my mother.

In this rush of emotion I decided to paint him as I last remembered him, with his white beard and bald head, which I could cover with a cap, his mouth tightened from incessant hard work, the brown eyes that I had inherited, his blunt, knotted hands, so much like my own, and covered with the same red hair. I knew I must also show the parent who had never stood in my way, but had always tried to help me, even though I doubted he ever understood my need to be an artist. No one on either side of my family had shown any interest in painting. I decided to paint him as soon as I settled in Amsterdam and I missed him so much I could have wept.

My mother stood in the doorway and I knew she would not

like that. When I had questioned his death, she had said, "It was God's will."

Now she held the Bible that was her strength and her support. Although she had been baptized a Catholic, she had become a devout follower of Calvin, and she had insisted that I read every word of the Old and the New Testament, which I had done by the time I was ten. Her face was wizened and wrinkled from age —she had never told me how old she was—but since she had married my father forty-two years ago, I felt that she was elderly, and so, must be treated tenderly.

She asked, "Son, what worries you?"

"I . . ." Her eyes, brown like mine and my father's, were sad. I did not want to add to that, and yet, I could not turn back. To give myself sustenance I glanced at her cupboard, her pride and joy. Like so many Dutch housewives she displayed her most precious possessions there. I thought, It was her one vanity. The cupboard was carved of the best wood and it held handkerchiefs, bonnets, and neckerchiefs her own mother had given her as a wedding present. There were also two dozen tablecloths and napkins that she had set aside for her children's dowries.

"Rembrandt, do you need any money?"

"Not at all. I have been doing so well lately I have been able to lend a thousand guilders to the art dealer, Hendrick van Uylenburgh."

"You must not be reckless. Often your father had to toil a year to earn that much and some years he earned much less."

"Do not worry, I am the fashion now," I said triumphantly.

"But you are very young. You are only twenty-six."

"Sit down, mother, and I will explain." I led her to the heavy Dutch chair next to the thick rectangular table with the bulbous legs that I had always disliked, but where she could put her beloved and comforting Bible, and seated her so that she would feel at home. Then I added, "I have many commissions now. More than I can do. A wealthy merchant, Nicolaes Ruts, wants me to paint his portrait, and this will lead to other such pictures. This work pays excellently."

"How excellently?"

"It has not been decided yet, but it will be worth several hundred guilders. And I have even better news." I felt like a conqueror as I exclaimed, "I have been asked to do the most important commission in Amsterdam, an anatomy by Dr. Tulp. He is the most prominent doctor in the city. With his support I cannot fail. Money is pouring into the city and Van Uylenburgh, who knows everyone, says he can sell anything I do."

"You must not boast. Pride will lead only to your fall."

"Mother, I want your blessing."

"Only God can give you that."

"I will come and see you often. As often as I can."

"You will come when it suits you. Rembrandt, you have always been the most stubborn and independent of my children."

I bent to kiss her to express my emotion, but she turned her cheek so that my kiss became a peck. She was afraid to express her feelings; she felt that they were sinful. Yet I saw a gravity in her eyes that told me that she cared, perhaps more deeply than she could ever reveal.

Then there was the last time I painted her. It was a few months before she died on July 14, 1640, just one day before my birthday, because of that I could never forget it, and as she sat I sought to use everything I had learned in her portrait. She looked very old now and I painted with patient care her shrunken features, her wrinkled skin, her toothless mouth, her thin lips, and her withered hands leaning on her cane for support, and with precious detail, the wedding ring on her bent finger.

I had to express her as she had suffered and endured. Her cape was a dark brown in contrast to the light that illuminated her aged face. My brush said she was one of millions and that she was like no one else.

When I allowed her to view it, she whispered, "Am I that ancient?"

I had worked passionately and I said, "I painted you as I saw you."

"It is God's will. Do your prospects still flourish in Amsterdam?"

Not as much as I had expected when I had settled there nine years ago, although I had just bought a large house on the Breestraat, which, I sensed, she thought was too costly, too big for my needs, even though she pretended it was as grand and fine as I felt it was. I said, "Mother, I am earning more money now than I ever did. Several thousand guilders a year, I guess, I cannot keep track of all of my commissions."

"If you need any money, I have some I have saved."

"Thanks, mother, but keep it for yourself. I have plenty for my needs. Do you like your portrait?"

She answered carefully, "Rembrandt, it is not a picture one likes. But I am glad you painted me. It is a pious act. God will be pleased."

When she died soon after I found my portrait of her hanging in her favorite place, in her bedroom and over the table that held her Bible.

Dr. Deyman's voice shook me out of my reverie. "We will continue the anatomy tomorrow evening with the dissection of the cerebrum."

I was glad that this session was over. I had an overwhelming need to transfer my sketches and ideas to canvas.

I worked without pause the next day, for I knew the corpse would not last much longer, and after many hours I had the start of a picture.

The second anatomy was less crowded and I saw no one in the audience that I knew, except Bonus, who still stood in the last row, although there were empty seats below him. Dr. Deyman was more matter-of-fact with the dignitaries absent, but when he dissected the cerebrum he held my attention. He had excellently formed hands and I loved to paint hands, his grasp was delicate yet firm, and I painted them that way. The body was still viable, although over thirty-six hours had passed since the hanging, and I gave it the most dominant space. I had to individualize him. I wondered why God had made blood such a vivid and beautiful color when it so often suggested death, which was portrayed by black. Perhaps I should ask the philosopher, as I had come to think of Spinoza, if I ever saw him again. I doubted that he would return to my studio after the way I had received him the last time.

By the third and last anatomy session there was little that I could use for my picture. The body had begun to decompose and now I had to depend mostly on what I remembered. Dr. Deyman could not ignore the deteriorating condition of the cadaver. He said abruptly, "It is useless to persist. God's will has been done. The criminal has been punished even as the practice of medicine has been advanced and this is to be honored with a painting to celebrate this occasion and the glory of the Surgeons' Guild. We will conclude the festivities with a sumptuous banquet for the guild members followed by a parade with lighted torches."

I did not attend any of the festivities; I was too busy working, but once again I was kept informed by Dr. Deyman.

A few days after all the ceremonies were concluded he visited me to see how his picture was progressing and to tell me, "We more than achieved our goal. The receipts from the three sessions of the anatomy totaled 187 guilders and 10 stivers. Public support was splendid. The money we earned will go to the purchase of fumigators, vessels, candles and sponges, and tobacco and beer for the attendants."

"And my fee, Doctor?"

He examined the partially completed painting for some time without answering, while I felt vulnerable. In my eagerness to do the picture I had started it before I had received my first payment of five hundred guilders, although I had insisted that I be paid in advance. I could hear myself breathing heavily and anxiously as I waited for his verdict, while I cursed the circumstances that made his words so important. He said slowly, "I see that you did follow your own course."

"Is that wrong?"

"That depends. It is not like *The Anatomy of Dr. Tulp.*"

"Did you want me to copy it?" I sounded shocked, as I was.

"It is not that. But the cadaver is so prominent."

"So are you." I hated myself for being forced to point this out, yet it was true. "Particularly your hands, Doctor. They are the center of the canvas."

He stared at them again and admitted grudgingly, "They are expressive."

"And they will be even more when I finish."

"I hope so. The first five hundred guilders will be delivered to you tomorrow. The second will depend on how the picture is finished."

I felt humiliated and yet relieved, and eager to change the subject. I asked, "What happened to the corpse? Did anyone mourn him?"

"Not publicly. No one would have dared." But when he saw my look of distress, he added less sharply, "However, we were not inhuman. On February 2, at nine o'clock in the evening, the body was interred with a fitting dignity in the South churchyard with a proper Christian burial."

That would have pleased my mother, I reflected, and as I remembered that I had painted those dear to me who had died, my father, mother, and wife, I wondered if that had kept them alive.

Dr. Deyman said, to make sure that I knew my place, "As I pointed out before, we are holding up the rest of your fee until we see how you finish our painting. We do not want an ugly picture."

IF YOU FEEL DESTRUCTIVE

If you feel destructive
Good
express it
Hostile is natural
walk into the shadow
and demolish it

—Stymean Karlen

BY the time I received my first fee for the anatomy picture the five hundred guilders were spent. I did not measure where this money went; my work absorbed me so fully I had no energy to consider my financial situation. I assumed that Daniel had used part of it for my painting necessities and Hendrickje the rest for our household needs. I was grateful that my assistant and my son did whatever I asked them to do and supplied me with oils, saw to it that my brushes were soft and pliant, that my canvas was placed in the best light and that it was properly covered at night for protection. I continued with my original concept of the composition and the anatomist and the anatomy remained the center of the picture. I also developed the color and contour of the corpse so that it was as potent as the dissection, so that even in death the man was still a powerful, vital figure. It took me two months of constant and arduous labor to finish this picture to my satisfaction.

After the delivery of the commission I was paid a hundred guilders by each of the eight men whose faces I had put into it, but not the second five hundred, as if the Surgeons' Guild was waiting to see what their members thought of *The Anatomy of Dr. Deyman,* and then Thyst came to my home. I felt he was using this situation for his own benefit, for he knew about the payment and his manner was demanding and abrupt.

He refused the chair I offered him, ignored my canvas of Jesus that I was studying in the hope I could resume painting it despite the absence of Spinoza, and declared, "Your ninety days of grace are over."

"Not yet, are they!" I exclaimed. "Have they passed that fast?"

"They are." His tone was positive. "I have kept a careful accounting, which is more than you have done."

I observed him again to decide how to reply but what I saw was not reassuring. His narrow green eyes, his pig-shaped snout, his long, pointed face seemed prepared to devour me. I also noted he had gained weight, and now there was gray in his hair—had I put it there? I wondered—but he strode about my studio impatiently and arrogantly. I thought of the fee I had been given for the faces in the anatomy painting and I said, "I can pay you a hundred guilders on account."

"No."

"Possibly . . . two hundred."

"You are ridiculous, Van Rijn. You owe me thousands of guilders and you offer a pittance. I need more just for interest and taxes."

There was the money I had hidden in the back of the canvas I was studying, but I could not touch it—I was saving it for a time when I might have nothing else—and I said, "I can only spare two hundred."

"You just received eight hundred guilders."

"The rest of it has to go to my other creditors."

"What about the first payment you received?"

"I used it for materials, oils, canvases, frames, food . . ."

He said skeptically, "I cannot accept your excuses any longer. Either you pay me a substantial amount or I will take action."

I was in no position to turn my back on him, as I longed to do, and so I replied, "Why not take one of my pictures as collateral?"

He did not seem interested, but when I insisted, although it was contrary to my own inclinations, he agreed to examine them briefly. When I showed him what I had done recently he disliked *The Slaughtered Ox,* he said it was revolting; he was not pleased

with my partially finished *Jacob Blessing the Sons of Joseph,* he found
the subject inappropriate for a pious Dutch household; and he did
not respond at all to my portraits of Titus, Hendrickje, and myself. They bored and exhausted him and my insistence that he
look at them exasperated him. After he viewed them superfi-
cially, he asked imperiously, "Have you sold anything else beside
the anatomy painting?"

I said brusquely, "That is a private matter."

"Not when you owe much of Amsterdam. I am aware of your
situation. Whose face were you doing when I entered? I want to
see it."

I showed it to him.

He regarded it intently, disturbed and puzzled, then said irritably, "The face is so dark. What I see of it. Who does it represent?"

"It is a portrait of Jesus."

He said critically, "It looks more like a Jewish rabbi."

I did not explain. I doubted that he would understand.

"Is it for sale?"

I had not thought of that possibility, I was involved in the face.

Before I could reply, not sure how to reply, he said harshly, "It
does not matter. No one will buy it." Having seen what he had
come to see, he added, "It is as I expected. You cannot pay what
you owe and you have no hope of doing so. Your affairs are in
a hopeless muddle. You spend far more than you earn." He made
that sound as if that were my biggest sin of all. "If you do not
sell your possessions soon and pay us, we will seize them. You
have pledged them as security for your debts and we are prepared
to go to the law to recover our money."

"Give me a few more months. Please?"

"No." Thyst's tone grew even more emphatic. "You have put
us off too long. And for the last time. All your creditors, even
Francen, who is your friend, are talking about instituting legal
action against you."

I cried out in desperation, "I could paint your portrait!"

He reminded me, "You said that my wife was not worthy of
your brush."

"I was angry, upset."

"It does not matter. I have commissioned Bol to paint us."

I was infuriated, I had to struggle to hold on to my temper, but I managed, the discussion was going badly as it was, and I said politely, "Perhaps you could consider something else from my brush. A landscape, possibly."

"If you were Titian I would think about it. I could always sell his work if I had to. But not yours—too much of it depreciates daily in value. As I said, if you do not make a substantial payment toward what you owe, we will put this matter into the hands of our lawyers."

"How substantial an amount do you require?"

"Two thousand guilders for each of your major creditors."

"Nothing less?" I asked incredulously. The amount was staggering.

"Nothing less!" he repeated severely. "Only then will we believe that you genuinely desire to pay your obligations to us."

When he was gone and I was about to return to my portrait of Jesus, the only work that I felt could comfort me in my dilemma, there was another knock on my door. Daniel, who had ushered in Thyst, admitted Ornia. This small, wizened creditor reminded me in his raspy voice that I had not paid him anything lately or delivered any paintings to him, although my six months were up and my obligations to him were increasing again. But he also refused to accept the pictures I showed him, even though that was part of our agreement. He said scornfully, "None of them are worth two hundred and fifty guilders." I replied that *The Anatomy of Dr. Deyman* proved that I was still in favor in Amsterdam and he retorted petulantly, "Deyman used you only because he could not obtain Lievens, Bol, or Flinck. Flinck is ill and Bol and Lievens were busy with other commissions. I want cash. That is my last word on the subject. If I am not paid soon I will attach whatever you own."

I contemplated visiting the Francens to find out of Thyst was right, Had they joined forces with my other creditors? If this was true, I knew I was in grave trouble. Then I decided this was too much of a burden to face in one day. I told Daniel and Hendrickje to collect all the bills I owed, while I sought to sustain myself with my work.

But now there was nothing of Jesus in me. I could not forgive my enemies as He had done. My hand felt lifeless as I applied it to the canvas and after a few aimless brush strokes I halted before I ruined what I had done already. I was staring out the window as the lamps on the Breestraat were turned on, hoping that the animated life on the steet would stir me out of my melancholy reverie, when Daniel and Hendrickje returned with a list of what I owed. My assistant added, "To the best of our knowledge, and as much as you have recorded."

I nodded and pushed their figures into my pocket without looking at them, while they withdrew, aware of my need for solitude. I reflected, An artist had to be a man of finance, a man of accounts, and acquainted with the law, but that has nothing to do with the consistency of paint, the colors of the palette, with my wrinkled face and the illusions of life, yet my eyes continued to look eagerly to make something out of existence. Except today, when I was too tired to even stand when I worked and I hated to paint sitting down. It was an inferior way of painting, painting was a physical activity, my exercise. I sat for a long time without moving, ignoring the cheese and beer that Hendrickje had brought me.

A face emerged from out of the mist surrounding me. I was recalling what Saskia said the first time we met. I was settling in Amsterdam and at a party in the house of Hendrick van Uylenburgh, my good friend and art dealer, he introduced me to his youthful Frisian cousin. And from the moment I set eyes on her I could not keep away from her. Saskia sat in the middle of the finely furnished parlor, expecting to be the center of attention. About twenty years old, I decided, flirtatious and animated, aware that she was the belle of the evening, proud of her silver bracelets, her cherubic features, her small yet womanly figure, her plump breasts and slender waist, her appealing round profile and high color.

She motioned for me to sit beside her and as I did, eagerly and yet anxiously, afraid that I would sound like a boor to such a cultivated and pretty young lady, she asked, "Are you the painter, Rembrandt van Rijn?"

"I am," I answered, puzzled. "Why do you ask?"

"Hendrick says you are the most respected artist in Amsterdam. That you have so many portrait commissions you cannot do them all. He tells me the saying is, 'Pray that he will finish and pay him.' That many important people have to wait a long time for their commissions."

"It is exaggerated." I tried to sound modest, although it was true.

"My cousin also said I must meet you and have you paint me."

"What do you think?"

She laughed and said, "Invite me to your studio and I will tell you."

When I did a few weeks later I was deeply in love with her.

Now Saskia was only a memory, but I had kept many portraits of her. Tonight I put my favorite one on my easel in the hope it would comfort me. It was my betrothal drawing and I read what I had inscribed on it; *"This is counterfeited after my wife as she was 21 years old the third day after we married on 8 June 1633."* Actually, we were wed a year later, but this was the moment I felt that we had become one.

Perhaps I had made her prettier than she was, I thought, as I gazed at this drawing; it was the most beautiful portrait I had ever done of Saskia. She wore an adorable large straw hat trimmed with flowers, and her face was tender and appealing, but this was the way I loved her.

These memories were painful to endure, and I did not want Hendrickje to see this sketch, a silverpoint on specially treated parchment, in a place of prominence, she was jealous of my wife. I put it into my closet with other precious works I stored there, and stuffed the bills into my pocket, still unable to examine them. I wondered how far I had drifted from what I had wanted to be when I had wed Saskia, how faithful I had remained to the ideal of the artist that I had set for myself secretly. I gazed again at the work I was painting, in the hope of gaining strength from them, but they did not suffice. They were what I desired to do but I was too tired and depressed to feel them.

The next day I visited Wilhem Beghen to find out if he had any news about my investment, but he kept me waiting in his outer office so long I felt that he did not want to speak to me. And when I was admitted to his presence he was brief to me, even curt. He said that he had only a moment to spare, that I must never drop in unannounced again—as if, from now on, I thought, he must be prepared for my visits—but inform him in advance, at least a week in advance, so he could furnish me with the right information. He was amazed that I suggested he return the money I had given him. "It is invested," he said in a tone of horror. "No, I have not heard anything about the two ships since they sailed. It is a long voyage to the East Indies and spices are difficult to obtain. That is why the price is so high when the voyage is successful. And, of course, there is always the danger of piracy, shipwreck, and other disasters." He sounded as pessimistic as he had been optimistic when I had given him the money and as he led me to the door, eager to be rid of me, I asked, "Is there any way I can determine the date I can have my profits?" and he regarded me as if I were mad and cried out, "You do not trust me!" I replied instantly, "But I do!" Although I no longer did. He closed the door on me so abruptly that I wondered, What had gone wrong with my investment?

I was too agitated to go home, and so I turned to the one man I felt might be able to resolve my tangled affairs, my lawyer, Louis Crayer.

To my relief, when I sent my name in to him, I was ushered into his office at once, ahead of several people who were waiting to see him, and he greeted me cordially and made me feel at home immediately.

His office, which was in the same district as Beghen's, had an excellent view of the harbor. From his large casement windows I saw a fleet of ships, newly arrived from the East Indies, and busy, crowded docks on which huge cargoes were being unloaded. Some day perhaps mine might be, too, I hoped; I had reveled in this incessant activity when I had made Amsterdam my permanent home. Crayer sat behind a neat, simple desk and faced the waterfront, and on the wall behind him hung four of my etchings of the Dutch countryside, which he loved as much as I did.

His tailored trousers and doublet expressed the pleasure he found in fine clothes, but it was his features that attracted me. He was forty, but his skin was still unwrinkled, his hair still brown, and I liked his wide forehead, his high cheekbones, his strong nose, and his carefully trimmed mustache and goatee. It was the appearance of a man I could almost trust. He was meditative as he greeted me and offered me a chair, yet his attention was concentrated, as if he cared about what I said.

I apologized for bursting in on him, but explained that my need was great, and he replied that he was glad he could see me promptly, and I realized that he was not surprised, that he had expected me. I told him about the new demands of my creditors —he had been my lawyer since I had inherited Saskia's estate— and he listened intently. When I finished he did not chide me as most people would have, but asked to see my bills. "All of them." After he examined them carefully and totaled them, he said, "Have you ever been able to assess what your collection is worth?"

"Are you referring to my own work?"

"Yes. But also what you purchased of other artists. Your sculpture, your collection of Italian and Dutch art, furniture, other possessions."

I shrugged helplessly and did not reply. I was overwhelmed at the thought of trying to assess the value of everything I owned.

"Do you have any record of what you paid for your things? You also possess Dutch, German, and Italian etchings that must be worth a large amount. Your collection of Durer etchings, for instance, is valuable. But you should know this." For an instant he sounded annoyed at me.

I rubbed my chin, feeling my prickly beard under my calloused hand, and said slowly, "I guess I paid about forty thousand guilders for my collection." I hurried to add, so I would appear less extravagant, "But, of course, I bought my things over a period of twenty years."

"I am aware of that. But your creditors may be less considerate."

"Do you think I should sell them?"

"You may have to. Before they do. But I doubt that you will get forty thousand on the open market. Once buyers learn that you are in need, they will offer as little as possible, perhaps only half, about twenty thousand guilders. But that might take care of what you owe."

"I do not think they will sue." I sounded more sure than I felt.

"I would not assume that." Crayer stood up suddenly—just my height now, he had a long torso but short legs—and he stared out the window at the bustling harbor. "Not all our ships come home." For a sickening moment I thought he was referring to my speculation and that he had knowledge of the result, then I realized he was commenting on the state of business, for he added, "Several of your creditors have had unexpected losses in the overseas trade. They are not as inclined to wait as they once were." He picked up the bills I had handed him and pointed out, "As far as I can tell, you owe about twenty-five thousand guilders. Even if you sold everything you own, you will still be in debt."

"Then my situation is hopeless," I cried out in my anguish.

He replied more gently, "Not hopeless. Not yet. But difficult."

I was grateful that he still did not scold me and I joined him at the window and whispered, "If I could only work without these distractions."

"That is why we must try to find a remedy. Obviously you cannot pay all that you owe in the foreseeable future."

Once again I felt lost but he had grown only more thoughtful.

"I will talk to your creditors' lawyers," he said. "We may be able to compromise."

"Thank you."

"Thank me when I have accomplished something. How is Titus?"

"He is beginning to grow into manhood."

"You must protect your son's interests."

As he said that, I knew what I must do. "Would you be his

guardian? I have been thinking about that for some time."

"I would be honored. But there is time for that. First, we must solve your present difficulties. Ultimately, they concern your son."

He walked me to the door. Suddenly I had a feeling of panic, as if once he shut the door on me, I would be isolated again, alone. I paused and asked, "What about my bills?"

"I will hold them for the time being. So I will know what I am talking about when I meet with their lawyers. Do not worry. I will find some way to keep you working. That is more important than anything else."

He sounded reassuring, yet grim, and I saw a new expression in his eyes, fierce and steady, as if a veil had been removed from them and he was determined to penetrate the tangled gloom of my life. "You are kind."

"Not kind, but not a fool either. Whatever I can do to aid your hand I will. I hate waste. For you to halt now would be a dreadful waste."

"What about your own fee?"

"We will discuss that when your affairs are settled satisfactorily."

I doubted they would ever be but as he opened the door I had another question I had to ask, "Did you see the young man I sent you, Spinoza?"

"Yes. I am representing him in his suit against his half-sister."

"Can he win?"

"It is possible. If the argument concerned only his rights to a share of his father's estate, I doubt there would be much difficulty. But his relatives claim that he is an atheist, and you know what a harsh accusation that is to fight. People have been hung for less."

"Do you think he is?"

"I am a lawyer, not a theologian. Fortunately, the suit I have brought in the young man's behalf will be tried in civil court." He pulled an official-looking document from his pocket and informed me, "I will read you my brief."

I listened carefully as he did.

Whereas Bento de Spinoza, as sole heir to an important capital left by his mother, is a preferred creditor of the estate left by his father, and whereas instead of insisting on his preference, said Bento de Spinoza has already paid off diverse other debts presented against the estate, therefore he should now be recognized as the rightful heir of what remains, and be allowed to take possession thereof.

I said, "He never told me any of these particulars."

"He is not one to talk about himself. I had to force it out of him, and only because I needed it for his defense."

Crayer took me by the arm to lead me out and I asked, "Did he tell you that I was using him as a model?"

"No!" He was surprised and he halted suddenly and said, "All he told me was that you recommended me. What subject are you using him for?"

"Jesus."

"Oh!"

"You do not approve?"

"Would that matter? Would that stop you?"

I smiled and said, "At least you have not said, Deplorable."

"How could I? Only you know how you will finally use him. Meanwhile, I will indicate your wish to pay your creditors but that you need more time. I will tell them that it is foolish to push you too hard, that they might get nothing."

"Do you think they will listen?"

"If they are rational."

I doubted that, just as I doubted that I would see Spinoza again.

Yet as Crayer said good-bye to me, he added, "I think the young man respects you. He mentioned your name with genuine warmth."

"Perhaps he thinks of me a little as a father."

"That is not likely. He does not sound sentimental."

"Give him my regards when you see him again."

"I will."

HOW CAN I QUESTION

How can I question
How can I not question

When appearance
And disappearance
Come at the same time

As the sun leaves the sky
The moon comes in

The loss and the find
Are a profound metaphor
That fits everything

—Stymean Karlen

I RETURNED to my portrait of Jesus, determined to paint Him as I visualized Him, whether or not I had a model that satisfied me. My meeting with Crayer lessened my anxieties about my finances and I could work once more. I reminded myself that I had painted many faces out of my imagination and I resolved to do this again. I did not like feeling dependent on anyone else. It was one of the reasons I had become a painter. But as I spent the next week with the canvas I grew confused.

There were still moments when I saw Spinoza as Jesus, but there were other times when Jesus became Spinoza. Yet I knew that was impossible. Even so, they were inextricably interwoven in my mind. Then I thought of Jesus as a rabbi, although I realized that it was unlikely now that Spinoza would ever become one. I asked myself: Should I ignore my original conception of Jesus? Should I paint Spinoza as Spinoza?

That increased my confusion and my brush faltered. This was

rare for me and I felt stricken with a painful disease: uncertainty. Then I remembered something that Crayer had said:

"Only you will know how you will finally use him."

With this in mind, I gained assurance and resumed my painting. I focused intensely on my memories of Spinoza and gradually he seemed to stare at me from out of the glass panel in my front window. The dusk was falling and I lit all my candles to see him clearly. That was not sufficient for my purpose; my studio darkened and I rubbed out what I had done on my study of Jesus, although it represented much work. Now I painted the background black so that the light would illuminate his face strongly. His features flooded my imagination and appeared to float on to the canvas. Then he was not youthful, and certainly not boyish, but possessed a new mature capacity for suffering and compassion. I thought, If this is true I might paint Spinoza appropriately after all. His pale olive skin, his dark hair, his fine head seemed surrounded with a halo. This worried me; it did not fit my present view of him. Yet his glance was trustful, but I knew this was my imagination—he had never given me the feeling he trusted me. Until he did, I doubted I could illuminate his features the way I desired.

I heard Hendrickje calling me for dinner. Spinoza's face vanished and I realized that I had been dreaming. My brush dropped from my hand as if it were paralyzed and I sat there feeling that my imagination, which I trusted usually, had betrayed me. I emerged from my reverie only when my son entered my studio to summon me to the table.

Crayer's comments reminded me of my obligations to him and I regarded Titus with more attention. I found him an attractive fourteen, but I was afraid that he had inherited his mother's delicate constitution. I took him by the hand to protect him and he was surprised, since such emotion from me was unusual, I was not one to express affection openly.

It gave him the courage to ask, "Papa, what was my mother like?"

I said, "This is not the time to discuss that. We will be at the table. Hendrickje will be serving us. It will not be appropriate."

"She cannot tell me. She did not know her."

I could not judge whether this was a criticism of her or a simple statement of fact, and I said, "Titus, that is not her fault."

"But my mother was an heiress."

And Hendrickje had come into my house, I reflected, because a friend of mine had recommended her as a housekeeper. At first I had fancied that she resembled Saskia, her features were also soft and round, but soon I realized they differed in many ways. Saskia had possessed the extravagant tastes of an aristocrat; Hendrickje was content with the simple needs of a humble servant girl. My wife had brought me a fortune, my mistress only herself. Yet Hendrickje kept my affairs better; Saskia had needed many servants and had been indifferent to the running of the house. I motioned to Titus that he sit and I joined him. I put my hand gently on his and I said, "Your mother was a pretty woman."

"Prettier than Hendrickje?"

"She was like a pink rose while Hendrickje is like a brown leaf."

"But you loved my mother more?"

"I love them both."

"You told me my mother was the prettiest woman you knew."

"She was very pretty." Titus' severity and persistence troubled me. I wondered if he had a grievance against my mistress. "And so is Hendrickje. In her own way."

"You married my mother. Not Hendrickje."

I said sternly, "You know that is impossible."

"Papa, is it truly?"

"Truly. If I did, we would lose half of your mother's estate. We must not keep Hendrickje waiting," I added, although Saskia had done that often to me, having no sense of time or money. "I will tell you more about your mother at the right time. Now you must treat Hendrickje as your mother. She loves you as if you were her own son."

"But I am not her real son."

"Never say that."

"It is true. You always say that I must tell the truth."

"It is half true. I will explain later." I felt clumsy and I stood up but when he followed me reluctantly, I asked, "Son, what is wrong?"

"Nothing. I asked about my mother. You brought in Hendrickje. Papa, do you think we will see Spinoza again?"

"I doubt it."

"I thought he liked us."

"Perhaps, but that does not mean he will want to see us again." Titus was confused but I did not explain. I led him downstairs without another word, anxious about how he would behave to Hendrickje.

He was casual. He ate all of the smoked fish and cheese she served us and I was relieved by his appetite and manner. Then Daniel informed me, "Master, I hear that Spinoza has returned to Amsterdam."

"I did not know he was away," I replied, with apparent indifference.

"He went to Ouwerkerk to prepare his defense for the rabbis."

"That is his business, not ours." I concentrated on the cheese.

"I still believe he wants to model for you, despite what he said."

I was curious about that but I acted as if it were of no consequence. I could no longer express a desire to paint him, I was in no mood to be rejected, and so I changed the subject and praised Hendrickje's cooking.

Later, when I reached across our spacious bed to caress her, she recoiled from me, wailing, "Titus wants to know what his mother was like and I cannot tell him! I do not know! Do you think he will forgive me?"

"There is nothing to forgive. I told him."

"I have tried to take her place but now I know that it is impossible."

"Calm yourself. He is only a child and asks childish things."

"He is growing up. Soon he will know about our relationship."

"He knows already. It is your person that matters, not your position."

"I doubt that," she cried mournfully. "I think your creditors are growing harsh because of your situation with me. It offends them."

"The lack of money offends them even more. Besides, Crayer

thinks he can reach a settlement with them so you must put that out of your mind."

"With bill collectors at our door almost every day," she whispered to herself, "and they are not good but cruel and eager to punish us."

"True, perhaps, but we do not have to punish each other." I drew her close to me and gradually my affection eased her agitation and she did her best to express her love for me, and I was satisfied.

Several days later Spinoza appeared at my door. Daniel admitted him, surprised but pleased, and led him into the reception room, for we were finishing breakfast in the kitchen. Hendrickje and Titus joined them at once and welcomed Spinoza as if he were a long-lost friend.

That was ridiculous, I thought, but I was also gratified by his reappearance, although I was determined to hide this feeling. I waited until I finished my herring and cheese before greeting him, to show that his arrival was not important. I recalled that he had broken his word to me, that a long time had passed since I had seen him, and that the willingness to model must come as much from him as from me. I started to scold him for his unexcused absence and Daniel halted me.

My assistant said, while Hendrickje and Titus smiled at the silent young man who today looked grave beyond his years, "Master, Baruch will not tell you, but he has been afraid to sit for you."

"Because he will fail me," I growled.

"Because he thinks that it will harm you. His position grows more precarious with the synagogue each day."

Spinoza said, "Daniel, I would prefer if you did not mention this."

"But," I said, "I should know if you are in trouble with the rabbis."

"That is not the way I would express it."

"How would you express it, young man?"

Spinoza was silent.

"Why did you come back here?"

"I am not sure."

"Was it anything that Louis Crayer said?"

"He gave me your regards. He was very kind to me."

I repeated, "Is that why you came back?"

Now the look on his face said, Do not ask me why I returned, accept it or not, but do not ask.

Hendrickje said, "You must be hungry. Would you like some herring?"

Titus volunteered, "It is good. Papa just ate some."

"Thank you, but I have eaten already."

I asked sternly, "Where have you been all these weeks?"

"Much of the time I was in Ouwerkerk. My father and mother and a brother and sister are buried in the Jewish cemetery there."

Daniel stated, "No Jew is allowed to be buried in Amsterdam."

"I know," I replied gruffly. "It is a barbarous edict."

Encouraged by my words, Spinoza added with a burst of feeling, "I wanted to pray for my family, and for their understanding. It is difficult to think rationally amid the tumult of Amsterdam."

"What about Van den Ende's home?" I asked jealously.

"It is filled with so many people coming and going that reflection is impossible there, too."

"You could have done that here."

Surprised, he said, "I thought you wanted me only as a model."

"That is true. But sitting would allow you time to meditate."

Daniel asked, "Have you given up living at Van den Ende's?"

"No. But most of the time I go there only when I need money for my bread, to teach Latin and Hebrew, the learned languages."

Hendrickje said suddenly, "Titus, offer the gentleman a chair."

Titus obeyed, giving him one of my favorite Spanish chairs.

But Spinoza only sat down when I and Hendrickje did, and then reluctantly, as if, now that he had made the decision to approach me, he was not certain he should remain, looking somber and withdrawn.

Daniel asked, "What happened when you met with the rabbis?"

Spinoza was silent until I said, "We will not criticize you," and Hendrickje nodded her head in agreement while Titus sat closer to him, to show that he approved of whatever this friend did.

Spinoza spoke softly, "Master Rembrandt, you asked me to settle my situation with the rabbis, but at the moment it is more unsettled than before."

Daniel said, "I heard that you met with Morteira."

"Yes. Several times."

"What did he say?"

For a moment I did not think that he would tell us, but when I motioned for him to continue and we all appeared sympathetic, he said, "Morteira said I am causing the synagogue considerable embarrassment."

Daniel suggested, "Such as living with Van den Ende, a freethinker?"

"That is one of the things that troubles him."

"And that you have attended Christian prayer meetings."

"That is untrue. I do not believe in their teachings either."

Hendrickje was shocked while Titus was puzzled, yet neither of them withdrew or spoke, as if his presence mattered more than his views.

He added, "While Van den Ende is unorthodox in his views, he is not an atheist, he insists that his daughter practice his Roman Catholic faith."

"Even so," said Daniel, "his school has a bad name in Amsterdam and you do not improve your reputation by teaching there."

But I, who knew Van den Ende, sensed this was not what troubled the rabbis the most. Manasseh ben Israel and Dr. Bonus were friendly with this teacher; I had met them at his home; it must be something else, something far more vital to Morteira. I suggested, remembering what he had implied, "Young man, is it your ideas that truly concern the rabbis?"

"Yes," he admitted slowly. "Because I do not agree with their teachings. I try to reason with them, to show them that God is not a personal being, but the world itself, that God is an all-embracing essence that inheres in all that exists, and they say I scorn the faith of my fathers."

Daniel said sorrowfully, "Because you scorn them. You were their best pupil. They expected you to become an illustrious rabbi."

"I would prefer to be a scholar."

(243)

Daniel asked anxiously, "Have they offered any remedy?"

"Manasseh ben Israel seemed willing to compromise if I kept my views to myself, but he is in England, and Morteira, who dominates the synagogue now, believes in the exact letter of the law. He says I must stop asking questions, attend services, and accept the ritual."

Daniel suggested, "You could keep your views to yourself."

"If no one asks me. But I will not lie," Spinoza said proudly.

"What will happen if you do not accede to these demands?"

"I will be summoned before the court of rabbis for trial."

And I, I thought, before the court of bankruptcy. I asked, "How much time have you to answer?"

"A few weeks."

"Then there is time for you to sit."

"If you still want me." He sounded surprised at that possibility.

"Was that not the reason you came today?"

He glanced at my new portrait of Titus, which I had hung in a place of honor since my son had asked about his mother, and said, "Why not use your boy for Jesus? As you paint him, he has the face for it."

"That is for me to decide. Besides, he is too young. My models have nothing to do with my personal feelings." I had been observing Spinoza all during the conversation in the hope he would reveal the expression and emotion I could use, and I was growing dubious. There were signs of suffering in his eyes but I missed the tenderness and the compassion that had attracted me earlier. Yet he appeared more eager to sit than before, and so I motioned for him to follow me to the studio.

Hendrickje was relieved, although still confused, and Titus wanted to help him sit, but I refused his aid and ordered him and Daniel to arrange my materials. I was very stern and they did this silently, obediently.

I had to find new ways to paint him now. I scraped off everything I had done before, particularly the work I had painted when I had depended solely on my imagination, and began all over. I felt that I had to consider more than Jesus; I had to use whatever was in Spinoza that had attracted me. He wore a white collar around his neck. Why? I asked. Was it an ornament? To show that he was still a Jew? As a propitiatory act? Was there any idea connected with it? The material set off his long, slender face and suggested a rabbinical student. I ordered him to take it off.

He did that reluctantly, saying, "I am not an ascetic, it is stupid to believe that sadness is good, that joy is evil. A wise man uses all the things of life and uses them to the full."

"Will you be quiet!"

"You have not changed," he said.

It did not sound like a compliment. I grumbled, "You have."

"How?" All at once he was interested, animated, eager to talk.

"You have suffered and it shows. We must work as long as the daylight lasts. Nothing is more interesting to human beings than human beings. I must paint your flesh tones more solidly." He seemed to be listening attentively, his head lifted just the way I wanted to paint it, and I continued, to keep him in this position, as I painted freely now, with quick, bold strokes of my brush. "Painters have exalted the beauty of Jesus' face, as if it were an idealistic Greek face they derived from classical sculpture, but he was a rabbi, introspective, young, humble, and understanding."

"Master, are you trying to convince me?"

"I am trying to convince myself."

"Do not plead for me anymore. It will do no good and they will not listen to you whatever you say."

My brush halted in midair and I scowled and shouted, "Who told you?"

"Amsterdam is full of malicious tongues. Why did you defend me, anyhow, since we hold contrary beliefs?"

I did not answer. It was pointless to explain an intuition, a feeling, an effort to illuminate my existence.

"I am not even sure why you paint me."

"Your flesh tones please me."

He said, more to himself than to me, "Morteira is wrong. I did not say the universe is callous, I said it was indifferent to man. Man is just another modest display of nature's works, not a superior object, and religion is an ostentation, essential however, for those who need it."

This was too much for me and I stopped completely and retorted, "But you do not need it, young man."

"No," he replied proudly.

"That is arrogant."

"It is rational."

We were too far apart after all, I thought, but his face was so alive and animated I could not resist it. Even as my reason said I should stop, I laid another layer of paint over his curly black hair, which was longer than I remembered it. I must go deep around his eyes, they were the essence of this youth, then do the fabric of his cloak. His flesh was soft, however strong his ideas. As I applied my paint more thickly, I told myself that painting was not a rational activity; it did not depend on reason but feeling, and there was no way to measure its value.

"I can tell, Master Rembrandt, that you do not agree with me."

"I am a painter, not a scholar."

"You have a library. I saw it in your reception room."

"Fifteen books. I do not have time to read, except the Bible. We must not waste any more time. I must use the sun while it is here."

Then, for an unmeasured time, neither of us spoke. A face emerged out of the darkness of the canvas that I felt looked more like Spinoza than Jesus, and yet, had some of both.

I paused to change brushes and he asked, "Are you tired?"

I saw that he was, for he shifted awkwardly, and since I did not want him to feel uncomfortable I said, "Yes. We had better stop."

He stood up, stretching his limbs with a deep sigh, and asked, "Do you like what you have done?"

"It is too early to tell."

"After all these months. And you said that before."

"I have to begin all over. I was on the wrong track."

I expected him to express disgust, or, at the least, dismay and disappointment. Instead, he asked quietly, "When do you want me to sit again?"

"In a week." I knew it would seem like an eternity. I could have toiled morning, noon, and night on this picture, but I did not want to tire him, or to make him feel too important. "Can I depend on that?"

"I will come as long as circumstances permit me."

I could understand that. In my fever of working I had forgotten about my financial difficulties, but now, without a paintbrush in my hand, they were vivid in my mind. "Good, I will expect you a week from today. Promptly. At ten in the morning. So we get the best light."

He nodded and said softly, "I should be prompt. I have decided to remain in Amsterdam and face my situation, however it turns out."

I DO NOT BELIEVE

I do not believe that a photograph
can be taken
of anyone whole
Only of what shows
Oh and how little that is
Only I know

It would take a
Rembrandt
to paint into the face
what is under the soil
of that person
and under the root

And what is now beginning
under all that
And what has died there
that is so paintable
And is still not all
Oh Rembrandt just saw
something else

—Stymean Karlen

JUST before Spinoza was scheduled to return for his next sitting, Crayer visited me with what he called "an interesting proposal." He met me in my studio so that he could view my latest work while we talked, and he explained, "Thyst told me that he would allow you a year's time to settle your obligation to him if you gave him a thousand guilders now."

Startled, I shifted uneasily in my chair, I did not trust the sound of this, while Crayer glanced at my work to avoid influencing my reply. After I collected my senses, I asked, "What about the other creditors?"

"He says that he can convince them to put off the proceedings."

"But I cannot give all of them a thousand guilders. I am not sure that I can even give him that much money."

"Thyst does not want you to. This payment is to be to him alone and is to be a secret."

"Suppose you tell the other creditors of this proposition?"

"He will deny it. He will say that I fabricated it. Nothing has been put in writing. No one can prove that he made such a proposal."

I pondered what to do while Crayer admired my newest etchings of the Dutch countryside. Finally, still undecided, I said, "It would take a severe effort to raise a thousand guilders." I was thinking of the eight hundred I had stored in the back of my canvas. "And it sounds like the wrong thing to do. He is proposing that I participate in swindling the others. Crayer, what do you advise?"

He shrugged and said, "I cannot advise. I can only tell you what Thyst proposed. This is a decision that only you can make."

"If I do not agree with his proposal what are the alternatives?"

"He will try to seize your possessions. Drive you into bankruptcy."

"Can he succeed?"

"It is possible. You did sign them over. But I could transfer this property to Titus. Put the title to the house in his name."

"Will that protect us from Thyst and the other creditors?"

"It might. That will depend on the authorities."

His tone was noncommittal and I asked, still searching for a solution, "Crayer, do you think that Thyst can be trusted?"

"Rembrandt, do you trust him?"

"No."

I told Crayer I would give him my reply to Thyst's proposal in a few days and I was grateful that he accepted that attitude without comment, and said, "Whatever you decide to do, I will support you. Good luck and may God bless you!" Then he was gone without having given me a clue as to his own opinion about this matter.

So, as I often did when confronted with a decision that perplexed me, I decided to take a long walk into the Dutch countryside near the city in the hope that the better air and more relaxed surroundings would help me find the right answer. I did not tell anyone in the household about Thyst's offer, but simply that I was going to sketch and since it was one of my favorite pastimes no one questioned me.

I was about to leave when Titus asked, "Papa, may I go with you? I will not say a word when you draw. I will be as quiet as a mouse."

I doubted this was possible, but I was pleased with his wish to be with me and I said, "Come along."

Daniel was leaving to attend weekly services at the synagogue and to find out what was happening to Spinoza, while Hendrickje was going shopping for dinner, and it would be better for Titus not to be left alone, and so I told them, "We are going for my favorite walk along the Diemer Dike to the Zuider Zee, and then, if we do not get tired, to the banks of the Amstel and Bullewijik rivers."

Titus assured me, as we left the house, "Papa, I will not get tired."

He tried to match my short, choppy stride, which was still longer than his, as we walked by the broad canal and over the hog-back bridge and past the open air market where Hendrickje did much of her shopping. I saw many picturesque faces there that I thought of as Jewish but I did not stop to sketch them; this was a day I resolved to devote to my son. My pace was fast for Titus and he did not have the breath to talk as we left the rough stone paving of the city and reached the earth path that ran beside the seawall and marked the start of the countryside. It was a cool but sunny day, good for walking, the air brisk and refreshing. I breathed deeply and he imitated me, striving to be grownup, although he was breathless. I realized that he was determined not to complain even if he collapsed from our exertions, and suddenly I slowed up and stopped at the dike.

He said, "I like being with you without anybody else along."

"I thought you were fond of Daniel's company."

Now that Titus had his breath back he was full of talk. "I am. When he does not lord it over me because he is older. But you are not his papa, although he acts like you are sometimes."

"Are you jealous of him?" I asked, amused and yet concerned.

"Not now," he asserted stoutly, "or of Hendrickje. You have never taken them here, have you?"

"There has not been any reason to," I replied, but that seemed to please him, for his fingers tightened around my calloused hand.

His eyes widened fearfully as a wave crashed against the dike and part of the sea swept over the wall and almost reached our feet. He cried out, "Papa, have you ever seen a break in the dike?"

I pulled him back so that he would not get wet and said, "Once. It was caused by a storm that came from the northwest. Part of the city was flooded. I thought the sea would engulf everything."

"Were you frightened?"

"It was overwhelming. I felt so insignificant, even trivial."

"I think some water is squirting through a crack now."

There was spray splashing over the dike, but it appeared secure. I dismissed this matter from my mind, for we still had a long walk ahead of us before we reached my destination. But I tried to heed Titus' opinions. "This dike needs repairs. You are observant, son."

He smiled, this was one of the best compliments I could give anyone, and he followed me eagerly. I did not pause until we reached the banks of the Amstel river, one of my favorite sketching haunts. Again I strode too fast to permit much talking, but I was curious to see how observant my son was here. This should test his vision.

He took in the horizon, which was as flat as the eye could see, with an anxious but puzzled gaze, as if he was eager and determined to observe everything that I did, but was not sure what to mention first. He asked, "Papa, did you bring your pencil and pad?"

"I always do. Hendrickje sewed pockets in all my cloaks so that I can carry my sketching materials without having to remember to take them."

"She told me. She is proud of her sewing. I am sure she will teach that to Cornelia but I am too grown up for that."

Now I had a pad and pencil in my hand, aware of my inevitable need, for I saw a man preparing to bathe in the Amstel and as he crouched to feel the temperature of the water—it was cold even in May—I sketched him, for his posture was animated, dramatic, and a little afraid. I saw a row of windmills across the river and as they moved in unison I drew them. Titus watched me intently, his eyes glued to my hands as if they were performing magic, although he had seen me sketch many times, but never in these circumstances, and I said, "You try, son."

Titus took the drawing materials so tentatively I wondered if the lessons I had given him had been wasted. In his hesitant fingers the sketching pencil looked like such a fragile instrument.

I added, "In drawing the greatest skill is often that of omission. Suggest as much as state. Not everything has to be put in."

"You do it so easily," he complained.

"After a lifetime of practice. It only looks easy. It is not." The fresh air had erased Titus' pallor and now there was color on his cheeks that heightened the beauty of his long curly hair and its reddish tints, and I longed to draw him with the pencil between his fingers. But first, he must do what I ordered. When he finished drawing the nearest windmill, it reminded me of my style when I had been a child. I did not judge it critically, I felt that would be unfair, but expressed my approval of his effort and said that he must sign it so we would know who had done this work. He did this with a flourish, writing, "Titus van Rijn" in a clear, proud script, and dated it, "1656," as was my custom.

Seeing my pleasure, I was smiling, he asked more boldly, "Papa, why do you avoid drawing Amsterdam? You never depict the city in your work."

"It is a question of taste."

"You do not like Amsterdam?"

"I love it!" I exclaimed. "But that does not mean I have to draw it!"

"Why not? Most people say it is the greatest city in the world."

"One of the greatest," I replied quietly, so I would not sound as if I were correcting him. "It has immense vitality, it is very large, it takes two hours to walk from one end of the semicircular canals to the other. When I settled here, I was fascinated by its excitement."

"Has that changed?" Titus was disappointed by my implied criticism.

"I realize now that some of its splendor is an illusion. That this town, however profitable it is for merchants, is built on marshes, that the weight of the city is carried by wooden piles, that moldering pine trees prop up the most flourishing trade center in Europe. It is a sobering thought. We live in a world built on mud. Shaky, soft mud."

"Yet you see many interesting faces on the street, Papa."

Titus was so enthusiastic I agreed. The bather had left, deciding that the river was too chilly, and when I put away my pad and pencil, so did my son. The breeze was gone and the windmills were motionless, but Titus was still attentive. I said, "We have given refuge to many, not just Jews, but Huguenots, English dissenters, Germans, Flemings."

"You approve of that, Papa? Some people say we are being overrun, that anyone can open a place of worship in Amsterdam. Even Catholics."

I added, "Also Lutherans, Calvinists, Mennonites, Remonstrants."

"Then why is our friend, Spinoza, in trouble?"

He waited intently and I realized that my reply mattered to him, so I tried to be accurate. "Belief in God is allowed in Holland but not disbelief. According to some of our Jewish neighbors and their Christian friends, Spinoza does not believe in God, and thus, must be punished."

"Do you think that he does?"

"How can I tell? Do we ever know what someone else believes?"

"Is that why you do not draw Amsterdam? You do not believe in it?"

"Much of it is ostentation, man-made, to display power and wealth, when actually, everything in our country is dominated by water. We are a nation crisscrossed by canals, rivers, ditches, dikes, and mud. Yet the country is good for a painter. The flat land gives a feeling of space. Trees, church spires, windmills,

(253)

farmhouses are vivid against our Dutch landscape and they are a natural part of it."

We were almost home when Titus asked, "What did my mother die of?"

I felt I could not put him off this time. We were also near the synagogue but I ignored the members who were leaving, although I was curious whether Spinoza was one of them. "Inflammation of the lungs."

"Not of childbirth?"

"Who told you that?" I was shocked.

"It does not matter. I thought maybe she died giving birth to me."

"And that you killed her?" I was angry now.

Titus nodded slowly, too emotional to speak.

"What nonsense!" I exploded. "Whoever told you that lied. You were born on September twenty-second, sixteen forty-one, and she died many months later, on June fourteenth, sixteen forty-two." I had a poor head for figures but some dates I could not forget.

"Was my birth difficult?"

"Only in that she could not nurse you. But Saskia was proud of you. We had lost two daughters in childbirth and when you lived we named you after her favorite sister, Tita, who had passed away the year before. The two daughters we lost and her weak lungs sapped her strength."

The sun set, the dusk fell on the street, and lights began to appear in the houses, but Titus said suddenly, "That worried me, Papa."

"You do not have to worry any longer. The illness that killed her started long before you were born. She was sickly for many years but she had such a good complexion that she looked healthier than she was."

I was relieved that Titus seemed satisfied with my explanation, for he asked eagerly yet anxiously, "Papa, do I look like my mother?"

"Yes, indeed. You have her eyes, forehead, and coloring."

"I always thought that my mother was a princess with her

golden hair, especially from the way you painted and drew her."

I did not tell him that occasionally I had idealized her, to express my love for her, something I sought to avoid in my work now. I said, "Son, she was my princess, too, but her hair was more of a reddish brown, like yours, although she tinted it yellow, to please herself."

I wondered about this awakening of interest in his mother, but he did not explain. When we reached our house, he said, "Papa, I am so hungry I could make a meal of bread, cheese, and a pickled herring. I hope Hendrickje was as lucky with her shopping as we were with our walk."

When Spinoza arrived promptly for his sitting the next day I was prepared to spend all our time working. Daniel had told me that he had seen him in the synagogue, which indicated that his friend was still a member of the congregation, and I was hopeful that his differences with the rabbis had been resolved amicably, that no further discussions would be necessary. Thus, I was surprised and annoyed when he entered my studio with a troubled expression. But he did not tell me what was bothering him; he greeted me politely and I responded the same way, determined to push on with my work. He was my model, nothing else, I told myself, I must treat him casually and concentrate on his appearance.

His posture was better, more relaxed, as if he had learned from his previous sittings, and he had discarded the formal clothes of the rabbinical student. Instead of a stiff white collar he wore a soft brown velvet collar, which was more paintable, a casual fur hat that I might have expected to see on my own head, and a long gray cloak that I could have worked in. This time I put my canvas aside—I had just seen something in his face that had escaped me until now.

I drew him three ways: as a possible Christ, a Messiah; then as I had viewed him the first time I had met him, as a potential rabbi; and finally, as he looked today, a Jewish student in search of his soul. The light was good despite the morning mist and the glow of the sun that emerged from the haze suggested a halo around his head, but I was tired of this conception and I discarded it. Yet this reminded me that in this work, at least, I had to paint Jesus as much as I had to paint Spinoza.

I returned to my canvas, shifting it back into position without a word while he sat motionless, unquestioning. I thought, I did not want to be a theologian or a philosopher or another Leonardo or a Michelangelo, I wanted simply to capture the essences of a face, a stone, a tree. Nothing more, nothing less, and, I added in my mind, nothing else.

In the meantime Spinoza did not say a word.

When, hours later, I finished the day's work, I felt I had come closer to the conception I sought, but that I had not yet found it completely.

Spinoza had sat a long time without stirring but he did not complain. After he stretched his limbs to remove his stiffness, he spoke for the first time in hours, asking, "May I see what you have done?"

He had been such a good model I could not refuse him, although the face was only half-done and I was still uncertain about the background and the clothes. "If you want to. Although it is far from finished."

He gazed at it intently, yet when he made no comment, although I did not want any criticism, I found myself asking, "What do you think of it?"

"You do not want my opinion," he answered. "You want my approval."

That was true but I did not like his saying so.

"Is this the way you see me?"

"It is the way I see you as Jesus. As far as I have gone."

"You make me look better than I am."

"Be patient," I said sarcastically. "If you insist I can still paint you as the devil."

He laughed. "That might be more appropriate for some people." Then he was sober again, as serious as I had ever seen him. "But it is not for me to tell you what to paint, just as I would not want you to tell me what to think." He bit his lip, as if he had said too much.

My curiosity was aroused and I asked, "Is there anything new?"

He pretended ignorance of my implication, asking, "About what?"

"Your situation with Morteira? Daniel seemed optimistic."

"Daniel means well and perhaps so does Morteira, but the rabbi has only added to my difficulties. However, that is not your problem."

"It is if it affects the sittings. Will it?"

"I cannot tell."

I sensed a fierce conflict in him, that part of him yearned to keep whatever was troubling him private, and the rest of him hungered to talk about it, to confide in me before he burst from holding it in. I said, "Whatever you tell me, I will not betray you to someone else."

He regarded me earnestly, then replied, "That is what Daniel says. But I do not want to worry you. It could damage your picture."

"A picture is always a worry. It is worse than a child for causing trouble and breaking your heart. But I have become accustomed to that. What is your trouble? Is it Morteira? Is he implacable?"

"How did you know?"

"I have painted him. What does he want now?"

"We had a private interview. Morteira suggested that if I return to the fold, give up what he calls my false ideas and become his student again, I would, by the grace of God, become a rabbi and eventually succeed him."

"That seems like a fair proposal."

"More than fair, from his point of view. Morteira also told me, confidentially, that this compromise, as he calls it, would include a gift of a thousand guilders a year to provide me with all the essentials I need, for as long as I need. For life, he assured me, if necessary."

"Is that what worries you?"

"It is a bribe!" he exclaimed. "I cannot take it!"

"What will happen if you reject his offer?"

"My trial will begin. If I am found guilty, I could be denounced as a heretic. They might even consider expelling me from the congregation, and possibly, if the authorities support them, as I think they will, from Amsterdam, too."

Yet his voice had grown softer as he told me this, as if he must not express any fury or hate or violence of any kind, it was against his nature, and this caused me to ask, "And you are not angry at them?"

"How can I be? They are so frightened that my views will bring down the wrath of the Dutch on their heads that I feel sorry for them."

"Then why do you not give in?"

"I must get along with myself."

That was within my comprehension. I was always being told that I must get along with patrons, art dealers, the multitude, how important that was, but I hated that, thinking, What about getting along with myself?

Spinoza said reflectively, "You can pretend to get along with others, but you cannot pretend to get along with yourself."

"What are you going to do?"

"I am not going to run away." His jaw stiffened and passion came into his voice. "That is the one thing I am certain of."

"Even if they threaten to expel you?" I was thinking of my own situation now. "You will still advocate your views?"

"I have no choice. Like yourself." He indicated my unfinished canvas to show what he meant. "Yet if you worshipped a totem pole I would not take it away from you. I might not respect you for it but I would not deprive you of your faith. Just as I will not be deprived of mine."

I knew I needed Jesus, I needed his compassion and mercy, for I did not find it anywhere else. I wondered what Spinoza needed.

"Master, you will be criticized harshly if you continue to paint me."

"No more than I have been already. That is nothing new for me."

"Your faith will be questioned."

"It already has been. Come, you must have some tea and cake with us or Hendrickje and Titus will be disappointed."

"Not today, thank you. I have too much on my mind to be good company. Will you give them my regards? They have been very kind to me."

"Of course. I will expect you next week at the same time."

He hesitated, as I expected him to, but when I took him by the arm and escorted him to the door gently, he said with sudden enthusiasm, "I am glad that your canvas is not a blank space anymore."

"And that I have the obstinacy of a madman," I joked, to hide the seriousness of the situation, and so that we could both feel better.

"Sometimes, Master, I think that you are the sanest man I know."

"I would prefer that you have that honor. A little insanity is good for an artist. It makes the supposed real world a little more bearable."

"Whatever it is, I hope you reach your goal."

"Whatever it is," I repeated. I could only think of one thing to say. "Good luck and may God bless you!"

Spinoza regarded me strangely, as if for the moment he thought I was ridiculing him, then, realizing by my expression I meant just that, he said, "Thank you. I hope you like the brown cloak I wore. I noticed that you favored yellow and I wanted to suggest that to your brush."

By the time Crayer returned for my reply to Thyst's proposal there was only one thing I could do—decline it. To my surprise, he was not upset but relieved. He did not ask for any explanations but said, "I did not want you to accept, but since the alternative could be bankruptcy, I could not advise you to turn down his offer."

I had prayed to God the night before, as much a declaration of my faith as an appeal for guidance and help, although that had been my purpose, too, and that had eased my doubts and fears and strengthened my determination to continue with my concept of Jesus.

"Thyst presented me with an itemized bill and you are badly in arrears. That was another reason I could not tell you what to do."

I said, "Could you transfer the title to this Breestraat house to Titus? As you suggested earlier."

"I will try. What should I tell Thyst?"

"Whatever you think is suitable. God willing, I may survive him."

"Amen."

WHEN DIMENSION EXCEEDS ITSELF

When dimension exceeds itself
and intensity outweighs
bearableness
resembling pain
Try it
to see if it be the materials
for creation

—Stymean Karlen

CRAYER returned a few days later to arrange the transfer of the title of my house to Titus. It was May 17, 1656, and I asked Hendrickje and Daniel to attend and to witness this meeting in addition to my son.

Hendrickje was gratified; she acted as if this signified that she was now a permanent part of my household; but Daniel was ill at ease.

He said, "I feel that I am intruding. This is a personal matter."

I replied, "It is essential that you join us. You know more about my finances than anybody else. If there are any questions concerning my creditors you can answer them better than I can."

When I added that his presence would be a demonstration of loyalty to me, Daniel agreed to share this difficult situation with me.

I felt better then, as if I had shifted some of the responsibility on to his shoulders, and yet, as we sat in the reception room while the lawyer arranged the papers for me to sign, I was sad. The necessity to transfer my prized house to Titus was a confession of failure.

Hendrickje and Titus served wine from the marble cooler while

Daniel reviewed my debts with Crayer and confirmed that they totaled more than twenty-five thousand guilders, possibly thirty —my affairs were in such a state of disorder my assistant could not be sure—and I saw my aging reflection in the mirror and disliked what I saw.

I felt that I looked more like seventy than the fifty I would be in two months. While Crayer, behaving with pious solemnity, uttered a prayer to God that this transfer would turn out for the best as he put the papers before me for my signature. Now everyone was silent as I signed my precious house on the Breestraat over to my son.

I tried to do it with generosity but there was an ache in my heart. While they drank a toast to this occasion, on Crayer's suggestion, the glass barely grazed my lips. I recalled how I had bought this mansion with such joy and a sense of accomplishment. But even then, although there had been an abundance of profitable commissions, I had had to struggle to raise the initial payment of twelve hundred guilders so that I could move in and take possession, and I had been forced to promise to pay the remainder within five years. But take no longer, I had been warned. This memory brought a rueful smile to my lips. I had been so proud of this reception room which was supposed to be for my guests. It featured seven splendid chairs, finely upholstered in velvet when my family home in Leyden had only three and they had been poorly cushioned.

Hendrickje said, "Heer Crayer, I trust this will end the Master's worries. These anxieties are not good for his health. I do not understand this business but he should not have such difficulties."

"That is why I am here," he replied, "to ease them."

Titus said, "It is still Papa's house. I will do whatever he wants."

Crayer said, "Let us hope this is all that will be necessary."

Daniel asked, "Do you think this transfer will succeed? Even the interest on the obligations is accumulating at a devastating rate. And the creditors grow increasingly impatient and irritable."

Crayer looked grave. His smile vanished. He said carefully, "It is a risk. Yet there is no alternative. It is too late to try anything else. A year ago we could have attempted safer measures, but today this is all we can do. However, I may be able to convince the creditors that we are doing this to protect their interest, too, that once the Master can work without the pressure of immediate obligations, he can earn enough to pay them all back eventually."

Even in my most affluent days I had never earned enough. I had always purchased copiously at auctions, I had spent as I had earned, I had done this without regard for the consequences. In that respect I could not blame anybody else. Yet I did not feel like a gambler, but like a collector. They waited for me to speak and I asked skeptically, "Crayer, do you think my creditors will accept your reasons for this transaction?"

He looked uncomfortable and he did not reply and I sensed that he desired to discuss this with me privately and I dismissed the others.

When we were alone he said, "As I feared, Thyst was furious when I told him that you could not accept his offer. He felt that he had been generous and that you betrayed him. This may make matters worse."

"Then why did you say I did the right thing in rejecting his proposal?"

"That would not have worked either. The other creditors would have come down on you whatever he promised. You do not have any choice."

Crayer's attitude had altered since he had suggested I transfer the title to my house to Titus and I wondered why. I watched him admiring my collection of sculpture, terrestrial globes, Indian fans, the Spanish chairs and the oak chests with their exotic, rare coins and medals, and I felt that he envied my possession of ornamental and beautiful things.

He said more consolingly, "This transfer might avert disaster."

"But you are not sure?"

"How can anyone be sure! It will depend on the authorities. And how much pressure your creditors will put on them. On—"

I interrupted, "What do you think Thyst will do next?"

"He will probably try to evict you."

"Do you think he will succeed?"

"It is impossible to tell. But I believe he will assemble the other creditors and ask them to agree to that course of action."

"Who do you think that will include?"

"Witsen, Van Hertsbeeck, Ornia, and Daniel Francen."

I said, surprised, "The Francens are my friends!"

"They will still want the three thousand guilders you borrowed from them. Or do you think that they are being unfair?"

I detected sarcasm in the lawyer's voice, as if my affairs were becoming too difficult and complicated even for him, and I replied, "Quite fair. They lent me the money without interest. I want to pay them back first."

"You may not have that choice." As Crayer saw the etchings I had done on my recent walk with Titus, his face lit up and he exclaimed, "How fine they are! How peaceful!" For a moment I felt that I had become a substitute for God. "If I could only afford them."

"They are yours," I said abruptly.

"You must not," he replied. "You need them for your creditors."

"I will sell them other things. They are your fee. Take them, please"—I thought, Before I change my mind—"or someone else will."

He was an inveterate collector, too, although on a less extravagant scale than I was, and as I handed him the two etchings he held them as if he were in a trance and whispered, "My God, you mean it, Rembrandt."

"Now get out of here before I change my mind!"

He stuffed the title to the transfer of the house in a pocket of his fashionable velvet doublet as if it were of little consequence while he affectionately held the etchings of the Dutch countryside as if he had found a treasure and murmured, "They are perfection itself."

"Nothing is perfect," I retorted, feeling that he was exaggerating. "Crayer, as a lawyer, what do you honestly think could happen to me?"

It was as if I had dashed cold water in his face. And his answer told me one of the reasons he had grabbed my etchings so avidly. However, he walked to the door before telling me, as if he did not want my response.

(264)

"Rembrandt, the law punishes insolvent debtors with imprisonment."

After I recovered from the shock of his pronouncement, I visited the Francens. It was the next day—I had tried to work during the previous twenty-four hours but my hands were limp and clumsy—and I decided that only etching would restore their vitality. Besides, I reasoned, I had promised Abraham etchings in return for his friendship, and I wanted to keep my word to him before it was too late. And I might hear the latest news about my financial situation and obtain some useful advice.

Daniel was absent and Abraham did not want to discuss business. When I said that it might take a little longer than I had expected to pay back the three thousand guilders that I had borrowed, he said, "No apology or explanation is necessary, I know you are strapped at the moment"—which sent a chill through me—"we expect the same treatment as your other creditors"—which added to my apprehension, yet he was smiling and greeting me warmly—"and you do not have to reward me. We lent you the money as friends, not to obtain favors."

He was so earnest as he sat by the window, and since the light was good and I had promised to draw him, I set to work without another word. This was something he could not resist. I put Abraham in the most congenial position possible, sitting him with his back to the window, through which bright sunlight streamed, while he held up a drawing to examine it in the best light. I included the art book on his table, the small statue of Buddha by his side, and the skull, which indicated that he was a licensed apothecary, but I concentrated on his features. The sun shone squarely on them, fully illuminating his face and the passion for art on it.

I drew him many times before I was satisfied and that was only when the chair he sat on became alive and I added trees in the window behind him.

He looked younger now in his enthusiasm, almost boyish, and I also strengthened his hands, particularly the one at the top of the drawing he was holding. I knew it was easy to give the bottom hand prominence but it was the top one that must suggest his intense love of my work.

He was amazed with what I drew. When I showed him the finished sketches his expression was as animated as if he saw a vision.

Abraham whispered passionately, "It is a miracle."

"Not quite," I muttered. "More like hard work." But I was gratified by what I had done. I had captured Abraham as I saw him.

I was no wiser about my financial affairs, although I felt differently since I had transferred title to the house to Titus. My son was sober these days, as if he had assumed a burden, too, and yet there was something pathetically childish in his effort to be more mature. He tried to act grown-up, but the situation was like a game to him and I was afraid that he would lose. Several days after I saw Abraham Francen, Thyst sent me a written summons demanding that I attend him. His tone was arrogant and I could not submit to it any longer. I could not endure more humiliation. I replied that I was too busy to see him, although I knew that it could spark his proceedings against me. Daniel delivered my answer and he said that Thyst received my refusal coldly, his glance as sharp as an ax, but had nothing further to say. My assistant was concerned about his friend. While I waited for Spinoza to return for the next sitting, he said, "If Baruch continues to differ with Morteira the consequences could be dire. With Manasseh in England, this rabbi dominates the synagogue and his natural inclination to rule is encouraged. I hope that Baruch does not antagonize him further."

Neither of them mentioned this when Spinoza arrived as he had promised. Daniel was eager to participate in this sitting but I said that it was not necessary, that his friend knew how to sit now. My rejection of his services made Daniel grouchy, but he became more agreeable when Spinoza said, "Do not worry. I am still a member of the congregation."

Once he sat for me, however, I realized that he did not feel as hopeful as he sounded. I sensed that he was suffering profoundly, for he was graver than I had ever seen him. But he was closer to Jesus. Then, after only an hour of sitting he fidgeted in his chair and he asked impatiently, "Master, how much longer will this take?"

"I cannot tell," I said irritably. "You know that."

"I am not certain how much I know," he replied bitterly.

This was so unlike him that I halted. I said, "Then you did decline Morteira's offer."

"I said that I would."

"I thought that would please you."

"No," he said sadly, "I got no joy from it."

"So now you cannot decide whether that was the correct thing to do."

"That is not the problem. I cannot sit now. There is sorrow in my heart. It will make your Jesus mournful and heavy."

"I will decide that," I said severely, but after a few more minutes of painting I knew he was right. Suffering without compassion was wrong for the vision I had; I was not even creating an excellent likeness of my model. Perhaps my wish to find Jesus in him was a vain quest. I put the canvas aside and said, "Maybe you are too learned for Jesus."

"Maybe."

"But no one has the right to be vain or arrogant, not even God."

He cried out, "Is that the impression I give you?"

"You are too wise to sit for me and I should have recognized that."

"Too wise?" He sounded incredulous. "I am not wise enough! Ever since you asked me to sit for you, I felt that, but you insisted. . . ."

"I saw something in you, I thought, that even you did not see."

"Whatever the reason, I cannot come next week."

"Because of what I just said?"

"I rejected the offer of a thousand guilders."

"I expected you to."

"Morteira did not. He was disgusted with me. He said I was disloyal. That he has long known of my evil ideas and ways and that he has tried repeatedly to dissuade me from them with all the kindness at his command."

His inner truth was hidden—I would have to be fortunate to penetrate it—but if I ever did, I felt, I might still fashion this portrait.

"So, as I said, I cannot sit. I go on trial next week."

He left quickly, wanting nothing else said or done. I had to speak to Daniel to find out the full extent of what was happening to him.

My assistant was shaken by what I told him and he said sadly, "Baruch has the finest intelligence in the synagogue and he does not realize that Morteira cannot match him and resents this. He should be more tactful."

"Should he lie? Surrender his convictions no matter what price is demanded?"

"It is one thing to preach but another to practice it. If Baruch is found guilty he could be cast out of the congregation. Even if it is done just to appease the Christian community. No wonder he did not want to discuss his situation with me. Master, was he adamant?"

"I could not tell. There are traits in him that evade me. Daniel, what do you think will happen at Spinoza's trial?"

"I do not think he will give in."

"Neither do I. But what then?"

Daniel ran his hand through his blond hair to give himself time to answer me as thoughtfully as he could. And when he spoke, it was with great care. "Unless he admits that his views are wrong, and I doubt that he will, considering his state of mind, Morteira will make sure that he will be found guilty. Morteira will preside at the trial."

"Is such a verdict serious?"

"Very. The consequences for Baruch could be quite grave."

The following morning I started another self-portrait, this time in the harsh manner of one of my favorites, *The Blinding of Samson*. I had painted the brutal knife in Samson's eye with all my power in the same year I had done a calm, contemplative portrait of Manasseh ben Israel, so no one would be fooled into thinking I took goodness for granted.

I was staring at the canvas trying to decide whether to continue with this caustic appraisal, the lines I had painted on the cheeks were more like scars than wrinkles, when Crayer hurried into my studio, and said angrily, "The authorities are idiots. They say that the transfer of the title is illegal, that they will not allow it."

I was not surprised, I had half-expected this, but I asked, "Why?"

"They considered it an act of bad faith. An effort to evade what you owe."

"I am not trying to do that. But I need more time."

"Your creditors are too influential. Witsen is still the burgomaster, Thyst and Van Hertsbeeck are wealthy and their money speaks loudly."

"Are there any alternatives?"

"Could you borrow more money?"

I said, "I doubt it. Borrowing has put me in this predicament. But I could pay off some of what I owe if they would only take my work."

Crayer said, as kindly as he could, "They consider that an uncertain commodity. They prefer cash, they feel it has a fixed value, although it, too, is losing value each year with the rising cost of things."

I slashed at my self-portrait with my brush, before, in my fury and desperation, I took a scissors to the canvas and cut it up into tiny shreds as I had done in the past. I muttered, "It is hopeless. No matter what I sell, I spend more. No matter what I save, I need more. My accounts are a muddle of confusion."

He nodded, as if, perhaps, that would make me feel better.

I asked, "What is the best thing that can happen to me now?"

"Something that would persuade your creditors to give you more time to lessen your obligations."

I doubted that was possible. Hendrickje was calling me for lunch, I could hear Daniel and Titus moving about upstairs where they were supposed to be working, and yet I felt so alone. But they must not know, I told myself, they must never know how much despair I felt sometimes. I blurted out, "Crayer, what is the worst that could happen to me? What is the very worst?" I had to know.

"You could apply for a liquidation of everything that you own."

"I do not understand."

"Then you will be declared bankrupt."

THE FIRST TIME IT TEARS

The first time it tears
you sew it
It is natural to sew it
It is torn

The second time it tears
there is some resistance in you
But you decide to conform
And do what all the proper people do
And you sew it

The third time it tears
you do not sew it Not a stitch
By now you have tortured your way
to your own philosophical truth
And you see through the false stitching

—Stymean Karlen

I SAT a long time seeking a solution to this new threat. When I did not reply to Hendrickje's repeated calls for lunch, she brought me beer, herring, and cheese, but I did not touch any of it. I had no appetite or desire to work, which was the worst feeling of all. I reviewed various courses of action in my mind, unable to look at any of the things that I was doing. Bankruptcy was a disaster I had not reckoned with until now. Yet I could not borrow more money, even if there was someone to borrow from, and I doubted that. I had no energy left to spare for such an effort. I could not face that humiliation.

Bowing when I did not believe in it, when it hurt, mumbling Yes, sir, No, sir when I did not mean it, did not like it, being humble when I hated that, begging when I felt like resisting, praising God when I longed to curse the devil, who seemed to be in more people than Jesus. I was so sick of asking for money I could have knocked my head against the wall. I wondered: Had Jesus ever borrowed money? That sounded sacrilegious, yet I thought: He must have pursued the usual activities during His life. Had that been why He had scorned the money changers? Driven them out of the temple? This idea struck my fancy and I contemplated painting this scene. First, however, I had to find some kind of peace within myself.

That night Hendrickje, Titus, and Daniel came upstairs together to find out what was wrong with me. They were alarmed. Not only had I failed to have dinner, they had not even heard me stirring in my studio.

And now I stared at them stonily with weary, bloodshot eyes.

Hendrickje asked, "Master, did Crayer bring bad news?"

I mumbled, "The transfer of the house was not allowed."

"Never mind," said Titus, "I did not want it anyhow. Papa, it is your house and I did not like the idea from the beginning."

"Thank you, son," I said, and stopped. That was all I could say.

Daniel was not satisfied, remarking, "Master, you are troubled by something else. The lawyer must have given you other bad news."

I felt as if I were about to be crucified and I told myself, Stop being foolish, you are too involved with Jesus, we are civilized in the United Seven Provinces, we do not crucify people, we merely ruin them.

Daniel persisted, "Is it that the creditors will not wait anymore?"

"If I could raise a few thousand guilders this crisis might ease."

Hendrickje cried out, "You must not worry. You must eat. You have not touched anything. Come, I will give you a hot meal."

I handed her a hundred guilders I had taken from my Jesus canvas and said, "That should pay for necessities. But do not tell anyone of it or they will want the money."

Daniel said, "Master, you need at least five thousand guilders to hold off your creditors now. Ornia was here this afternoon, demanding money, and I told him that you were at The Hague speaking to a prospective patron. I implied that it was one of the royal family, and he went away impressed. But that will last only a short time."

"So we will find a new excuse next week," I said wearily.

"Master, I am running out of excuses. Ornia also said that Thyst is talking about taking action and so is Witsen and Van Hertsbeeck. Only the Francens seem willing to wait any longer for what you owe them."

Titus said, "Papa, we could eat less, save money that way."

I smiled despite my pessimism. Titus ate too little as it was, but I appreciated his desire to help me. But now I had to find other relief from the pressures that threatened to overwhelm me. I said abruptly, "I am going to visit Frans Hals in Haarlem." I thought, He will tell me how to face my crisis, he has experienced bankruptcy and lives in an almshouse now. "I must discuss painting with him. He is the best painter I know."

Hendrickje was as skeptical as Daniel about my reasons for this sudden decision, while Titus wanted to go with me, but I said that was impossible, and I dismissed their objections. I was able to eat the *hutespot* Hendrickje had prepared, now that I planned to do something I looked forward to doing. When Daniel asked, "What should I do if your creditors call while you are absent?"—I had said I would be gone a few days—I replied, "My affairs are in Crayer's hands. Refer them to him. I will be back for Spinoza's next sitting. Until then, I expect you and Titus to take care of my studio and not allow anyone into it. That is important. What I am doing here is private."

"No one, Papa?" asked Titus, pleased with this responsibility.

"No one, son. Not even Crayer, and certainly not Thyst or Ornia."

At least, as long as I was not bankrupt, I could keep them away.

Hals had given me his address on his last visit to Amsterdam and the next morning I took the *treskechuit*, the canal barge that was drawn by horses and men along the side of the Haarlemmermeer Poldar, the largest lake in Holland, which extended fourteen miles to Haarlem. It was a painfully slow journey to this large town on the coast west of Amsterdam and near Leyden, although

Holland was a small country. Indeed, I reflected, for once not in a mood to sketch, but still trying to observe the land, a forty-mile square would cover the most important cities in Holland: The Hague, Amsterdam, Leyden, Utrecht, and Haarlem. The sky was bright, there was not a cloud in it. A day, I thought with joy, excellent for viewing. I could see for miles and as I gazed at level land I realized once again why Holland was known as The Lowlands, there was not a hill or even a mound to be seen anywhere. It was as if God had flattened out the earth with a majestic sweep of His hand. Then my attention was captured by the bulb fields that stretched as far as I could see. I had never been afflicted with the tulip fever and the passion for speculating in them that had swept the country but as I approached Haarlem, their beauty fascinated me. The tulips were an ocean of brilliant colors, divided like a checkerboard into neat patterns. I could understand why the natives of the town were proud that they were the center of the tulip industry; they had created a kingdom of flowers out of a huge oozy swamp. They had fought a continual battle against a harsh climate and the ever-present enemy, the sea. Then I saw the Church of St. Bravo, the tallest object in Haarlem, and I knew I was at the city.

Dusk fell and I decided to visit my fellow painter the following morning. I took a room in an inn in the middle of Haarlem, on the great market square, but it was difficult to sleep, there was so much noise in an adjoining tavern. I decided that it was probably a banquet given by the local civic guard, it was so boisterous, and since I knew they could go on for days I resigned myself to the incessant revelry.

Nonetheless, I was irritable the next morning, for the festivities had kept me up most of the time, and I approached Hals' address uneasily.

The almshouse, Groot Heiligland 62, was a short distance from the market square, which was the heart of Haarlem, a dingy, two-story building of doubtful character, a mixture of brick and heavy stone.

The attendant who answered my knock, a wizened old man, toothless, bent but spry, informed me, when I asked to see Frans Hals, "The painter has not been here for several days. He is at the inn The Learned Man. The civic guard of St. George are having a banquet there and Hals can never refuse a free drink and there are many at The Learned Man today."

By the time I reached the festive tavern, which, I realized, was the place that had kept me up most of the night, I hesitated to go in. The banquet was even noisier, the flags that hung out in the street shrieked with self-importance. A young officer of the guard staggered out and bumped into me as I stood in the door-way, his breath as foul as the gin he had been drinking, and muttered, "I warn you, I would not go in, there is not one sober man among them. It is not safe, they are all drunk."

I waited until a boy came by and gave him two stivers to give the following message to the painter, Frans Hals: "A fellow artist wants to meet with him outside the inn."

A minute later the lad returned, whining, "The old bastard hit me in the eyes. He said I was a liar, saying that the artist was someone who was trying to get him to return to the Old Men's Almshouse."

The boy's cheek was bleeding and he ran away after he gave me this message and I had to go in myself. I entered apprehensively.

At first I could only see a few feet in front of me. The banquetting room was filled with tobacco smoke, the latest craze in the Netherlands, and the mist on the windows dimmed the light. Most of the candles were out, having been knocked down during the boisterous festivities. Finally, moving between the swashbucklers, who reminded me of the stout, middle-aged, self-important burghers I had painted in *The Night Watch,* with their drinking, shouting, and singing, I found Hals sitting in a corner. He was cursing a fat, elderly barmaid for refusing to give him any more brandy to drink. She was glaring back at him and I stepped between them, although I was not sure that was wise.

She shouted, "Get out of here, you old stinker, you smell!"

I was wearing painting clothes but I had washed this morning. Then I realized that she was screaming at Hals, who had not budged. I pushed her away, and for a moment I thought that she would strike me, but when I put a stiver into her hand her anger vanished and she waddled away.

I sat down next to Hals and asked, "Have you been here all night?"

"Go away." He motioned wearily and glared at me through bleary eyes.

"I am your friend," I said. He did not seem to recognize me.

"No one is my friend. No one will give me anything more to drink."

"We are fellow members of the Painter's Guild."

"Did Ruisdael send you? Or De Hoogh?" he asked suspiciously. "They are always worrying about me. But I will outlive both of them. Even though I am over twice their age. I am almost eighty, did you know?"

He exaggerated a little but I did not correct him.

"Do you have any stivers for the woman? But no, you would not have. You are a painter. They never have any money. Who are you?"

Was he so drunk? I wondered.

"You look like one of the guardians of the almshouse. Old, stern, righteous. Always trying to tell me what to do. I will outlive them all. You, too, whoever you are."

This was too much for me and I leaned over and screamed in his ear, "Hals, I am Rembrandt, Rembrandt van Rijn! Remember?"

He replied drunkenly, "What would he be doing here? He lives in Amsterdam. He is still in demand. He does not need me."

He fell into a stupor and I shook him until his head rose from his chest. Then I pushed open the window near us, although several of the civic guards protested that I was spoiling their party, and gradually the air from the street cleared his head and he could see me better.

I asked imploringly, "Do you recognize me now?" Was he so far gone?

He peered at me intently, and then said slowly, "Your chin is thicker. You look older. Rembrandt, did the guardians of the almshouse send you?"

"No. I came to see you for myself, not for anybody else."

"Excellent. Marvelous. I do not believe you."

"Hals, have I ever lied to you?"

He admitted reluctantly, "Not that I remember. Why are you here?"

"I want to talk to you about various matters."

"I have no money. I am bankrupt."

"I know. That is one of the reasons I am here."

He regarded me suspiciously again and said, "You cannot help me. I hear that you are deep in debt, too. These rumors are plentiful."

"That is why I am here," I stressed. "I want your advice."

"Advice?" His laughter was so mocking I could hardly endure it. "No one asks me for that, even about painting. Not even Ruisdael or De Hoogh any more. When I failed to interest you in their work they turned away from me. How can I help you when I cannot help myself?"

"I admired their work but I could not do anything about it. Hals," I raised my voice to be sure he heard me, "I am facing bankruptcy, too."

He said, "Get me another beer."

"Another?" He smelled like he had been drinking for days.

"Do as I say. It will clear my head."

I obeyed him and he drank the beer down with one gulp. Then he stood up, leaning on his cane for support, and stated, "Pay no attention to the civic guard. They will go on drinking for days. They allowed me to join them because I painted them."

"Was this your fee?"

"Yes. But I can outdrink any of them. Even at my age. You want to know what it means to be bankrupt? I will show you."

He led me past the sprawled bodies and the litter of bottles that cluttered the smoke-filled inn, limping a little as he leaned on his cane, but apparently recovered from his drinking. Yet by the time we reached the almshouse I realized his legs were shaky, for the moment we entered his room he sat down, while I surveyed his surroundings.

His quarters were more like a cell than a room, his furnishings a small, cramped cot, a rickety, square table, two wooden stools, but I was glad that the window was large enough to give good light and that he had an easel with a canvas on it. He was still working.

(277)

Suddenly he grumbled, "I have to piss, I have been drinking for two days." And while he went to the outhouse to relieve himself I examined what he was painting. It was a study similar to his *Woman's Guardians of the Old Men's Almhouses,* and the five elderly starched ladies were angular, formal, self-righteous, far different from the ribald, boisterous figures he had done in his earlier days. His brush had become heavier, darker, like my own, I thought. I also observed that he was using just a few tints: yellow-ochre, red, white, some charcoal-black, and blue and green, but not much of these colors. This was the soberest painting of his I had seen. Then, as I looked closer, I realized it was not flat or tedious as I had thought at first, but that the women filled the surface as they were, pathetically aged, hard. He still possessed his feeling for faces. Each of the five women were delineated in a highly individual and unique manner.

"Not much like my groups of civic guards," he declared, as he hobbled back into the room. "Is it, Rembrandt?" He was quite sober now.

"Not at all. It is dark."

"Too dark, the good ladies say. But they will have to take it as I paint it or use it for their fireplaces."

"They would not do that!" I exclaimed in horror.

"Who knows," he said indifferently, "they like to be flattered as much as anyone. And I do not flatter. I have not the time nor inclination for it. Sit down. Are you hungry? I have a little herring, cheese."

"No, thank you. I ate before I came here this morning." I did not trust the greasy dishes he reached for, and I stood, it was more comfortable.

"What is troubling you? You said that you wanted advice."

I asked carefully, "Hals, could you work after you were bankrupt?"

"Why not?"

"Your confidence must have been shaken. You must have lost heart."

"I did not have to go bankrupt to have that happen."

"Yet you are still working."

"As you see. When the good lady governors of the almshouse

supply me with paint, canvas, and a subject. I have found several good pictures out of this experience. It is having to depend on others that I dislike. I am given a few guilders each week but there is never enough for my needs. That is why I accepted the invitation to the banquet of the civic guards. The drinks were free."

"What about your family? Could they not help you?"

"My ten children, my seven sons!" He laughed as if they were an absurd joke. "I do not like them. They think that my carousing has ruined the family name, although all of my sons and my brother, Dirck, are painters. They are having a difficult time supporting themselves and do not want to be bothered with their old, drunken father, although I can paint better than any of them, drunk or sober."

I knew his brother's work. It was competent, that was all. I asked, thinking of my problems with Spinoza, "Have you ever painted a philosopher?"

"A Frenchman, Descartes. Was he an ugly man!" Hals added with satisfaction. "And I showed it. Why do you ask?"

"Was he difficult to portray?"

"No more than anybody else. Once I stopped him from talking."

I thought, Perhaps that would help me with Spinoza.

"Descartes was confusing. One moment I felt that he did not believe in God, the next he sounded like a pious Catholic. But, Rembrandt, you did not come to Haarlem to ask me that, did you?"

"No," I admitted. "Were the bankruptcy proceedings harsh?"

"Harsh enough. They took all my work. It was dreadful."

I noticed a sparrow on his windowsill and the bird did not fly away as Hals approached it, apparently expecting something.

He said, "I feed it for company, it does not criticize me, and now it comes every day, but I forgot yesterday, I was at the banquet." He brought out a dish with some crumbs and cheese and gave it to the bird. The sparrow ignored the cheese but ate the bread.

I asked, "Do you have enough money?"

"The governors give me five guilders a week for necessities." His voice grew aggrieved. "It never leaves me enough for liquor."

Suddenly I offered him twenty guilders, but he refused it.

He said, "I cannot take a loan. The obligation is too painful."

"It is not a loan. It is a fee for your advice."

He gave me a cynical grin, but his pride was appeased, for he pocketed the money and said, "I know a fine tavern where we can drink in peace."

"Not now, Hals. When did they take formal possession of your work?"

"After they went to law."

"Did they seize everything?"

"Yes, except what I was painting. They cannot touch work in hand."

He was surprised that suddenly I was more cheerful, but I had just learned of a possible way to save my Jesus portrait. I insisted that he dine with me and a few minutes later, while he sat over steaming mutton, a delicacy, and cabbage, he ate a few mouthfuls of the meat as a courtesy to me, his host, ignored the vegetable, and drank the strong double beer as if this were his meal. For dessert, I ordered cheese tarts flavored with wine and he disdained them, saying, "They are too sweet. Did you know that Rubens, with all his elegance, admired my work?"

"Yes, I did. As I admire it, too."

"Not many people do these days. I have not had a paid commission since I was put in the almshouse. I am painting these severe-faced women for my room and board. Believe me, Rembrandt, do not allow them to possess you and they will if you become bankrupt."

I realized now that what I had expected from him, a kind of wisdom or encouragement, or comforting conclusions, was impossible to get. The will to sustain myself would have to come from myself. I said brusquely, "Hals, do not tell anyone what we discussed."

"There is no one to tell. Ruisdael and De Hoogh seldom visit me since I failed to aid them in Amsterdam. They are afraid that I will ask for money and I am considered a relic of the past."

"Do you need any more money?" I felt guilty that I had given him only twenty guilders. "I can spare it."

He put his hand on mine with more affection than he usually

allowed himself and said softly, "If I was rude before, I was tired."

I handed him another twenty guilders without a word and he accepted it just as silently.

But as the sun fell strongly on my face his animation returned and he exclaimed, "Rembrandt, I have a proposal! Let us paint each other!"

His face did not have a regular feature on it, and I would not change it for a fortune. But how could I paint him? I could not remain in Haarlem and he could not live in Amsterdam.

As I hesitated, he asked glumly, "What is wrong?"

"I have to be back in Amsterdam to face my creditors," I said, and, I thought, to paint Spinoza. "Unless you could join me there."

He reached for another jug of beer, which seemed to sustain him better than anything else, and muttered, "Perhaps it was not such a good idea."

"It was a wonderful idea. But . . ." I halted. What could I tell Hals that he did not know already?

He embraced me fervently when we parted, as if he did not expect to see me again. He looked very old while we said good-bye.

I came home three days after I had left to find Daniel more upset than I had ever seen him. Before I could join him, Hendrickje, and Titus at dinner, he indicated that he had to speak to me privately and urgently. I assumed that it was about my creditors and that he wanted to spare my family, but after I closed my studio door behind him, pleased that everything was as I had left it, he blurted out, "Spinoza has been found guilty."

I replied, "That is no surprise."

"The punishment is. He has been reprimanded severely and he is forbidden to enter the synagogue until he repents and admits his errors. He has been given one month to do this."

"What will happen if he does not submit?" Daniel was very agitated.

"He could be expelled, and excommunicated."

I doubted that Spinoza would recant his views, it was not in his nature, but I sought to put the best face on the situation, saying, "Meanwhile, he can continue to sit for me and perhaps we can persuade him to compromise."

"Master, modeling is forbidden, too." Daniel sought to stand upright but he looked bowed by the weight of his words. "The *niddui*, the small ban that he has been sentenced to, states that for thirty days he is to keep ten paces from everybody, and in turn everybody is forbidden to have anything to do with him. No one is to drink, eat, or speak to him."

Shocked, I said irately, "My God, the Dutch authorities must have put enormous pressure on the rabbis for them to evoke such a stern sentence."

"What will the Gentiles say?" Daniel replied sadly. "I hear it said wherever I go in the Jewish community. Even my father reminded me that despite all his Christian friends, we are here only on sufferance, and that no good Dutchman can tolerate a man without faith, an atheist. He has forbidden me to have anything to do with Baruch."

"Are you going to obey him?" Daniel was striding up and down my studio in such a frenzy I feared he would throw himself out the window.

"If I do not, he will stop paying my fees to you."

"We will manage." I said that without thinking; I had been considering this prospect for a long time. "Have you seen Spinoza since the verdict?"

"Once. At Van den Ende's, where he is still residing."

"How is he?"

"Stunned. Stricken. He never thought it would come to this."

"Do you think he will give in?"

"Master, do you?"

I did not reply, standing silently, reflecting about how Spinoza must feel, battling single-handedly a multitude amid the glares of irate folk who watched him from afar as if his soul was evil. I wondered if a spark of compassion glimmered through the infernal certainty of Morteira's vanity. Or was he as self-righteous as Thyst and Ornia?

"Master, what are you going to do? I cannot imagine Baruch coming here any more to sit. And you have enough problems as it is, without adding to your burdens. He will surely stay away from you now."

I stared at the picture to which he had added much. The features were his, but the expression was Jesus. I must put more shadows behind the eyes. I said, "There are some things that are alike. Morteira is stupid, as is Thyst and Ornia. I will decide what to do about my model later."

"He is so shaken I doubt that he will even talk to you."

"Yet you do not think that he will give in."

"Master, I did not say that."

"It is in your manner, in your anguish, in your despair."

"He is so stubborn, so righteous."

As Jesus had been, I thought. Suddenly I realized that I had ignored the most vital fact of all: Did Spinoza still consider himself a Jew? If he did not, he was wrong for Jesus. I knew I had to find this out before I could paint him anymore. I said, as I prepared to join Hendrickje and Titus for dinner, "Do not tell my family about the ban. That would only hurt and confuse them."

"They will have to find out eventually."

"I will mention it at the proper time. Did any of my creditors harass you while I was gone?"

"No. I think they believed my story that you were at The Hague."

"Then you feel that Ornia told that to the others."

"Yes. Gossip is common in Amsterdam. Especially when it can be malicious. The spreader feels so virtuous. How did you find Hals?"

"Still working. Still trying to do what he likes. He thinks he is ignored now, but Hals has profoundly influenced my generation of artists."

"Even you, Master?"

"All of us. Who have any sense. Who have eyes to see." But now my mind was elsewhere. I was wondering what to do about Spinoza.

IF GOD WERE MY NEIGHBOR

If God were my neighbor
Could I befriend Him
In a neighborly way
No I could not
He would know more
about me
Than I would know about
Myself
That is what is wrong
With my neighbor
   He thinks He is God

    —Stymean Karlen

WHEN no creditors visited me the next few days I was relieved.

Evidently they believed Daniel's story that I had gone to The Hague for a profitable commission and that I might have money for them after all and they were allowing me time to earn it. Grateful for this, I decided that I had exaggerated my anxieties over my debts and I returned to my portrait of Jesus. My visit to Hals remained vivid in my mind and reminded me that our own work came first and that strengthened my hand.

Gradually, as I reworked the profile of Jesus and the moment of illumination on his face and the shadows behind Him, I left the foolish noises of a slanderous and turbulent world. I refined the features and while I was content I felt suspended in time.

One morning I realized that I was painting around my subject but not within Him. Spinoza had not returned to sit, and although he had warned me that he would not, suddenly his absence infuriated me. This portrait had to have a living model.

I summoned Daniel, who was sketching in the attic with my son, and asked him, "Have you seen your friend again?"

"Not since the ban started. It is forbidden."

"I know that," I said curtly. "Is that the best you can answer?"

"Master, do not reproach me. I warned him to be careful."

"Careful? Careful? Is that the only thing you know?"

"It is the prevailing sentiment in Amsterdam."

"That does not help my portrait. I need its model."

"His ban is only for thirty days and part of it has passed already. Maybe, by the end of the *niddui,* he will be able to sit for you again."

"You know, Daniel, that he is not inclined to give in. But I cannot finish this work without him. Is he still living in Van den Ende's house?"

"As far as I know. I have not heard that he has moved elsewhere."

"Spinoza must sit tomorrow. This picture cannot wait any longer."

"Do you want me to approach him?"

As Daniel suggested this, he looked so fearful I said, "No, this is my responsibility," trying to sound more courageous than I felt. Now that I was committing myself to visit him, I realized that it could bring scathing criticism down on my head and worse difficulties, but I had gone too far to retreat. I added positively, before I could change my mind, "I will go tonight when he is likely to be home."

"Master, it could be dangerous."

"Daniel, no one is going to attack me for visiting Spinoza."

"I am not so sure." When he saw me frowning, he added, "But that is not what I meant. The city streets are poorly patrolled at night."

"I must go see him since he will not come to see me."

"I do not like you going alone. You will be vulnerable to attack."

"Do you want to come with me? I am too close to finishing to stop."

I expected him to refuse, since this could damage him even

more than me, but I owed him that courtesy. He said, "I have no choice."

"No one is compelling you to go."

"He is my friend. I have known him all my life."

I did not tell Hendrickje or Titus where we were going, I did not want to worry them, and although she was surprised—I seldom went anywhere at night—she did not question me. She was preoccupied with Cornelia, who was teething; she was trying to keep our daughter from crying and using Titus to help her. While he regarded this as a childish activity and preferred to go with us —I refused to take him, I did not want to make his future any harder for him than it was already—and so he treated his sister's tears as another way to express his superiority over her.

They were so much at home in the house I tried not to think of what would happen to them if I became bankrupt and lost it. I was glad that the days were long in June and there was still light in the sky.

We walked silently, lost in our thoughts. The sun had shone all day and the air was still warm and it was a balmy twilight. The streets were empty except for a few pedestrians and an occasional coach. Two armed guards watched us suspiciously until I gave each of them a guilder.

Daniel whispered to me, "Master, that is too much," but now they bowed and wished us a safe journey and did not remind us that everyone who walked at night was obliged to carry a lantern or a torch.

We reached Van den Ende's large three-story house, which resembled mine in size and shape, just as night fell. A servant was lighting an oil lamp in a recess of the building and he was not surprised that the Latin professor was having visitors. But when I said, "It is Spinoza we want to see," the short, swarthy servant's face grew pale and anxious.

Daniel asked, almost hopefully, "He is not in?"

"I am not sure. If he is in, who should I tell him is calling?"

I stated more assertively than I felt, "Rembrandt van Rijn."

"The painter?"

"Yes. Do not keep us waiting. I do not have much time."

Yet it seemed an interminable time before anyone returned. I was on the verge of giving up this quest, which I sensed, Daniel preferred, when someone opened the door. It was not Spinoza, but Frans van den Ende.

I saw that this product of a Jesuit education, whom I knew, was tense as he greeted us. Usually this tall, lean, fifty-year-old professor with his regular, smooth features was of a cordial disposition, but tonight he was stiff, defensive, and inhospitable.

I said, "My business is with Spinoza."

"My servant told me. I wanted to make sure who it was."

Daniel exclaimed, "Is he in any danger?" Van den Ende was nervous.

"There have been threats. Against both of us. It is claimed that I sowed the seeds of atheism in Spinoza and other young men. Which is absurd if you know him. He is too strong-minded to be influenced. And I am still a Roman Catholic. But there is much fear and hysteria about."

I asked, "How is he?"

"As well as can be expected, considering what is happening to him. You are the first visitors he has had. He will be surprised."

I said curtly, "He is my model for a work. I need him to finish."

"So I hear. A portrait of Christ, I believe. Is he suitable?"

"Professor, I came to see Spinoza, not to be questioned. Is he in?"

"Yes. I will ask him if he wants to see you. He seems to prefer solitude these days so he can resolve his reply to the ban."

Van den Ende forgot to close the door as he left to speak to Spinoza and so I entered, tired of having others order my life. Daniel followed me in more cautiously and as we mounted the stairs to the attic I was surprised that Spinoza lived in such humble, monastic quarters, usually it was the students who lived on the top floor, not the teacher. Then I heard him arguing with Van den Ende and, while I disliked being an eavesdropper, I was too involved to allow such scruples to halt me. I told myself, I must not humor him, I must be firm. He must sit again.

Spinoza was saying, "I told the painter I could not model any more."

"I do not think that he will want to take that for an answer."

"Want? Want? Too much wanting ruins a man. What about what I want?"

"Do you truly know, Baruch?" Van den Ende asked critically.

"I want time for study and reflection. Not to be tormented."

Impatient, I strode in and pretended that it was the natural thing to do. I was even more surprised by Spinoza's actual quarters. They were sparser than Hals's. It was one of the smallest rooms I had seen. If I stretched my arms I could touch both walls. I wondered: How could he work here? Yet he appeared to feel at home in this monastic severity and simplicity, although it was like the cell of a monk. It contained only a cot, a plain table, one stiff-backed chair, and a shelf with books. Many of them were in Latin and I could not read their titles; I had forgotten most of what I had known of that language, it was of no use to a painter.

Daniel trailed me hesitantly, as if he felt he was intruding, and we stood, as did van den Ende, for there was no place to sit.

I expected Spinoza to order us out; he was annoyed by our presence, while Van den Ende was dismayed, as if I had betrayed him. Then Spinoza, seeing that I was trying to be friendly, rose to his feet to show that he did not wish to quarrel either and waited for me to speak.

Two candles on his table shed a fitful light and told me that I had neglected the darkness; I must paint him by night, too. It gave me the impetus to blurt out, "You should not have deserted me."

"Deserted you? Am I not accused of enough crimes without that?" He was offended and distressed, as if I had charged him falsely.

"You failed to return just as I was on the verge of finishing. Do you think I labored so long and hard to allow you to indulge yourself now?"

That amused him and he laughed.

Daniel was still uneasy and Van den Ende was irritated but I was pleased. At least he was not angry at me. I said, "It is time we returned to the portrait. One or two more sittings and it should be done."

He became somber and just as I was thinking, The difficulty is, the picture does not matter as much to him as it does to me, he asked, "Do you honestly believe that it will be an appropriate view of Jesus?"

"Yes. I told you that before. I do not waste my time."

"Perhaps the portrait is worth finishing."

Daniel said, "I thought you did not believe in Jesus' divinity."

"That is true. But He was a remarkable man. Reason tells me that He could not have been resurrected from the dead, but I have much sympathy for His teachings. I admire Him as a rabbi, as a teacher. Christ could have communed with God. He had the spirit and the capacity to do that."

Spinoza's features radiated such a glow from the enthusiasm with which he spoke that I felt that however he might differ with me on faith, he was a God-intoxicated man, and this was what I needed. I stated, more positively than I felt, "I will expect you tomorrow."

For a moment it was as if we were engaged in a wrestling match, for he regarded me severely, but when I returned his gaze with a steadiness and assurance that I did not feel, he assented.

I sighed with relief but Daniel looked even graver.

Van den Ende said abruptly, "Baruch, it seems to me that you are allowing the painter to force you to sit for him."

Spinoza replied with sudden emotion, "He is not forcing me to do anything I would not do of my own free will. I admire Christ. That I believe that the Scriptures are full of human fallibility does not make me an atheist as my enemies say. My faith is in nature."

I felt that Van den Ende resented anyone having more influence with Spinoza than he had. It was the professor's support that bound them, I thought, not similar beliefs. The Latin teacher's freethinking was an attitude to lift himself above others, but Spinoza's ideas were his own, without an ulterior motive, whether they were right or wrong. I turned to the door, motioned for Daniel to follow me, and declared, "Spinoza, we will share our experiences for the duration of the painting. But no longer."

He replied, "For the duration of the painting. But no longer."

He was prompt the next day and I went to work at once, feeling that we had very little time left. I had exaggerated when I had told him that I could finish in one or two sittings but now that I had experienced his regard for Jesus, I could see the end in sight. If only the world did not interfere, I prayed, and I decided to depict Jesus as I might have depicted Spinoza, as a Jewish student studying to be a rabbi.

I dressed him in a dark fur-trimmed cloak and a large broad-brimmed soft felt hat that I found in my storeroom. I could not think of God as an abstraction as he sounded in Spinoza's mouth; I wanted no distance between me and God. And despite his determination to be a man of reason, I saw suffering on his face. There was also a self-searching going on within him and I also painted this. Whether or not Spinoza considered himself a Jew, he was, no matter what Morteira asserted.

He did not talk much. He realized, as I did, that circumstances could limit our time and that words could distract and delay me.

When I finished this sitting, he said, "It is so dark."

"We are a world of mud, mud, mud. Wherever I walk there is mud."

"We are also sky, sky, sky. Why is the work so dark?"

"Dark because it is dark. We are still a land of mud. We take our earth from the water. Our cities would be under water if not for the dikes. As it is we are eight feet below sea level and mostly mud."

"You should be a theologian," he said. "You argue so passionately."

I changed the subject. "Would you like some tea before you go?"

"No, thank you. Will you give my regards to your lady and to your son?"

"I will be happy to."

"When should I come again?"

"When does your ban end?"

"In about two weeks." He was startled by my question. "Why, Master?"

"Come when you can. When you will be comfortable. It helps the work."

He said spontaneously, "A week from now. As we arranged originally." Then his face clouded. "Unless I am prevented from coming."

"What should prevent you?" I asked with apparent innocence.

"The Calvinists support the rabbis. They could try to stop me."

"I doubt it," I said strongly, although I shared his apprehension. We were so close to completing the portrait it would be criminal to halt now. "We Dutch prize ourselves on our tolerance."

"Not with anyone they fear may upset their religious views and order."

I thought of Jesus, who had done that, and it reaffirmed my feeling that I was on the right path. I said, "I will expect you in a week. Thanks for sitting. Two or three more times and we should be done."

"At Van den Ende's you said you only needed one or two more sittings."

He sounded upset, as if I had deceived him, and I replied quickly, "That was an estimate, not a conclusion. You must trust me, as I trust you." I was still not sure that he did, but he repeated that he would return a week from today and I called Daniel to escort him to the door.

No one had approached me about my debts since I had returned from Haarlem and I was starting to think I might be left in peace to paint for a while longer, when Hendrickje informed me, two days after Spinoza had sat for me, "Pastor Hoag is below. I tried to put him off but he insists on seeing you." She was on the verge of tears. "Master, he is very stern. I fear that he has come to separate us."

"It must be something else, girl." I was angry at the pastor for alarming her when I had assumed that her fears had been buried.

"Rembrandt, you will not desert me, will you? Not now?"

"Not ever," I stated. "There is nothing that he can do to us."

"He can excommunicate us. Ban us from the church."

"His church," I reminded her. "We can always attend Ruismeer's."

"I hope so. Do you think the pastor knows about Spinoza?"

"Everyone knows. It is the chief subject of gossip in the city. But what have you heard?" Her voice had grown strained.

"It does not matter. I am sure the neighbors lie about him. He is such a nice young man, he could not consort with the devil."

"That is an old wives' tale," I asserted strongly. "Show Hoag in. And do not worry. We will attend Ruismeer's services this Sunday."

That eased her fears and she ushered in the pastor and then withdrew, while he stood in the doorway menacingly. I did not ask him to sit and he did not want to. After a perfunctory greeting, he strode about my studio as if he were in search of something. Then, as he saw the picture for which I was using Spinoza, he halted suddenly.

He exclaimed incredulously, "It is Jesus! I recognize him!"

I did not reply. I was not interested in his opinion.

He said quickly, "You use the wrong model."

Curious, I asked, "Who would you suggest? Jesus Himself?"

"Do not be sacrilegious. You should use a man of the cloth."

"Yourself, for instance, Pastor?"

He frowned heavily at my skeptical tone and said, "Why not? I am the same faith. My piety is unquestioned. I would be a good model."

Good God, no, I thought with horror, do not be absurd, Hoag, you are the last man I would choose, you have nothing of Jesus' compassion and understanding, not a drop. But he was so serious I sought to be tactful. I said quietly, "I am sorry but I have a model already."

"You need my devotion. My knowledge of Christ."

His persistence was stretching my temper to the breaking point and he was wasting my time. I said more curtly, "Your face does not appeal to me."

He was insulted and his tone grew harsh. "I have tried to overlook your sins but this picture mocks what Christ stood for."

"Is that why you came? To be a critic? To judge my work?"

"I have come to pass judgment on you." Now he was consumed with righteousness and spite. "As I was warned, this portrait reveals that you have abandoned our faith. You paint like a heretic."

Outraged, I cried out, "It is a lie. I am as good a Christian as anyone. I have done more religious pictures than anybody in Amsterdam."

"When you use a heretic to sit for you? You are blasphemous."

I wanted to change the subject and ask him how his pigeons were faring but before I could mention them he rushed on.

"It is not how much you paint but what you paint. I came here in good conscience to warn you not to have anything more to do with Spinoza."

"Who told you about his presence here?"

"Everybody knows. And that he is a heretic, an atheist. He has no respect for God. If the Jews do not get rid of him, we will get rid of the Jews." Hoag's voice became contemptuous, vindictive. "They are here only because some soft-headed burghers think they can profit from their knowledge of how to trade with the Spanish and Portuguese. If I had my way I would send them off without another word." He gloated as he added, "And we will if the Jews do not cast him out."

"Then you think there is a possibility he will be allowed his views?"

"You never can depend on what Jews will do. I hear some members of the synagogue think that he has been punished enough. Idiots."

"What will you do if he is let off with his present punishment?"

"I will demand that all Jews be expelled. As they deserve. This heretic questions the heart of our faith. That cannot be tolerated."

I was shocked into silence. He was so vehement that for an instant I felt that God would punish me by ordering the heads of my brushes to fall off, my oils to turn to water. Yet as I glanced about my studio nothing appeared changed, except his rage, which had increased.

"And you have not been forgiven for your lust with your housekeeper." Before I could reply, he snarled, "I would have thought after we condemned your indecent behavior with her, you would have learned your lesson. Instead, now you owe everybody in Amsterdam money and cannot pay them back."

I shouted furiously, "That is none of your business!"

He said piously, "Whatever affects my congregation affects me."

"You read me out of your church."

"Not yet. You are still on our register, despite your immorality."

I said vigorously, "Then strike me off your records."

"Van Rijn, are you serious?" Hoag was appalled by my defiance.

"Very serious. I can always find a church that will accept me."

"Like Spinoza," he sneered, "a congregation of one. Believe me, painter, Jesus will make sure that I live long enough to spit on Spinoza's grave and see to it that his doctrine is buried with him while his soul rots in hell. And your misalliance will be punished, too."

"Get out!" I ordered.

"You would not dare." His eyes were narrow slits in his rigid, bony, pallid face. He was a mixture of indignation, scorn, insolence, and hysteria. "Several of your creditors belong to my church and they will regard a blow against their pastor as a blow against themselves."

"I will throw you out if you do not go!" I was so angry I trembled from my rage. I was glad that my arms were still strong and muscular.

We stood face to face and then, as I stepped toward him threateningly and he tripped in his haste to evade my onslaught, I stated, "Do not come back, for you will not be admitted."

He screamed, "When I do, heretic, it will no longer be your home!"

After my fury had abated, I sent Daniel to summon Crayer so that I could find out the state of my business at this moment. Meanwhile, Hendrickje wanted to know if I had struck Hoag, since he had fled in such a terror and rage. She was trembling and tearful, unable to contain her anxiety.

As she stood in the studio, I said, "I did not touch him. But I should have. He was obnoxious and obscene."

"Was it about us?" she asked fearfully. "I heard him screaming."

"He saved his harshest vituperation for Spinoza."

"Maybe that young man should not model for you anymore."

"Do you advocate my giving up my conception of Jesus too?"

I regarded her sadly. Was she as craven as the others?

"Master, I am thinking of you. The pastor's spite could harm you."

"No more than we will harm ourselves by doubting each other." I took her in my arms and only then did her trembling cease and her tears subside.

Daniel returned with the news that Crayer preferred to see me in his office. That increased my concern, but I tried to remain calm as I approached him. I was admitted to his presence as soon as I arrived, which was a comfort, and I put on such a cheerful expression that he cried out, "Then you did obtain a profitable commission in The Hague!"

I said, "Would that make any difference in my situation?"

"It might." But when he saw me gazing at my muddy boots, then at my etchings proudly displayed on the wall behind him, but not into his eyes, he sensed the truth and he muttered, "If you cannot satisfy your creditors now there will be the devil to pay. They cannot be put off much longer. Two more have appeared and the old ones grow more impatient daily. I wanted to see you here because my records are here."

"Is there any way to determine how much time I have left?"

"I talked Thyst into allowing you thirty more days, but once that is over, if you do not satisfy him, he will take legal action."

"How much money do you estimate that I need?"

"Five thousand guilders. At the least. As I told you before."

I wondered if I could trust him. My mind ran on, Was that what Spinoza was asking himself? Tomorrow, I yearned to say, everything will be better, but I knew that was not true. I had come to Amsterdam with such fine plans. Perhaps I would be better off alone.

Crayer said, "I do not know what else to advise."

"Thank you." I walked to the door to terminate our meeting.

"Thanks for what, Rembrandt?"

"For trying to establish some order out of the chaos of my affairs."

"You do not know how to defend yourself. But we will defeat them yet."

I did not believe him and I wanted to say, What do I do now? I could hang myself from the nearest tree, but that would leave Hendrickje and my son in a worse state. I could crawl in the mud but no one would give a damn. I excused myself, saying I would try to find the necessary capital in the next few days, that there were several possibilities. That apparently satisfied him, for he replied that he would strive to hold off my creditors a little longer, and that we must be resolute.

The place I felt I had the best chance to raise money was my investment with Beghem. I visited him the next day; I sent my name into his office with his clerk, who returned with the news that his master was in conference and that I should come back in about a week. I could not afford to wait and I pushed my way past the protesting clerk and walked in on the merchant, who was conferring with Daniel Francen. I was shocked to see them together; I wondered if they were talking about me. But I was too desperate to retreat; ignoring Francen, I demanded an accounting from Beghem.

"What accounting?" he retorted. He looked amazed at my request.

"Of the money I invested with you."

He replied sanctimoniously, "Not all our ships come home. It is a long voyage to the East Indies, the waters are infested with pirates, the risks are great. Your bottoms could have been lost at sea."

"You promised me that I would double my investment in six months."

"You are misinformed. That was never guaranteed. Now will you please excuse me. Francen and I have important matters to discuss."

As he rose hurriedly and maneuvered me to the door he made me feel like a savage and I asked, "Where are the ships I invested in?"

He gave a hopeless shrug of his shoulders and said, "I do not know."

I turned to Daniel Francen for help, but he gazed at me as if I were childish and foolish while Beghem, once he had pushed me through the door of his office, said sharply, "Tell your creditors that you suffered losses at sea. At least, you did not squander that money."

When I recovered from this shock, I went to Van Goor to try to convince him to sell my new pictures. I felt it was my last hope of raising the necessary money and I was encouraged that he was willing to see me.

He was hanging a collection of Lievens' work in The Adam and Eve gallery, and he indicated that this was what could have happened to my pictures if I had listened to him. Although I was dismayed by his taste, I did not respect my former friend's present work, I tried to sound hopeful as I asked, "Would you consider looking at my new paintings?"

"At your Jesus?" he answered. He brushed a speck of mud that I had brought in from his immaculate clothes. "Is it for sale now?"

"I have not decided."

"You will never sell the Jesus. The Jews will not buy it because they do not believe in Him and the Christians will consider it sacrilegious."

"What about my self-portraits, one of my son, my housekeeper, a fine slaughtered ox, several new biblical subjects, others?"

"There is no market for them. The price of your pictures is still falling, and possible patrons have heard that you are facing bankruptcy. They will not buy anything now, for they expect to be able to obtain your work cheaper soon. Today, no one even wants your art collection."

The picture dealer seemed to enjoy telling me this, reminding me that I was to blame for my own misfortunes, that I should have followed his advice.

Then he said, "However, I have heard from Don Ruffo recently. He is still interested in more work from your hand. Your *Aristotle* and *Homer* still pleases him and he is interested in the sketches you sent him."

"Why does he not order a commission from them? I sent him a dozen."

"He wants to see more sketches. It will take several years

before he will be able to decide what he wants next. The trouble with you, Van Rijn, is you never worried about tomorrow."

As his voice rumbled on I recalled how I had dunned the House of Orange eight times before they had paid me. "What about the newly completed Town Hall? There must be commissions for that."

"There are, but your theology is wrong. You are never in the pews of the Reformed Church anymore and the town fathers cannot commission official works from a man who lives in sin with his maidservant and paints a heretic as Christ. They cannot trust what you will paint. It is too bad, for you can paint effectively when you want to. If you had used your gifts intelligently, you could have been rich." He turned to talk to two younger painters who had studied with me once, whom he was exhibiting next week, not bothering to usher me to the door or to say good-bye.

Frightened by what I faced, I called my family into conference to discuss what could be done. I included Daniel, as I sat at the kitchen table with Hendrickje and Titus, for he knew more about what I owed than anyone else. The thirty days Crayer had won for me were almost gone, and Hendrickje served my favorite prune soup and fresh fowl, a delicacy, but I could not eat. I summarized my situation briefly.

Titus asked, "Papa, will we have enough to eat?"

"I think so. I have money left that I may be able to keep out of the hands of my creditors. And I can always paint for cheese and herring."

"You would work on the streets, Papa?" Titus was amazed.

"If it will feed us." I was not joking, although he thought I was. I had no intention of starving, even if I had to steal to prevent that.

Hendrickje stated, "I could hire out. Earn some guilders each week."

"Who would take care of the house? No, we will manage somehow."

Daniel said sadly, "My father stopped the money for my instruction. He says I disgraced him by seeing Baruch during the *niddui*."

"Never mind. One more mouth to feed will not make much difference."

Hendrickje beamed at Daniel to show that she agreed with me while my son was indignant that my assistant could consider deserting us now.

I asked Daniel, "Do you worship God?"

"I worship . . ." He halted suddenly, embarrassed.

"Careful!"

He grinned in spite of his anxiety and he said, "I worship art."

"You must not. It will betray you."

The bitterness in my voice silenced them. We finished supper without anything having been said that suggested a solution. But one thing was unanimous. Whatever happened, we must stay together.

Spinoza came early and begged me to finish with this sitting. I said reprovingly, "You know that I cannot work by the clock," and he replied, "I do not know whether I will be able to return again. I cannot promise."

I did not pursue this. Today I felt an extraordinary drama and emotion stirring within him and I wanted to capture it before it vanished. The light that emerged from his inner self illuminated his face with a gentle glow. I thought hopefully, He is approaching an awareness of his suffering, the compassionate understanding that suggests my Jesus. But I was not yet certain whether this was sufficient for my work.

I painted until we were both numb and my eyes felt as if they would fall out of their sockets. Finally, near nightfall, I had to stop before I ruined what I had done. He did not complain and, though he did his best to cooperate and I used all my craft and feeling, I saw that he still lacked what I needed to complete my vision of Jesus. This had become one of the most difficult pictures I had ever painted.

Spinoza asked, "Master, is it done?"

"Not quite."

"You will never finish," he said with a sudden burst of pessimism. "You will never be satisfied. As long as you have it, you have Jesus."

He could be right but I could not admit that—it would sound like a confession of weakness and self-indulgence. "When will I see you again?"

"I told you when I arrived that I did not know, but you ignored me."

"One more sitting, maybe two, and then, with luck, hard work, and God's blessing, it might be finished."

He paused to view the picture again and he said in wonderment, "I am beginning to think that it has more of me in it than of Christ."

"It has both," I said stoutly. "You were both Jewish students studying to be a rabbi. But the eyes are still a little heavy and the eyelashes are too long. It is not important that you be recognized."

Spinoza nodded in agreement and added, "I will return if I can. If I do not, it will be because it was impossible to do so."

I asked, "Your thirty-day ban is up soon. Are you going to give in?"

"Would you, Master?"

I shrugged and said, "I cannot answer for you."

"What about your own situation? I hear that it is precarious. I was warned that my presence here could make it worse. It was one of the reasons I did not come before. I felt it would be bad for you."

"It would be worse if I did not use you for Jesus. Besides, my situation is unpredictable." I preferred to talk about his. "What will happen to you if you do not give in?"

Spinoza pondered a moment, then replied quietly, "I will be rejected probably, one way or another. Expelled or imprisoned, or both."

"Yet you are willing to face that?" I asked in wonder.

"I have no choice. No one is going to force me to do anything that I would not do of my own free will."

But a forlorn expression had appeared on his face, as if he felt betrayed and deserted. Then his inner strength refreshed him and he regained his composure. There were indestructible things in him, I thought, and I yearned to paint them. Yet it was too late. My hands ached from my hours of toil and their fatigue would ruin whatever I felt. I must save what I had just seen for another sitting.

He said, "But I must not be harsh on the rabbis. Whatever they do to me, it will be because the Christian community has forced them to do it."

"Then you do not hate them?" I asked in wonder.

"Why should I? I loathe quarrels but not people."

I doubted that I had such compassion. When I thought of Hoag and Thyst and Beghem and Van Goor and some of the others I felt had driven me against an unsurmountable wall, I was filled with a growing and consuming rage. I escorted him to the door and suddenly I put my hand on his to express my affection, and to comfort him.

He responded with a gentle, sweet smile and said, "I would appreciate if you would give my regards to your lady and to your son. Their kindness to me will help me to avoid despair."

In a few days I would be fifty while he was not yet twenty-four, and yet, in some ways, I felt that he was wiser and more mature than I was.

After he was gone I sat staring at the unfinished painting, wondering whose identity I was truly seeking in this portrait of Jesus.

HANG ON

Hang on
Hang on to the kite

Do not let go
However strong the wind

the kite will hold you
However weak the wind

the kite will bring you
down safely

Hang on
Hang on to the kite

Life is the kite
is

—Stymean Karlen

THE last two weeks of July became the most crucial of my life. There was not a day that I did not think about them. I could not work during this period. I sat in my studio, reviewing the events that had brought me to my knees, praying to a God that did not appear to hear me.

On July 15, 1656, I was fifty.

On July 20, 1656, I was bankrupt.

On July 27, 1656, Spinoza was excommunicated.

Now, the next day, I waited for the arrival of old Thomas Haringh, the warden of the Amsterdam Town Hall, to supervise the inventory of my possessions so they could be put up for sale at the appropriate moment.

Inevitably, however, my mind moved backward to the links in this chain of events that threatened to strangle me.

I awoke on my birthday aware of impending disaster.

Twenty-four hours before, Crayer had told me gravely, "Rembrandt, there is no putting off your creditors any longer. Therefore, I am petitioning the court, in your name, for a legal cession of estate." When I looked puzzled—I felt that he was taking the path of least resistance—he added, "It is a kind of leniency granted to unfortunate and *bona fida* debtors. Otherwise, debtors not protected in this way are imprisoned."

Today, I thought wryly, I am supposed to celebrate that I am fifty, but I feel like a hundred. As I sat up in bed my joints were stiff, my arms ached, my eyes were misty, and my mind was painfully stuffed with the confused circumstances of my existence.

Hendrickje, who had waited until I arose, determined not to disturb me, although she had been awake for hours, tenderly took my hand when she saw that I was getting out of bed and whispered, "Happy birthday."

But I was not happy, I thought angrily, even my model was being taken away from me. Spinoza had not submitted when his ban had ended, and he had not returned to sit for me; I doubted that he was in Amsterdam while the synagogue authorities were deliberating what to do about him.

Hendrickje said, "We must celebrate."

That was the last thing I felt like doing. I was dressing in front of my long Venetian mirror and I disliked what I saw before me. Perhaps, I reflected, my appearance was merely the cover of a book, but the cover was worn, frayed, and rotting away. My face had grown thicker, my wrinkles deeper—it was a harshly used face no matter how gently I painted it—my nose was more bulbous, there were large pockets under my eyes, my eyelids drooped, and my cheeks had become swollen, fat, and pendulous.

After Hendrickje gave me breakfast and while Titus's and Daniel's good wishes still echoed in my ears, I told them that I did not want any celebration. I intended to spend this birthday as I preferred—working.

I put aside the memories of the many self-portraits I had done, even those of recent vintage, and I began this one as if I were starting all over. But at the end of the day I felt that I had not accomplished anything. In my determination to be honest I was painting the most unfavorable image of myself that I could. This portrait was revealing a painter who was a broken man, on the verge of ruin, who had nothing to look forward to. Suddenly this likeness was wrong. I could not allow my enemies to think that I was beaten, that they had me at their mercy. The features I had painted were clear and correct, but again, wrong, without heart, neither flesh nor blood but merely method. With a violent stroke of my palette knife, I scraped off what I had painted. I remembered that when I was young I could paint an excellent likeness in a few hours—now I doubted that anything satisfied me.

When I could not work on my portrait of Jesus either or anything else the next few days I waited for the next blow to fall.

It came in the form of a petition from the court. I read it aloud to Hendrickje, Titus, and Daniel as we sat around the kitchen table.

> Rembrandt van Rijn, residing in Amsterdam, respectfully makes known that he, the suppliant, through losses suffered in business, as well as damages and losses by sea, has come into such difficulty that he cannot satisfy his creditors, and that through these same creditors, namely the Lord Burgomaster Cornelius Witsen, Christoffel Thyst, Issac van Hertsbeeck, Daniel Francen, Gerbrandt Ornia, Hendrick van Uylenburgh, Geert Durex, Gerrit Boelissen and the others ought to take this into consideration, and the situation is actually so that he is threatened with attack by the aforementioned, for which reason the suppliant is obliged to address Himself to Your Honorable Magistracy petitioning that immediate letters of cession with *commitimus* be sent to the Court of Amsterdam.

Hendrickje said, "It sounds as if you are the one who is protected."

"Do not be deceived," I answered. "Although Crayer has worded the petition cleverly, it declares that I am insolvent. Anything of mine that is sold from now on will go to my creditors."

Titus said hopefully, "Papa, it does not sound that bad to me."

"It is. However it is put, this document means that a receiver will be appointed to institute the liquidation of all my belongings."

"Will we be forced out of our home?"

"Yes. When they find a buyer."

"Papa, I have saved some money. Five guilders and ten stivers."

"Is that why you did not get me the oils I wanted?" I asked irately.

"They would not give me any credit and I thought you would need the money. You say that you want me to be grown up."

Not so fast, young man, I thought. You are only fifteen and your face is still beardless. But he was pushing the money into my hand and I could not refuse him, it would hurt him. I thanked him for his contribution as I put this money on the table for our common use.

Hendrickje took thirty guilders she had saved and hidden in the cupboard with her precious linens and gave it to me, and Daniel added what he had left from his father's last allowance, twenty-five guilders. Then I thought of what I had stored in the back of my portrait of Jesus. I did not recall the exact amount, but I estimated that it must be at least five or six hundred guilders, enough for us to survive a few weeks, perhaps longer. But I did not add it to the money on the table, as I did with what Hendrickje and Titus gave me. I was afraid to tell anybody else about this money. I felt that would cause it to be taken away from me. I divided the sixty guilders into two parts and handed Hendrickje thirty for the household and told Daniel to keep the rest for an emergency.

Everyone was so quiet and somber while we ate that suddenly I sputtered, "I am not discouraged, I am not discouraged," although I quickly realized that the very reiteration indicated that I was.

The following day Crayer came to my house—this time, I thought, to soften the blow—and said, "I am sorry about the situation you are in, Rembrandt, but it is the best that I could do under the circumstances. And, at least, I have kept you out of prison."

I thanked him again for his efforts on my behalf and asked, although I had not done any the past week, "Will I be able to work for myself?"

"I am fighting for that and for Titus' share of the estate."

"Whatever happens, my son must be protected."

"I am glad we agree. Now that you are placed under receivership, the court will appoint a guardian for your son."

We were sitting in the living room, which also served as a reception room. I offered him some wine from my marble cooler, but he refused. I asked, "Will I have anything to say about who is Titus' guardian?"

"Your wishes may be considered. And since you suggested before that I act as your son's guardian, they may accept that. If you do."

I nodded. Any help at this moment was welcome. "What is next?"

"As you know, I admire your work, but . . ."

"But what?" He was squirming uncomfortably. "Tell me what I face."

"There will be an inventory in a few days. Of everything you own, works of art, personal and household effects. Nothing will be omitted."

I was not as shocked as he assumed I would be; I had expected this to happen. I asked, "What about the work I am doing now?"

"What about it?" Irritation crept into his voice. I was distracting him from essential matters. His manner made that clear.

"Frans Hals told me that when he became bankrupt he was allowed to retain whatever he was working on. In effect, works in hand."

"So you went to see him, not The House of Orange at The Hague! And I thought!" He threw up his hands helplessly. "You must not lie to me!"

"I did not lie to anyone. Someone else spread that story, not me."

"With your connivance. Oh, well, it made no difference eventually."

It had to me, it had consoled me. I would never forget the day I had spent with Hals. "Crayer, it is important that I be allowed to finish what I am painting."

"Is it your portrait of Jesus?"

I nodded reluctantly.

"Rembrandt, there is much criticism of that picture."

"That is ridiculous. Virtually no one has seen it."

"You know what I mean." He added, with as much kindness as he could summon, yet, I felt, determined to justify his own view, "Personally, I do not agree with the pastors who condemn you for using a Jewish model, especially one they consider a heretic. I find Spinoza a pleasant and agreeable young man who has never thrust his opinions on me. But your concept worries them and they have influence with the civic authorities. If you were painting something else it would be easier to win support." When he saw my jaw set stubbornly, he continued more firmly, "However, I will do what I can. I may be able to keep this work in your hands."

If not, I thought grimly, this picture could be destroyed. That possibility brought a pain to my stomach as vicious as any I had ever felt, but as I bent over to hide it from him, I said, "I do not intend to sell it so they cannot say that I profit from it."

"Under any circumstances?" he asked wonderingly.

"Under any circumstances," I repeated for emphasis. "It is not for sale."

Crayer said in amazement, "I think you mean it. Even if it would save you from bankruptcy."

"I mean it. This picture belongs to me." And to Jesus, I thought.

"Your creditors may feel otherwise, but I will do my best to keep it in your hands. Be sensible, cooperate with the inventory, and it will make matters easier for you." But now I was not listening to him, I was deciding where to hide the picture during this trying time.

After his polite farewell I hid the portrait of Jesus in my store-room with my other unfinished works. Then I developed a daily routine of wandering from room to room to view my possessions before they vanished in bankruptcy, and because of that, I examined them with a new and deeper passion. At night I barred the doors, bolted the windows, but when I was notified on the 27th of July that the inventory was to start the next day, I could not look at my things anymore.

I told Hendrickje, "Dust the frames, scrub the tile and take the paint spots out of the carpet, polish the brass and copper and silver, and wash the windows. I must show them that we are proud of our home."

She did as I ordered and I also wanted to keep her occupied, for Daniel had just rushed into my studio to tell me that Spinoza had been excommunicated today and I had to know what this meant, and I did not want any tears or hysteria from her while I decided how this affected me.

When Hendrickje was gone I ordered Daniel to tell me the details. I was not sure that he could. He paced up and down my studio as agitated as I had ever seen him. His blonde hair was unruly, his fair complexion was florid with emotion, and he looked ill.

"Is it that bad?" I asked finally, when he seemed unable to speak.

"Worse, Master. I never thought it would come to this."

"I thought only Roman Catholics excommunicated their members."

"Who do you think they copied it from?"

"Is the edict irrevocable?"

"Yes. Listen." He read the declaration exactly as it was worded.

The elders hereby make known that they have been long since cognizant of the wrong opinions and behavior of Baruch Spinoza, and have tried by various means and promises to dissuade him from his evil ways. But as they effected no improvement—obtaining on the contrary more information each day of the horrible heresies which he practiced and taught, and the monstrous actions which he committed—and as they had many trustworthy witnesses who in the presence of the same Spinoza reported and testified against him and convicted him, and after investigating the whole matter in the presence of the rabbis, they finally decided with the consent of the rabbis that the same Spinoza should be excommunicated and separated from the people of Israel. Accordingly they now declare:

After the judgement of the Angels, and with that of the Saints, we excommunicate, expel, curse, and damn Baruch Spinoza with the consent of God, Blessed be He, and with the consent of the Holy Congregation, in front of the Holy Scrolls with the six hundred and thirteen precepts that are written therein, with the ban with which Joshua banned Jericho; with the curse which Elisha cursed the boys, and with all the curses that are written in the Law. Cursed be he by day and cursed be he by night; cursed be he when he lieth down, and cursed be he when he riseth up, cursed be he when he goeth out, and cursed be he when he cometh in. The Lord will not pardon him; the wrath of The Lord will rage against this man, and bring upon him all the curses which are written in the Book of the Law; and the Lord will destroy his name from under the Heavens; and the Lord will separate him from all the tribes of Israel. But you who cleave unto the Lord your God, you are all alive this day.

We command that none should communicate with him orally or in writing, or show him any favor, or stay with him under the same roof, or within four paces of him, or read anything composed or written by him.

When Daniel finished he was even more agitated, while I thought that the edict was overwrought. It bore no relation to the young man who had sat for me, yet in the eyes of the synagogue he had committed a heinous crime and must be punished and cast out. I wondered if this matter would have gone this far if Rabbi Manasseh ben Israel had remained in Amsterdam. I asked, "Do you know how Spinoza received this ban?"

"No one has seen him recently. He may have left the city." Daniel added bitterly, "He will have to. The Christian Church authorities have approved of the excommunication and they have persuaded the civic officials to expel him from Amsterdam. Baruch is banished from the city."

"For how long?" I thought with horror. I would never finish now.

"For the time being. The exact length is not specified. The Dutch religious and civic authorities want to show they applaud the ban."

"Where do you think he went?"

"It is rumored that he is in Ouwerkerk but no one is sure."

"What do you think he will do?"

"I think he will wait to see how the public reacts and if the uproar dies down he may return to Amsterdam. But I am not sure that will be wise. I have heard threats against his life and no one will protect him now."

I did not have time to meditate about Spinoza's situation; there was a messenger downstairs with the reminder that the inventory was starting tomorrow and that everything must be ready for it. I was angry; they had already notified me that they were coming on the 28th. Did they think I had to be impressed and intimidated? My impulse was to ignore them, but Daniel, who had heard the news with me, said, "Master, you must not. If you are civil to them it is possible that you may be able to save what you are working on." I thought with satisfaction, So my portrait of Jesus did matter to him. I had not been certain of this, but I still wondered if he was equally concerned with Spinoza's participation in this picture. There was no answer in his distraught eyes, only a need to present an inventory of my effects in the best possible light.

The rest of the day and long into the night Daniel and Titus sought to put my possessions into an attractive order, to prove to me that my things would not suffer any harm, when the loss of one item was a kind of death.

And Hendrickje cleaned the house until she was sure it was spotless.

Old Thomas Haringh arrived promptly. I was glad it was sunny; that would show my collection in the best light. I knew the warden. A few years ago I had etched a portrait of his son, the lawyer Jacob Haringh, who was called "Young Haringh" to distinguish him from his father. The elderly civic employee, with his wavy white hair and heavy, round face, was a personage in the city. In his position as warden and concierge of the Amsterdam Town Hall, he was responsible for carrying out the inventory and the sale of my household effects and art collection. He was the auction master of all movable property in bankruptcy cases.

I was waiting for him at the door and he greeted me with a delicacy of sentiment, as if my self-esteem must not be damaged by what he had to do. I responded as civilly as I could, considering the circumstances, and apologized for the five steps he had to climb to enter my house.

He was breathless already and I said, "I hope this task will not be difficult." He replied, "Not at all, it will be a privilege to view such a fine collection," and I realized that he regarded himself as an art connoisseur, too. He was accompanied by two young men who were to do the actual work and he did not introduce them.

After Haringh recovered his breath I took him for an inspection of my house while Hendrickje gave his helpers beer in the kitchen. Daniel and Titus followed us at a respectful distance, should they be needed to move something. Haringh wanted to start with the ground floor.

So I showed him those things first and he exclaimed, "This chamber looks like the storeroom of a dealer in antiques! The old arms, the statues you have collected from all parts of Europe. I did not know you had so many objects besides paintings."

I was surprised, too. I had never itemized my collection and I saw many things that I had forgotten about.

Then, as I escorted him up the stairs that led to my salon, I saw the mark that I had made fifteen years ago when Saskia had died. In my rage and heartbreak I had kicked the top step with my heel and the imprint, the scarred and scratched wood, was still visible. I thought, What have the stairs learned in all that time? Was it how kind or unkind a footstep could be? God had not returned the dead to me. But now I needed his sympathy. I took him into the vestibule, where he counted twenty-four pictures by Brouwer, Seghers, and Lievens.

He said, "I did not know you admired Lievens. I heard . . ."

I interrupted, ". . . that we were enemies. It is common gossip. Lievens and I studied together in Leyden. We were close then. I have a high regard for the work he did when he was younger."

He noted fourteen paintings that I had done. He was amazed that so much of my work was unsold but I did not respond to this.

He was enchanted with my anteroom with its green velvet-covered Spanish chairs, my Raphael, Palma Vecchio, Giorgione, and Van Eyck. "You have unusual taste," he said. "They must have cost a fortune."

I had never thought about these pictures in that way. What I loved I wanted. What I wanted I had obtained. When it was possible. I did not answer his implicit question.

The size of my salon and the number of objects of art in it evoked an awed silence from him as he admired the casts, the bronzes, the china and the glass, the sixty-four portfolios of engravings and drawings by Dutch, German, Flemish, and Italian masters that I had collected. But his most passionate attention was reserved for more of my pictures that hung in this chamber. I felt that he was paying a last tribute of respect to a funeral cortege, but when he said, "I have admired your work for a long time, I wish you could do a portrait of me as you did of my son," I realized that his regard was genuine.

I ignored why he was here and I replied, "I would be honored. I will paint you when you have the time. I hear you are a very busy man."

He said emphatically, "I will make the time."

For a long time we stood there as if nothing mattered but the work around us. Finally he whispered apologetically, "I am sorry, but I should see your studio."

I said, "It is just a large workroom. With unfinished pictures. However, if it is necessary I will show it to you."

"I am sorry but it is. The law requires that everything be listed."

"Even unfinished work?" I remarked, as I took him into the studio.

"That depends."

"On what?"

He did not commit himself as he followed me into my studio, but he was disappointed by how little was being done. Surprised, he said, "I thought you were painting a portrait of Jesus. There is much talk about it."

"What kind of talk?" I asked anxiously.

"Most say it is sacrilegious, a few think it is superb."

"It does not matter. It is a private picture, work in progress, in hand, not for sale, and it has nothing to do with the inventory."

"I hope your view is upheld, but the authorities may differ with you." Haringh tried to sound kind as he added, "If not enough money is raised at the auction to satisfy the creditors they may demand that it and all other work in progress be included to make up the deficit."

"What about the necessity to earn a living?"

"I think that will be considered. When can I sit for you?"

I could not be penitent, yet I did not want to refuse him. The man standing quietly in the shadow of the empty easel certainly did not suggest any sinister design and there was a uniqueness in his expression that was worth depicting. And his son had paid me promptly. I decided to bargain. I said carefully, "I must have a free mind to do you."

"Which means . . . ?" He paused and waited for my proposal.

"I can only draw you properly if I feel that the portrait of Jesus that I am working on remains in my hands. This is vital to me."

He considered what I said, then replied, "Rembrandt, I am not a heartless wretch. I will do what I can to make that wish of yours possible. But I cannot assure you that will happen. Others have to be consulted and will make the decision. I can only advise."

"You will be listened to if you stress that I cannot pay all my debts unless I can continue to work. The auction will not accomplish that."

I felt audacious, but he did not seem to resent my demand, for that was what it was, however I expressed it. Fixing his weary brown eyes on me and nodding wisely, he answered, "You should be allowed to earn a living." He added virtuously, "Like a good Christian."

"Then we will arrange a time for you to sit."

"Yes. Meanwhile," he said apologetically, "I will have to ask my men to list everything that is within the walls of this house."

"Do whatever is necessary," I said curtly, to hide my emotion.

"Everything is so clean. I had heard . . ." He halted awkwardly.

"That I was dirty, untidy, slovenly."

"People talk too much. I trust you will excuse the inventory."

"Of course. My assistant will show your men whatever is necessary."

During the inventory I invited Haringh into my reception

room, where Hendrickje served us tea and cake and we discussed the work of Hals. The auction master said his portraits were the best in Holland, except for mine.

But the reality was that after the inventory my treasures were draped in tarpaulins and other coverings to protect them from damage and to signify that they no longer belonged to me. I had owned some of these things since I had settled in Amsterdam twenty-five years ago and the thought of doing without them made me ill.

Hendrickje, Titus, and Daniel gathered in the kitchen to console me.

My son said, "Papa, they should not expect you to be like other fathers. You are separate from them. You should do what you want to do."

I answered, as I also saw Hendrickje's concern, "You are right. And we will go to Ruismeer's church this Sunday. Daniel, did the men question the inventory? Did they act as if anything was hidden from them?"

"Not to my face. I showed them everything except the unfinished work. They were surprised by the size and quality of your collection. They said it is one of the finest in Holland, worthy of The House of Orange. Here is the duplicate list they gave me."

As my eye fell on the multitude of items, I, too, was astonished by the scope and strength of my collection. The number of works that I possessed of other artists was large and of a high order. I read the heading: "Inventory of the Paints, Furniture and other items contained in the house of Rembrandt van Rijn Living in the Breestraat by the St. Anthony Water Gate," and then I skipped to individual items.

> One small landscape by Rembrandt
> One moonlight scene by Jan Lievens
> Two naked children in plaster
> One still life retouched by Rembrandt
> Four Spanish chairs in Russian leather
> One painter's studio by Adrian Brouwer

Suddenly I could not go on. My vision blurred. I could hardly see my hand in front of me. I was terrified that I was going blind. Hendrickje, seeing me rubbing my pupils, brought me a cloth soaked in warm water and applied it gently to my aching eyes. Gradually the pain ebbed and I could see clearly again. Then, looking again at my family's faces, at their varied expressions, at a world I could view again, I sighed with gratitude. I embraced all of them, Daniel, too, who responded awkwardly but with affection, and asked him, "Do you think I will see Spinoza again?"

Now Hendrickje and Titus wanted to know what had happened to him and when I told them, they looked at me with consternation.

Titus cried out, "Does that mean he will not come here any more?"

"I do not know."

"Could the rabbis have been wrong?"

"It is not for me to judge. But I think he has faith, in his own way."

Hendrickje was so upset she almost scalded herself with the tea she was brewing, exclaiming, "Does he have to shake his fist at heaven?"

"Who knows? Will you speak to him if he does return? It is forbidden to Daniel."

"Will Daniel speak to him?" she snapped, prepared to argue with me.

Daniel replied slowly, "As I told the Master earlier, I have no choice. I have known Baruch all my life. He lived next door to me."

I thought of how odd it was that Spinoza had been born just around the corner from me and had resided there most of his life, that I had drawn his teachers, known his friends, that we must have passed each other many times before we became acquainted —I had visited the synagogue often to use its members as models while he had worshipped there—and now there was this dreadful interruption. Suddenly I was exhausted from what I had endured the past two weeks and I cut short the speculation about Spinoza, saying, "We have had a long day. It is late. We must go to bed."

After Titus and Daniel went to their separate rooms in the attic Hendrickje asked me, as she undressed, "How can he be so wicked when he behaves so kindly? I will beseech God to look mercifully upon him." I did not answer. I donned my nightgown and prayed, "Please, dear God, for the love I bear You, have forgiveness for our friend."

Hendrickje lay down beside me a minute later and had a new question for me. "Master, what will you do about this picture if he does not return?"

"I will not be able to finish it." I took her hand and entwined her fingers in mine to express my feeling for her.

"Will the sale be soon?"

"I do not know. Nothing was said about the date." I could not bring myself to think about it. I wondered, Was my work simply the scars and scratches I had made on the stairway of life? And would they fade and vanish in time? As had so many of the friends I had known? Yet I realized that this painting of Jesus had to be Spinoza or no one. I knew that with a certainty that I did not possess for anything else.

TITUS SAYS

Titus says
Papa
no matter what they do to you

You will always live to paint
You will always paint to discover
You will always discover to paint
And you will always paint to live

Papa that makes a very good circle
Circles always complete themselves
And so will you Papa
No matter what they do to you

                                   —Stymean Karlen

I BECAME so involved the following month with my bankruptcy, the inventory of my possessions, and the plans for their sale that I was unable to find the time, energy, or emotion to work. I was also upset that there was no word from Spinoza. It were as if he had vanished from the earth. Without his presence I could not finish my portrait of Jesus and I lacked the faith to start anything else. Without faith I was lost.

Hendrickje ignored my orders to feed me frugally with vegetables and dairy products that were cheap, and instead served me fresh meat and fowl, while Titus and Daniel ate sparingly so that I could eat better. But I did not have any appetite and their efforts to encourage me failed.

Just as I feared that my dire situation would never end, Haringh and Crayer agreed to visit me in an attempt to ease my tangled affairs. It was the first time they were seeing me together and I awaited them with eagerness, yet apprehension. I prayed, If only they could restore to me feeling, energy, and a will to work. The sterility that had settled on me was inexcusable; I could not forgive myself or those who had pushed me into this predicament. I felt that my creditors were trying to put me into a world where there was no hope and no desire.

They were business acquaintances and they talked gravely about the possibility of a new war with England, and how it would damage trade. I could not endure such distractions so I interrupted them, grumbling, "Nothing seems to get settled. I have no idea where I stand."

Haringh said apologetically, "Other people have to be consulted. The law moves slowly in such matters."

"I cannot work. I still do not know whether it is allowed."

Crayer replied, "It is allowed. I believe. Haringh, am I correct?"

"Within certain limits." The auction master had returned twice to verify the inventory, it was so large, and to discuss the proposed portrait, and he seemed honestly concerned about my inability to work. But also, I sensed, not quite sure of himself as he added, "I think."

Hendrickje was serving them the usual tea and cake that I gave guests, with Titus carrying the tray, while Daniel was in my studio preparing it for Haringh's first sitting, and suddenly I felt this was in vain, I would never be able to work again, and I stood up abruptly and shouted, "Are you trying to excommunicate me, too?"

Even Hendrickje was startled, and Haringh and Crayer looked stunned.

It was Titus who answered, murmuring, "Papa, even if you do not go to church much, you are a good Christian."

"Christians excommunicate all the time!" I growled. "If I am forbidden to work, that is what it is, whatever they call it!"

Crayer said, seeking to appease me, "We sympathize with you." And as Haringh agreed with a nod of his head, he went on, "But you must not do anything that is unwise."

I said, "Such as using Spinoza as my model for Jesus?"

Crayer looked pained that I had mentioned this work while Haringh stated solemnly, "That is not the subject at issue."

"It is with me," I retorted angrily. "If I am not free to depict

Him as I see Him, I cannot portray you. The same hand is needed for both."

Crayer and Haringh glanced at each other to decide how to answer, but I felt human again; I had spoken out, I had stopped being humble, that was not becoming to me, or natural, and there was not a blank space in front of me anymore; it was filled with objects to draw and paint.

When Crayer saw that I had no intention of being contrite, he asked me, "What would you like us to do?"

My possessions were still draped, but in this instant they lost their ghostly grayness, and I replied, "Settle my affairs. Find out what I can do. Otherwise, this uncertainty and delay will kill me."

Hendrickje whispered, "Begging your pardon, gentlemen, but the Master has not been well. He sleeps very little, he eats hardly anything."

"That is enough!" I said severely. "My health is not the issue!"

Titus said, "Papa, she is right. I have never seen you eat so poorly or not work for such a long time. It is not the way you used to be."

Hendrickje cried out, "Gentlemen, he must paint again or he will die!"

I was silent. I could not dispute her. She was telling the truth.

Titus said, "Hendrickje and I could sell his new work. In our name."

Crayer said, "Haringh, his son makes a good point. Is it possible that Rembrandt could work for Titus van Rijn and Hendrickje Stoffels?"

Everyone was silent while the auction master considered this proposal. After a minute of reflection, he said slowly, "Other things would have to be settled first. Then something like you suggest might be possible."

"What other things?" I asked, still impatient with the delays.

"First, the sale of your effects. You own three hundred and sixty-three lots and they include seventy of your paintings."

"Seventy? I did not know I had that many in the house."

"And that does not include work in hand."

So we were back to that again, I thought grimly. I stated, "That

(319)

is the issue. Otherwise, I cannot start any new work."

This statement caused the auction master to look somber and uneasy.

Crayer added, "He is right. You cannot auction a work in hand."

Hendrickje said, "Your portrait, Heer Haringh, would be just that."

I declared, "Even if I am reduced to the barest essentials, I must be allowed to continue with what I have started. To support myself."

Titus said, "Hendrickje and I can sell it. Why should his creditors get his new work, too? They should get enough from what is already here."

I was proud of my son, but I was afraid to show it, it might cause him to disobey me. I said, "Heer Haringh, I would like to begin your portrait today, but at the moment my hands are bound."

He said grudgingly, "I will do what I can."

"In what way?" asked Crayer.

My lawyer was demanding again, I thought with relief, on my side.

"What do you mean?" Haringh asked, growing puzzled and irritable.

"It must be made clear that Rembrandt is allowed to support himself."

"That does not depend on me. The creditors are demanding that enough money must be raised from the sale of his effects to meet their claims. If it is less, they will want it from other sources."

Crayer said, "His collection must be worth forty thousand guilders."

"Our estimate is closer to twenty and with the bad business situation, that may not be realized. Our Court of Insolvency has been presented with claims exceeding thirty thousand guilders. So, even after the sale, he may still owe much money."

"I will work," Titus said stoutly.

"So will I," Hendrickje added just as enthusiastically.

The auction master smiled indulgently and even Crayer was

not impressed by their support, for he said, "That is not sufficient. A better remedy must be found. Haringh, what is the view of his creditors?"

"The Francens are willing to wait, the others are not. Then there is another problem. Although this house has been put up for sale, there have not been any offers. No one wants to pay what it costs. It may take years to dispose of it. It will be a struggle to sell it. As it will be for the effects. Many feel they are too costly, extravagant."

He was also inferring that I had been extravagant to buy them, but they had been necessary to me, not simply to enjoy them, which I had, but to learn from them. I did not explain, I knew that would be futile. Instead, I suggested, "Heer Haringh, would you like to sit now?"

"But you said . . . ?" He left the rest unspoken but implied.

I had seen something in his face that was worth sketching after all, and I added, "You said that you will do the best you can and so will I. Titus, make sure Daniel has prepared the studio and, Hendrickje, make more tea and cake for our guests. We must not be inhospitable. Crayer, would you like to join us in the studio? See how they have stripped me?"

He declined, saying he had to be in the Orphans' Court this afternoon for the settlement of Spinoza's suit against his half-sister—he had no idea what the verdict would be—and as he thanked Hendrickje for her courtesy, Haringh said, "Crayer, prepare your plea and I will present it to our Board of Insolvency with a recommendation for clemency."

Now Haringh was welcome in my studio and, with all my materials in place, thanks to Daniel, his presence reminded me that I was an artist again. He did resemble his son, I realized, and gradually, as I etched his face, I forgot everything but the work in front of me. His black cloak, his white ruff and cuffs were appropriate to my view of him, and the sun that came in from the window behind him lighted his head so that it stood out strongly against the darkness of the background. I resolved to make this portrait one of the finest I had etched. Not quite like any other I had done and yet to show that I was still master of my craft.

He sat silently and motionlessly and when I told him that there would have to be another sitting, he said, "Master, whatever is your pleasure."

That Sunday, in gratitude for the restoration of energy and emotion to my soul, I took Hendrickje and Titus to Ruismeer's church. No one tried to stop us at the door as I half expected and feared.

Ruismeer's service was simple and he preached: "We Christians must treat everyone with charity and mercy. Wherever those are found, there Christ really is, and when they are lacking, there Christ is not. By the spirit of Christ alone can we be led to the love of charity and mercy."

The pastor approached us afterward and thanked us for attending and Hendrickje regarded him with a worshipful attention, as if he were one of Jesus' disciples, while Titus was excited by his interest.

He said to me, "I am glad you are better. I heard you were not well."

I replied, "Pastor, that was exaggerated. May we come again?"

"Whenever you want. You and your family are always welcome."

I was considering a new self-portrait several days later, dissatisfied with the pessimism of the one I had begun on my fiftieth birthday, trying to decide what approach to use, when Spinoza returned.

Titus rushed upstairs to tell me that he was at the door, not sure whether I wanted to see him under the present circumstances, and that Daniel had remained with Spinoza to keep him from having a change of heart and fleeing and I was in a dilemma. I did not want to show Spinoza how eager I was to paint him, yet I could not endure the thought of losing him, perhaps this time for good, with work still to be done.

Titus cried, "You must not hesitate. I do not think he will wait long. He keeps looking over his shoulder as if someone is following him."

"Was he glad to see you?"

"I think so. But you know how reserved he can be. He is almost solemn now. I am glad to see him. Papa, you are not?"

"It depends." I strode down the stairs, seeking to avoid scuffing them in my anxiety, excitement, and doubts. But when I saw Spinoza standing in the doorway, speaking to Daniel, and I observed his flowing black hair, thick, even eyebrows, his dark, lustrous eyes, his long straight nose, his beautiful mouth and his finely formed red lips, his attractive, almost handsome face, whose inner light was heightened by his suffering, there was nothing for me to do but to surrender to my need to paint him. I led him to my studio while Daniel and Titus followed eagerly.

Hendrickje joined us there and blurted out, "You are back! Unhurt! It is a miracle!"

"I am grateful for your concern, but I do not believe in miracles."

"Now the Master can paint you again. He missed you very much."

"Not that much," I growled. He must not think that he was essential.

Daniel, the only one of us who did not appear pleased, but worried, said, "I thought the civic authorities banished you from Amsterdam."

"They did. But nothing happened. And since the suit over my father's estate was being settled I came back from Ouwerkerk for the verdict. The length of my banishment from the city was not specified."

"What happened with your suit against your half-sister?"

"I won. The Orphans' Court decided the case on its merits."

"So now you have your father's house, furniture, and other effects."

"No. I gave everything to my half-sister except my bed."

"Then why did you contest her claim?" Daniel was surprised.

Spinoza smiled gently and said, "Because I was right."

"But you have no money of your own. And no way to earn it except as a teacher and that is not likely to be possible here."

"All I need is a good bed with furnishings."

"Baruch, how will you support yourself?"

"Grind lenses, probably. I like to work with my hands and it is monotonous enough to give me the time to concentrate on my ideas."

"You will earn very little."

"It will be enough to live on," he answered simply.

I said urgently, "Then you will remain in Amsterdam until I finish?"

"Master, I am not sure. Do you truly want to finish this picture?"

I realized there was truth to what he was implying, but I merely grunted and turned to see if everything was in place for his sitting.

Hendrickje, believing that he was hesitating for other reasons, hastened to add, "Young man, we were threatened with excommunication several years ago. But we survived and never lost our faith."

He said sadly, "I have lost my faith. Did they sentence you?"

"No." She blushed, embarrassed now by what she might reveal, and added, "They tried to punish us in other ways, but we were threatened with it."

I said, "And I have been threatened with damnation."

Spinoza said, "I do not believe that. You are trying to comfort me."

"Some people consider me a heretic."

"With your belief in Jesus? They must be stupid, misinformed!"

Daniel was still anxious and he pointed to the stripped studio and said, "The Master has suffered since you were here last, too. He has been declared insolvent. Soon his treasured prints, drawings, paintings, costumes, and curiosities will be in the hands of the auctioneer."

My executioner, I thought bitterly, but I was pleased with Daniel's passion. Perhaps he could become a painter after all. Then I saw Spinoza stir restlessly and uneasily, and I said, "Clear out. All of you. I must work now. While there is still good light in the sky."

The severity of my tone was not to be disputed. They retired to the kitchen while Spinoza sat by the window and I took the precious picture from where I had hidden it. But I could not start from where I had left off. He had altered drastically and so had I. This required the most careful attention. And suddenly I had to ask—I had to know—"Spinoza, why did you return? It will not improve your situation in Amsterdam."

"That does not matter. You have put so much of yourself into this work that I thought it was a crime to prevent you from finishing it."

"I have put you into it, too. Sometimes, I think, as much as Jesus."

"I am no Jesus. I do not wish to be a martyr. What I did, I had to do."

"As He had to do. I will judge what you are."

But while I observed him over and over the next few minutes, my final conception escaped me. Now, however, I knew that there was nothing more fatal for this picture than delay. Yet I could not go on like this. If I could not trust my hand, I could not trust anything. Then I realized that I did not know the most vital thing of all about him. I asked abruptly, "How do you feel about your excommunication?"

"What is there to feel?"

"Young man, I am not dangerous."

He smiled, and yet he suddenly looked wounded and angry.

"Then you do not forgive them?" I prodded.

"That is not necessary. If they want to regard me with scorn, I cannot stop them, but that does not mean that I have to feel the same way. Scorn is an indulgence I do not have to succumb to. I try to be rational."

"You are not angry at them?"

"Why should I be angry? Jews have suffered greatly for their faith."

Sorrow mixed with compassion came into his lustrous eyes and he seemed transformed by his experiences of the last few months. I was grateful to Daniel for having saved a fine, clean brush from the inventory, a fresh jar of turpentine, a palette with the essential colors—I was using as few as possible to keep the picture from becoming dirty or heavy—for I wanted this painting to speak for itself. No explanation, no apology was necessary now. I was going to have a good afternoon after all.

(325)

We worked in absolute stillness—he was trying, I sensed, in his own way, to suggest what I saw in him—and I painted his inner qualities: spiritual, poetic, meditative. "Just a minute," I whispered, as he moved suddenly, his body cramped. "Take no notice," he replied.

"Sssh." He was also a rich plastic material in his remembering, expressing, reflecting. A light shone out of him and I felt I was coming close to the source of his soul. But not quite, for all at once there was bitterness in his eyes rather than the compassion I had seen.

I had lost track of the time but we must have been working several hours, for suddenly he said curtly, "Quickly, there is not much time left."

Yet the answer was in him, whether he considered himself a Jew or not now, and I thought, Jesus chose to be a Jew rather than a Roman, which, at this moment, struck me as significant, and I said, "Be patient. With God's blessing and hard work it should be finished soon."

"You mean I will have to come here again? I am not sure I can."

"Only once more," I pleaded. "We are almost there." And we were, I decided, as I examined the portrait. "If we could do the final sitting at night it should convey the final tone of the picture."

For an instant Spinoza regarded me as if I were a lunatic, and then he said, as he gazed at the painting and apparently saw something in it that he had not seen before, "You suggest, The question is not how to die, but how to live." He approved with a nod of his head, thoughtfully.

"How to be. How to be. Young man, when should I expect you again?"

"Tomorrow night. If the authorities do not interfere."

"You told Daniel that you had nothing to fear."

Spinoza said mournfully, "There have been threats against my life. I did not want to worry your lady or your son."

"Where are you staying?"

"At Van den Ende's. No one should betray me there."

I asked wonderingly, "Who would want to attack you?"

"Rembrandt, there are many fanatics about," he said grimly.

"Christian, Jewish, others. To question the nature of God is to question them."

"I will see you tomorrow night. Come, I will take you to the door."

"Master, that is not necessary."

"Do not tell me what is necessary. Young man, this is still my house."

I was so tired after he slipped out of my house into the growing darkness that I could not tell whether I was close to my intention. I must have sat in front of the picture for hours, for by the time I responded to Hendrickje's call to dinner it was black outside and I saw the stars.

When Daniel asked, "Is he returning?" I replied brusquely, "Tomorrow." I did not explain, except to add, "In the evening. It will give me the best perspective. Were there any messages while I was working?"

Titus said, "Crayer and Haringh are coming in the morning."

"Did they tell you why?"

"The auction master spoke about his sitting but I think they have news for you, Papa. About the insolvency and the sale of your work."

"Did you tell them about Spinoza?"

"Not a word. Did you want me to?"

"No. You did the right thing." I did not want to sound like a conspirator, especially with the others regarding me suspiciously, even Hendrickje, so I said with the utmost sincerity, "It is just that I do not want anything to interfere with the picture."

Daniel said hopefully, "Then it is almost finished, Master?"

"Almost. Now I have to persuade Haringh to allow me to keep it."

THREE HERETICS

Three heretics
each in a different way
Rembrandt Spinoza Jesus

Three heretics
each assassinated
in their own time
each in a different way

Three heretics
each resurrected by time
each made famous by time
Rembrandt Spinoza Jesus
each in a different way

—Stymean Karlen

HARINGH and Crayer came early, when I was still at breakfast, as if their news could not wait. They declined my invitation to join me at the table and I left my meal reluctantly. This was the first time I had eaten heartily in weeks—I had taken a close look at my portrait of Jesus on my way downstairs—and it was better than I expected, perhaps one sitting away from finishing after all, and I looked forward to working on it. But I tried to hide my impatience with them and I took my guests to my reception room, and as I sought to make them feel at home, the auction master came to the point quickly. He said, "As I promised, I recommended to the Amsterdam Board of Insolvency that they treat your situation with clemency and they have come to the following conclusions."

While he paused to gain breath and emphasis and Crayer

waited attentively, I asked impatiently, "Will I be able to keep my work in hand?"

"Patience, friend," said Crayer. "We will come to that."

"In time," said Haringh. "First things first."

This was first, I thought, and I found it hard to control myself.

The auction master resumed solemnly, "I think the Amsterdam Court of Insolvency will grant your petition for a *cessio bonorum.*"

"That I applied for," Crayer said triumphantly.

I did not feel victorious as they did and I said, "It sounds to me as if I am still regarded as a bankrupt."

"You are," said Haringh. "An undischarged bankrupt. You will still be forced to relinquish to your creditors the proceeds from the sale of your entire estate."

"I know that." I wondered why he was so pleased with himself.

"But you will be allowed to retain your personal freedom."

"I will not be imprisoned?"

"That is right," Haringh said proudly.

I said, "But, Crayer, you informed me earlier that I would not be."

He replied, "That was my intention, but now we are sure you are safe."

"You will not be imprisoned," Haringh repeated, to be sure I knew what he had achieved. "And you will be allowed to retain such things and possessions as are needed and required to earn a living."

"When will my effects be sold?"

"As I told you, it will take some time, possibly a year, perhaps even longer. The market is depressed, the creditors may want to wait, and they are creating other difficulties. And the law moves slowly."

"What about my work in hand?"

"We will come to that. We intend to circulate the following advertisement as an expression of good faith and to conciliate the creditors." He read a paper: *"The Trustees of the Insolvent property of Rembrandt van Rijn will sell his art and collection as soon as possible."*

While I questioned why they were congratulating themselves on what they had accomplished, I did not feel they had improved my situation much, Crayer announced, "Moreover, Titus will be protected. The Orphans' Court has appointed me to be his guardian, as you desired, and I plan to arrange for Hendrickje and your son to become art dealers so that you can work for their company as an employee and adviser. They will collect whatever money you earn and pass that on to you as a salary."

Puzzled, I asked, "Does that mean that I can continue to work?"

"If my proposal is accepted, and Heer Haringh thinks there is an excellent chance it will be, you will still be able to earn a living."

"However," Haringh warned, "You will lose everything you own now."

I was starting to understand and I said, "Except what is unfinished."

"That is what you wanted, is it not?"

Suddenly I was overjoyed that I had not finished my portrait of Jesus.

Crayer said, "We want to keep you painting."

Haringh added, "But you must realize that you will be allowed to retain only enough of your earnings to provide the bare necessities of life."

My joy faded. I wondered if Jesus had ever doubted Himself, had ever felt that He and His works would be extinguished. I felt my faith fading.

Crayer, sensing that, declared, "Since you have used up most of your son's estate in your efforts to hold on to your house and possessions, I am petitioning the Court that Titus be the principal and preferential creditor."

By now I would have given much to return to my work, my head was such a muddle, but I realized that this was vital. I asked, "Does this mean, that in spite of my bankruptcy, Titus will inherit something?"

"Yes. If my petition is allowed and I think it will be."

Haringh said, intending to be kind, "You will probably remain an undischarged bankrupt but Titus should be protected. Crayer is clever."

"Very clever," I mumbled. I was glad for my son but still shaken by the realization that my bankruptcy was irrevocable

and that my collection was lost forever. I repeated, seeking sustenance somewhere, "But I can retain my work in hand?"

Crayer said, "It was a struggle to achieve that, but we
did."

Haringh said, "I can sit for you now. I have a few minutes to
spare."

I hesitated, exhausted from the ordeal I had just endured, but
he was eager to sit and he had done his best for me, and so, to
express my gratitude, I nodded. But after Crayer departed,
pleased with what he had accomplished for my son, I could not
concentrate on Haringh's features. Although I saw decency as
well as self-interest on this burgher's face, rectitude in addition
to self-righteousness, my mind was on Spinoza. His expression
suggested what I desired to say about God and man; there was
none of that on Haringh's countenance. So I darkened the background and kept his face subdued. He was surprised that I
wanted another sitting; he said that he did not have any more
time to spare from his official duties. But when I assured him that
I would do my best to complete his portrait in the next sitting,
he agreed to come once more, but only once more.

While I waited for Spinoza I worked on another self-portrait.
I disregarded everything I had done in the past, and especially the
harsh view of myself that I had projected in the last one. I could
depend on this sitter, I thought wryly, and this was good practice
for the work I would have to do later, I was exercising my hands
and eyes, but gradually, as I became engrossed in my subject, the
picture became important in itself. I recalled what Titus had said
and I put myself in the sitter's chair with a grandeur that caused
me to sit as if I were a monarch granting a royal audience to the
viewer. I felt pleased with myself when I presented my body,
appropriately enough, I reflected, with a massive and imposing
strength that gave dignity and authority to my face. The sun was
setting and I painted its golden glow full upon my skin. I was
saying simply and directly, Do not count the old man out, I am
not surrendering, whatever happens. I was determined to show
that emotionally and spiritually I was not ruined. I was no longer
concerned with whether it was a physical likeness. And as night

(331)

fell and as the darkness sustained my hand I did not care what others would think of it.

When I joined my family at the dinner table I felt better than I had for some time and I looked forward to finishing my portrait of Jesus.

We were eating fruit that Hendrickje had bought for dessert—I had given her fifty more guilders from my savings in the back of the canvas—when we heard the sounds of a scuffle outside and shouts for help. We ran to the door, the Breestraat was usually quiet at this time of the night, but as I flung it open we saw Spinoza trying to push away a would-be assassin. This was on the darkest part of the street, where the light was faintest between two widely spaced lamps, and as Spinoza recoiled from the assailant I saw a knife flash in the air and strike downward at him. Then, as the would-be assassin saw us approaching, it was evident from the fury with which he attacked Spinoza that he intended to kill him, he fled. It was so dark that I could not tell what he looked like, and he escaped down a black alley before either of us could pursue him. And Spinoza needed our help.

He was bleeding and staggering and Daniel and I, holding him on each side, led him into my house. Automatically, I expected the worst, but once he sat down, his legs trembling, the most I could see was a rent in his clothes and a cut on his neck where the attacker had gone for his throat. Hendrickje washed the blood off his neck with a clean cloth while we gathered around him and I asked what had happened.

Still shaken by the attack, he whispered, "I was coming from Van den Ende's house where I have been staying temporarily. I said I was going to the theater. Some of his pupils are putting on *The Medea* and I did not want to be followed. Ever since I returned to Amsterdam I have had the feeling that someone is trailing me."

Daniel asked, "Then why have you remained in the city?"

"Once I won my civil suit I took that as a sign that I could safely."

"To walk the streets at night? You know that is dangerous even under the best of conditions."

"The Master asked me to sit then. I have not been attacked before."

I said, "You should have carried a lantern or torch as is required."

He said, "I did not want to be seen."

I asked, "What about the town guards? Were none of them about?"

Daniel said cynically, "They are never around when you need them."

"Besides," Spinoza said, "the assailant was waiting for me outside this house, as if he expected me. He was like a madman when he came at me, snarling ferociously and calling me many vicious names."

"What did you do?" I asked.

"Nothing. I let my hands hang down very still to show that I did not wish him any harm. I told him quietly that he was wasting his rage."

I shuddered. No wonder he had barely escaped with his life. Yet he was not a fool. "What kind of a knife was it?"

"A thick, long one. Perhaps a kitchen knife or a small sword. I could not tell. The light was bad and everything happened so quickly."

"Did you recognize him?"

"No."

Daniel inquired nervously, "Was it anybody from the synagogue?"

"I doubt it. He screamed at me in Dutch. He was in a dreadful rage."

I asked, "Who do you think ordered it? The synagogue? The Church? The authorities? An unaffiliated fanatic? Or some other source?"

Spinoza said gravely, "I do not know. I prefer not to know."

"Yes," said Hendrickje, "it is better if we do not know."

"Who tried to assassinate him?" I asked incredulously.

"Your lady is right, Master," Spinoza said. "Knowing will not serve any useful purpose and will only arouse tempers already too agitated."

He grew weak and I was afraid that he was going to faint.

Hendrickje told him to put his head between his legs—that should bring the blood back to his head, her mother had taught her that—and when he did, he remained conscious but he still felt faint. I cried out, "He needs a doctor but no one will come at this time of the night!"

Daniel suggested, "I could call Bonus."

This aroused Spinoza a little and he mumbled, "He will not come. He is a devout Jew and I am cast out. I will be better soon."

He did not look better as he sat limply, complaining that he was dizzy, nauseous, and Daniel declared, "Bonus lives nearby. The worst that can happen is that he will decline to treat you."

My assistant was gone before Spinoza could stop him and I was glad. I did not trust our ability to help the patient and even Hendrickje, who knew many home remedies, was not sure what to do next. Titus said food might help, but Spinoza had no appetite, a feeling I knew intimately.

While we waited anxiously I thought that this was the end of my picture and Hendrickje examined the wound again, it was bleeding slightly. She applied cold water to it and that stopped the flow and his head cleared. He looked very young now and I felt that she wanted to mother him and I suggested, to take his mind off what had happened to him, "Hendrickje, give us some cheese, herring, and beer."

Titus said, "Heer Spinoza, I will eat it if you will."

"I am not hungry." Now, however, he looked a little distracted and a little better and he sat up and some color returned to his cheeks.

Hendrickje put the food in front of him as she did for me and Titus, and gradually, as we ate as if we were famished—although we had eaten a large dinner—to encourage him to eat, he nibbled on some cheese.

I felt better when I heard Bonus' voice at the door.

The doctor was arguing with Daniel, saying as he entered, "I am surprised and disappointed that you even hesitated to call me. If he is ill, I will tend him. Despite the ban. I delivered him into the world, I cannot desert him now. His father, may he rest in peace, would never forgive me. Where is he? Is he bleeding profusely?" Bonus did not finish as he saw his patient sitting at the kitchen table. His wig was askew, his cheeks were flushed, and he was still in his bedroom slippers, but he examined Spinoza as if nothing else mattered. He did it with thoroughness while we waited anxiously. After he surveyed the wound he complimented Hendrickje on the skill with which she had treated it, and said, "It does not need a bandage, it is only a scratch."

I exclaimed, "Then what is wrong with him, Doctor?"

He smiled knowingly and said softly, "Shock. And fear."

Spinoza sat upright abruptly and cried out, "I was not afraid!"

"Not of death, perhaps, my young philosopher, but of pain."

"I can endure that. It is violence, unreason, that I fear."

Bonus asked intently, "Was your assailant Jewish or Dutch?"

I intervened, for Spinoza clearly did not want to answer. "It was too dark to tell. It could have been a madman, a thief, a minister, a civic guard. Assassination has many faces. It is enough that he has recovered."

"Yes," said Spinoza. He stood up and added with a sudden resolution, "Master, now we can finish the portrait of Jesus of Nazareth."

Although I desired that devoutly, I said, "You must be too weak."

"I must sit. I gave my word."

I asked Bonus, "Doctor, is he strong enough to sit?"

"It depends on the circumstances."

Spinoza said, "I know I can sit for an hour, maybe two. The Master promised me that he will be finished then. And I will not be able to come back again."

I had not promised anything but I was in no position to correct him. I said, "Doctor, an hour would be a great favor to me."

"Only an hour," warned Bonus. "His body has had a great shock."

"Thank you."

"May I see the painting?"

Good God, I thought, another critic, but I said, "If you want to."

"I have heard so much about this work I wanted to see it for myself."

I escorted him to my studio while Spinoza assured Hendrickje,

Daniel, and Titus that he was fine and joined us. Bonus surveyed the portrait with the same thoroughness that he had given to his examination of Spinoza and said in wonderment, "You have captured the Jewish soul!"

Spinoza said, "That is one of the reasons I came back."

"Master, you must paint my daughter. She is being married next year. Would you portray her and her husband when they are betrothed?"

A Jewish bride, I thought, and I could celebrate my own feeling for Hendrickje in it. I said, "I will consider it. At the proper time."

"Bless you. I hope you will forgive this interruption." He turned to Spinoza and added, "Young man, you must be more discreet. Many in the Dutch community as well as the Jewish are disturbed by your views."

After Doctor Bonus was gone, Spinoza said, "No one should be disturbed by what I think. I am only trying to discover the truth."

"You threaten their faith. For many, that is unforgivable."

"Master, you do not seem to mind. And you are a devout man."

"I will mind if you do not sit as you are supposed to."

He had put himself by the window, but I moved him to where the shadows were deepest, where the darkness strengthened the light on his head.

Spinoza was saying to himself, as if to reassure himself, "Those who excommunicated me are more to be pitied than blamed."

I worked to express that in his eyes, imagining him sitting in the synagogue, as Jesus must have done, seeking a reconciliation with its members and meditating on the mysteries of the universe.

While I painted the emotions that came from within him, he still had a need to express his feelings, saying, "I am not going to allow a stupid attack to stop me. If anything, it makes me more eager to sit for you. I am not going to be intimidated. Just as I would not attack anyone, I would not be attacked myself."

"Neither would I," I replied. Confident of my conception now, for once his words helped my brush. And as I thought, the darkness added light and strength to his face and blended with my initial view of him. I added, "You are a Jew no matter what

Morteira decrees. It is your nature. As it was Jesus' nature, whatever Hoag says."

"Who is Hoag?"

"A pompous, righteous Calvinist pastor who calls me a heretic."

"Master, I never said Jesus was not a Jew. Any other view is false."

I felt closer to my intention and knew that my choice of a model was right after all. My Jesus was rejected, despised, and cast out, and this young man had suffered the same fate and was an outcast now, too. Yet in spite of all the suffering he had endured he was still compassionate, and I sought to suggest this conception rather than to state it.

He said suddenly, "I have never denied that I am a Jew. My family have lived here longer than most Jewish families. We were among the first to settle here. But I have often thought that the Jewish people would be better off if they could return to Israel and have it as their homeland. Then they would not have to depend on the charity, usually unwilling, of other countries. Now they have to worry about what their neighbors think. I feel sorry for them."

I would feel sorrier for myself if I did not finish this work the way I wanted to and I hushed him. I saw the color leaving his cheeks and I was afraid that he was going to faint and I felt that I had very little time left. Yet I must not hurry, I warned myself, however eager I was.

I donned a velvet beret and that helped my hand, and that Daniel and Titus had supplied me with the palette that I needed, and I used my beloved yellow. Delicately, I whispered to myself, this golden color, even as it delineated his features must suggest his inner self.

I strained so hard to convey this vital aspect of his person that I felt a pain in my chest. I should stop, I thought, this could be a warning, but I could not stop. I might use money poorly but paint was my life. I tried to ignore the knifelike stab in my chest.

Oh, God! I exclaimed to myself, This will be the final irony, to be deprived of my conception when I am so close! Then the pain went away and I reflected, We were survivors, Spinoza and I. I assured myself that it no longer mattered who dominated this picture. Jesus would understand. His spirit shone through the face of this Jewish student.

Spinoza was just about to stand up, drained from the intensity with which we were working and the strain of the attack, when I halted.

I did not explain why but I called my family, who were waiting downstairs in the kitchen. They came as one, marching into my studio in the order of their age, Hendrickje, Daniel, and Titus.

Then I told my assistant to prepare the varnish and they knew.

"Finished," Daniel said.

"Finished," I said.

Spinoza spoke with the same wonderment that Doctor Bonus had expressed. "You make me think as well as breathe. It is as if I am listening to my inner voice. You have seen and painted what I truly am."

I was gratified that I had conveyed his nature and emotion accurately and passionately, but I did not want him to think that this was just his experience. I reminded him, "I have also depicted you as Jesus. This is my portrait of Him as a young Jewish student."

"As a would-be rabbi?" Titus asked.

"Perhaps. Son, do you like this portrait?"

"Like is not the word for it, Papa. You make us care. Which is more important."

Hendrickje said, "Master, I hope that you feel better now."

"I feel fine." I was deeply pleased by Titus' understanding but I couldn't tell him; such a demonstration of emotion made me uncomfortable.

"You did not push our young friend too hard?"

Spinoza answered, "No, my lady. No more than I did myself. Daniel, do you think that I look like Jesus now?"

"You look like the Master sees you. This painting is the work of his imagination. You are fortunate that he has a powerful one."

I said, "To preserve a likeness is not an obligation." Besides, this painting was an act of faith. But I hoped that his soul shone through his face. "Spinoza, you are not the only heretic in the room. My work has been accused of that many times. I take it as a compliment."

Daniel reflected aloud: "Three heretics—Rembrandt, Spinoza, Jesus." He added, "What a trinity!" The idea amused him and he laughed.

For an instant Hendrickje was offended, but when she realized that he did not intend any blasphemy, she asked, "Master, what are you going to do with this portrait of Jesus?"

Until now I had planned to keep it for myself. Then I remembered that my need to restore her faith and mine in the compassion of Christ had started me on this long, arduous, and passionate work. I said, "Hendrickje, it is my gift to you. My wedding present."

"What shall I call it?" she asked, tears of gratitude coming to her eyes.

"Portrait of Jesus Christ as a Young Jewish Student."

Spinoza said, "That is appropriate."

We shook hands on that and said good-bye. I had a feeling that we would not see each other again, that from now on we would travel in different directions. Yet I watched him from the window while Daniel and Titus escorted him to Van den Ende's house with brightly lit torches and I waited eagerly and anxiously with Hendrickje until they returned with the news that he had arrived safely.

What did I believe?

I thought, if my work did not answer that, I had wasted my life. I wrote on the back of my portrait of Jesus, "Work in hand." I was so engrossed in what I was doing I forgot about the money stored behind the canvas. I had expressed my love of God with the soul of the most saintly person I knew, and if he were a heretic, than so was I, and I felt as devout as anyone.

I lay down beside Hendrickje, who was waiting for me, who never fell asleep until she was certain that I was next to her, although often I went to bed hours after she did. As I felt her hand in mine, soft and gentle against my hard, calloused flesh, I prayed to God that He grant us more affectionate years together. If my picture did not please Him, I doubted that anything else I did would. I fell asleep wondering whether I would ever be satisfied with what I had done.

A few days later Crayer and Bonus wanted to buy this portrait of Jesus, but I refused to sell it. I loved its tenderly contemplative expression, and it belonged to Hendrickje now. Then a week after I had finished this picture it vanished. I had no idea where or how.

The five hundred guilders I had stored in the back of the canvas was gone, too, but that did not upset me the way the disappearance of this picture did. Money had never made me happy and I had obtained a new commission that should be sufficient to support an undischarged bankrupt, but I missed this portrait of Jesus poignantly. It was like my dearest friend had been taken away from us. And I knew that I would never quite paint like this again. And one other thing shocked me.

Scrawled on the side of my house in foot-high black letters was painted one word: *Heretic.*

My eyes blurred from staring at it and all that day I was terrified that I was losing my vision and that I would never be able to work again.

Then I remembered what Daniel had said and I repeated it to myself, Three heretics: Rembrandt, Spinoza, Jesus.

Hendrickje, Daniel, and Titus cleaned the wall of my house that evening, and at eight the next morning—I could tell by the bells ringing in the nearby church at St. Anthony's Gate—I made another appointment with my God. I began another portrait of Jesus as a young Jew, this time studying to be a rabbi, while I prayed that the portrait of Spinoza would survive somehow. I had to work. It was an act of faith. My eyes were still a little blurred, but I could see enough and I was also working by touch and intuition and my love for Him.

HISTORICAL NOTE

WHILE this novel is a work of the imagination it is based on these facts. Rembrandt and Spinoza lived in the same part of Amsterdam at the same time, possibly on the same street and certainly within walking distance of each other. They visited the same synagogue; Rembrandt to use its congregation as models; Spinoza as a member and a student.

Rabbi Manasseh ben Israel was Spinoza's teacher and a good friend of Rembrandt's. He lived near the artist, he sat for him several times, and Rembrandt agreed to illustrate a book written by the rabbi.

Rabbi Morteira conducted the examination and excommunication of Spinoza, and also sat for Rembrandt and was a friend of the artist.

Crayer served both the artist and the philosopher at a similar time.

Biographers of each man have speculated on the likely probability that Rembrandt used Spinoza as a model for his studies of Jewish students and for biblical figures such as Saul and David, but this can only be supposed.

Rembrandt's difficulties with the Reformed Church, his bankruptcy, and Spinoza's excommunication occurred as depicted in *I, Rembrandt.*

Spinoza's exile continued for the rest of his life and he died at the age of forty-five. Rembrandt remained an undischarged bankrupt to the day of his death at sixty-three and outlived Titus and Hendrickje.

Neither of them ever stopped working.

Spinoza's words are read everywhere and Rembrandt's *Aristotle Contemplating the Bust of Homer,* which he sold for five hundred guilders, was bought by The Metropolitan Museum of Art in New York on November 15, 1961, for $2,300,000.